FIELDS OF FIRE

BOOK TWO OF
RISE OF THE PEACEMAKERS

Kevin Ikenberry

Seventh Seal Press
Virginia Beach, VA

Chris Kennedy/Seventh Seal Press
2052 Bierce Dr.
Virginia Beach, VA 23454
http://chriskennedypublishing.com/

Publisher's Note: This is a work of fiction. Names, characters, places, and incidents are a product of the author's imagination. Locales and public names are sometimes used for atmospheric purposes. Any resemblance to actual people, living or dead, or to businesses, companies, events, institutions, or locales is completely coincidental.

Cover Art by Ricky Ryan
Cover Design by Brenda Mihalko

Ordering Information:
Quantity sales. Special discounts are available on quantity purchases by corporations, associations, and others. For details, contact the "Special Sales Department" at the address above.

Fields of Fire/Kevin Ikenberry -- 1st ed.
ISBN: 978-1648550249

For My Girls.

Chapter One

Ten Years Ago

Snowmass

James Francis stood with his hands on his hips and watched the final loads reach the ramps of the *Independence*, the oldest and largest of Intergalactic Haulers' fleet of long-haul ships. The last time the ship had been on the planet, almost forty years prior, he'd been a younger man serving under Don Yerkes—one of the finest men he'd ever known, and the father he'd never had. For a long moment, he closed his eyes and breathed in the fresh, cold air. Snow covered the planet's continents for almost the entirety of its year. In the sinus-clearing breath, all the memories this particular planet held swarmed around his mind like lightning bugs on a warm summer night. In them were humor and sudden, wrenching pain.

Katie. Oh, Katie, I'm so sorry.

The woman he'd fallen in love with—at first sight, standing in the deep snow smiling down at him by starlight—was many light years away on Earth. As much as he wanted to be there, he couldn't. People needed him. Intergalactic Haulers moved everything from produce to agricultural equipment to construction materials across the galaxy to support Human colonies throughout the Union. On the surface, the Haulers performed a vital logistical mission. What most people didn't see was the real primary mission of his company—the safe return of Human mercenary personnel when proxy wars and contracts turned south. Don Yerkes had been but a teenager at the time of the Alpha Contracts, but he knew well the cost. His father, as well as Snowman's, had died on their missions. Rumor had it his father's company, Matty's Moonshiners, died of starvation on a distant planet because the Jivool they'd been paid to fight severed the Moonshiners' logistical chain. Out of ammunition and fuel, they lingered and slowly died, unable to do anything other than submit situation reports over the GalNet every few days. The reports stopped coming a month later. Two months after that, word reached Snowman's mother that the entire company was dead. He'd vowed to never let that happen again and had focused his early years on every type of retrieval training he could afford before signing on to the *Independence.*

The mission took James away from Katie and his beloved daughter Jessica. While he and Katie tried, in vain, to keep Jessica from knowing the full nature of the business, she'd found out on her own and come looking for employment when she finished high school. The company's officers told her they wouldn't hire her without a college degree, so she went to college early. The board asked for his recommendations, but he did nothing. As much pain as it caused to play dead and remain lost to his own daughter, with the company's board of directors repeatedly saying he was missing in action while he ran missions all over the galaxy, losing Katie had nearly crippled him.

Her last message, encrypted and protected by an ancient program Snowman had secured from the elSha themselves, relayed the news. He'd been expecting it for a while, given the diagnosis, but Katie had once again exceeded every expectation of the medical professionals and lived with Stage Four cancer in several organs for more than a year out of sheer determination.

Jessica was a sophomore at the University of Georgia at eighteen years old and on track to graduate in a year and a half. From there she'd likely pursue a career as a mercenary, if the Haulers didn't answer her inquiries. His orders to the company were definitive—Jessica would not be a Hauler. It brought a measure of happiness and equal panic into his heart that she would likely be a mercenary with some other company. She needed to learn and gain experience, especially if his predictions came true.

One day, Jess. One day you'll understand what's going on, that what I'm working on is so important I can't tell anyone, even your Mom, what I'm really doing.

Snowman ground his teeth in sudden frustration. Katie entered hospice not long after Jessica's departure back to school following her summer break. According to her message, she had a couple of weeks to live at best. Through the message routing scheme he'd developed for their personal communications, it had taken a month for the message to reach him. When it came, he'd already found out about her passing through official company reports. He'd buried his head in his hands and wept before reading it a thousand times over.

My Snowman,

By the time you read this…heh. I always hated those words, ever since you handed me that sealed envelope with your own letter in it. Do you remember that? Gods, what stress even seeing that thing on my desk brought. Well, you can guess the rest. The hospice workers from Atlanta have arrived and are making me comfortable. They were angry at me for delaying their help, but they would never have understood why I did what I did.

Jessica excelled on her VOWS, just like you said she would. She'll graduate UGA in a year and a half—before she turns twenty-one, also like you predicted. She's already signed on with Lemieux's Marauders as a mech pilot. Pierre recently retired from active service, and he's turned it over to his son, Marc. I hope that boy knows what he's doing.

I never told her I was this sick, but I planned for her to get Ellie like you asked. The things we do for family—even the things they'll likely never know or appreciate until we're gone.

I never told her a lot of things, and while it hurts to think she might die without knowing the truth, you were right to protect her. To protect us. As you said, the threat is real and must be stopped. I hope you can do that when the time comes. I wish I could be there by your side, my love. I ask only one small favor. When it snows, and you feel that first breath of cold air in autumn, think of me. My only regret as I lay here now is not seeing snow one more time. When I do, I can't help but think of you, my Snowman.

I love you, Jimmy.

Katie

The proud redheaded woman he'd met on the plains of this very planet had kept his secrets to the grave.

How many more will it take?

A shuffling sound came from behind him, and Snowman turned to see the small Veetanho move through the snow to stand next to him.

"I am sorry, Snowman."

He nodded but barely trusted himself to speak. "Thank you, Reecha."

"Katie was an incredible Human. My children were privileged to have her as nest-mother to them." Reecha sighed and scratched at the fur under one eye. "I was honored to call her my friend."

Snowman took a deep breath and let the tears he'd been holding back come. "It hurts so much."

"That pain will subside over time. Grief is a burden we gradually cast aside."

"I cast aside my *family*, Reecha."

"I know you did," she replied, "and you worry it will be for naught, though you also realize you're most likely correct in your assessment."

Snowman took a breath and looked down at the snow between his feet. "That might be the case, but I'm working toward something. You've arranged for the relocation of your entire colony, but Veeka tells me you're intending to stay."

Reecha chittered. "She did, did she?"

"You know I can't leave you behind." He turned and looked down into her eyes. "Your colony needs you."

She raised her paws and shook them in an all-too-Human gesture. "Please, Snowman. They will be fine under Tcheya's leadership. I raised my granddaughter well. Once they're away from the Dream World Consortium, things will inevitably improve. They may face some hardship in the early years, but I'm confident they will thrive."

"You won't come with them?"

"No," Reecha said. "I'm staying behind. I have to know what they're up to, Jimmy. As you would say, something stinks. I'm not the only one who has made this choice."

Snowman nodded. "Veeka told me the DWC hired her, and she's staying behind. She didn't say what she's supposed to be doing."

"They hired her to be the Veetanho liaison to the local committee. Snowmass cannot remain a Dream World without a representative from each of the original colonies," Reecha said. "As long as one member of the colony remains behind, the claim is valid and protected. Should the Dream World Consortium's motivations and actions become transparent, we reserve the right to return to the world and stake our original claim. As long as Veeka is here, we have that right."

"But you'll be here as well. And a few others?"

Reecha glanced up at him and a tiny smile curled her mouth. "I'm remaining behind, yes. But the committee will not know that."

Snowman took a deep breath, held it, and released it slowly as the pieces came together in his mind. "You think they'll show Veeka the…well, we call it a dog-and-pony-show. Inspecting and looking after only the places they want her to see, that won't provide you anything useful for your gut feeling."

"That's what I'll be investigating, where they can't find me."

"That's pretty risky," Snowman said. "I gotta tell you, I don't think this is a good idea."

"Says the man with a plan he will tell no one." Reecha chittered a laugh. "You've actively deceived the Mercenary Guild and the Merchant Guild for the last ten years. Who are you to tell me I cannot disappear on a world I know like the back of my paw?"

"That's not what I meant, Reecha. I think you should leave this behind. They've been nothing but awful to you and your colony from the very beginning. Come with me and forget this planet."

Reecha breathed deeply, and a small cloud of steam erupted from her mouth with her words. "You are family, Jimmy Francis, and you have a place with us as long as you live. But since the Zuul mercenaries have been here, things have changed. Thirty-eight years of constant deployment of their forces to 'keep the peace' in a place where no one wants to come. Where the living is too hard. They're protecting something. I have to know what it is and maybe stop them. They won't find me. Veeka will not let them know, and I will not be alone."

"I don't like it, Reecha. Katie would..." Sudden tears welled up in his eyes. The horizon blurred, and he wiped them with the back of his gloved hands. "Ah, dammit."

Regret, shame, love, pride, and a host of other emotions raced through his mind in an instant. He hadn't been there when it really mattered. She understood, and she still loved him to the end. While there should have been a measure of solace in that knowledge, the hole in his heart wouldn't mend.

He felt Reecha's paw grasp his left hand. He took it, squeezed, and the little Veetanho returned the squeeze. "You have taken good care of me and my children, Jimmy. Allow me and the children to do the same for you."

"What do you mean?"

"The caves. You know which ones I'm talking about?"

He nodded. "For what?"

She looked at him for a long moment. "I will not ask you to tell me what you fear so strongly. I will only ask you this: will there be a fight?"

He took a long, ragged breath and nodded. "If I'm right, like something no one's seen in a very long time, Reecha. I hope I'm wrong."

"Hope is not a strategy, Snowman. I know Katie taught you that." Reecha smiled again. Her eyes glistened as her smile faded into something more feral. "If you think there will be a fight, you must prepare for it. The caves provide you storage space and more. Use them to your advantage."

"If you come back here, I mean your people, they won't—"

"They aren't coming back. Even if I solve this problem tomorrow, my colony will not return to Snowmass."

Snowman frowned. "Then why would you risk Veeka's life in town?"

"She can handle herself," Reecha said.

"That's not what I asked."

"For something greater. The same reason you're looking at a future you may not see. The same reason you plan and work behind secure curtains, trying to make sure no one else sees what you're thinking or planning for. Veeka knows why she will remain. She also knows why I will remain. We have the same mission, Snowman. The Dream World Consortium offers a great product, but it's a cover. They're clearly after something nefarious. Maybe it's resources, maybe it's simply territory, but they're planning something against the Union itself. I've watched them slowly regulate this and deregulate that. None of it makes sense. I've seen the companies come and go. *You've* seen it! You've even hauled some of them here. You have to understand what's at stake here, Jimmy. They're taking in colonies of every species in the galaxy and making promises they have no intent to keep."

Snowman kicked at the fluffy white precipitation at his feet. "Why not call in the Peacemakers?"

Reecha barked a laugh. "The DWC contracts are airtight and perfectly legal. They would find nothing wrong with the DWC boilerplate—that's its name, right? Anyone who signs the contract believes they're being given the keys to a fully livable planet, but all they're really getting is trouble. Mark my words, old friend. Until the DWC tries to eliminate a colony by force, the Peacemakers will do nothing about them. Whatever they're doing will not be discovered until it's too late. Maybe even until after whatever you're chasing happens. I will not wait for them. After the arrest of Guild Master Breka? I do not trust the Peacemakers. Neither should you, Snowman."

* * * * *

Chapter Two

Taal's Fury

Hyperspace

42 Hours to Snowmass

Tara Mason set the slate aside and rubbed her tired eyes. Standing watch aboard the newest ship in Force 25's inventory probably wasn't a normal course of action for a mercenary company commander to do, but it felt right. Her charges, most of them, were asleep in their quarters as the MinSha frigate made its way to their first targeted planet. She hadn't been able to sleep well since departing Victoria Bravo. The sudden stress of command manifested itself in a desire to catch up on all the news reports from across the galaxy.

They'd called it the Omega War, and its aftershocks were still being felt across the galaxy. From what she understood, the Mercenary Guild was all but destroyed, as were multiple companies from Earth, including the Four Horsemen themselves. Based on what little intelligence she had regarding the status of other units, Tara couldn't help feeling that Force 25, in its unique status, was one of the most powerful and capable mercenary companies in existence. Had their mission not been of the ultimate importance, it would have been a nice capability to exercise. Many of her leaders privately wished they could use their position for greater profit, and Tara understood. For her, though, duty was most important, and that meant finding Snowman.

James Edward Francis was the founder of Intergalactic Haulers, one of the most well-known and well-respected long-haul companies in the Galactic Union. For the entirety of his business dealings, he'd also run a search and rescue service for mercenaries and, surprisingly, some very black operations across the Union itself. All her searches for additional information, including the ones she'd had her near-AI assistant Lucille run, had proven fruitless. Pulling watch, she'd reviewed the official internal after-action report from the Peacemaker operation on Parmick with great interest. Young Peacemakers straight out of the Academy, with the help of the well-hidden Peacemaker Nikki Sinclair, had taken on a corrupt mining operation and found a connection to a common enemy, Kr'et'Socae.

The former Enforcer's whereabouts were unknown once again. Despite that, his touches and machinations seemed to be almost everywhere. More than once, she'd asked herself the question: how far could his reach extend? What was his endgame? Possibilities existed in too many directions at once, and while she could tap the Peacemaker Guild's intelligence as necessary, they'd decided their best play was to lie low and scour the files of Intergalactic Haulers for clues to the whereabouts of James Francis—the mercenary commander called Snowman.

<<Tara?>>

She didn't look up from her slate. "Yes, Lucille?"

<<I have completed the maintenance checks of the equipment aboard *Taal's Fury*. Ninety-one percent of the equipment is fully operational. The remaining nine percent are within tolerances for limited operations, and on schedule for completion, provided we can

gather some repair parts at Snowmass. I have added the request to the files for Captain Gray and his initial landing party.>>

Adds validity to our landing request. Tara reached for the bulb of coffee secured to her chair. "Anything that can give that guy an opportunity to look around and keep his mouth shut is helpful."

Lucille didn't respond.

Harmon Gray commanded the remnants of Gray's Goblins. Tara knew of them only by reputation, which was good, but in the run-up to the Omega War and the capture and detention of Human mercenary companies, most of his unit had attempted to defend themselves in a ground fight on Sprocja. It hadn't gone well, and Gray wouldn't talk about it. Behind his stoic demeanor was a quiet, analytical mind. Almost clinical. He took in copious amounts of details, rationalized them, and presented them in a clear and concise manner. The trouble was, like most Human mercenary commanders, he had issues with the doctrine and tactics of other mercenary races. Sometimes to a fault.

"Have there been any more discussions between Gray and Lieutenant Whirr?"

<<Four today,>> Lucille replied. <<They have also run two simulations. To disastrous effect.>>

"Disastrous how?"

<<It only furthered their arguments that each were wrong in the conduct of the attack,>> Lucille said. <<I recommend throwing them against the Oogar. The last Marauders mission.>>

Tara drew a breath and held it. Lucille liked the mission because it was incapable of being won without significant communication and firepower. The Marauders had taken so many casualties they'd only been able to escape with one CASPer and a heavily damaged sled. Jessica Francis had made their escape possible, with help from Lucille, which brought the whole episode full circle, in a way. Still, the mission made her think of Hex Alison. His loss more than a year before was something she still felt, though it had brought his brother Xander into her life. Hex had sacrificed himself for her and the others on Araf. Every day she lived, she owed him. While it was painful to relive parts of his life via simulation, Lucille was right. The developing factions of her forward force needed to come together.

Gray and the MinSha lieutenant led only a portion of her forward forces. Gray's CASPers joined with the remnants of two mech companies under the overall command of Major Vuong, her tactical executive officer. With a career in armored mercenary forces well behind her, Tara couldn't shake the feeling that having mech infantry forces only was a bad idea, but she knew it was a necessity. Back on Victoria Bravo, the rear detachment of Force 25 worked the more corporate aspects of the business and what they referred to as depot-level maintenance. A major component of those operations was the determination of why Cochkala armored forces had decimated the best of humanity's current armor. The tanks of the Victoria Forces had been no match for smaller, faster armored sleds with seemingly far less firepower and maneuvering capability. Once they could figure that out, they could reinstate tanks for Force 25. Until then, CASPers were her only combat forces. If they had to go toe-to-toe with a heavy force, the outcome would likely not be favorable.

Their primary mission, thankfully, likely wouldn't involve heavy direct combat. Tara scoffed at the thought and realized the likelihood they'd find a fight was high enough that training and simulations were time well spent. In hyperspace travel, there wasn't much else for combat forces to do, and sitting around created the age-old problem of idle hands creating trouble. Trouble was something no commander wanted but would have to address. Sometimes forcefully.

"Load it up, Lucille. Send a message to the commanders and the XO, I want everyone in the simulation—even if they're sitting on consoles and tapping buttons."

<<Acknowledged,>> Lucille replied. <<Captain Gray and Lieutenant Whirr are in the forward galley and away from comms.>>

Tara looked up over her console. The only other being on the bridge was Maarg. Her large, elongated head was covered by an absurdly large set of headphones that both looked strange and made Tara jealous. Sometimes the ability to shut out the rest of the world and get work done trumped everything else.

With a tap, Tara engaged the communications switch at Maarg's console. The TriRusk had taken a liking to classical music from Earth. Tara listened for a moment and tried to place the sweeping string melody, but couldn't.

"Maarg? Sorry to interrupt, but I need a favor."

The TriRusk chuckled. "I was wondering how long that would take."

"What do you mean?"

Maarg turned in her seat and removed the headphones. Her dark eyes twinkled, and her mouth twisted in the approximation of a smile. "Why would I be sitting up here working when I could work in my quarters? The commander of a mercenary unit shouldn't be pulling watch. You have other things to do."

Tara frowned, but she knew Maarg was right. "Sometimes a commander needs a time and place to think, Maarg. And I should do the things I expect others to do. If I don't, I'm not much of a commander."

"That's a very Human approach to leadership," Maarg replied. "Don't get me wrong; it's not a bad approach. But pulling two watches a day? That's a hundred percent too many, Tara."

Tara caught the slight change in Maarg's voice and laughed. "You sound like your father."

"Direct and obnoxious?" Maarg laughed. "That was exactly my intent. I'll finish your watch, on one condition."

Tara's eyebrows raised. "And that would be?"

"Run the simulation from inside Deathangel 25. Sitting on console allows you conveniences you don't have in combat. If you want the others to do what you want them to do, it may require you to show them first."

Truer words were never spoken.

Tara unbuckled her seat harness and pushed up gently. In the ship's microgravity, she caught the back of her chair, spun on one axis, and pointed herself at the hatch. With a gentle tap on the seat, she propelled her body toward the hatch. "Thank you, Maarg. You're right."

"Of course I am." Maarg grabbed her headphones and tucked them into a bag at her side. "Now leave me to my Vivaldi, will you? I really like this guy."

Tara moved through the hatch as the familiar strains of one of the *Four Seasons* pieces rose to a crescendo behind her. The light airiness of the music brought a smile to her face that faded the minute the inner hatch opened. Down the circular passageway, about where the forward galley would be, came the sound of an argument about to turn sour.

* * *

Jackson Rains ducked out of the small quarters he shared with Major Vuong and propelled himself across the passageway. He rapped on the opposite door twice. A moment later, the door slid open, and he looked inside. The small, white-furred Veetanho lay curled on the only bunk in the room, reading her slate.

"I'm still jealous you have your own suite." He smiled at his partner Vannix. "Granted it's smaller than mine, but I'd love the privacy."

"I know you would. For the fourth time, I'm not interested in trading." She twitched her whiskers at him.

Rains pointed at the slate. "What are you reading now? Smutty MinSha romance novels?"

"Do what? Those really exist?" She laughed. "I mean it takes one to know one, right? You must have a few."

He laughed, and it felt good. "Nope. I stick to non-fiction like a good Peacemaker should."

"Oh, please. I'm actually reading the memoirs of Hr'ent. It's a pretty fascinating story of how he became an Enforcer."

"I bet. Dude had one helluva a reputation. I wish I'd met him." Rains braced himself in the door with both arms. "I wish I'd met him."

"Me, too," Vannix said.

"Is that why you're reading it? Or are you searching for something?"

Vannix sat up. "He trained Kr'et'Socae. Did you know that?"

Rains blinked. "I didn't. What else have you learned?"

"I just got to that part at the end of Volume One," she said. "Are you headed to the sim?"

"Yeah." He grinned. "I have to admit, I kinda enjoy driving a CASPer. You think I can get Guild Master Rsach to add them to the inventory?"

Vannix chittered a laugh. "He's pretty open to new ideas. I mean, who would've thought you Humans could actually be good Peacemakers?"

"Kiss my—"

There was a click from the ceiling-mounted speaker near the open hatch. <<Peacemaker Vannix? Will you and Peacemaker Rains please report to Hangar Bay Three? Tara would like to brief you on the simulation prior to initiation.>>

"I wonder what that's about?" Vannix asked, her brow twitching up over one eye. "You think our prediction is coming true?"

"Maybe. It's not the veterans from Victoria, though. I think it's the newbies."

"Technically, Gray's Goblins and the others aren't newbies." Vannix pulled herself up to a sitting position and set her slate to one side. "They're an accomplished mercenary force in their own right."

Rain nodded and ran one hand over the stubbly black hair on his scalp. He took a breath and let it out slowly, shaking his head. His thoughts bubbled to the surface and out of his mouth. "There's too much going on. It's almost overwhelming."

"You mean Kr'et'Socae? What he's trying to do?"

"That's part of it. I mean, did you read the reports from Parmick?"

Vannix nodded. "Those young ones did good work."

"Jyrall and Larth? They're exactly one year behind us, Vannix. That doesn't make them young ones."

"Not in age." She stood and brushed the fur on her arms with her paws. "They aren't exactly mature. The pranks they played?"

Rains laughed. "Well, true. But it sounds like they grew up a little on Parmick."

"Indeed. They aren't done yet, much like the two of us." Vannix gazed at him intently for a minute. "We're making a difference here, Jackson."

As usual, she'd cut through the static in his head like a knife. He'd been wondering the same thing since they'd departed Victoria. Vannix and Maarg's deep dive into the files of Intergalactic Haulers had provided their first clue in the search for Snowman—the planet Snowmass and its connection to the entire Francis family. He'd taken up a more operational focus in working with the CASPer forces and learning their tactics. He harrumphed. "I haven't felt much like a Peacemaker recently, you know?"

"It's not kicking in doors and flashing the badge all the time." She reached for her blue Peacemaker vest and slipped her arms into it. With one arm she locked the small weapons' locker holding her sidearm and slipped the key into one of her vest pockets. He noticed her badge wasn't pinned to the exterior of the vest as his was.

"Where's your badge?"

She twitched her head toward the locker. "In there. Everyone on the ship knows who we are."

"I suppose that's true." He glanced down at the platinum badge on his dark blue coveralls. As was the custom, each badge featured a tree from the being's home planet. It was both a reminder of his home and his duty to protect that world along with the others. His badge featured a cypress from the bayous of Louisiana where his adopted family lived.

Stay true, Peacemaker.

I'm trying, Bes.

"It helps me, though."

Vannix pushed herself toward him and caught his arm with her paws. She looked up into his face. "We all have to do what we must, Jackson. Wear your badge if it makes you happy. It's not like you don't have the patches on your shoulders."

He flushed, suddenly embarrassed. "I'm being silly, huh? I know the badge doesn't make the man and all that. It's just—"

"Sssh." Vannix twitched her whiskers again and laughed. "My vest says Peacemaker on the back, too. I lock my badge up because it's precious to me. It will be there when I need it, I promise. Now let's get going."

He nodded. "Thanks, partner. Let's get to the sim."

"You're just excited to fight a CASPer again." She grinned. "I wish I could see what that's like sometime. And not from your camera feeds—like inside."

"A Veetanho CASPer?" Rains chuckled. "Now, *that's* pretty scary. Considering recent events—something like that might have been dangerous if Peepo'd had them."

Vannix shrugged. "Maybe that's why she was so interested in Humans? Those suits are pretty spectacular for what they allow you to do. But I don't think she counted on you being so damned unpredictable."

"It's a good thing for all of us we are."

* * *

Harmon Gray bit hard enough on the inside of his lower lip that he tasted blood. The overwhelming urge to get in the MinSha lieutenant's face, against all sense he had for self-preservation, didn't hold back his tongue.

"Lieutenant Whirr?" Gray let the air in his lungs out slowly and drew a quick breath. "Do I need to draw you a fucking diagram?"

The MinSha warrior, even in the null gravity of hyperspace, stood tall on her rear legs. "Excuse me?"

"You heard me. CASPer tactics are not, and I say again, *not* limited to the doctrinal constraints of traditional infantry. They're more in line with armored forces than even mechanized infantry. To put them in a line formation, marching forward shoulder-to-shoulder, tosses us back several hundred years. We're talking Napoleonic Era bullshit. Stand in line here. Fire at that line over there. Reload while they fire at you. No use of maneuver. No use of flight. Limited, harassing use of artillery. With a CASPer and well-trained operators, we can do all three things at once."

"I am not arguing that, Captain Gray." Lieutenant Whirr's posture relaxed, albeit slightly. "My argument is that CASPers function as the infantry, much like my platoon. While we cannot fly, we can shoot, move, and communicate as well as you do. CASPers give you an advantage over traditional infantry, but it is not the kind of advantage you can expect to have in every fight. Sometimes sheer mass, surprise, and other factors will prevent victory."

Gray forced himself to relax. "I respectfully disagree, Lieutenant Whirr. You're entitled to your opinions, but CASPers are much more than traditional infantry, and we will continue to use them in ways that best suit the situation. Individual operators in their CASPers are much more valuable than infantry soldiers."

"You're insinuating that because we do not possess powered armor solutions, MinSha and other infantry-based forces are less valuable than yours?"

Here we go again. Dammit.

"That's *not* what I'm saying," Gray said. He glanced around the MinSha's imposing thorax and saw Tara Mason floating their way. "Colonel on deck."

Lieutenant Whirr assumed a rigid position of attention and locked her head and eyes straight forward, not unlike a recruit facing a drill instructor. Gray merely turned his upper body and nodded at the approaching commander.

"Ma'am."

"Another argument?"

Gray glanced at Whirr. The MinSha said, "We were having a discussion of the value of traditional infantry versus that of mechanized infantry."

"Powered infantry. Specifically, CASPers," Gray added. "I was trying to get Lieutenant Whirr to understand—"

"Enough," Mason said. "Everyone is entitled to their opinion, Gray. It's not your job to change anyone's mind. We're a unit with multiple capabilities, and it's our job as leaders to understand those differences and use them to our advantage, rather than argue over who's right and who's wrong."

"Yes, ma'am," Whirr said. The MinSha's iridescent ruby eyes flashed over at him.

Gray nodded and then shook his head. "There are fundamental differences in this—"

"I said enough, Captain Gray." Mason clenched her jaw and closed the distance between them. "Differences work to our advantage. You need to stop trying to get everyone to fight your way. Understand?"

He felt heat rising in his neck and face, but Gray simply replied, "Yes, ma'am."

"We're running a full unit simulation in twenty minutes. I want all your soldiers either in their vehicles or plugged into the sim." She looked away from him to the MinSha lieutenant. "I realize our ability to work all your folks into an active role in the sim is limited, but I want them to see the whole unit in action and understand what their role is. That role, to clarify for both of you, is neither traditional infantry nor a specific maneuver force. The tactics we develop and apply in combat situations will be fluid, dynamic, and work toward a common goal."

"Kicking ass," Whirr said.

Gray laughed. The very concept of a MinSha not only understanding Human idioms but quoting and using them correctly never failed to surprise him. Since the Alpha Contracts, Human impact on the culture and operation of the Galactic Union had been nothing short of extraordinary.

"We'll be ready." Gray nodded at his commander.

"No more 'discussions,'" Mason replied. There was a hint of a smile on her face. "And never couch an argument as a discussion, Gray. Only a real idiot wouldn't know the difference between the two."

"Sorry, ma'am," Gray replied. "I've always believed professionals can disagree without argument."

"They can," she smiled at him, "but only when they're willing to acknowledge and accept the other party's position, even if they don't agree with it. You have eighteen minutes to get into the sim. I suggest you get about it."

*****

Chapter Three

New Perth
Snowmass

Citsym had seen the first licks of flame and the rising gray cloud of smoke from his office a mere hour before. Atop one of the forested hills surrounding the sprawling colony, one of the planetary control and measurement units, or PCMUs, burned for the third time. He'd scampered to the surveillance network office only to find the camera systems had failed, again, to catch any sight of the culprits behind the attacks. In frustration he'd returned to his sprawling suite and watched the sun rise over the valleys as the fire burned. The Zuparti scratched idly at the soft brown fur on his arms and clenched his maw in frustration. Behind him, the doors to his suite slid open. He didn't need to turn around to identify the visitor. A faint whiff of a flowery perfume, one of the curious habits of Humans, wafted to his sensitive nose almost immediately.

"What is it, Sophie?"

Sophie Pryce was the oldest granddaughter of Johann Pryce, the first colony leader. As the contracts for the Dream World stipulated, the leadership rotated between the founding species and had, as such, passed to Citsym upon the death of his father fifteen years before. Sophie towered over him, as many Humans did, and her pretty face and blonde hair gave her the appearance of a much softer, friendlier person than she was in reality.

"PCMU Sixteen, again. Arson, again." He saw her blurry reflection in his window. She looked down at her slate. "Cameras were all negative, of which you're aware. The fire crew has the unit extinguished, and the surrounding brush fire is seventy percent contained."

Citsym sighed audibly. "Had they hit the unit during a drought, the fire would have already threatened the colony."

"I had the same thought," Sophie replied. "While it doesn't change the nature of the attacks, that decision alone suggests the culprits are concerned for the welfare of the colony. For me, that rules out the intent as terrorism."

"They're terrorizing our operations, Sophie. They're terrorists to the colonial government, and that's the label we will continue to give them. Have you ordered the media accordingly?" He turned and saw she wore a simple Human pantsuit in a light blue color that accentuated her slender shape. By Human standards, she was beautiful. By Zuparti standards, she was as shrewd and ruthless as they were. He liked her immensely.

Sophie smiled. "They have a crew on site and are focusing on the quick response of the fire team and the colony leadership. And, of course, the good fortune of favorable winds and climatic conditions only provided by Dream Worlds. Standard package."

"Good." Citsym nodded and turned back to the view of the surrounding mountains. The thin haze of smoke appeared much smaller and less intense than it had been two hours before. "Please relay my compliments to the fire team. I want the PCMU team ready to go in there as soon as the fire marshal says we're clear to begin operations."

Sophie tapped her slate. "If you'll forgive my prescience, I've asked Commander Krukk to be here in five minutes. I believe the time has come to reevaluate their contracts."

"And you would ask them to do what?"

"Install the remote strike systems again."

Citsym frowned and turned back to her. The displeasure on her face was obvious. "We've talked about this. Many of our PCMUs operate in popular recreation areas or protected natural habitats. The Trenta Knights' deployed systems are singularly terrible and unreliable. I will not have another incident, Sophie."

Four years before, when the terrorist attacks began in the outlying colonies, the Zuul mercenaries had immediately suggested the solution of remotely operated kinetic strike platforms. Capable of identifying a target and slewing an active weapon system to the target within two seconds, a remote operator could engage the target immediately and without warning. A picnicking Human family was targeted by one of the systems, and the young Zuul mercenary on the console had carelessly swung the platform to clarify the image in the cameras and brushed the trigger. The resulting weapon's fire had wounded the father, mother, and two of the children. The third child died when struck by one of the magnetically accelerated projectiles. Social uproar skyrocketed high enough the Zuul mercenaries took the systems down voluntarily, even paying a fee for defaulting on a specific clause of their contract.

Pryce undoubtedly intended for them to reengage the systems—with more control measures this time—and leave them in place. Their rules of engagement would be much more stringent, but they wouldn't take them down again. The fee for a second default would bankrupt most planets.

But the Human was both vicious and correct. If it took the death of innocents to scare the rest of the population into good behavior, so be it. He glanced up at her cold blue eyes and saw the faint hint of a smile on her lips. She knew he was on the verge of capitulation.

"I've ordered a recovery crew to scour the site for evidence."

Which means you've ordered them to emplace it.

Citsym stroked the side of his face. "You've identified who is to blame?"

"I will," Sophie replied. "You must break eggs to make an omelet, so to speak."

He frowned. "Carry out an investigation only, Sophie. When we discover who is behind these attacks, we will deal with them on an individual level."

"There could be many of them," she replied and looked out the window. "Today it's a fire at our remote units. Tomorrow it could be something closer, more valuable. I know you disagree with me, Citsym, but we must eliminate the culprits before this situation grows any more dire."

The icy delivery of her words caught his attention. She met his eyes with a hard stare, and he understood immediately. "What have you done, Sophie?"

"I've hired professionals to deal with this situation. Colonel Krukk and his lazy band of miscreants are perpetually late to the game and, frankly, cannot be expected to do anything other than rumble about in their old tactical vehicles and find nothing. I want results, Citsym. I've arranged for someone experienced in these matters to assist us."

He let the comment about the mercenaries' laziness go. Things had been very different for the mercenaries under their new commander, but old wounds seeped pain. Her grandfather's inability to handle them approached legendary status. As ineffective as the previous mayor had been, she more than made up for it. "And what was Ch'tek's response? Hmm? He has operations going in multiple locations to find the benefactor behind the attacks on Victoria Bravo and Araf."

Sophie laughed. "Benefactor. Listen to you, Citsym. You speak as if you're afraid to mention his name. Like he's some boogeyman set to come out of the shadows and eat you up if you say it."

She wouldn't understand. Being Human, and notwithstanding more ruthless than most, she didn't understand the disgraced Equiri's reputation and history. He was afraid of Kr'et'Socae. Given their intelligence reports on those sites and what had taken place at Parmick, there was little doubt in Citsym's mind that the former Enforcer's hooves appeared to be everywhere at once. What they didn't know, nor would they entertain, was the idea that both Victoria Bravo and Araf were Dream Worlds. Araf was in the purest sense of the term—having been the third planet the Consortium undertook for terraforming. Victoria Bravo had been the corporate office for the region, and while not necessarily an indicator of operations in the area, the office space was established and occupied at the time of the attacks, and the building took heavy damage. If Kr'et'Socae knew about the captured Information Guild server housed there for the shortest of time, he could rightly surmise that the DWC also had their paws in many pools at the same time. Citsym didn't know if that was a good thing.

"He presents a great unknown to the overall situation, Sophie. Despite the board's feelings, I think he is well aware of the DWC's actions, and it is only a matter of time before he comes looking."

The door chimed behind Sophie, and she turned. Citsym, too, moved in the direction of the inner sanctum's door. The newly appointed Zuul commander, Colonel Krukk, entered. Like his recently departed father, Krukk carried the familial black and brown coloring on his face, accentuating his bright brown eyes. He wore a sleeveless armored vest to protect his chest cavity, and two sidearms that looked like Human-styled .45 caliber pistols with inlaid gold handles hung at his side. The traditional golden eagles of a mercenary commander adorned the shoulders of the vest. With his guild in disarray, Krukk kept order and discipline in his large, capable company through impressive drills and regular field exercises. All in all, it was a refreshing change from the laconic command style of his father and predecessor.

The recently deceased Colonel Krut hadn't necessarily been a bad commander, just lazy. From the time of their first contract signing through his death only a few weeks before, the older Zuul hadn't taken an interest in the training and discipline of his mercenaries—instead leaving that to his subordinate commanders. None of them, save for his son, had taken the initiative to train them for combat operations. Granted, their contract for protecting Snowmass had never been thoroughly challenged in over thirty years. No situation had ever arisen that the Dream World Consortium's leadership and board of directors couldn't solve, until now.

"Colonel Krukk," Citsym said, his pleasant tone that of a practiced diplomat. It was far too early to tell if the young commander knew the difference. "We were discussing this recent attack and our possible course of action to respond. Do you have any additional information for us?"

The Zuul nodded solemnly at Citsym and then again, less formally, at Sophie Pryce. "Mayor Citsym. Miss Pryce. I've dispatched a reconnaissance team along with the fire suppression teams. They're within two thousand meters of the PCMU now and will reach the unit within the next thirty minutes. I have them scanning everything. Visual, audio, and everything in the electromagnetic spectrum. I'm confident we will find something to trace or something to identify the attackers."

"You must pardon my skepticism, Colonel, but this is the fourth attack in the last two quarters. We've yet to find anything even close to being identifiable." Sophie frowned and glanced at her slate. "The identity of these attackers is a critical piece of information that you and your forces have yet to provide."

"These investigations take time. We embed my people within the fire prevention teams and out of the public eye, Miss Pryce." Colonel Krukk shook his head and cleared his throat with a deep rumble. "You trusted me to run my company, and service our contract, in a different manner than my father chose to. This is one of those areas where I require your commitment to my methods. I will get the information you want, but I require your patience most of all."

"And you have it." Citsym glanced at Sophie. The blonde Human didn't appear appeased. He took a quick breath and added, for good measure, "You have our full support, Colonel. We merely request constant communication."

"Which I've given you," he replied. He took a calculated breath, Citsym saw with admiration, before he continued. "My soldiers are doing the most complete work they can. I've overseen their progress and processes myself. Our foe is very good at what they do. Forgive me for saying so, but I've only encountered such trace-free work in the Veetanho mercenary companies I've worked with in the last ten years."

"Veetanho?" Citsym felt his brows rise in shock. "There are twenty-five Veetanho left in the colony. Four of them serve on the board of directors. Are you insinuating that someone from this tiny cohort is a terrorist?"

Krukk shook his head. "No, Mayor, I'm not insinuating anything. The level of stealth and non-attribution for these attacks is simply at that level of complexity. Finding them will be difficult. Frankly, it could be a deception operation meant to derail our intelligence gathering. Given the current status of our remote sensors? Positive identification of any type would be miraculous."

Sophie flared. "We told you to update your capabilities, Krukk. Your father before you as well. You've done nothing!"

"Jeha-built sensors do not come cheap, Miss Pryce." Krukk bared his teeth at her. "Given the status of our contract, there is no profit margin to cover that expense. Were you willing to let some of my platoons pursue other contracts instead of sitting here babysitting New Perth and the other—"

"Babysitting?" Sophie roared at him. The petite Human stepped toward the Zuul commander with enough energy and fury that the dog-like alien actually retreated a step. "Your contract was for the security of the entire planet. Your company has been here for decades, Krukk. You can't expect me to believe you've had no money for research and development during the entire time. You've spent your money on trips to Karma. Your soldiers have as well. If they spent their wages on the economy, there could be enough to facilitate such requests."

Krukk laughed. Paws to his belly, the mercenary commander howled with laughter, further infuriating Sophie Pryce. "You want us to spend our money on *this* economy? To fatten your purses so you can occasionally shower us with your benevolence? Spare me, Miss Pryce. This contract reaches its competitive status in three days, and there is no one in their right mind who would stay on this planet solely for the scraps from your table."

Citsym almost nodded. The Trenta Knights had serviced the contract on Snowmass for over forty years. Had it not been for a meager mining operation they oversaw on the southern continent, the Zuul mercenaries would likely have left the icy world behind. Instead, they mined a large palladium deposit as needed to support their power cells. Had they the initiative, the deposit would be worth millions of credits across the Union, but the Zuul mercenaries appeared content with what they'd been able to obtain. What they earned, they spent on wages and equipment. The palladium mine could have driven them to a point rivaling the most powerful mercenary companies in the galaxy, but Krukk and his family had sat on it like a nest egg. They wouldn't operate it at anything close to its potential, nor were they willing to sell.

"I trust you're preparing your recommendations, Colonel?" Citsym asked. His voice was quiet enough to signal both the Zuul and the Human to back down in their tone. "The colony board is certainly interested in what you have to recommend for the next ten years."

Krukk met his eyes and nodded solemnly. "My family is preparing them as we speak. They will be ready at the time and place of our continuation hearing."

Citsym's eyes narrowed. "Your father, for the last three hearings, shared the recommendations with this office and the board of directors more than a week in advance."

"We will have the recommendations at the hearing. You will see them at that time. No earlier. Much has changed with the way the Trenta Knights will conduct business." Krukk put his hands on the belt holding his sidearms. "The last thirty years have given me great pause, Mayor. Now that I run the company, changes must be made."

"I'm hoping your changes will not adversely affect our longstanding relationships," Citsym stated. "I believe we have much to gain by working together."

"Quoted like a Dream World Consortium executive, Mayor Citsym. Working together is only possible when all parties wish to do so." Krukk turned to Sophie Pryce and bared his teeth again. "There are certain entities on this planet, spread through the colonies, who do not share your optimism or professionalism. The pursuit of profit drives them in differing directions when the deals are signed."

"How dare you accuse my family of—"

Krukk shot out a hand and pointed a singular claw level at Sophie's face. "There will come a time when your family's pursuit of profit and the goals of the Dream World Consortium will part ways. When that happens, no paltry mercenary force providing security will save you."

Awkward silence fell as the two immovable beings stared each other down. Citsym allowed it for almost fifteen seconds before he cleared his throat theatrically and waited for them to look in his direction.

"It's not often that the mayor's office has to issue official decrees, but I believe the time has come for us to start several things. Foremost, Colonel Krukk, your forces are to continue their investigations with the full cooperation of the occupants of Snowmass. To that end, I am instituting a colony-wide curfew which includes our outlying communities. No one shall be allowed outside their domiciles from 2300 hours local time until sunrise. To enforce this policy, you will post roving guards throughout New Perth and the other communities. You will also emplace your remote gun platforms to protect every PCMU located within three hundred miles of an established community. This will protect the units themselves, but your operators must be properly trained and restricted from opening fire unless positive identification has been achieved. To do this"—he turned to Sophie—"the Dream World Consortium's remote camera reporting system must be engaged."

Sophie opened her mouth and closed it quickly. Citsym knew her mind was racing with the possibilities and trying to reason out if the use of the planet-wide surveillance system fell under the auspices of the colonization agreement between New Perth and the DWC. "There's nothing specifically against allowing the network for your use. Especially those systems monitoring the environment near the communities. I believe we might be able to support that request."

Citsym smiled. He'd expected that precise response. They might have the colony over a barrel, to borrow an expression he'd heard years before on Earth, but that didn't mean they didn't feel threatened. Dream Worlds hadn't been well-received since the three-sided showdown on Araf ended with the deployment of a Human Peacemaker who'd simply stepped in and put the two mercenary units down instead of negotiating a truce.

The times truly are changing. I wonder if that's for the best?

"Good. I suggest we get to work, then," Citsym said. "As the stormy season approaches, we have no choice but to figure out our differences and protect our colony and planet. With the Union teetering on the brink, I believe we have no other choice. Eventually, even little outposts like ours will be the center of attention for those looking to gain at the expense of others."

"And in the meantime?" Sophie asked. Her desire for blood simmered just below the pretty veneer.

"Colonel Krukk? Ask your men to find Veeka and have her come to my office immediately," Citsym said. "I'm quite interested in who she thinks may be behind these attacks, and why. If you'll excuse me. My next appointment has arrived from off-world, and I do not wish to keep them waiting."

*****

Chapter Four

Force 25 Corporate Headquarters

Lovell City

Victoria Bravo

The ravages of recent battles hadn't stopped the explosive growth of the Victoria system. Designated by several guilds as a commercial trade zone, the Earth-like planet's population and economy boomed. Amidst the tremendous growth of Lovell City, the downtown district continued to repair itself from the attacks surrounding a building in the cosmopolitan downtown district that had once belonged to the Dream World Consortium. Expelled by Governor Watson for activities against the planetary articles of confederation, they'd departed in a hurry, leaving the building and several hangars at the starport in their wake. As it developed, another brand-new corporation had taken over the building and the additional hangar space at the starport. The Force 25 Corporation's new acquisitions rivaled those of the Four Horsemen on Earth before the revelation of the Mercenary Guild's ultimate deceit. Yet the actual presence of Force 25 on Victoria Bravo was relatively small by comparison to their larger, more storied counterparts.

Controlling the office building and its administrative, research and development, and special projects spaces, along with the starport facilities, and the converted MinSha cruiser in orbit was a daunting task. With their commander and chief executive officer, Tara Mason, deployed forward on the search for James Francis, the operations at Victoria Bravo fell to a few trusted individuals. While founded as a Human mercenary company, there was nothing exclusive about the organization. With close friends across the many species of the Galactic Union, Force 25 aimed to create a new standard for species interaction filled with respect and mutual cooperation.

"Gods, Bukk!" Xander Alison exclaimed. His counterpart, the ant-like Altar operations officer, skittered back in equal shock and dismay.

"I'm sorry, Xander," the tall alien said through his translation pendant. "I had no idea you and Lieutenant Colonel Ibson were still here. It's almost 1800 hours local time. The bar has been open for an hour. I was getting worried about you."

The amused tone of the Altar's voice wasn't missed. Both Alison and Ibson smiled at first, and then laughed aloud. Hunched over a large rectangular worktable in the special projects department, the Humans stood and stretched their backs in various ways.

"We needed the interruption," Xander said. "I didn't realize it had gotten so late."

"The fun never stops," Ibson said as he placed both hands behind the small of his back and stretched again. Dressed in the black fatigue pants of the company duty uniform and a gray T-shirt, he moved well despite the large braces on both knees. The devices were the last visible reminders of his being trapped in the Victoria Forces command center during the second battle for Victoria Bravo. "I think we deserve a drink, Xander. Since he scared the shit out of us, I think the first round is on Bukk."

The Altar bristled. "I bought last night, Xander. And you bought the night before that. Thunder Six here"—he pointed at Ibson with one claw—"owes both of us a drink, I think."

Ibson flushed while Alison laughed. "I agree. Drinks on you tonight, my friend."

"Fine." Ibson rolled his eyes. "I'll buy. Just make sure you get the cheap stuff. I'm pretty sure there's a bottle of Jeremiah Weed in the cabinet."

Alison made a sick face. Bukk waved his upper two arms in mock supplication. "Please. Anything but that. I've heard the mechanics say the flyers could operate with that as a primary fuel. And it tastes...well...awful."

The three of them laughed again. As it trailed off, Bukk leaned over the table. Several fragments of armor lay strewn across the work surface. "What have you found?"

During the second battle, the Cochkala attackers had deployed multiple wheel-based skiffs. The angular, low-riding vehicles carried both an impressive laser weapon and targeting system behind seemingly impenetrable armor.

"It's like nothing I've ever seen." Xander Alison was the chief financial officer of the company and had already used credits and cooperation to widen the recruiting net for the nascent mercenary company. His business acumen was formidable, and yet from his former life in mining and recovery operations, he'd seen all kinds of metallurgy from across the galaxy. "By composition, it resembles Besquith armor at the molecular level, but there's a mixture of other components. As a composite, it's pretty damn strong."

"And it's lightweight," Ibson pointed out. Jamie Ibson had been a career officer of the Victoria Forces, the militia-like force protecting the colony during its formative period. After the first battle for the planet, he'd assumed command of the entire force when its previous commander, Brian Watson, ascended to the governorship. During the second battle, he'd commanded his forces with great skill until the Cochkala targeted the command center. He'd been the only survivor, by sheer luck. "We're talking half the weight of a similar sample of our armor."

"No wonder your weapons didn't penetrate it," Bukk replied. He leaned closer and peered at one of the larger samples. "You said molecular level. I take it you've analyzed them with every sensor suite on the planet?"

"Even the ones we had to bribe entry to—like the hospital's imaging machines. We're still trying to identify the other components. We're seeing lots of carbon, which isn't surprising, but it's still not completely identified," Alison said. "It almost resembles—"

"Diamond," Bukk said, leaning even closer to the sample. His compound eyes were a few centimeters from the armor. "Not just any diamond, either."

"What do you mean?" Ibson leaned closer. Alison did the same.

"I can see in a wider spectrum than you can, Jamie," Bukk replied. "There are indications of diamond here, but it's not a typical, one hundred percent carbon diamond."

Alison shook his head. "That would explain part of it. Where would the Besquith, or whoever had this armor designed, get something like that?"

Bukk straightened. "You have about twenty kilograms of them upstairs in your safe, Xander."

"Sonuvabitch," Alison replied. "They're TriRusk diamonds."

Bukk nodded solemnly. "Yes, or something very similar. There may be other sources for synthetic diamonds in the galaxy. It's an exceptionally big place. I've never encountered diamonds being integrated into armor, and while I wouldn't think it to be cost effective based on the worth of the gems themselves, the way it's been manufactured suggests it was done for very specific reasons."

"Lighten the armor. Make it harder for us to penetrate." Ibson nodded. "That's the obvious thing."

"Then what are we missing?" Alison raised up and ran a hand over his chin.

"They're red diamonds, too." Bukk scratched at the armor with one claw. "This relates back to what Peacemaker Vannix forwarded us from Stormwatch."

"Parmick." Ibson shook his head. "That whole operation was tied to Kr'et'Socae, too. Fuck me."

Alison turned to the Altar. "This is a limitation we still have to overcome. You could see that with your eyes. We were using Human technology and Human eyes. We missed this completely. I'm glad you came down here and surprised us."

"It was my pleasure watching Thunder Six 'lose his shit,' as your expression goes."

Ibson smiled and pointed at the armor. "Across the entire organization, we need to leverage our strengths better. Not just in combat operations. I'll take care of everything I touch. You two need to do the same."

Bukk straightened up to his full height. "I'll engage the others. Most of our interspecies forces are deployed forward, but as we bring in new recruits, we must integrate them to this way of thinking. Whether or not they're Human."

"Agreed," Alison said. "Meantime, what are we going to do about this?"

Bukk looked at Ibson first, who said, "We believe the TriRusk are in danger. We need to send a secure message to Captain Kurrang and the Peacemaker guild master. Copy it to Colonel Mason."

"Vannix already reported that her guild was 'taking measures' to protect the TriRusk," Alison replied. His brow furrowed. "What if this is all a giant feint? That Kr'et'Socae is faking us out?"

"What do you mean?" Bukk asked.

"Parmick? I mean, come on. That place is a shithole and was tapped out years ago. Do we think he really went in to get the red diamonds just to put them into composite armor?"

Ibson shook his head. "The report Vannix was allowed to show us said otherwise. It was a forgery operation. He was using the dust to synthesize fake diamonds. If he gets his hand on TriRusk diamonds, he could produce near perfect currency and disrupt the entire galactic economic structure."

"But we're finding the same synthetic red diamonds in armor. Doesn't a currency destabilization mission seem farfetched to you? They're in the armor here. That's more suspect, to me. Like he's playing at something against our combat forces," Alison said.

"There are industrial diamonds and cosmetic diamonds, Xander," Ibson replied. "Who says you can't use synthetic red diamonds this way? I mean, it was tremendously successful against our armor. They cut us to shreds in minutes, and there was nothing we could do about it."

"And without sampling the Parmick gems, we can't say that the two are the same," Bukk replied. "We can isolate a sample here, of course. But we must send for samples from Parmick."

"I know, I know." Alison waved his hands and shook it off. "Sorry. I was just thinking out loud."

"Aside from sending a report to everyone and their brother, is there anything we can do directly to support operations on Weqq?" Ibson asked.

Bukk turned to the soldier. "That would be up to you for forces. We don't have sufficient transports to get there at the present time."

Ibson was already nodding. "And we don't have the force structure I'd want to go in there. We have no idea what they might end up facing, either. Unless we're asked, I recommend we focus on things here. We have recovery and cannibalization efforts going on with all the damaged and destroyed vehicles to oversee, and recruiting to attend to. The response to our campaign for recruits has been surprising so far."

"But what about this?" Alison pointed at the armor. "Is there something more specific we can do?"

Ibson looked up at his Altar counterpart. "Is a red diamond, synthetic or not, harder than a regular one?"

"I don't know," Bukk replied. "That might be an excellent place for our research efforts to begin."

"Research?" Alison's eyebrows rose comically. "What are you two thinking?"

"Reverse engineering," Ibson said. "There's a forge on the riverside of Lovell City. We'll go over there, talk metallurgy with their folks, and see if we can get the compounds right."

"I'll see about getting industrial diamonds," Bukk replied. "The Flatar battalion was hired to protect petroleum operations in the southern highlands. There are all kinds of weird biologics down there. The likelihood of them having diamonds for their drilling rigs is near-certain. I can take the flyers out for cross-country maneuvers and return by nightfall. Combined with the TriRusk diamonds in our possession, we should be able to generate some good data once we determine exactly what it is and how we can use it."

"You're going to reverse engineer it? Why?"

"Two things"—Bukk pointed at the armor fragments—"metallurgical investigation will show us who made it and maybe even where. We can use the files from the Trade Guild, provided they'll permit our request. Given the situation and the threat of additional attacks, I'm sure Governor Watson would seek an injunction if they denied our request."

"What if the Trade Guild wants to know what we're doing? What are you going to tell them?" Alison picked up a fragment of the armor and twisted it in the light. The ragged metal did have a trace of red, but it was fleeting, as if turning the fragment under the light changed both the reflectivity and its albedo. He'd never touched any metal so lightweight yet durable. "This stuff is unlike anything I've seen and likely either sought after or protected by its manufacturers. Are you planning to steal the manufacturing data? Make it ourselves?"

"Weren't you discussing cash flow the other day?" Ibson grinned.

"I was, but corporate espionage really isn't the way a mercenary company needs to do business, Jamie." Alison was smiling as he said it. "But that would be a few steps away, right? I mean, if we can figure out how they did it and make it ourselves?"

"Then test and outfit our vehicles and CASPers with it?" Bukk asked with a chittering laugh. "What an excellent idea."

They smiled at each other for a moment. Alison knew the others thought the idea was both profitable and worth pursuing, no matter the expense. The true cost of their very lives had come by the sacrifice of others. None of them were about to put another Human in harm's way again without the best equipment and weaponry credits could buy. And if it wasn't available, they'd do it themselves.

That was the Force 25 way.

There was a knock on the door behind Ibson. He turned and opened it. Lieutenant Danny Lee stood on the opposite side. His coveralls were grimy and dirty; there was no doubt he'd come straight from the maintenance hangars. The former mechanic had been part of Drew Morris' tank crew during the battle for Victoria Bravo. Now, the experienced young officer played a major part in the effort to recover and strip every vehicle and CASPer they could from the battle-damaged hulks. He wiped sweat from his brow with the sleeve of his coveralls.

"You wanted to see me, sir? Gentle…" He looked at Bukk.

"Stop worrying about pleasantries." Bukk laughed. "I would never be considered a gentleman in any language or culture."

Ibson nodded. "Come in, Danny. We were just discussing something that might interest you. Ever worked with enemy armor before?"

The young officer smiled. "There's always a first time, sir."

* * *

Taal's Fury

Dropship *Mako 15*

Simulation

"I'm a CASPer pilot, not a flyer pilot!" Irene Mata tried not to panic as the flyer was buffeted through a strong Victorian wind.

Gods, this thing is too realistic.

To her left in the copilot's seat, Captain Mike Carter grinned and leaned back against the seat. He oozed calm and confidence, but he wasn't the one trying to control a disc-like flying machine with four ducted fans that didn't want to move in the same direction at the same time.

"Stay off the throttle and let her settle in the wind, Irene."

The wind from the east ripped at the open cockpit, and the flyer pitched hard to one side. "Shit!" Mata said, but the disc stayed in stable flight. She took a deep breath and forced herself to relax while keeping her hands on the controls.

That wasn't so bad. She tried to find a rhythm to the breeze as they flew across the valley toward the three buttes on the far side of the Swigert River. She'd grown up kayaking the river with her family. Further west, downstream from Lovell City, there were impressive Class Four and Five rapids almost year-round. Her parents loved the river, and looking down on it, seeing the sun catch the ripples like a blanket of diamonds, her racing heart calmed. In a kayak, the first time she'd raced into the throat of a Class Four rapid, she'd been terrified. Her father had been on a rock midstream and pointed at the familiar notch. In most cases the path through a rapid looked like a triangular notch pointing downstream. She'd oriented the tip of the kayak at the notch and paddled like hell. Every nerve came alive, and she'd seen things almost before they happened. Her anticipation of the movements of the water had helped her propel the kayak through the rapid faster than she'd believed possible. The kayak spun in the calmer water and she'd looked up into the happy eyes of her father—his arms raised over his head in victory.

Relax, honey. Just relax and think ahead. Stay ahead.

"Stay ahead," she said under her breath. "Stay ahead."

Carter's voice came through the earphones of her helmet. "Much better. You're ahead of the aircraft, Renee."

"What does that mean?" She smiled tentatively and risked a look at her friend. "Ahead of the aircraft?"

"You're thinking ahead. Anticipating. Kind of being one with it. Not letting the wind or anything else get to your focus." He laughed. "Which means watch where you're going."

Like finding the notch. I got this.

Mata turned her attention back to the horizon and stabilized the flyer's path with a coordinated movement of stick and control yokes.

"Almost like the simulator," she said with a laugh.

"Almost," Carter replied. "Turn a hundred and eighty degrees and let's enter the pattern at Lovell City."

"Copy," Mata said. She turned the flyer around, pointing the nose back toward the starport. "Never thought I'd take up flying full time."

She'd been a qualified CASPer pilot since the age of eighteen, until the aftermath of the second battle for Victoria had left the remnants of Force 25 struggling to field the traditional armor forces and the flyers that had been so integral to the Victoria Forces. There were only a couple of tanks remaining in the arsenal, and none of the flyers or qualified pilots for them.

"You're a natural, babe."

Her face flushed. "We said not while on duty!"

"Sorry, I just couldn't help it," Carter replied. In the days following the battle, they'd taken solace in each other. No one in the leadership had said anything about their barely private relationship. Expectations were that they keep things professional even as he trained her to fly. As much as they both needed each other, Force 25 needed them, too, and neither wanted to jeopardize their employment or their sense of duty. "But you are a natural. Just keep it smooth and watch for ground effect with this wind. Flyers respond much different than dropships."

"Says the dropship pilot." She smiled and kept the flyer level in another stiff gust. "Don't you want to take over the controls?"

"Nope," Carter replied. His relaxed posture never changed. "This one is all yours. You have to solo land sometime. Might as well be today."

"In a gale force wind?"

He laughed. "If you can land in this little breeze, you can land in anything, honey."

Mata shook her head and focused on staying ahead of the flyer. The distance to Lovell City closed much faster than she thought it would, and within a minute they passed over the outer marker to the starport, and she pressed the transmit button.

"Lovell Center, Foxtrot 22 at the outer marker. Transit to final and landing, Force 25 Pad Alpha. Over."

"Foxtrot 22, Roger. Cleared direct to Force 25 Pad Alpha. Maintain present altitude and speed. Lovell Center, clear."

She depressed the transmit button twice instead of responding in the affirmative and kept her focus on the approaching landing pad. Over the starport she lowered the flyer's altitude and slowed to hover over the pad and gently bring the flyer down in the buffeting winds. All three wheels of the landing gear touched the tarmac at the same time. Mata recognized the sensation even as her hands flew through the vehicle shutdown procedures by memory. She turned and smiled at Carter and saw him watching her with pride and love in his eyes.

"Well, instructor?" she asked.

He unbuckled his harness and sat forward, extending a hand for her to shake. "Congratulations, Lieutenant. You're Force 25's first newly certified flyer pilot."

"Thank you, sir," she said with a barely concealed wink. "I trust you'll be ready to celebrate in earnest when we get home?"

Carter grinned. "There's a small crate of Italian wine fresh from Earth with our names on it. And you're off the flight schedule for the next two days."

"Whatever shall we do?" Mata laughed.

Carter grinned. "If we were home, I'd buy one of those new cabins up on the bluff. Stuck here on the ship? I'm sure I can think of something."

* * * * *

Chapter Five

Taal's Fury

Drop Bay Alpha

Tara climbed into the cockpit of her Mk 8 CASPer and paused before bringing the cockpit shell down in front of her and locking in for the simulation exercise. Part of her didn't want to go through another simulation, but the sudden forming and explosive growth of the Force 25 Corporation had brought so many new players onto their team that she and the other combat commanders had no choice but to run simulations to identify tendencies and mitigate risks when operations were conducted for real. Without actually counting it up, she was certain the amount of time she'd run simulations since signing on with Jessica Francis and the small band of soldiers Selector Hak-Chet had pushed forward to help the Peacemaker's final commissioning mission totaled more than the simulations she'd run in her previous five years of mercenary service. Prior to meeting Jessica and Hex Alison almost two years before, she'd always thought hyperspace transits were meant to be spent sleeping, eating, and generally fucking off. After studying the results of her previous missions without simulation training compared to those where training had taken place, she'd converted. Idle hands in transit meant lifeless hands on the battlefield. While she couldn't mitigate every risk or circumstance, she could ensure her people were ready for operations and not stuck trying to remember how to shoot, move, and communicate.

Tara tapped a sequence of commands on the CASPer's forward instrument panel and brought up the suit power and network connection. Almost immediately there was a faint *click*, and a synthesized female voice filled her ears. <<Simulation is ready, Tara. Waiting for everyone to connect.>>

"Thanks, Lucille." She engaged the cockpit close switch and the CASPer's heavy front swung down and locked into place. The exterior camera system linked to the server, and the familiar dark forests of an unnamed Oogar planet came into view. A thin smiled curled one side of her mouth as she remembered Hex and his easy smile and incredible fighting spirit.

<<All stations are connected, Tara. As you wanted, the Peacemakers are sitting this one out and observing.>>

Tara nodded, but her mind was firmly in the past instead of the present. *If I had a few dozen like you, Hex.*

"All stations, this is Deathangel 25," Tara called over the simulated radio connection. She'd never asked how Lucille accomplished such a complete and total simulation. The visuals were near perfect in almost every situation they'd practiced. The Oogar mission used actual imagery she'd collected from the multiple vehicles and CASPers in that particular fight. While Lemieux's Marauders had effectively met their end, their experiences lived on in a way she and the others could benefit from. Especially when her subordinate commanders, who hadn't seen this mission, could be dropped in and forced to work together or fail spectacularly with no physical cost. Pride and hubris not excepted. "Let's work with the new SOP for callsigns and brevity codes. I'm in observation mode above and behind your forward line. For this exercise, Major Vuong in Avenger 6 will be the field commander. Take all cues and commands from him."

<<All stations, standby for drop protocols. Thirty seconds.>>

From the data, Lemieux had dropped his entire combat force in one dropship. Given their tactical makeup, Tara had Lucille adjust the simulation for the two dropships attached to the outer hull of *Taal's Fury*. Other than that, her forces would face the same mission that had cost Lemieux's Marauders, and Hex Alison, dearly. She'd seen it far too many times to fight it objectively, as had Jackson Rains and Vannix from their respective stations. Yet as an evaluation tool for her newer commanders and their troops, it would do nicely.

Tara tapped the communications panel. "Maarg? You out there?"

The young TriRusk replied, "I have Jackson and Vannix here with me, Tara. You're on speaker, so they can hear you."

"Good." She smiled to herself. "Jackson, I want you evaluating Gray and his CASPers. They're First Platoon—callsign Reapers. Keep in mind they're Mk 6s and not as fast as what you've been working with. See how they shoot, move, and communicate."

"Copy, Tara," Rains replied. "I'm looped into their net now."

"Vannix, you've got Lieutenant Whirr and her infantry. They're Second Platoon, and the callsign is still Mantis." She chuckled. "I can't believe they wanted to keep it after Victoria Bravo."

"Not everyone thinks it's derogatory. The MinSha thought it was lucky," Vannix chittered, "especially after what happened to me."

Tara nodded. They'd almost lost the Peacemaker because of Governor Watson's impatience and incompetence. He'd tried to lead an infantry platoon into combat against the Cochkala, and they'd caught the young Veetanho in the crossfire. Only a concerted effort to rescue her, combined with a powerful sacrifice, had removed her from the field in time to save her life. If the MinSha infantry thought that constituted good luck, Tara wouldn't contradict them.

"Sounds good to me. Maarg? You've got Third Platoon. They're calling themselves the Misfits."

"Good band. I kinda like their music," Maarg replied.

"What?" Tara shook her head in disbelief.

<<The Misfits were a rock band in—>>

"Not now, Lucille!" Tara closed her eyes and shook her head. "Maarg? They're irregular forces, to say it best. Find out what they're doing and how they're trying to fight so we can help or change their approach."

"Affirmative," Maarg said. "However, I should point out that Oogar, Pushtal, and Flatar forces have never actually fought together before—at least on purpose. Never under the command of a Human, for sure."

"Then we make it up as we go," Tara replied. "Lucille, drop them to the surface. Let's see how this plays out."

* * *

Location: CLASSIFIED

Peacemaker Guild Contingency Headquarters

Guild Master Rsach set aside his slate and rested his eyes for a long moment. Outside the tiny window of his private quarters, the sky was a mixture of oranges and reds heralding the day to come. He'd awoken early to reread the mission report from Parmick and found himself reading back through the early records of the Enforcer program and his oldest and best friend, Hr'ent. They hadn't been so close during their time at the Academy. At one point late in his life, Hr'ent had visited and told him there'd been a time or two around graduation he'd thought about taking Rsach's life. There was no doubt the Oogar had been serious as they'd shared a drink in his quarters on Kleve. Rsach knew there'd been no excuse for his behavior as a candidate, and throughout his formative years he'd tried to live to a higher standard. The only thing that mattered was why Hr'ent had saved his life on Godonnii Two and then given his life for the guild a few scant months ago.

While it was true that Hr'ent was terminally ill at the time of his final posting to the consulate on Luna, he'd volunteered not only to sniff out the Mercenary Guild's attempt on Rsach's life, but he'd laid important groundwork for the future of the guild. As he lay on his couch, slate in pincers, the memory swam up in his consciousness with such clarity it surprised him. Five years before, his friend had returned to Kleve for the last time.

* * *

"You're certain about this?" Rsach returned to his couch and motioned for the enormous Oogar to sit. "I have to admit, I'm uncertain. Can they handle it?"

Hr'ent sat on a flat bench and stroked the side of his snout. More white hairs than purple caught the low light of the guild master's office. The telltale signs of age caught Rsach by surprise until he remembered his own struggles with aches and pains throughout the typical day.

"Why are you looking at me like that?" Hr'ent's voice was a low growl.

"I'm just wondering how we got so old," Rsach replied. His mouth twisted in a grin, and he laughed. After a moment, Hr'ent relaxed and joined him. They smiled at each other, and what little tension there was between them boiled off in an instant.

"Speak for yourself." The Oogar flashed his teeth. "I still exceed the standards for my physical fitness."

Rsach cocked one of his antennae. "You should pass it the day you die. I doubt your Enforcer treatments will ever stop working."

The Oogar shook his head, and his dark eyes brightened. His mouth opened once and closed again with a snap. After a moment, he looked at Rsach and then beyond him out the wide windows of the Kleve offices. Hr'ent had never been the silent type, and that meant something else.

"What's wrong?" Rsach asked. He leaned forward and set his eyes at as close to the level of his friend's as he could. "What is it, Hr'ent?"

"I ordered that it be withheld from you, old friend." Hr'ent chuckled. "My last annual physical showed several abnormal growths in my lymphatic system."

Rsach dissected the words carefully. Oogar didn't have a lymphatic system in the traditional, albeit Human, sense of the word. They had a healing structure of similar design, and that was the area of concern. "Your body can't heal as it did before? Even with the Enforcer treatment?"

"That cocktail of nanites and wonder drugs won't stop this, Rsach. It's cancer. Stage III. Catching it early like this is normally a good thing, but unless it actually responds to treatment, it will continue to get worse. The Enforcer treatment has kept it at bay and will likely continue to do so. I've been told my time could be as little as six months, and as much as five years."

Rsach sucked in a breath and sagged perceptibly in the chair. "I had no idea."

"I just told you I had it withheld." Hr'ent chuckled, but the sound turned raspy and sad. "Graa'vaa knows. As does Tellah. But we've kept the news close to our family."

"I'm honored you think of me that way," Rsach said. "Your news goes no farther than me."

"I appreciate your discretion, Guild Master."

Rsach rippled in flash agitation. "Stop that, Hr'ent. I'm your guild master, yes, but we're far beyond those customs and courtesies. You're as much my brother as any of my clutch mates. I don't say that lightly."

"Nor do I take it that way," Hr'ent said.

"How long ago did you find out?"

"Four months."

Gods! Rsach tried not to explode.

"You've known for four months and didn't tell me? You said as little as six months."

"I wanted to make sure I wouldn't die. The cancer hasn't sped up or metastasized, so I came to tell you my time is limited." Hr'ent shrugged. "We attempted holistic medicines and the like on Uuwato with no success. There appears to be nothing I can do to stop it. For the first time as an adult, I feel truly powerless."

"So this visit wasn't purely a social one?" Rsach smiled at his old friend and felt a pang of sadness ripple down his segmented body.

"Before we both become emotional wrecks, I suggest we discuss our business. You first?"

Hr'ent nodded. "I've been talking with Hak about Humans. It's time to admit them to the Academy again."

Rsach made a click with his jaw in disapproval. "You're aware of the situation regarding the last candidate? Will Cartwright?"

"I am"— Hr'ent nodded—"and I simply want to turn your attention from what you've read in the files to things I've seen with my own eyes. They're capable fighters. They're unpredictable to a fault. Most importantly, they don't give up. I believe the right candidates are available to become the first Human Peacemakers. I have four files I'd like you to review at your discretion. I'd like to set up official interviews."

Rsach understood. "Hak-Chet put you up to this, didn't he?"

Hr'ent opened his enormous palms in a gesture of guilt. "I said I would talk to you about it, and I am. I've observed two of them in action and am quite impressed with them. Several of them come from Human mercenary families. A few are outliers, definitely, but all four candidates are worthy of admission to the Academy."

"What if I'm not ready to admit them?"

"Then you're making a huge fucking mistake, Rsach. The type you haven't made since the Academy. Can we not go there?"

Rsach laughed. His friend was correct, and there was nothing he could say except what came to mind. "I'm very interested in the Humans, actually. I've ordered a consulate constructed on their moon, Luna. I'd like to have a close presence observing them for the next several years. You want Humans in the guild? I think you're the Oogar for the job."

"Why?" Hr'ent stared at him. "What are you cooking up?"

He laughed. "You know me too well."

"Then cough it up, Rsach."

* * *

Rsach rippled up to a sitting position and set the slate on the nearby table. With a stretch and an abdominal movement that replicated a Human yawn, he sat for a moment with his eyes watching the sunrise. Hr'ent's recommendations had proven opportune, even if unorthodox. For Hr'ent, his time on Luna had been well spent prior to the interception of the Mercenary Guild's intent to assassinate Rsach. By that time Hr'ent's health had failed enough he asked to have the honor of bringing down the attackers but letting their handiwork stand. He'd performed both his final missions admirably. Should the state of war in the Union calm down enough for the guild to return operations to Kleve, Hr'ent would be inducted into the Hall of Heroes for defeating the assassination attempt and, if all went well, for helping to change the scope of the Peacemaker Guild itself.

Rsach moved to his desk and tapped on the slate controls there. The message took him only a couple of minutes to compose and revise. When he'd finished, one pincer paused over the send button for a long moment.

If I do this, everything changes. We cast our lot not as representatives of peace, but truly as enforcers *of peace.*

He snorted and twisted his mouth in a snarky smile. The Enforcer program continued, but there had only been six of the enhanced Enforcers ever treated and sent out into the galaxy. Four of them were dead as a result of their field operations, including Hr'ent. One,

Captain Dreel, still remained aligned to the Guild. One had turned his back on everything good and just for personal profit and chaos.

Finding Kr'et'Socae had taken over as the top priority of the High Council. While there were other missions and roles they had to pursue, the arrest and execution of the disgraced Enforcer was primary. He'd overplayed his hand with the actions at Parmick, and the only possible continuation of his plan would be an attack on the TriRusk at Weqq. He would certainly go after them for the innate ability of some of their offspring to synthesize diamonds. Having them remain on Weqq, but with a contingent of Enforcers and mercenaries to protect them, played well for the Peacemaker Guild, but it also meant Kr'et'Socae had to be stopped should he appear ready to fight. That appearance, though, wasn't guaranteed.

Rsach reviewed the plan as the first tendrils of light filtered across his wide desk. Dreel and Kurrang were overseeing the protective actions at Weqq, where things appeared to be ahead of schedule. The young Peacemakers, Jyrall and Larth, had followed a path blazed by Jessica Francis and were gaining allies to help them pursue the leads they'd found on Parmick that pointed to Kr'et'Socae's whereabouts. Jessica herself remained with the Depik as his personal liaison to their recovery efforts, if only to keep her out of the line of fire. Her father was still missing, and the effort to find him and his information had been transferred to Force 25 under the command of Tara Mason. All these missions connected in his mind, but there were two others that also bore watching.

Cast a wide net. Is that the phrase?

Rsach chittered a soft laugh and leaned back against his couch for a long moment, steepling several sets of pincers across his chest.

So many things were in play. So many avenues of information and misinformation.

Have I done all I could?

The thought stopped him for a long moment. A guild master couldn't be everywhere at once, yet the history of the guild itself told stories of those who'd gone before him and lost sight of the overall goal. Peace across the Galactic Union wasn't entirely possible, but the lawful conduct of its citizens was a goal worth reaching. For centuries, the Peacemakers had been less funded, less manned, and less capable than their counterparts across the guilds. When the Mercenary Guild foundered after what the Humans had called the Omega War, the doorway to opportunity was open. All the guild had to do was step through. Peepo and her minions had provoked humanity and crumpled under their assault. Rsach had no such intentions. There were many corporations and entities in the galaxy who believed the Humans to be cause for concern. The Peacemaker Guild wasn't one of them.

Rsach turned back to the message and added a CLOSE HOLD classification notice and a subject line. Hr'ent had called the operations plan Project Crusader. There was no sense in changing it, and it made Rsach smile as he finally clicked the send button. If there was one being in the galaxy he fully trusted to have the best interests of the Guild in mind, it was Hr'ent Golramm.

Rest for you, old friend. I shall enjoy seeing you again in the great beyond.

Message sent, Rsach leaned back and turned his face to the rising sun. The warmth through the tiny window paled in comparison to what he'd grown used to on Kleve and even in the administrative halls of the Academy on Ocono. A guild master's day was not one of peace and quiet, but of carefully scheduled meetings and briefings.

His last few solitary moments of the day would be spent in thought and curious anxiety. A report from Hak-Chet should arrive before the day ended, as would the latest from the MinSha lieutenant colonel who'd become a trusted friend and confidant of Jessica Francis. One followed the carefully concealed trail of the Dream World Consortium. The other, his oldest friend in the Guild, tread much more dangerous ground. While a guild master should be oblivious to worry, Rsach was not. He'd lost one good friend in the course of the last few months. Losing another would be more than he could take.

* * * * *

Chapter Six

Unnamed Planet

Simulation

Inside the cockpit of Deathangel 25, Tara closed her eyes and bit down hard on her bottom lip. The urge to take over the simulation, to tell the others what to do and how to do it, rose in the back of her throat, but she kept it down. Failure was a bitter pill, and there were far too many newer members of her unit who needed to taste it.

Better now than when you can't say goodbye or when the bullets are flying.

She touched the camera feed controls in her CASPer. "Lucille, can you put me onboard with Major Vuong? Feed me his audio and visual channels?"

<<Stand by,>> Lucille replied. <<The feeds will go live in ten seconds. Are you certain you want to do this? I believe the sensation could be very jarring for you, Tara.>>

"I don't want the haptic feedback, Lucille. Just his feeds. If I'm trying to follow his movements and getting my ass kicked by every movement and inertial response, I can't imagine I'd do anything other than puke my guts out. I just want to see and hear what he's seeing and hearing."

<<Understood. Thank you for the clarification.>>

For a moment, Tara wondered if Lucille could have fed everything Vuong did inside the CASPer, then realized just as quickly that she could have. The near-artificial intelligence that was Lucille had become a vital part of the team. While Tara had followed the recommended procedures from Jessica to restrict Lucille's abilities, there hadn't seemed to be a decrease in her operational capability. Aside from a few moments of relative indecision, Lucille had performed within the bounds of what Tara and the others knew. Lucille performed the work of a dozen trained operators and specialists in a fraction of the time. She was an essential member of the crew.

"Lucille, ensure you're collecting data from the simulation. I don't want you playing NPCs or influencing what they do. Let everything play out like it did for the Marauders. This is purely up to our assets on the ground."

<<Understood, Tara. I am collecting information as requested and will not engage,>> Lucille replied. <<Feeds are active. You are riding with Avenger 6.>>

The screens changed, but not before Tara used her far-seeing sensors to watch the Oogar's initial charge through the forest push toward Gray's Goblins on the far right of the CASPers and MinSha infantry. None of her forces could see them, which was just as well. She watched the snarling purple wave descend on her unit and thought not of what her people were feeling, but of Hex Alison watching everything he loved come to an end in the next scant minutes.

I can't imagine living through what you did, Hex.

I hope you found peace, because there's nothing like it here anymore. I have Xander to grieve with now, but I can't help thinking I failed you.

How did the Marauders win this fight?

Vuong moved with the MinSha infantry. The female warriors scrambled forward at a speed he couldn't have matched without his

CASPer and its jump jets. Their target was the fallen Raknar where Marc Lemieux had encountered Jessica Francis, but none of those directly involved knew the whole story. Tara wasn't sure how much of it they should know, but she was sure someone would put two and two together. Someone would ask questions and try to figure out why Tara had selected this mission to evaluate her leaders. Her answer would be simple. When everything turned to shit and people were dying despite their best efforts, leaders either pushed through on the mission, or crumbled and made excuses for their failures. She was determined to see who did what in the worst of circumstances.

With the Raknar as their objective, Vuong had each of his platoons move on a different azimuth to the target. The MinSha infantry squad of twelve warriors came in from the north through the marshland near the fallen Raknar's feet. From the south, he'd positioned Harmon Gray with his six CASPers to sweep through the heavier forest. The tactic was solid, given that Gray and his soldiers were experienced CASPer pilots with upgraded, state-of-the-art Mk 6s. Marc Lemieux had played the scenario the same way, though, and how Vuong and Gray played out the next several minutes would say much about their ability to handle complex operations.

The outlier was something Lemieux's Marauders hadn't had, nor something Tara had ever tried to field. Other mercenary units had done so, but the Misfit platoon was something she'd never tried to wield. Interspecies units worked for some commanders, but mixing the different capabilities and equipment fielded by each mercenary species wasn't easy. The Misfits had an Oogar platoon leader, Quin'taa, a Pushtal heavy weapons specialist, a Flatar/Tortantula pair, two Humans in CASPers, and two refurbished tanks that could only provide artillery support. They'd only had the few weeks since the formation of Force 25 to train and work together. How they'd perform in a combat simulation was anyone's guess.

Something was missing, however. "Lucille? Did you remove the flyer support from the sim records?"

<<For this exercise, yes.>>

Tara shrugged. While they'd likely have both dropship and flyer support available during a real mission, not having it would test the ground forces' ability to see and control the battle space. Much like not having herself and Rains in CASPers and Vannix and Maarg flying *Molly* would test how Vuong and the others fought on their own. Letting go of command wasn't easy, but there was no other way to really evaluate Force 25's new abilities.

"Avenger 6, this is Mantis 6. Have the Raknar in sight. Negative sensor contacts," Lieutenant Whirr reported over the channel.

"Mantis 6, Roger. Secure the northern side of the wreckage and report any hostile contacts." Vuong's answer was sure and confident. "Reaper 6, what's your status?"

"Moving west from drop location. ETA on site is three minutes. The forests are thicker than kudzu over here," Harmon Gray drawled, and the laconic accent made Tara smile. Granted, it was a funnier report because she'd learned what kudzu was not long before thanks to Jackson Rains.

"Secure the east side of the wreckage and link up with Mantis elements on the perimeter," Vuong directed. So far his actions were about perfect. Tara knew better than to expect that to continue as the situation developed.

"Avenger 6, this is Misfit 6. Southern side of the wreckage is secure."

Tara took a deep breath and let it out slowly through her nose. The main mass of Oogar would come from the northeast. Lemieux's Marauders had used that avenue of approach because it was faster on level ground with little cover. They'd paid a price getting into the perimeter around the Raknar and had only been saved because the feral Oogar didn't approach the fallen mecha out of what Jessica reported as a strange reverence.

Chalk up one point for Major Vuong.

"Contact!" Harmon Gray reported. "I've got Oogar on my right flank. Unknown number. Turning to engage."

"Mantis 6, move to support by fire. Let's close the Oogar flank," Vuong replied conversationally.

He sounds bored. Tara shook her head. *Just you wait, buddy.*

On Vuong's command display, several of the Reapers' icons turned red and winked out in rapid succession.

"Avenger 6, we're being overrun. There're hundreds of—" Gray's radio call terminated as his CASPer went down.

He never knew what hit him.

"Avenger 6, Misfit 6, moving to support."

"Negative. Hold that side of the perimeter. The Raknar is our objective, and security is paramount," Vuong snapped. The emotionless tone was gone. He was clearly trying to visualize the attack and his response, and he could tell he was about out of time.

"Contact front!" Whirr reported as the Oogar wave slammed into the MinSha infantry. In seconds the snarling purple onslaught overran her squad. At the front of the formation, Avenger 6 went down firing without saying another word.

As his command feeds died, Tara said, "Lucille, give me back the overall feeds."

<<Engaged. Misfit 6 has withdrawn from the objective.>>

Tara watched the icons pulling back toward their initial drop point. What none of them could see was the mass of Oogar swirl completely around the Raknar at a respectful distance and charge south. They would overrun the Misfits in a matter of minutes.

"Well, that was interesting." Tara smirked. "I thought they'd perform a little better than that."

<<Simulation terminated, Tara. All forces are standing by for instructions.>>

"Get them out of their cockpits and into the hangar bay for a hasty after-action report. Reboot the sim, too. They'll run this a couple of times today."

<<Is that a prediction?>>

Tara laughed and opened Deathangel 25's cockpit. "No, Lucille. After that performance? It's a fact."

* * *

New Perth

Snowmass

Summer on Snowmass was a short break from the perennial winters that embraced the higher latitudes where the main landmasses were. The equatorial regions, where water maintained its liquid form year-round, were devoid of any type of hospitable terrain. Those areas that existed were little more than smooth lava structures from the creation of the continents several hundred million years before the Dream World Consortium's terraforming efforts. The continents themselves had turned into cold, yet forgiving environments capable of supporting a multitude of lifeforms year-round. The addition of snow domes that protected crops in a controlled atmosphere to allow year-round, sustainable farming gave the colonies more than enough provisions to stabilize themselves and their populations. Further south, where the water flowed, equatorial storms relentlessly pounded the barren islands and rendered any type of artificial settlement impossible. The further occupied colonies were geographically separated from the stormy zones, the better for everyone. As such, living in wintry conditions for eight months a year was the norm for New Perth and its sister cities.

The brief summer, more a combination of a rainy spring and a cool autumn, ended typically in a period of warm, dry weather the natives called the Tissenta. With the warmth came festivals and markets to celebrate the mid-year harvests of rare delectable vegetables pulled from the rich volcanic soil. Rare tubers, excellent for long-term storage, were the most sought-after choices. Fortunately, there were plenty of suppliers. While a sizable portion of the harvest went offworld, the rest stayed with the colonists, and they celebrated and ate their fill for a fortnight before the first snowfall. Carts full of the tubers and the more Human-friendly fare filled the market square. Amongst the swirling crowd of faces, both the families of Zuul mercenaries and the few remaining Veetanho circulated openly, sharing smiles and goodwill as only a closely-knit colony could in the face of open warfare. On Snowmass, as with many planets on the far reaches of the Galactic Union, the troubles of the Mercenary Guild and its perilous war on humanity seemed distant and unreal.

A dark-furred Veetanho dodged Zuul and Human children playing football in the street. The older female chittered a laugh and pirouetted as the hexagonal-patched ball skidded toward her. As it did, her left leg shot out, catching the ball perfectly with a sharp spin. The ball arced several meters through the air, past the surprised open maw of a tan-colored Zuul pup playing goalie, and into the makeshift netting, to the cheers of the Human children. They briefly ringed the Veetanho, who touched her paw to their closed and open hands in celebration. The ball skidded into action again, and the children dispersed from around her. She moved quickly across the corner of their playing field toward a cart holding bushels of a long, skinny legume she'd taken a liking to years before.

The familiar face of the Human farmer smiled in greeting. "Honored Veeka! I was wondering when you'd come by. Strange not to see you during the early days of the festivals."

The Veetanho nodded and reached across the display to clasp her paws around the Human's hands. "Mister Balyeat. There are two things as certain as the Tissenta. One of them is that I won't let a bushel of your green beans escape the festival."

Balyeat smiled. He was tall, bald, and with his heavy chin covered in dark, thick hair, he seemed far older than his age. He'd taken over the family farm and its three domes at eighteen, when most of his counterparts were scratching their itch for action by joining the passing mercenary forces. Many of them hadn't lived more than a few years. The young farmer's contented smile said he felt no regrets in his choice of life's work. "I've saved you two this year. I have to ask, what's the second of the two things as certain as the Tissenta?"

Veeka grinned up at him. "Why, that I have you and your family to dinner before the snows come, of course. I've perfected my dumpling recipe with Stephanie's recommendations. I'm eager to show them off to you. I think they're quite good."

Balyeat grinned wider. "Say the word, Honored Veeka. We graciously accept."

"Pshaw." The furry alien waved dismissively. "That is how you say it, yes? We're friends, Nathan. It would honor me to cook for you and your family. Does two days give you enough time to close up the booth and prepare for the trek north?"

"Certainly." His smile faded slightly. "The winter looks especially harsh this year. Has there been any discussion over lowering the precipitation levels again?"

Veeka shook her head. From her position on the governing board, she was bound not to discuss their plans. "The levels, as you know, have been set for a decade." Her voice was low, and while she smiled at her friend, her words weren't happy. "They've assured me that these fluctuations will subside. I have great hopes that the winter won't be as significant as before."

The reality was that it would be worse, most likely. She saw the recognition in Balyeat's eyes even as he smiled and nodded, thanking her profusely.

"Thank you for looking into it, Honored Veeka. Our friends and the families they support in their farms will be very interested to hear this news." Balyeat's eyes twinkled. "We'll have to ensure that our perimeters and inner structures are ready."

Veeka shook her head slightly. "I trust you'll know what to do for you and your families. I'm sure we'll find a way to make things work here."

The farmer nodded once more, and the business part of their conversation faded to pleasantries again as Balyeat handed her a bag of green beans with the promise he would deliver the bushels when they had their dinner. They would visit more, she assured him. His eyes flickered past her head and over her left shoulder. She didn't need to hear his words to know what was coming. The old soldier in her never fully retreated.

"How many of them, Nathan?"

"Three. They have rifles slung over their shoulders," he replied. "They're walking this direction with their eyes on you, Veeka."

"They believe they have a lead on their terrorists." She curled one side of her mouth under in a smirk. "I'm not surprised they're summoning me."

"But at gunpoint?"

She chittered. "You said their rifles are slung. They're lazy mercenaries, Nathan. Remember that when the time comes. Plowshares to swords."

Balyeat's face turned cold and hard. "If it becomes necessary, Veeka."

The three Zuul mercenaries came up behind her. By their scent, she recognized two of them as lower level mercs, pups barely off their first tour of duty. Their leader would be in the center. As they closed the distance, she caught a whiff of day-old bread and recognized it for what it really was. The local wheat beers never failed to cause her nose to wrinkle in distaste. While there were several Zuul who liked to drink more than others, there was only one who limped on a long-injured right leg. Sergeant Turlyq was a burly brown- and gray-haired Zuul with sad brown eyes and ears too large for his head. There was no doubt it was him, but Veeka turned with poise and grace instead of the barely controlled rage she felt burning in her stomach.

"Sergeant Turlyq? Is there a problem?"

The Zuul bowed awkwardly. "Honored Veeka. His Honor, the mayor, has requested an audience with the members of the Board."

"A meeting? Unscheduled meetings aren't allowed by—"

"No," Turlyq barked. "Individual audience. His Honor, the mayor, wishes to discuss the emergency this morning and communicate the results of our investigation."

Interrupt me again, cur, and I will rip your entrails out through your mouth.

She inhaled sharply and calmed herself. "I see. I'm to understand that this audience is now?"

"Yes," Turlyq replied. The two pups at his sides had a glimmer of fear in their eyes. In another lifetime, Veeka would have relished such an opportunity and fed their fears appropriately. But to do so would only exacerbate the situation and bring further scrutiny upon her and the other Veetanho. Intuition told her that the Zuul believed a Veetanho was behind the recent attacks. Truth be told, they'd never trusted the Veetanho, even before Reecha and the main colony withdrew from the Consortium. Veeka and a handful of others had stayed to avoid legal disputes that would cost millions of credits, but they'd also stayed behind to observe the Dream World Consortium and their leadership. Something in their dealings hadn't set well with Reecha all those years before, and her guidance to Veeka and the others had been crystal clear.

Discover the truth.

Veeka exposed her teeth in an approximation of a Human smile. "Very well, Sergeant Turlyq. I shall report to the mayor's office when my business here is finished."

"I am sorry, Honored Veeka. The mayor's summons is immediate, and we are to escort you."

She wanted to laugh, but she held it in. Every free pair of eyes in the market followed her every move. The two pups made no move to secure their slung rifles. They didn't consider her a threat, nor did they want to incite anxiety in the populace. Veeka felt the stares of her fellow colonists like a hot wind on her face, yet she also knew in their racing minds the seeds of doubt had been planted. The doubt wasn't fixed on her, but on their collective leadership.

Whoever was responsible for the attacks on the PCMUs had done exactly what they'd wanted to do. History told many stories of colonists suppressed by their governments who'd ultimately revolted and determined their own destinies. The key was to involve the general public in the cause. The Dream World Consortium had given them all the ammunition necessary to generate sympathy among the populace. Unreliable weather and diminishing trade deals weren't enough. Sacrifice was necessary.

Unfortunate, but necessary.

* * * * *

Chapter Seven

Office of the Colonial Mayor
New Perth
Snowmass

"Honored Veeka." Citsym rose from behind the obsidian topped desk in the central office. The Zuparti practically danced around it to greet her. "I am sorry to summon you so dishonorably, but haste and necessity forced my hand. I needed to speak with you immediately. You're the senior Veetanho in the colonies and there have been some…unfortunate revelations according to Colonel Krukk's investigators."

Veeka's whiskers involuntarily twitched. "And what might those revelations be?"

Citsym directed her toward a chair facing the desk. Instead of sitting behind it, he sat in an opposite chair as if he were a friend carrying on an innocent conversation. Citsym paused and let out a nervous titter. "Well, allow me to come quickly to the point. There is no easy way to put this, Veeka. Colonel Krukk believes the culprits behind today's attack were Veetanho."

"I assume you have some type of proof?" Veeka folded her paws across her lap.

"As in physical proof? Well, no," Citsym said. "Krukk's team is certain that the sheer lack of evidence points directly to a Veetanho operation."

Veeka let out the laugh she'd been holding since the confrontation in the market with a bark. "You *have* to be joking, Citsym."

The Zuparti frowned. "Sadly, I'm not. As difficult as this situation is, I'm inclined to believe Colonel Krukk's investigators."

"Without proof?" Veeka squinted at him.

"Can you prove otherwise?"

Anger seeped into her thoughts, and she let it rise. Given recent history, an accusation against her kind was part of almost every news cycle. On Snowmass, however, it was almost a declaration of war. "This entire line of questioning is repulsive. Without physical proof of any kind, you're inclined to believe the findings of soldiers who can't be trusted to clean up their own waste. You place them over the small contingent of my people who have supported New Perth for decades. You support your mercenaries, who were responsible for the deaths of innocents, over the Veetanho I represent to the Dream World Consortium's local board? Then you're placing the soldiers, these mercenaries, in a position above the very colonists you claim to represent."

Citsym flinched and raised his tiny paws, palm out, as if warding off danger. "I didn't mean to be accusatory, Veeka. I'm trying to ask you for cooperation and assistance."

"I see." Veeka took a long breath. There was little doubt in her mind that Citsym had meant to be accusatory, just as there was little doubt in her mind that his new steps would be to pump her for insights and information. "I have little help I can give you, Citsym. With as small a contingent of Veetanho as we have on Snowmass, I know them all intimately. None of them are capable of this kind of attack."

"They don't have the experience? Or the formal training?"

Oh, there it is. Why not accuse me directly?

"I resent that, Citsym. My experience in the mercenary forces is over eighty years in the past, and I've done nothing but openly support you and this office for the last fifty years, since the bulk of my people gave up on the contract and fled."

"I've always appreciated your support, Veeka. But this situation grows larger than my abilities or those of this office." Citsym leaned back against the heavy desk with a sigh.

"The Consortium's board?" Veeka asked.

"They're concerned about their reputation after the debacle on Araf and the intervention of Peacemaker Francis."

"Their reputation?" Veeka laughed and shook her head. "This situation, as was that on Araf, is about the Dream World Consortium delivering the products they promise and properly servicing their customers: the colonists. Us. If the DWC wants to secure their reputation, they should focus on deliverables."

Citsym frowned even deeper. "You're speaking about the complaints from the high latitudes."

"They promised us longer growing seasons, Citsym. The standard season appears to be down to just fifty-four days. The domes and facilities built to provide geothermal energy barely create enough heat to keep our colonists from freezing to death during the hard months. The rich soil they promised us hasn't materialized, despite our best efforts. We're relying on soils and fertilizers shipped in from across the galaxy. This is hardly the paradise world they promised us."

"You're insinuating that we don't care about our colonists."

Veeka paused, noting the change in Citsym's words. Whether purposeful or not, his allegiance seemed tipped toward the DWC. "And you're insinuating that I'm behind the attacks on your PCMUs. I led the original site surveys and oversaw their installations."

Citsym pushed off the desk and gathered his paws in front of him. "This is going nowhere. Perhaps I should start over."

"I think that would be an ideal situation," Veeka replied. A simple restart to the conversation wouldn't be enough. Citsym was a consummate politician and able to turn phrases and give assurances easily. He seemed more troubled, and increasingly flustered, by telling the truth.

"I need your help, Honored Veeka."

Pressing on the nerve, she replied, "Then you should have called me, rather than having me fetched by your mercenaries. The only thing they didn't do was point their weapons at me, Citsym. From that moment to your request for help just now, the entire tone has been accusatory."

His chin lowered toward his chest. "You have my deepest apologies, Veeka. These attacks have strained my abilities."

There it is. She almost smiled at the admission. Instead, an option flashed through her mind, and she latched on to it.

"If you'll allow me to inspect the site?" Veeka asked. "Perhaps a more trained eye can be of assistance and actually move the investigation forward?"

Citsym brightened. "I appreciate your candor and your offer, Honored Veeka. Thank you."

"I have always supported the colony, Citsym. I wish for its continued growth and success."

And I'll do everything I can to make sure of it. Even undercut you if I must.

"The best interests of the colony and its citizens are paramount," Citsym replied solemnly. "I take any threat against them seriously."

"As do I," Veeka replied. A door opened behind her, and the immediate scent of Human perfume attacked her nostrils. Her nose involuntarily twitched in disgust, a response Citsym undoubtedly saw before he glanced over her shoulder.

"Yes, Sophie?"

"My apologies for the interruption, Mayor Citsym. You have a scheduled conference with the mining union from down south in fifteen minutes, and you asked for time to review and sign the proposals for additional exploratory drilling in the far north. The Science Guild representatives should arrive this afternoon."

Citsym rocked back on his tiny heels. "Ah, yes. Thank you for that, Sophie. Honored Veeka and I were just culminating our discussion. Please make arrangements with Colonel Krukk allowing Veeka to inspect the PCMU fire site this afternoon."

Pryce's carefully controlled face broke for an instant, her eyebrows rising perceptibly. She recovered quickly. "I'll see to it, Honored Veeka. We are grateful for your assistance."

Veeka nodded solemnly at Pryce and then Citsym. "Thank you for your time, Mayor. I shall report my findings to you by sundown."

"I welcome your insight, my friend. Your colony thanks you." Citsym returned her nod, and she took that as a dismissal.

Veeka smiled at Pryce as she turned for the door. "Miss Pryce," she said, ensuring the smile didn't encompass her whole face. The Human disgusted her, as had Pryce's grandfather, Johann. His passing should have been a great moment for the final desegregation of the colony, allowing free trade and interaction. It had taken only two years after his death to fully accomplish what he'd been unable to start. Given the chance, Sophie Pryce would follow in his xenophobic footsteps, of that Veeka was certain.

* * *

When the door closed to the outer office, and the Veetanho could no longer hear them, Citsym met Sophie Pryce's glare with a stern look of his own. "What was the meaning of that interruption?"

"I was merely keeping you on schedule," Sophie replied. The innocent look she attempted to plaster on her face nearly caused Citsym to laugh aloud. "You've mentioned on many occasions how time seems to slip away during your workday."

Citsym said nothing. Her intent had been obvious. Like her father, Sophie Pryce didn't care for the Veetanho. After the departure of most of their colony over forty years ago, the elder Pryce had conjectured openly that they'd continue to conduct operations to undermine the colony. His fears had been unsubstantiated, and only amid the recent unrest had the specter of the Veetanho returned. He'd thought it unfounded and tried to remain neutral, but what little evidence there was pointed to them as the culprit. Yet Veeka's words were true. There was no other Veetanho on the planet with the combat experience she had. If she wasn't the one behind the recent attacks, then either something far more nefarious was at play, or the Zuul mercenaries were less than honest. Neither of the outcomes would surprise him, nor did Sophie Pryce's actions.

"You've ordered her followed, haven't you?"

Pryce nodded. "I believed it was the more prudent action. If she's behind the recent attacks, we'll know fairly quickly."

Citsym stroked the hair on his chin. "Have you ordered an evaluation of the closed-circuit monitoring system?"

"Of course. Her actions for the last two weeks—the extent of the video recording and archive system—have been almost impeccably on a schedule."

"With any dubious activity?"

"No." Pryce barked an awkward, pained laugh. "She invites friends over to her place and cooks them meals. Up at dawn and in bed early. Never leaves her place in the off hours. Almost boring."

"Then why have you ordered her followed?"

"It's too perfect."

"Maybe she is…what have you called it? A home something?"

Pryce curled one side of her mouth up in a smirk. "A homebody. She seems to fit the bill. But I still say it's almost too perfect to me."

Citsym frowned. "What aren't you saying?"

"I don't trust her," Sophie replied with a shrug of her shoulders.

"Tell me something I don't know," Citsym replied. "You share your father's distaste for the Veetanho."

"Among other things."

Citsym chuckled and then openly smiled. "I trust your judgment, but if there's nothing there, we must let her be. She's agreed to investigate the PCMU scene."

"Why? That's like letting a fox into the henhouse!"

"I don't understand the analogy, Sophie." Citsym shook his head. "You're saying your distrust for her means I shouldn't let her investigate on my behalf? She's been nothing but personally honorable in her dealings with this office for forty years."

"That doesn't mean she shouldn't be followed," Pryce said with her eyebrows raised, an almost comical expression to the Zuparti.

"Fine, leave your orders in place," Citsym said. "I have a full calendar for the afternoon, but cancel all my evening activities. I require personal time to deal with the stress of this situation."

A faint hint of color tinged Sophie Pryce's cheeks. He knew she suspected he had a mistress in New Perth for whom relieving his physical stresses was a constant need. Little did she know that he in fact had *four* mistresses. But he had no intention of visiting any of them that evening if his timetable held.

"I understand, Mayor Citsym."

Citsym smiled and rubbed his paws together. "Now, while Honored Veeka and her escorts inspect the PCMU, let us continue to business of New Perth, Sophie. The time is coming for us to make good on the promises of our fathers."

* * *

Taal's Fury
Hyperspace
Emergence T-12:00:30

It had taken four iterations, but Force 25 had finally prevailed in the simulation. All her troops were tired. From the cockpit of Deathangel 25, Tara could see their fatigue from a distance. Yet in their exhaustion, there was a sense of hope. From her earliest days as a mercenary, she knew readiness was everything. The ability of the unit to perform when necessary was paramount to everything else.

Training came in three phases. The first phase was the crawl phase. Introducing new terms, new tactics, or new equipment meant not only a significant investment in training time, but also in rehearsals. At the crawl stage, a unit couldn't be expected to perform to the standard required. But given enough iterations, a unit could move to the walk phase.

In the walk phase, a unit could perform its mission to standard with both help and multiple iterations. The more successful the training mission, the less assistance would be required. Able to perform the mission more to standard than not, the walk phase was a critical transformation for unit readiness. In theory, a unit transitioning from the crawl phase to the walk phase meant proficiency at all the required tasks. Once proficient in individual and collective tasks, they could move as a unit to the run phase. Reality told Tara that proficiency in all tasks was like perfection and therefore unattainable. Yet what she'd seen in the course of eight hours of simulation time gave her hope.

The extended time in this simulation also gave her and the remainder of the unit the need for rest. Emergence from hyperspace was half a day away, and she needed every single being ready for any situation they would face upon arrival at Snowmass. She ordered her subordinate commanders to place everyone on a rest plan for the remainder of the day, but a mercenary unit commander could hardly ever rest. So Tara pushed away from Deathangel 25, leaving the shutdown procedures to Lucille, so she could head to the bridge and make sure the ship was ready for emergence before getting some rest herself. Once satisfied everything was in order, she retired to her quarters and turned on Vivaldi's *Four Seasons.* Tara stripped out of her coveralls and used one of the large, prepackaged waterless bathing towels to wipe herself down. She dressed in a red University of Nebraska sweatshirt and black shorts before getting a bulb of red wine from her cooler and moving to her bunk to read Lucille's analysis and after-action report from the simulation.

<<Tara? May I bother you for a moment?>>

"What is it, Lucille?"

<<You asked that I monitor further discussions between Captain Gray and Lieutenant Whirr.>>

Gods. Not again.

Tara undid the strap holding her to the bunk and set her slate aside. "Where are they?"

<<They are not arguing. They are discussing an idea that has merit. I believe this is a most fortunate development. Would you like to know what they are discussing?>>

Tara thought about it for half a second. "No, Lucille. Let them do their thing. If they talk it out and can present it in a way that I understand and buy in to it, that would be great. If they devolve into an actual physical altercation, that's when I want to know. Okay?"

<<I am detecting irritation in your voice, Tara.>>

Tara sighed and pushed her head harder against the cushions of her bunk. She sipped from the red wine bulb, an Argentina Malbec from Jessica's private, but shared with her, collection. "I'm tired, Lucille. That's all."

<<I have communicated to all commanders that you are not to be disturbed. I have also let the commanders know that I have placed the same notification for their own connections.>>

Tara smiled. "That's one way to take care of us, Lucille."

<<Looking out for the mission can be done in many ways, Tara.>>

"Very true." Tara yawned. "I guess the reports can wait until tomorrow."

<<That is a most prudent course of action.>>

"Did you just use prudent and course of action in a sentence together?" Tara laughed. "You sound more and more like Jessica every day."

<<That is hardly a derogatory statement, Tara.>>

Tara's eyes closed. The bulb of red wine spun away from her hands and tumbled gently in the microgravity to hang suspended above her bunk. Snuggling down in the covers, she said, "You know I didn't mean it that way. Jessica is my friend, Lucille. She is..."

* * *

"You really think Tara will listen to this?" Harmon Gray rubbed his sweaty short hair with one hand and squeezed a shot of cold water into his mouth. "I mean, you know her better than I ever will."

The MinSha lieutenant hung from angular rungs that covered almost every flat surface on the inside of the *Taal's Fury*. He'd assumed the rungs were meant for the massive mantis-like creatures to move in any direction, not unlike the loops and stirrups in most Human ships to allow for both movement and stillness when required in microgravity. He'd never been so close to MinSha in his career, and their collective grace and power awed him. In the bowels of one of their combat cruisers, filled with a crew of Humans, MinSha, and several other species not exactly known for fighting together with success, the ranking MinSha officer stared at him with her ruby compound eyes. Her antennae twitched in what he'd learned was amusement and exasperation. For the life of him, Gray couldn't figure out how those emotions could be so close together.

"I do, Captain Gray."

"It's ballsy." Gray laughed.

"I do not have an equivalent saying for that in the MinSha language. My translator calls it 'aggressive.'" Lieutenant Whirr flexed the claws on her left forelimb. "I believe, though, that both our languages understand the context of the word 'sore.' I have never practiced with a weapon for that length of time before."

Gray laughed. "Neither have I, but I think we're in for more of that as long as we're with Force 25, Lieutenant."

"I understand if this is not possible in Human customs and courtesies, Captain Gray, but I would appreciate if you could simply call me Whirr. While my rank is important to convey the duties I perform as a commander, we consider the use of it extremely formal in the MinSha, and it typically signals an…ass chewing? Is that the correct term?"

"You…" Gray covered his mouth with one hand and let the laugh come. As far as he was aware, MinSha didn't have an ass except in a metaphysical way. "You got it right, Whirr."

The MinSha's antennae bounced in laughter. In that moment, she was no longer a massive alien capable of ripping him apart with her claws. They were comrades and, more interestingly, friends. Gray kept the smile on his face. Whirr asked, "Is there anything else we should do? I mean, besides simply talking to her?"

"We should let Major Vuong know before we speak to her." Gray took another sip of water. "You know, that whole chain of command thing."

Whirr nodded, an exaggerated move of her long neck and wide head. "I understand that, Captain Gray."

Gray snapped his eyes to hers. While the MinSha didn't recoil, there was an element of surprise to the flick of her antennae and the tilt of her face. He relaxed his face and smiled. "If I'm going to call you Whirr, please return the favor. My name is Harmon, but I prefer my friends call me Harm."

Whirr's head tilted further in a curious mix of confused puppy and dangerous insectoid monster. It was all he could do not to burst out in laughter. Whirr replied slowly, "Then we are friends, Harm? Despite our arguments?"

"Our arguments have led us to this, Whirr. A possible solution for a combined weaponry approach to combat. I guarantee you no one else is fighting like this. It might be the thing that sets Force 25 apart. Or it won't work, and we'll either survive to keep arguing about it, or slake our thirst on Fiddler's Green. Are you familiar with that?"

"I am. Though the concept of an empty canteen took some getting used to," Whirr replied with a laugh. "Tara ensured we all had a copy of the poem before the second battle of Victoria Bravo. I believe it was prescient."

"Meaning what?" Gray asked.

"That come what may, she'd like us to all be together rather than in the cold, dark void," Whirr replied. "If being in Force 25 does nothing else, I will be glad to serve alongside my friends and family."

* * * * *

Chapter Eight

Taal's Fury

Snowmass

Emergence

<<Emergence in twenty seconds.>>

Tara tapped her console. "All hands, this is Colonel Mason. Brace for emergence in fifteen seconds." Transmission complete, she sat back in the modified bridge chair and closed her eyes. One moment, the white, featureless hyperspace environment was there outside the bridge, and the next, she saw the swirling colors behind her eyelids. There was a perceptible shift around her. Bile rose quickly in the back of the throat and receded. She opened her eyes to see the distant yellow star of the Snowmass system shining in the distance. The bright white and blue world beckoned in the distance.

"Emergence," the MinSha watch officer said from her position forward and to Tara's left.

<<Confirm emergence. All systems nominal,>> Lucille reported.

"Thank you," Tara said to both. "Stand by for—"

The bridge lights flashed blue, the MinSha alert signal, and a klaxon brayed.

"Collision warning! Collision warning! Brace for impact!" the watch officer called.

Tara pushed herself back in the chair. "Where is it?"

<<Emergence port side. Zero point five kilometers distance. Evasive action engaged.>>

Sudden G forces piled on as every thruster along the port side of the frigate fired at once. Tara grabbed the arm rails of her chair and struggled to stay upright for several seconds, then the thrust cut out.

<<Clear. Vessel emerged at 0.75 kilometer spread. That is twice as close as normally happens with emergences.>>

Tara stabbed the transmit button on her console. "All clear, all clear. Sorry about that, everyone. Recover from emergence protocols. We're two days and sixteen hours from Snowmass. Bridge, out."

The MinSha officer turned at her console. "Colonel Mason, you have my apologies."

Tara waved a hand in the alien's direction. "Not your fault. You did an outstanding job getting us out of the way."

"Thank you." The MinSha paused as if to say something else, but the communications system crackled to life.

"*Taal's Fury*, this is the *Strong Arm*. Thank you for your prudent and fast maneuvering. We are in your debt."

Tara pointed at the watch officer to reply. While universal translators did a good job camouflaging voices to a certain extent, having anyone know there were Humans aboard a MinSha vessel wasn't something Tara was prepared to acknowledge.

"*Strong Arm*, thank you for reaching out to us. Safe travels."

The other voice replied. "And safe travels to you, travelers."

Tara squinted. "I've never heard that before."

<<It is a standard parting phrase from the Cochkala, particularly those with a long history of space travel. You know the *Strong Arm* is

the Jivool-registered ship mentioned in the Peacemaker reports from Parmick, yes?"

Tara took a quick breath and let it out. "That's right. I thought it sounded familiar."

<<What would you like me to do?>> Lucille asked.

"Are there any open receiver ports you can exploit?"

It took a moment, and then Lucille replied, <<Negative. I tried 453 entries on four ports. I could not penetrate the vessel. The flight plan they filed for Snowmass lists New Perth as their destination, but there is no other information.>>

She sighed. While more intelligence on the suspicious vessel would have been nice to have, there was no sense in making a further attempt for fear of being found out and risking reprisal. "Stop trying, Lucille. Monitor them and see what they're doing. I want to know if they release any ships or attempt to land anywhere on the planet."

<<You believe this is directly related to Kr'et'Socae and his operation on Parmick and not a simple coincidence.>>

"Until we know what they're doing, it's a coincidence to see them here. What's more interesting is that they're still broadcasting and using their name. I would have expected them to change it."

<<Ship signatures are difficult to change, Tara. Perhaps they've simply continued operations with this vessel as a deception operation?>>

Tara shrugged. "I suppose it's possible. That's why we'll observe and report what we find. Use any channel necessary on any outbound ship, Lucille."

<<Acknowledged. What are your directives for the crew, Tara?>> Lucille asked.

She bit her lower lip for a moment. "Initiate the rest plan first."

<<Rest plan transmitted. After the near collision excitement, there may be issues with personnel skipping the sleep period, Tara.>>

"Can't be helped, Lucille." Tara scratched her eyebrow with one hand. "Set the initial landing party brief for eight hours from now and relay that to Captain Gray and Lieutenant Whirr. I'd like the intelligence team there as well."

<<Done. There is a request for a meeting from Captain Gray. The subject is blank, but he has requested Lieutenant Whirr's presence, and she has accepted.

Interesting. Maybe they've buried the proverbial hatchet?

"Fine. Let Captain Gray know they can speak with me an hour prior to the briefing."

<<That will cut into your rest period, Tara.>>

"Can't be helped, Mom." Tara smiled. She heard the MinSha watch officer chitter a soft laugh.

<<You know I do not appreciate your sarcasm, Tara.>> Lucille huffed. <<I have alerted Captain Gray and Lieutenant Whirr. May I speak privately, please?>>

"Sure," Tara replied. She dug quickly into the left sleeve pocket of her dark green coveralls and retrieved her personal headset. After positioning it, Tara touched it to activate the connection. "I'm here, Lucille."

<<Captain Gray and Lieutenant Whirr are meeting with Major Vuong at this moment. I thought you should be aware.>>

Tara frowned slightly. "Lucille, I understand you're concerned for the mission, but the crew should be able to meet and discuss anything they want at any time. I don't want any surveillance on them."

<<I understand. They are discussing tactics and strategy; that is why I thought it was important to bring to your attention.>>

A flicker of recognition caused Tara to blink. "You're not sure who to trust."

<<The personnel changes notwithstanding, there have been several adjustments made. Working with the personnel isn't an issue. I am merely trying to consider all the variables in play and bring them to your attention, Tara.>>

Tara massaged her temple for a moment. There was a twinge of a headache starting, and she really didn't want to deal with that, or discord between her near-AI assistant and the crew. Lucille wasn't really hers, but for the duration of the mission they were interminably linked. Since Jessica's message to throttle Lucille's abilities, she'd performed almost as before, but she asked questions. Determining the parameters Tara wanted enforced was important, but the extra effort grated on Tara's mind after a while. "So what are you really wanting to ask me, Lucille?"

<<Once we arrive at Snowmass, what do you want me to do?>>

"Everything you've always done: monitor, investigate, and inform. You connect to thousands of systems faster than I can flip a switch. As long as your actions remain outside of detection or attribution, I'm good with you digging deep, Lucille. Like always."

<<Thank you, Tara,>> Lucille replied. <<To that end, I have cataloged every information source I have for the Intergalactic Haulers. I have found four more entries for the Snowmass region. I believe there may be a base or installation of some type there based on the communications in the archive.>>

Good to know. We can start there.

"Have you adjusted our identification?"

<<I have. We are still transmitting the *Taal's Fury* identification, but I have added a series of clearance codes to the underlying signal. I am not using the Force 25 codes, for multiple reasons. The most important one is with the current unrest in the Mercenary Guild, the company's official certification has not been approved. It remains awaiting signature.>>

"Gotta love bureaucracy, huh?"

<<More sarcasm? It would seem to be, as I know you do not love what you call bureaucracy.>>

"You're correct, Lucille." Tara laughed. "I'm not a fan of red tape whatsoever. Keep searching the Haulers' archive and maintain all active searches through the GalNet. I want to know as much as we can about Snowman's dealings on this planet and any clue where we can find him."

<<Understood. I am receiving message packets now, including intelligence from active MinSha searches ordered by Queen Taal. I will review and summarize them for you when you wake up from your sleep period. Major Vuong would like to schedule a meeting with you prior to arrival. I believe this is based on the conversation just completed with Captain Gray and Lieutenant Whirr.>>

"Schedule it, Lucille. And no more spying on the team unless you detect any type of aggression or threat. So we're clear, bitching and moaning aren't threats. That's life with soldiers."

<<I understand, Tara. Quin'taa is on his way to relieve you on the bridge. I will ensure you are not disturbed for the next seven hours.>>

Tara grabbed her slate and quickly finished logging a summary of her watch time, including the bridge incident. When she finished, the Oogar mercenary squeezed through the bridge opening and assumed a standing position near the watch officer's station—the only place on the bridge he could fit.

"I have the watch, Colonel Mason," Quin'taa said. He nodded and tapped a huge fist to his breastbone—the multi-species sign of respect.

Tara patted his massive upper arm. "Thank you, Quin'taa. The watch is yours. Lucille is active and available if you need her. I'm going to get some sleep."

"I understand," Quin'taa rumbled. "Good soldiers sleep and eat whenever they get the chance. I hope you rest well, Colonel."

"Thank you, Quin'taa." Tara pushed toward the hatch and didn't look back. Quin'taa's words stuck with her regarding sleeping and eating. The habit of a good soldier. She smiled to herself. After so many years of mercenary life, she could finally say that about herself.

A good soldier, yes. Now I can become a better leader.

I hope.

* * *

Taal's Fury

Jackson Rains drank from a chilled bulb of water and rubbed his head. Transition from hyperspace never failed to give him a headache. He rummaged through his bag for the analgesic tablets the pilots called CASPer Candy and palmed two of them, tossed them into his mouth, and drank more water.

"You doing okay there, partner?" Vannix asked from the open hatchway of his quarters.

"I wish." He closed his eyes and rubbed his temples again. "It will fade in a little bit, but right now? Not so much."

He turned and saw the small Veetanho staring at him. They'd been partners since leaving the Academy, and friends for longer than that. All that came through in the look she gave him, but he could tell something was troubling her. Hanging around and wanting to talk wasn't something she did lightly.

Rains waved to her to come inside and close the door. "What's on your mind, Vannix?"

She floated toward the small desk built into the bulkhead of Rains' stateroom. She touched the desk, rotated gracefully into position, and pushed her feet down to snake them through the angular rungs below. She looked impossibly smaller in the accommodations built for the MinSha. "There are a few things, really."

"Like what?"

"We're Peacemakers, Jackson. Yet here we sit practically embedded within a mercenary company. We should be working on our overarching mission." Vannix scratched her forearms simultaneously, "I'm worried our orders from Guild Master Rsach are taking us away from the real fight."

Jackson spun and hooked his feet into a matching rung. "Away from the fight?"

"This whole business, Jackson. We're sitting here cooling our heels while the Mercenary Guild collapses and the whole Union construct crumbles toward entropy. Guild Master Rsach wants us to find Snowman. Why? What does he possibly have that can mean this much?"

Jackson shook his head. "You read up on the ceasefire, correct? The guild is completely involved in the situation."

"But we're not." Vannix frowned.

Rains laughed. "For someone who went through the Academy saying you just wanted to do the job, you seem to suffer from a fear of exclusion."

"Maybe." She rubbed one ear. "But I'm wondering if we'll find Snowman at all. We've gotten nowhere since we hooked up with Tara."

"I disagree, partner." Rains reached down into a leg pocket of his coveralls and withdrew a small tan notebook with a pencil strapped to it. "I've been taking some notes along the way."

"Where's your slate?" Vannix blinked.

Rains pointed to the cabinet above the desk where she sat. "Up there. I've been doing a few things old school."

"Old what?"

Rains waved his hands dismissively. "Human expression. I mean I've been doing things in a way that's old-fashioned, maybe archaic. Does that make sense?"

She didn't respond, instead she bent down and removed a similar pad and thicker type of writing utensil from her vest. "More than you know."

"We're not cooling our heels," Rains said. "The whole presence of Kr'et'Socae confirms that. He's behind the operation Jyrall and Larth stopped on Parmick. He followed me to Araf. It's only a matter of time before we run into him or his cronies again. When, not if, we do, who better to be embedded with than one of the most powerful mercenary companies in the galaxy?"

"I suppose you're right," Vannix replied. "But there's one thing I really don't understand, Jackson."

"What?" He saw the glimmer of ferocity in her eyes and felt his shoulders hunch forward involuntarily. "What do you not understand?"

She leaned back against the desktop and draped one small arm across the wide surface. "You've never told me the full story of what happened on Tyun when you found him and confronted him."

"It's classified as need to know by the guild, Vannix."

"And I'd say this situation requires that you tell me, and maybe even Tara and the others. I *need to know* why a disgraced Enforcer wants to rule the galaxy. And why he wants you dead."

Rains sighed and his head slumped forward. "All right, Vannix. I'll tell you, but call Lucille and ask if Tara's awake. I really only want to tell this story once."

Vannix tucked her notepad into her vest pocket and tapped her slate. "Lucille? Is Tara still awake?"

<<She is, Peacemaker Vannix. However, I have asked that she not be disturbed unless the discussion is urgent.>>

"I've asked Peacemaker Rains to share his interaction with Kr'et'Socae," Vannix replied. "He's agreed to brief us."

<<Understood. I am summoning Tara now. Please secure the space you're working in to allow for the distribution of classified information. Tara is on her way and will be there in five minutes.>>

"Very well. Thank you, Lucille." Vannix looked at Rains for a long moment. "Kr'et'Socae may try to gain some type of foothold amidst the instability, but his business with you is personal, isn't it?"

Rains nodded slowly and raised his eyes to hers. "You have no idea."

* * *

New Perth
Snowmass

Veeka turned to the two Zuul mercenaries accompanying her and pointed at a large smudge of residue. "Did you test that?"

"No, Honored Veeka. We have not."

She nodded and withdrew a swab from her belt, collected the grayish-white residue, and held it up. "Bring me your slate, soldier."

The Zuul with brown fur and a white blaze running vertically between his eyes offered his slate, which was connected to a chemical compound sniffer wand. He extended the wand over the swab for several seconds. A satisfying series of beeps told her the slate had identified the compound.

"This says the compound is Xi'Tal'ch'quan, Honored Veeka."

She ran a paw under her chin. "Hmm, why would a MinSha explosive be placed on this PCMU? There hasn't been a MinSha on the planet in months, and this thermal compound is primarily used by their special forces. That makes no sense at all. Does it?"

She looked up at the Zuul and his darker furred companion shared a blank look. "No, it doesn't," the brown one replied.

"Nevertheless, it's a clue," Veeka said. "There's not much else here. Some vegetation disturbance. I suppose it could be MinSha, but they've certainly covered their tracks well. We must head back to your headquarters and query the colony administration. If there have been any MinSha sightings or transports in the region for the last several months, we should be able to identify them."

As they made their way back to the city, Veeka's slate beeped, and a transmission from the mayor's office connected automatically.

"Honored Veeka?"

She smiled. "Mayor Citsym. I trust they've briefed you on our findings?"

"They have. We are indebted to your experience and knowledge, old friend," Citsym replied. She could hear the giddy smile on his face. "We're looking into any recent MinSha presence on the planet. There have been multiple landings at the remote colonies in the last six months."

"Some of them might coincide with other attacks on PCMU sites and networks, then," she said.

"Indeed. We're working that as we speak."

"I'm thankful to have found something useful. If you require nothing more of me, I shall retire to my domicile for the rest of the day," Veeka replied.

"Rest well, old friend. Thank you again for your assistance."

"Thank you, Honored Mayor. I'm available, should you need me." The line clicked off, and Veeka turned to see her escorts already moving away to their headquarters without her. She turned down the hill and made her way through the long-needled evergreens to a hiking path that lead to the central avenue of New Perth. She wound through the residential district toward the central square but ducked into a narrow street and climbed partially back up the hill she'd descended from the PCMU site. Her home was a small cabin with an angular roof. With its windows left open to take in the warm late autumn air, she caught the smell of something cooking on the stove.

The fur on her neck stood up, but she kept walking toward the cabin. Along the path, she stopped and peered into several rows of potted herbs and spices. The smells made her smile amid her anxiety until her eyes found an impression in the soft dark soil.

Zuul.

Damn you, Citsym. You and your hired curs.

A square-bladed shovel lay in the dirt nearby. Her weapons were inside the cabin, but there was nothing else she could do. She stooped and wrapped her digits around the handle of a modified shovel and moved toward her patio and the door she'd left open, as was the colony tradition. Crime had never existed on Snowmass, but she distrusted both the Trenta Knights and their own government.

Her grip tightened on the handle as she pushed through the open door. On the small stove, a kettle of soup simmered. She moved past the kitchen to her sitting room. A dark figure sat in the far corner, away from the light.

"It's about time you came home, Veeka."

She loosened her grip on the shovel and set it aside. "What are you doing here, Reecha? You gave me a fright."

Reecha laughed. "You think you could've taken me down with a shovel, my student?"

"Never," Veeka said. "You made aiticos soup? I haven't had that in years. At least not the way you make it."

Reecha stood and crossed the room. They grasped hands and sniffed each other's faces before the elder Veetanho wrapped her tiny arms around Veeka's neck. "Snowman taught me this. It's called a hug."

Veeka returned the embrace. "I know what it is, teacher. I've missed you, Reecha. Your soup making skills aside."

Reecha laughed, and they released each other. "No one prepares aiticos soup this way anymore. The key to a good soup, Veeka, is the correct ingredients simmered slowly, and gently raising the heat to a near boil. Place a lid on the vessel and let the soup rest while the spices release their particular fragrances. Then the soup will be complete and the feast can begin."

"You're not just talking about aiticos soup." Veeka smiled. She knew the answer even before her oldest friend, whose mere presence was the greatest secret on Snowmass, smiled in return.

"Not in the slightest. There are many more courses to prepare, Veeka," Reecha said. "A ship approaches from the emergence point searching for Intergalactic Haulers across our networks."

"Do we know why they're searching for him?"

"Not yet. As soon as we know more about them, we'll find our answers. Until then, we have much to do. Let us begin."

* * * * *

Chapter Nine

Taal's Fury

Vannix touched the side of a pyramid-shaped elSha security device and waited for the red lights to turn blue, indicating the stateroom was secure. She glanced up at Tara. "We're ready."

Tara looked to Jackson Rains. "We're secure, and Lucille is monitoring through my headset. Are you good with that?"

"I am." Rains took a deep breath and sighed so hard his shoulders pitched forward slightly. "I haven't told this story to anyone but Guild Master Rsach. The official record is different, too. There are some things he didn't want revealed immediately."

Vannix reached across the narrow table and patted his forearm. "There are no devices in the room save Tara's headset, and it's secured to Lucille. Only the three of us will hear the story, Jackson. It's important we fully understand why Kr'et'Socae followed you to Araf. Whatever he's planning, there's a keen interest in you. You can't deny that."

"No, I can't," Rains said. He looked up at Tara and then to Vannix. "I don't know what he's planning to do, but his interest in me is personal."

Tara reached for a bulb of water attached to the magnetic tabletop. "How so? You said you tried to arrest him."

"I tried and failed to do so." Rains smiled ruefully. "He's after me because I killed his chosen mate. That's the kind of thing an Equiri carries to the grave."

"Tell us, Jackson," Vannix breathed. "Tell us everything."

* * *

Two Years Earlier

Tyun

Peacemaker commissioning missions fill many needs across the Galactic Union. A mission can run the gamut from health and safety missions to combat operations. Over the course of history, there was virtually no mission a Peacemaker candidate hadn't undertaken in pursuit of their platinum badge. There had been other Humans before him to undertake a commissioning mission. Only two had completed their missions and worn the Peacemaker badge. Several other Human candidates had been killed in pursuing their mission objectives or quit the program during their mission. To that end, Jackson Rains had chosen a simple, important mission.

Much of the Peco arm of the galaxy had the reputation of being a lawless frontier. The reality was more troubling. Rules and regulations existed across the varied colonies and settlements of just about every known race. Where their rules and regulations became matters of law were much more difficult to define than in most areas, except for combat. There the rules were clear and definitive. For a financial crime, particularly embezzlement, the rules were vague enough that most species didn't elevate their concerns to the Peacemaker Guild, but handled matters on their own. Or most of the societies preferred to engage in the proxy warfare of hiring mercenaries to fight their battles. Only in the rare case of interspecies crimes would they ask the guild to step in and investigate wrongdoing.

The alleged crime Rains was investigating seemed almost too good to be true. A Zuparti trading company and a Cochkala textile manufacturer were accusing each other of embezzlement. As his classmates scanned the blotters for incoming requests to hang their proverbial hats on, no one touched the simple conflict. In hindsight he should have recognized their trepidation as a sign of the difficulty of the mission. Instead, he'd gone to the guild master with the special request to work both local accountants and barristers to determine what he called "ground truth" and see where the chips fell. Rains had sold the guild master on resolving the conflict by declaring he could do it in a matter of days, if not hours.

After a third week of negotiation and discussion that barely moved the accusatory needle in either direction, he'd called a recess and gone on a long run to clear the rising stress threatening to strip his faculties. Instead of wearing his Peacemaker coveralls, he'd gone to his rented room and dressed in exercise gear. Without a weapon on his person, he'd taken off and deviated from the main thoroughfares. About thirty minutes into his run he turned a corner and saw several Equiri hustle inside a dingy bar called Raem's. They glanced his way and dismissed him, but there was something suspicious about the group. When the door to the establishment opened more than two hours before its posted opening time, a larger coal black Equiri had opened the door.

What if that's Kr'et'Socae?

The disgraced Enforcer's escape from the maximum-security prison on Kleve three months earlier had made galaxy-wide news.

He hadn't been seen or heard from since the daring operation. There had been several Equiri involved, and before he could glance in their direction again and attempt to capture a mental image, they disappeared into the bar. He'd kept running, but spun back toward his hotel, intent on grabbing his slate and weapon before returning to see what he could see.

An hour later, the bar's door was unlocked and guarded by an armed Equiri. At a café across the thoroughfare, Rains sat at a table, drinking an alien version of coffee that irritated his tongue and picking through an amalgamation of local foods that vaguely tasted like pizza. His eyes and slate trained on the bar, he believed it was only a matter of waiting for the right moment to capture some type of intelligence. He hadn't had to wait long. The Equiri guard denied entry to a quartet of Cochkala, who chirped and squealed at a pitch irritating enough to annoy Rains a good thirty meters away. Their protests stopped when the door opened and a black Equiri with a white blaze between his eyes peered out at them.

Gotcha.

Within a few seconds the recognition program on his slate cut through the local government system and positively identified the Equiri as Thraff, a known associate of Kr'et'Socae and one of those suspected of assisting in the escape. A quick glance at known friends and associates positively identified two more of the Equiri he'd seen earlier and implicated a third. Given the data on Kr'et'Socae, Rains believed he had enough probable cause for an arrest attempt, but Tyun didn't have a Peacemaker office, and the regional barracks was a 170-hour hyperspace transition away. In that amount of time, he knew Kr'et'Socae would move on and disappear again—that was his *modus operandi*, his way of doing things.

I have to do it on my own.

But caution prevailed. With no support, he decided to wait and attempt to gather more intelligence first. If Kr'et'Socae disappeared again, he had a confirmed sighting the Peacemakers could act on through their intelligence networks. Every little bit helped.

Aside from his mission, Rains spent his afternoons for the next several days running more than he'd ever enjoyed, but he identified both that the dingy bar was the fugitive's base of operations, and that they did indeed have a ship on one of the remote landing pads. The additional four kilometers on his running path was agony, but he'd seen several shipping crates of various sizes. By their markings, it was everything from cleaners and solvents, to mining supplies. He never got close enough to inspect the containers. Running didn't really allow him to carry his slate without attracting attention. His weapon, however, fit under the running jacket he wore even on the warmest days. On the third day, a loading party of Cochkala teemed around the ship and the adjacent pad amidst a roaring downpour. Departure appeared imminent. As the local sun set, Rains made it back to his hotel, intending to shower and change into his coveralls. After alerting the local security force, he would head to the bar and confront Kr'et'Socae. He'd even believed the Enforcer might surrender peacefully—until he opened the door to his hotel room.

Thraff sat on a modified couch by the wide wall of windows with his empty hands clearly in sight. Rains froze, and something powerful slammed the door from behind. He bounced off the jamb and back into the hallway. Another Equiri, this one a shimmering gray with a white blaze across its left shoulder, reached out and grabbed him by the jacket and flung him into the room.

Fuck!

He rolled and grabbed the pistol from its concealed holster at the small of his back. Rains came up into a firing position facing a smaller brown Equiri carrying a stun stick already pulsating with wild blue energy. Rains found its center of mass and fired three times in rapid succession.

"Aaah!" the brown Equiri gasped and fell backward.

"No!" Thraff roared an instant later and came up from the chair. Before Rains could turn in his direction, Thraff bludgeoned him in the head.

Sometime later, Rains woke in a dark room and realized he wasn't alone. Torrential rain fell on a metal roof above him. It was cool and damp. They'd tied his wrists to the chair with a metal chain of some type. He carefully wriggled his wrists, trying not to give away his conscious state as he tested the bonds.

"Good," a deep voice rumbled like thunder from behind him. "You're awake."

Rains turned his head slightly to look over his right shoulder, but he couldn't see anything. "You're making a mistake, Kr'et'Socae."

There was a laugh as the massive Equiri swept around Rains' left shoulder and stood menacingly over him. "A Peacemaker Candidate doesn't scare me. That you are Human and resisted the impulse to rush into a potential conflict for several days is laudable. Yet you were preparing for an arrest with certainty of conflict without ever having called for assistance. Stupid."

Rains snorted. "Staying in place is stupid. You should be running."

"Oh, I should? Tell me, great Peacemaker Candidate Jackson Rains. In your two years at the Academy, have you gained so much knowledge that you can tell me what to do? You certainly haven't realized when a Peacemaker should keep their mouth shut."

"You should have sent better lackeys to get me, though. I killed one of—"

Kr'et'Socae's left hind hoof came up faster than anything Rains had ever seen and kicked him once, devastatingly hard, in the chest. He gasped for breath as he fell backward, and the chair slid across the floor. His left wrist crackled sickeningly. Pain exploded. Breathing hurt. On the wet floor he thrashed and struggled to breathe as Kr'et'Socae knelt in his face.

"You killed my *mate*, Rains. By Equiri law, your life is in my hands. If I kill you, there is nothing your guild could do about it, save etching your name into the wall outside the Hall of Heroes. Another Human Peacemaker Candidate who failed. Especially a male, when not one but *two* females of your species have accepted their commissions. Their commissioning missions were much more significant than trying to settle a winless embezzlement case." Kr'et'Socae laughed and shook his head. His ebony mane gleamed in the low light.

Rains sucked in slow breaths. His entire rib cage ached, and there were doubtless broken bones of all sorts around the impact zone. The pain was too great. Rains could do nothing as the Equiri motioned to someone else.

Thraff appeared with a large pneumatic hypodermic needle. Without warning, he slammed the injector into Rains' thigh. Whatever had been in the syringe shot into his body like warm, thick maple syrup. The injection site burned, and Rains bit his tongue to stop himself from screaming. Tears leaked out of his eyes and ran down his cheeks in hot, damning trails.

"Hurts?" Thraff laughed. "Good, motherfucker. That's for Sa'texia."

"What?" Rains struggled to speak through the pain. "What was that?"

"Don't you worry about that, Candidate," Kr'et'Socae said. "As a matter of fact you're probably getting very sleepy about now, right?"

Rains' vision swam, and his eyelids felt like lead. Everything faded. He drew a deep breath, hoping the momentary shot of pain would clear his mind for an instant. "We'll find you."

"No you won't, Rains." Kr'et'Socae smiled, but his blazing eyes burned with hatred. "You'd better hope I don't space you the minute we get to orbit. I'd take great pleasure watching your body burn through the atmosphere."

Rains struggled to speak again but couldn't. His head fell to the wet floor, and blackness overtook him.

* * *

Taal's Fury

There was silence around the small table. Tara watched for a long moment and finally saw a crack in Rains' carefully manicured veneer. There was genuine pain and regret in the young man's face. It was far different from the surly, arrogant Peacemaker she'd first met.

"What happened next?" Vannix asked. "Did they load you on their ship?"

Rains shook his head and sniffled. "No. They left me there on the floor. Nobody knows how long I was out. An Enforcer team came to investigate when I didn't show up for the next day's proceedings. Blue Flight got them there in five days. They found me and stabilized me. I didn't wake up until we were halfway back to Ocono."

"Gods," Tara said. "They knocked you out for almost ten days. Whatever was in the cocktail they gave you was more than a tracer compound."

"Yeah," Rains replied. "But whatever it was, it contained experimental medical nanites, too. When I woke up, there was no evidence I'd been kicked or that they'd broken my wrist. I was good as new, but with no evidence Kr'et'Socae or his buddies had even been on the planet. They cleaned everything better than a Veetanho team would have done. My slate. My local files. Everything."

"What about when you got back to the Academy?" Vannix's eyes narrowed at him. "Why did you turn into such an asshole?"

Rains took a deep breath and drummed his fingers on the table. "Funny thing about that. The embezzlement investigation died the minute the Enforcers showed up. I mean like it never even happened. Guild Master Rsach thinks Kr'et'Socae might have engineered the whole thing to get a Peacemaker deployed so he could trace them and ultimately make a play against the council or even himself. I think he was right."

"But you were just a candidate," Vannix said.

Tara leaned forward. "Which played even more into Kr'et'Socae's hands. If it had been an experienced Peacemaker, they would have called for backup."

Vannix blinked. "Wait. Who approved your mission?"

"Selector Hak-Chet." Rains grimaced. "Yeah, I've thought about that a lot, too."

"What do you mean?" Tara asked.

Vannix turned to her. "Jessica, Nikki, and Jackson all had missions that were chosen by Hak-Chet, or he manipulated them."

"That's a pretty strong accusation." Tara replied. "Humans as Peacemakers were one of his responsibilities, right?"

Rains nodded. "On the recommendation of Enforcer Hr'ent, no less. But he had a hand in all this. I'm wondering why. What's his long game?"

"There's no way of knowing," Vannix replied. "And now he's off on some mission. Something a Selector hasn't done in five generations."

"Meaning what? He's supposed to be simply choosing candidates for the Academy all the time? He's a Peacemaker, right? Why wouldn't he go on a mission supporting the guild?" Tara asked. The looks on the two young Peacemakers' faces were equally disillusioned. "Have you two spoken to anyone else about this?"

"No," Vannix replied. "We've just compared notes, Tara. We're not making an accusation of impropriety or anything like that."

"Something just stinks." Rains grunted.

Tara nodded. "Maybe. But maybe it's your attitudes about it?"

Rains glared at her. "Meaning what?"

"By even engaging in questioning Hak-Chet's motives, you're attempting to assign blame. That means you've chosen a side. I didn't think Peacemakers were supposed to do that."

"We're not," Vannix sighed, "but we should consider everything."

"Which is exactly what we're doing." Rains paused. His mouth opened and closed quickly. "Unless we're *not* doing it. Just because something doesn't make sense—"

"Doesn't mean it's wrong," Vannix finished. She chittered a laugh and turned to Tara. "One of our classes at the Academy taught us that. The old saying is something like there are two sides to every tale, right?"

"Something like that," Rains smiled.

Vannix's nose twitched in mock irritation. "At the Academy we learned that not all tales have sides. Some are amorphous. Some are linear. Others twist and coil around themselves. Our job is to see every angle and consider them equally."

"And I haven't done that," Rains said. He sighed and slumped forward as they all quieted. Tara saw the young man close his eyes for a long moment and then open them. When he spoke, his voice was barely a whisper. "I've blamed everyone but myself for what happened. When they didn't celebrate me like I thought they should, I blamed everything. All the way through graduation. Yeah, I did the coursework and all the chickenshit stuff. Walked across the stage, too. But when it was time to show up for duty, I walked away. I believed I wasn't good enough for them. Or anyone."

"Until I dragged you out of that bar," Vannix said.

"I didn't even get that woman's slate address!" Rains snorted and laughed. "No thanks to you, partner."

"You're welcome." Vannix laughed.

They smiled at each other for a moment until Lucille broke their reverie. <<May I say something?>>

"Of course, Lucille," Tara replied.

<<Peacemaker Rains? From what I have observed over the course of our time together, you are more than good enough to be a Peacemaker.>>

"Thanks, Lucille." Rains sighed with a thin smile on his face.

<<However, I calculate the appearance of the *Strong Arm* at almost our precise moment of arrival was not coincidental. The connection to the actions at Parmick and to Kr'et'Socae suggests our gambit to have you appear in two places at once isn't working.>>

Tara frowned. "They could be looking for something else, not knowing Jackson is here. But it's just as likely they know. They're following the same clues. And following us."

<<I have confidence my efforts to screen our manifest have been successful, Tara. How they are following us, I do not know without scanning all personal communications.>>

"We're not going to do that," Tara replied. "Not yet, at least. If Kr'et'Socae turns up here to take his personal revenge, we'll know for sure. Until then, we let the situation develop and keep our eyes open."

The two Peacemakers nodded in agreement. Rains looked to his partner and then to Tara. "There's just one more thing."

"And that is?" Vannix asked.

"I want to go down there, to Snowmass, as a Peacemaker," Rains replied. "I mean fully. Since we signed on with you, I haven't felt much like a Peacemaker. Don't get me wrong, driving a CASPer is fucking awesome, but this time I want to avoid that as long as possible."

"We can use a cover story about paying for transport." Vannix turned to Tara. "The appearance of two Peacemakers will draw some attention away from our mission, especially at an official level."

Tara nodded and smiled. "Let's do that. We'll brief the team in the morning. Right now I want the two of you to get some rest."

"Yes, ma'am," Vannix chittered.

Tara reached over and put a hand on Rains' forearm. "And, Jackson? Thank you for sharing. Lucille's right, too. You're pretty damned good, and we're lucky to have you both with us. If you ever tire of being a Peacemaker, I'd hire you as a CASPer pilot any day."

"I'll take that as a compliment." Rains smiled.

Tara grinned at him. "That's exactly what I intended."

*****

Chapter Ten

Force 25 Corporate Headquarters

Victoria Bravo

Ibson rapped twice on the jamb of Xander Alison's outer office door. He knew the chief financial officer was deep in the kind of meetings where all the participants prayed either for death or a sudden emergency interruption.

"Come in," Xander called from the inner office. As Ibson walked in, Xander held a finger to his lips and then grinned and pointed to a nearby seat. He took a breath, and the smile on his face faded in an instant. "Lieutenant Governor Peterson, I'm well aware of our status as a mercenary organization. I'm also aware that we're a registered corporation of Victoria Bravo. As such, we're entitled to do business with whomever we please."

Ibson rolled his eyes. To say the metallurgists at the forge had been excited to see what they possessed would have been a vast understatement. While they had more than a fair share of work to accomplish, their excitement to dissect and then reverse engineer the unique compound armor had derailed their production for a day and a half. Other businesses, especially those following the construction efforts, were rightly peeved. Yet he also knew the Victorian-owned businesses would have understood the delay after having lived through two attacks in the span of a few months.

"I understand, Lieutenant Governor Peterson. Rest assured our little science project, as you called it, is complete for now, and the forge expects to regain their lost production schedule within twenty-four hours. You can also rest assured that continued harassment of our legitimate business interests on this planet may trigger a physical move. We'd hate for it to come to that."

Xander bounced his head from side to side and rolled his eyes. With one hand he mimed holding up a rope to hang himself, and Ibson snorted out loud. For a colony supposedly grateful to be alive thanks to the efforts of Force 25, the government wanted more than a pound of flesh from the fledgling company's coffers and was seemingly willing to do anything for it. Xander sat forward, his face serious and a flush of red blood creeping up his neck. "Let me be very clear, Peterson. Neither this company, nor any company of Victoria Bravo, will pay that kind of tax to you or your government. Especially when our company is trying to make sure those bastards don't come back to finish the job. Then again, maybe that's exactly what you want."

Xander withdrew his headset from his right ear and tossed it angrily on the desk in front of him. Ibson grinned. "I take it that went well."

"They want us to pay a fee to all the companies whose orders we preempted by working with the guys from the forge." Xander leaned back and stared at the ceiling. "I hate bureaucrats, man."

Ibson laughed. "I told you Watson would find some way to nickel and dime us to death. It's his revenge for not being a very good mercenary."

"I thought he was a colony militia leader, not a merc."

"Precisely." Ibson grinned. "He just thinks he's better than all of us. That's what's going to eventually doom this colony, Xander. I really think we should prep a move plan."

Xander sighed. "Bukk said the exact same thing two weeks ago. He says the incoming guilds and their emissaries are polluting the very ground they intend to build on—metaphorically speaking."

"The Altar are not a true political race," Xander said. "Gods, how I envy them."

Ibson leaned forward. "So I have news for you. The kind that'll make you forget about Peterson and his stupidity for a little while, at the very least."

"You found a match for the armor compound?"

"It's a Besquith-Jeha design for mining tools, first put into use at a little mining operation nobody ever cared about some fifty years ago."

Xander sat forward. "Parmick?"

Ibson grinned. "Yep. They tried to make something hard enough to mine the red diamonds from the rest of the godsawful rocks and ore under the planet's surface. When it didn't work—that whole diamond versus diamond thing—well, somebody figured out it had another use."

"But they kept it quiet." Xander rest his chin on his hands. "But who? Who would have found this and both kept it quiet and been able to have it mass produced? Peepo?"

Ibson shrugged. "Not sure, honestly. The trail kinda goes cold for a while, but it warms up at Kr'et'Socae. He's the one behind the skiffs and the Cochkala attack on Victoria Bravo. We're certain of that. If we find whoever was behind the armor development and how Kr'et'Socae intercepted it, we'll have that piece of the puzzle figured out."

Xander wiped at his nose and leaned back again in the black leather chair. "But why did they develop it from tools into weapons? You know, plowshares into swords and all that?"

Ibson squinted and then nodded. "That's from the Old Testament, except in reverse, am I right?"

Xander nodded. "It fits. Something built to dig and separate ores and diamonds, and now it's been converted into an almost impenetrable armor. Have we found anything that gets through it?"

Ibson nodded. "We have, but with some interesting data."

"Like what?" Xander asked. He reached for a slate and tapped on it. "I need to know what we can put into our inventory and how much it costs. What have you got?"

Ibson withdrew a slate from his tanker's jacket and tapped on the screen. "Sending you the list now."

"Copy," Xander said. "You want anything to drink?"

"I'm good, thanks," Ibson said. "What else is going on?"

"We're getting a lot of interest from the recruiting side. Are you sure you're not wanting to bring on more troops?"

"You're the CFO, Xander. Can we afford it?"

"Not really." The younger man ran a hand through this sandy blonde hair. "I just don't want to be short troops if something else happens."

"We're good," Ibson said. "Unless we get some qualified mercs coming through these parts, I'm okay with separating the wheat from the chaff."

Xander didn't reply for a moment. His eyebrows furrowed as he scanned the list Ibson had sent. "There are really damned exotic weapons on here. You can't have tested them all."

"No. We used the data from the forge and accessed weapons testing charts from manufacturers all over the galaxy," Ibson said. "I think it's a good start in identifying what could work if we face that armor in combat again."

"But there's nothing in the current Human inventory, save some really rare MAC rounds manufactured on Earth, that has a prayer of penetrating this armor more than three inches, Jamie."

Ibson nodded. "I know. We need those MAC rounds and a miracle, Xander. Otherwise anybody with that compound armor might be able to stop any size Human combat force with ease. If this is what Peepo and her minions were after, no wonder there's so much intercepted comms traffic saying Humans were lucky. I'm thinking we were."

Xander nodded. "We were lucky, Jamie. But if Kr'et'Socae had enough of an inkling about this to deploy it against us, he had something else in mind entirely. That's what scares me."

* * *

Taal's Fury

Snowmass

<<Orbital insertion maneuver complete. *Taal's Fury* has achieved a circular orbit with minimal eccentricity at a height of 265 kilometers.>>

Tara didn't look up from her console. "Thank you, Lucille. Ensure your collection programs are running by SOP."

<<Acknowledged.>>

"Alert the leaders and the Peacemakers. I'd like to see them in Bay Alpha in fifteen minutes for pre-mission brief."

<<Acknowledged. I have GalNet connections active on multiple channels. Snowmass has a global communications satellite relay system. I have access to this network and seventeen others at the present time. There are Dream World Consortium servers available in the downstream, Tara.>>

That's a trap.

Tara flinched at the sudden thought, but she realized it was Jessica's voice in her head. There was no way the Dream World Consortium, given all the negative press and their financial losses, would put their dirty laundry out on the GalNet for everyone to see.

"Lucille, is there a planetary news agency? Something reputable?"

<<You recognize that query is invalid given the state of media in this century, Tara.>>

"I do, and my query stands. Is there someone down there reporting somewhat honestly on the DWC?" Tara drummed her fingers on the console and tried not to frown. Lucille either didn't do what she'd done before, or the restrictions placed by the programming Jessica had sent slowed the near-AI down considerably. While she missed the old Lucille, the one with all the answers ready before the questions were asked, she couldn't risk loosing the controls placed upon her. There was too much at stake.

<<There have been numerous fires at scientific monitoring stations over the last six months. While not explicitly stated this way by the governing body, there are some Aethernet entries that align these events with terrorism.>>

Interesting. Not everyone is happy in paradise. Business as usual with the Dream World Consortium.

She held back a laugh and unbuckled from her console on the bridge. The full bridge crew of four was there. The MinSha pilots could completely command the vessel without her, so she intended to make her way off the bridge without comment.

As she moved across to the hatch, one of the MinSha said, "Colonel leaving the bridge."

She couldn't help but turn and respond. "Ops, you have command of the ship. I'll be in Bay Alpha with the leaders for the pre-mission brief."

Taal's Fury wasn't a massive ship like Tara had originally thought all the MinSha frigates and cruisers to be. She was a fast ship and more thoroughly designed and organized than anything Tara had ever seen. While Humans gravitated toward open spaces and pleasing lines, the MinSha used every space effectively, while still providing all the comforts of home. It was a different home than Humans were used to, but the ability to have a private room, internal plumbing that could be modified for multiple species' use, and all types of food to sustain a diverse cast of soldiers and support personnel struck her as nothing short of extraordinary. And technically, it was hers.

As she floated through the main passageway toward the stern, there was a constant hustle and bustle around her. Supplies moved via pallets attached to magnetic tracks on one side of the hemispherical shaft. MinSha crew members darted to their stations—each passing her with a tap of a fore claw to their armored thorax. Humans moved through the maelstrom with ease, some conversing and interacting with the MinSha in the same relaxed banter of soldiers chewing common ground together. All in all, it was a bit surreal, but Tara reasoned to herself that the entirety of the last couple of years had been surreal.

I never expected this.

Gods. I'm commanding a mercenary company on a MinSha ship. How much more surreal does that get?

No sooner had the thought crossed her mind than another voice, another memory, bubbled up and placed everything in perspective.

You want to command a unit? Then understand the other thing that matters in combat is you get as many people home with all their fingers and toes as possible. That's how you measure success as a commander. Let the history books say what they will; what matters are those around you.

Tara made her way down the connecting spine to Bay Alpha. The angular rungs built for MinSha claws proved to be useful handholds and hard points. Inside the hangar bay were the storage and maintenance racks of her CASPers. The interior wall of the hangar was the maintenance area. On the bulkheads fore and aft were twelve CASPers—the Reapers toward the bow, and the Hammers aft. In the center, around a maintenance table used for weapons system troubleshooting, the figures of her commanders either stood with their feet under the ever-present angular rungs, or hung free and mostly still in the microgravity.

Small talk died quietly as she approached, but there were no angry or disappointed faces in the crowd. Even Gray and Whirr seemed to talk in as normal a manner as soldiers could muster. That, she decided, was good enough for her.

Maybe they've just realized we're about to drop folks on Snowmass and decided to put their game faces on. Either one works for me.

"Good morning, everybody," Tara replied. Ship time followed Galactic Standard, but on Snowmass, the New Perth colonial seat rested just inside the terminator of light and dark making its way across the planet. "We're on New Perth time from now on for synchronization. Lucille will sync our clocks every six hours automatically. All watches and operations will follow the timing standards. Everybody got that?"

There were murmurs of assent, and both Human and alien heads nodded vigorously. She couldn't help but smile at them.

"In case you haven't figured it out yet, I'm not much for ceremony, but there are some things that never change. This is an operations order briefing. Whether your prior units or species have done anything similar to it, I can't say. What I know is, it's the standard for operations in Force 25. We'll follow a very simple format: Situation, Mission, Execution, Command and Signal, Service and Support. This format is a few hundred years old on the Human side, and it works just fine. Maarg, as our lead intelligence officer, will give the situation brief. Because we have Peacemakers attached to us, and not just for show, they'll provide a portion of the situation brief, and they'll also cover a little bit of ground when we get to execution. The last two paragraphs are pretty standard fare, but we'll cover them anyway. Any questions?"

There were none. Tara locked eyes with Maarg, and the young TriRusk consulted her slate. "In the interest of keeping this short, Snowmass is a Dream World Consortium planet. It has a total population of just over seventy-five thousand souls. They're spread between sixteen colony cities across the four continents. The largest colony is New Perth, which is also the seat of the colonial government. The government comprises the mayors of all colonies, a board of advisors, and the colonial leader, who's traditionally the mayor of New Perth. The current mayor is a Zuparti named Citsym, and he's assisted by his chief of staff, Sophie Pryce, a Human. They're overseeing the finalization of the DWC contracts for the second phase of terraforming and dealing with some other more pressing issues I'll cover in a moment.

"It's the equivalent of autumn across most of the populated areas of Snowmass now. Winter is days away, and it will swirl snow and ice for the better part of eight months. In that sense, our timing for this mission is good. Where we've chosen poorly is there's widespread discontent on Snowmass. Over the past several months, various DWC installations and machinery emplacements have been attacked by an unknown party. While no one has officially claimed credit for these actions, there's an undercurrent of suspicion, given what the DWC did on Araf—which you should all be familiar with. If you haven't read the document I sent you on it, do so before you go planet-side."

Jackson Rains half-raised his hand. "Mercenary forces on the planet?"

Maarg flashed a glance at Tara, who kept her face still and calm. The young TriRusk didn't need anyone to keep her on track, and the question Tara had planted with Jackson Rains both deepened the trust of the new recruits in the intelligence process and kept the briefing moving. Most mercenary units didn't bother with intelligence at all. Bridging that gap was an important step.

"The Trenta Knights. The entire company is headquartered here on Snowmass. It's all Zuul, with about six hundred mercs in the unit. They're also spread across the continents, but the most sizable units are on the northern continent, stationed at two camps outside of New Perth. Camp One is to the north of the main city compound, and Camp Two lies on the banks of the Tentio River. They've held this contract—solely, I might add—for over forty years. The same folks who are suspicious of the DWC are equally sure the Knights are up to something nefarious. As we get closer, we'll try to determine just what that might be. Any questions? Peacemaker Vannix?"

The small, white-furred Veetanho stepped forward. "From a legal aspect, the Knights' contract with the Mercenary Guild is one of the oldest contracts still in continuous enforcement. They've rewritten it several times and are approaching the next renewal cycle. That could be a point to create some discord between them and the Dream World Consortium. As for them, well, they own the advisory board in total. Originally made up of representatives from the Zuparti, Humans, and Veetanho, the Veetanho almost completely left the colony over forty years ago. There are still some Veetanho on the planet, including the one who is the primary source Jackson and I wish to investigate. If you've read the Intergalactic Haulers' archive, you'll recognize her name: Veeka."

A rumble of surprise moved through the group. Gray raised his hand. "The same one? She's still alive? She was a helluva warrior, according to everything I've read in those files."

"That she is," Vannix said. "Finding her is critical to the success of our mission. I believe she has information that could assist us in finding Snowman, but I'm also worried the Dream World Consortium is so desperate to pin the source of the attacks on someone that they'll choose her because she's an obvious target. Given the downfall of the Mercenary Guild and General Peepo, it's not surprising to think there are many who would challenge even the most legitimate Veetanho. Even myself."

Jackson Rains stepped forward. "To that end, Vannix and I are going in as full-fledged Peacemakers. The recent attacks have caught the attention of Guild Master Rsach, and he's tasked us to investigate—at least that's what we'll tell people. Given the Dream World Consortium's history with Peacemakers, we're counting on them doing something stupid."

He glanced at Tara as smiles turned to chuckles, and the chuckles became open laughter. She nodded at him approvingly. The young man had certainly turned things around over the course of the last year.

"Thank you, Peacemakers." Tara nodded at them. "And let me be exceptionally clear on something, for the good of the group: you may be Peacemakers, but you're a part of this family. As a deputized agent of Guild Master Rsach, I can assure you that any attack on you is an attack on all of us."

Tara heard, "Hear, hear!" from several of the leaders, including Harmon Gray.

"Now, our mission is fairly simple. We're going in to get whatever information we can find on Snowman. That includes working any angle, including government, mercenary, and general populace. Given the unrest, it's a safe course of action. The Peacemakers have already told you the angle they're intending to use via the governmental agencies. Maarg and Lucille will continue to scour information sources from here. Neither of them can get to the surface for obvious reasons. Likewise, I'll be here on the ship, but in constant communication with the initial ground team."

"What's the initial ground team going to do, Tara?" Vannix asked.

Tara pointed to Gray and Whirr. "Captain Gray is still the commander of Gray's Goblins, at least according to the Mercenary Guild's servers. Lieutenant Whirr will become, on paper, the executive officer of the Goblins. They'll blend in, essentially. Take on provisions, fuel, ammunition. The intent is to be just another mercenary company looking for resources. This is likely to arouse the Zuul's suspicions, which is exactly what we want. The last thing we need to focus on for execution are the outlying targets on the northern continent. There are a couple of sites we'll be watching from orbit, but I'm planning to order the Misfits into a reconnaissance mission once we see what the Zuul are doing with the ground situation."

"Ma'am? Have we had any communication from home? Specifically regarding air support?" Gray asked. The unit's flyers and dropships had been badly depleted during the second battle on Victoria Bravo.

"No, Harm. We're on our own as of now," Tara replied. "That's the general synopsis of things as of right now. We'll take a few minutes to go through each group's tasks and objectives. Once we do that, we'll talk communications updates and schedules. Again, Lucille will handle most of that, but I want us to have a contingency plan in case things go to hell in a handbasket down there."

"Which is exactly what you're expecting, right?" Jackson Rains smiled. There wasn't a shred of malice or sarcasm in his face. Tara snorted and let a matching smile form on her face.

"It wouldn't be a Force 25 combat mission without everything going to shit, would it?" Tara laughed. "One of these days they'll give us an easy mission, right?"

Lieutenant Whirr rose to her full height, her antennae bobbing in laughter. "Oh, I hope not."

The group dissolved into laughter, the kind of laughter a good commander lets their soldiers have, and Tara Mason did just that.

*****

Chapter Eleven

Office of the Colonial Mayor

New Perth

Citsym looked up from his slate and the morning briefings from the Trenta Knights, the Dream World Consortium's remote stations, and the other colonies. Sophie Pryce entered the spacious office carrying two large cups of coffee. He'd taken quite a liking to the strong, bitter liquid and preferred it black. Pryce crossed the distance and handed one to him, which he took and cradled in both hands.

"Thank you, Sophie." Citsym slurped the hot liquid and made a satisfied sound before leaning carefully back in the chair. "Anything to add to the morning briefings?"

Pryce sat in a chair opposite him and stared at him for a moment. "How long have you known there were illegal Veetanho on the planet?"

"This is a partially Veetanho-led planet, Sophie. There have always been—"

"Cut the shit, Citsym. I'm talking about Veetanho reported having left the planet and who are here illegally," Pryce said.

"Are you saying I know something about the attacks? Or that you've found the cause of them yourself?" Citsym slurped the coffee again and smacked his lips. Sophie continued to stare at him.

"I have a report, without confirmation, of a Veetanho meeting with Honored Veeka yesterday at her home." Pryce consulted her slate. "The physical description doesn't match a single Veetanho in the current planetary database."

Citsym snorted. "And how many transports arrived in the last week with Veetanho aboard?"

"Twelve. Immigration services catalogued all the visitors," Pryce snapped. "This one wasn't."

"You're making a tremendous assumption, Sophie."

"Oh, am I?" Pryce laughed and turned her slate around. "I plugged the parameters of the physical description into the archive. This is what I found."

Citsym leaned forward, staring at the image on the screen. His coffee cup involuntarily trembled in his hands, splashing hot liquid onto his paws. "Gods, that can't be true."

"What if it is?" Pryce asked. "Reecha would have been in line to be the mayor of New Perth before you. If she is here, I'm afraid the contracts and articles of confederation for the colony would require you to step down."

"I'll do no such thing!" Citsym said with a sneer, set the coffee cup down on the obsidian surface of the desk, and wiped his paws on his fur. "If she returned to claim her right to this position, she could have incited the recent attacks."

"That's my assumption, Citsym." Pryce turned her slate back to her face and tapped on it several times. "Either she's returned to Snowmass to attempt action against this office, or she's been here all along and is orchestrating the attacks and discontent across the entire planet."

Citsym rubbed his face with his forepaws. "We have to find out her intentions."

"No we don't," Pryce said and tapped the slate again. "I've commandeered your schedule for a few moments, Honored Mayor. There's an urgent meeting you must attend on behalf of your future tenure in this office and the needs of the Dream World Consortium."

Citsym's mouth dropped open in shock. "You've disengaged all recording protocols, yes?"

"Of course." Pryce smiled. She looked like a feral Tortantula standing over her prey. "There are two beings outside who deserve an audience and can likely provide a solution to this situation."

"And how much will it cost me?"

Pryce grinned. "All things have their price, Citsym. Staying in office until you die is worth the credits, don't you think?"

He had to agree. With one paw he reached forward for the steaming cup of coffee and greedily slurped more into his mouth. The exquisite taste made him close his eyes in pure caffeinated ecstasy for several seconds. When he opened his eyes, a haggard-looking Zuul with gray around the end of his snout stood next to a shimmering gray Equiri sporting a white blaze across one shoulder. They both stared through him in return.

"Honored Mayor Citsym, let me introduce Lmott and Qur'atta."

Citsym's eyes widened. He recognized the name Lmott from communications between the Dream World Consortium and a certain subset of customers. The Zuul's brother, Lmurr, had died attempting a contract to assassinate Peacemaker Jessica Francis on Weqq sometime before. There was little doubt Lmott also partook in the family business and, by his appearance, was better at his trade.

The Equiri, though, he hadn't known until the mention of his name. One of the known associates of the disgraced Enforcer Kr'et'Socae, Qur'atta also had a lengthy series of experiences on the shadier side of galactic activities. His coal black eyes were emotionless as he stared down. Citsym met the gaze, and the significance of their presence and the solution to his problems materialized inside his mind.

"Well met, gentle beings." Citsym smiled and allowed the sarcasm to permeate his delivery and face. Both visitors snorted, and the tension broke slightly. "I doubt any of us have ever truly been gentle, have we?"

"I understand you have a situation that requires dealing with? A rat problem?" Lmott asked. His voice was high in pitch, but gravelly and hoarse. "I've had a lot of experience with them over the years."

Citsym nodded. "I imagine you have. Yes, we have a situation on our hands. But I'm uncertain of the intent or the players just yet."

"That doesn't matter," Lmott replied. "We'll find this Reecha and determine what she knows and anything she's done before we kill her."

"You work as a team?"

Lmott glanced up at Qur'atta, who didn't speak. The Zuul returned to looking at Citsym with a gleam in his eye. "My associate has his own mission, but in this particular case, our target is the same. This Reecha, as Miss Pryce indicated, is a clear and present danger to your operations on this planet. My associate believes she may have other information."

"Like what?" Citsym blurted.

Qur'atta stepped forward menacingly. His voice was a deep rumble that shook Citsym's chest. "You do not have the need to know, Mayor. I suggest you never ask of it again."

"Y-yes," Citsym stammered placatingly. "I shan't. Please forgive my question."

Qur'atta stepped backward, but his eyes never left Citsym's. The mayor worked his tongue in his suddenly dry mouth as the Equiri glanced at Lmott.

"Now," the Zuul said with a grin, "I believe we should discuss our fee. And I believe you're going to be thrilled with the price we quote you to rectify this little situation in a couple of days. Isn't that right?"

Citsym shot Pryce a glance and saw her openly smiling at the visitors. Her eyes flicked back to meet his, and he saw one corner of her mouth tuck under slightly in disappointment. He pulled himself more erect in his chair and smiled his best smile.

"Of course, gentle beings. Now please sit, and we'll find the solution that suits us all best, like civilized beings would do. Present company excluded."

* * *

Transient Landing Facility
Snowmass

The instant the hatch opened and the cool morning air filled the cabin, Harmon Gray smelled snow. It wasn't coming immediately, but the frosty autumn tinge in the air was unmistakable, and he fought a pang of homesickness. Instead he took a second, deeper breath as the ramp lowered.

"Harm? Is something wrong?" Whirr asked. She looked at him with one antenna askew, like a raised eyebrow. "You seem to be breathing heavily."

Gray laughed and took another deep breath and exhaled. The wisps of steam from his mouth made him smile wider. "Smells like snow."

Whirr cocked her head to one side. "I've never seen frozen precipitation before. I've heard stories of it, but I must tell you I smell nothing in the air. The weather forecast said nothing about precipitation."

"No, no," Gray said. He waved a hand dismissively. "It's not happening now, but that cold bite in the air? That's the smell of snow. It's coming. Most of the upper latitudes of both hemispheres have already seen measurable amounts. Down here in the temperate zone? Yeah, it's coming. Only a few weeks at most."

Whirr said nothing. Instead the MinSha warrior appeared to gaze over the transient docking facility. "I see no signs of unrest."

Gray swept his eyes across the facility, noting it was quiet and surprisingly vacant. "I thought they were just finishing harvest?"

"That is what the Dream World Consortium reported," Whirr replied. "I was expecting more transports."

Gray nodded. "Yeah. See any of the Zuul?"

"Not yet," Whirr replied. "Lucille could cross reference the video system across the colony. She has their normal operating routines on file. Most of them don't come near the docks. I think that may be by design."

Gray didn't reply. Not having the mercenary force present at the docks would allow for the ease of movement of goods through customs and the like. Were they present, the question of legitimacy would undoubtedly rise, but in their research on Snowmass, nothing ever had. The Trade Guild gave the New Perth facility on Snowmass its highest possible recommendation. He'd had to look deep into the historical record to find anything damning against the Zuul.

"They keep the mercs away from here because some of them get frustrated with the easy life," Gray said. "At least that's what I gathered from one report I saw. It would make sense. If they're unhappy and want to leave, it would be easy to sign onto an outgoing vessel." He'd done that himself at sixteen at the Colorado Springs starport instead of picking up produce from the farmers' markets downtown and returning to the family homestead near Alma. "It brings a question to mind, though."

"As in, if everything is so nice and wonderful here, why would anyone want to leave?" Whirr chittered. When Gray snorted and smiled, she said, "I'm glad we think alike. Makes this assignment much more fun than simple fact-gathering."

Across the tarmac, Gray saw a Human dressed in dark blue coveralls and a baseball hat walking toward them holding a slate. He watched for a moment and quickly determined that the approaching official was female, unarmed, and all business. She didn't look up until he and Whirr made their way down the ramp. Her face paled, and her mouth threatened to fall open in shock. To her credit, the brunette regained her composure and made eye contact with him.

"Commander Gray?"

He smiled at his old rank and extended a hand. "Harmon. Nice to meet you."

The young woman shook his hand firmly and let it go to consult and tap on her slate. "I'm Chief Yale; welcome to Snowmass. We got your supply request a couple of hours ago, and my teams are working up what we have available for you."

"Much obliged." Gray smiled. He paused, waiting for her to look up again. "I'm sorry. You said your name was Yale?"

"That's right." The woman frowned. "Am I missing something?"

"A first name." Gray grinned wider and winked.

"Oh!" Yale laughed and smiled in return. "Emily. Emily Yale."

"Very nice to meet you," Gray said. He gestured at his partner. "This is Lieutenant Whirr. She's my executive officer and will handle the loadouts and drop shipments. We have more gear to grab."

"That you do," Yale replied. "Honestly, it may be two to three days before we're able to get everything you've requested here to New Perth, sir."

Gray shrugged. "We expected that. Can't be helped. We appreciate every effort y'all can make."

"We'll do what we can." Yale nodded at Whirr. "It's nice to meet you, Lieutenant."

"You've never seen a MinSha, have you?" Whirr asked.

The young woman swallowed visibly and shook her head. "No, ma'am."

"Do not fear me, Emily Yale. We're here for materials and will soon be on our way. Though I was under the impression there are other mercenaries operating here?"

Yale took a breath and some color returned to her face. Without looking away from Whirr, she replied, "The Trenta Knights. They're a Zuul company and have been here longer than I've been alive."

"We know." Gray smiled. "I thought we'd see them here."

"Not likely," Yale responded. Behind her there was a commotion, and four figures turned around the end of an old shipping container and marched directly toward them. At the front was a stunning blonde woman in a business suit. Yale's voice faded out as she turned to see the entourage approaching. There was no mistaking who the blonde was, even at this distance.

Sophie Pryce. Now we're talking.

As she approached, Sophie Pryce beamed. "You must be Captain Gray of Gray's Goblins. I do hope our landing teams have taken good care of you."

She didn't bother to acknowledge Emily Yale or anyone else on the tarmac. She'd also completely ignored Whirr, which should have been impossible, given her size and the collective MinSha reputation. Instead, she'd locked in on him because he was a Human mercenary commander who'd transmitted what was likely the longest and most detailed request for supply Snowmass had seen in the last thirty years. She'd followed the money and, thanks to Lucille and the careful ministrations of Force 25, that led her directly to him.

"And you must be Miss Pryce." Gray stepped toward her and extended his hand. She took it much more firmly than Chief Yale had and pumped up and down twice before dropping it.

All business. Time to turn on the charm. If this part of the plan is going to work, that is.

"It's a pleasure to meet you, Captain Gray. Your reputation proceeds you. I'm sorry to hear about your recent troubles. The situation regarding your unit's demise was unfortunate, from what I've read."

Gray smiled thinly. If she'd read anything, she'd gotten ahold of the mission report required by the Mercenary Guild. While not classified by any means, reading it in her civilian capacity meant the Trenta Knights were either openly sharing their information or incredibly lax in their security procedures. He surmised it was a mixture of both.

"Unfortunate is a good word. Starting all over again was not what I'd imagined, but we've been able to rebuild a new company with much different capabilities." Gray smiled. "Hence our request for resupply. Snowmass was the nearest world capable of providing the bulk of our needs."

Pryce smiled in return. While she was attractive to a fault, the look in her eyes was dangerous. Deadly. "Well, we're very interested in assisting the Goblins with their needs. How long will you be staying?"

Bingo.

"Depends on how much of our supply request is met and whether we have any luck recruiting." Gray shrugged. "I figure we'll stay until your winter arrives. A few weeks at most, by the smell of the air this morning."

Pryce laughed. "Oh, you're familiar with that scent?"

"I grew up in the mountains of Colorado. While that wasn't typically as much snow as you get on this planet, it was enough to recognize when winter is right around the corner, so to speak."

"Indeed." Pryce's smile softened slightly. "I've always wanted to see Colorado."

"It's certainly still there. Surely a woman in your position gets vacation time?" Gray grinned.

"Not as much as I would enjoy." Pryce's face returned to its all-business set. "There's always so much work to do for the government."

"As there's always work to do for a mercenary company," Gray said and turned to Whirr. "May I introduce you to Whirr? She is my executive officer."

Pryce's eyebrows rose a fraction. Humans and MinSha weren't the likeliest of combinations. She nodded solemnly. "It's a pleasure to meet you, Whirr."

Whirr bowed her jaw toward her thorax. "Likewise, Miss Pryce. Thank you for responding to our request with such enthusiasm. We are aware of the sophistication of some items."

Pryce nodded. "We will certainly do what we can to honor them. Your unit's reconstitution effort could be very profitable for us, should you have the credit to support it."

Gray raised his hand. In his fingers was his UACC. "Please feel free to scan it for a credit check."

"That's quite all right," Pryce replied. Her attempt to deflect was poor for a diplomat. Gray leaned in a little.

"I insist."

Pryce took the card and slipped it into a reader attached to her slate. There was a faint chime, and Gray watched her mouth actually drop open a millimeter before she composed herself. "Well, I believe your credit is good, Captain Gray."

Gray kept his face straight. He knew the exorbitant amount of credits listed on his account was a fabrication, but there was still more than enough in the company's coffers to cover anything in actuality. Maarg assured him she could produce the full balance, if required. For some reason, Gray believed the young TriRusk's abilities after watching Sophie Pryce's carefully crafted image crumble.

"There have been some silver linings to our recent troubles," Whirr said. "As we explore new opportunities, we have a chance to create the company we need to handle unique situations."

Pryce cocked her head back to Gray. "Are you currently pursuing contract work?"

"Not officially," Gray replied, "but we never stop looking for opportunities. It's more than a simple matter of credits, though. Situational benefits are certainly something we'd pursue."

Pryce smiled. "Would such situational benefits include, how do you put it…taking a knee?"

I'll be damned. That was way easier than I thought it would be.

Tara's plan had been simple. Put forward a huge, diverse supply list for a larger mercenary company to reconstitute its assets. Added to the size of *Taal's Fury* in orbit and the obvious intent for the survivors of Gray's Goblins to stick together, the hope had been to introduce the possibility of the Goblins replacing the Trenta Knights in the long-term protection contract. He'd thought it was possible, but having himself and Whirr as the supposed command team should have been a challenge. Most Human colonies didn't trust the MinSha for fear of conquest or unprovoked attack.

Sophie Pryce wasn't fazed in the slightest. She was willing to consider the possibility with little more than a tarmac conversation. Harmon Gray knew two things in that instant: one, Sophie Pryce was a dangerous Human being with a severe distrust of the Trenta Knights. Second, there was something she wanted, and she saw the Goblins as a means to that end. Either way, Force 25 had the in they'd been looking for.

"A few years ago," Gray began, "I would never have imagined taking a knee in this business. Given recent events? A long rest sounds like a refreshing idea. Especially with your winter approaching."

"Why's that?" Pryce asked, her eyebrows raised quizzically.

"I'm a Colorado native. That means I like a little snow."

"We have more than a little bit." Pryce smiled at him. There was a genuineness in it that made Gray grin in return. "There really are some beautiful areas to explore, especially in the northlands."

"You'll have to show me sometime."

Pryce beamed. "I might just do that, Commander Gray."

"Please. Call me Harm."

"Then I'd be pleased if you'd call me Sophie."

"I'll do just that, Sophie," Gray replied. "Is there a time you'd like to meet and discuss contract prospects?"

Her slate buzzed and the pleasant look on her face vanished. "I'll be in touch, Harm. Right now I'm sure you have business to conduct here, and I have a full schedule today."

Sensing an opportunity, Gray tilted his chin toward her. "This evening, perhaps?"

"Perhaps." Pryce smiled. "Whirr. Harm. A pleasure meeting you. I look forward to our future discussions."

"As do we," Whirr replied. Her antenna bobbed at Gray in obvious amusement at the developing situation. "As do we."

"One question?" Sophie looked at her slate again. "There were Peacemakers on your ship?"

Gray shrugged. "We hauled them and a small shuttle. A nice little fee. They landed about an hour ago."

"Any idea what their business might be?"

"We were asked to ferry them to our next destination, no questions asked," Gray replied. "They had no idea we were coming to Snowmass until we emerged."

"Interesting," Pryce said. She tapped at her slate. "I have some time this evening, Harm. Would you care to meet over dinner?"

I was wrong. That was way *too easy.*

"I can. Whirr will be busy with second shift during maintenance," Gray replied.

"That's too bad," she replied without taking her eyes off him. "I'll send you directions. Does 1800 local work?"

"Perfectly," Gray said as they parted ways. He glanced up at Whirr and saw that she was thinking the exact same thing he was.

"This stinks like a GenSha in the rain, Harm."

"Oh yeah it does," Gray replied. "You got that whole conversation recorded, yes?"

"SOP."

"Send it to the boss right now." Gray put his hands on his hips and stretched his back. "And warn our friends. Something's up."

*****

Chapter Twelve

New Perth

Snowmass

Jackson Rains relished the return of gravity. Even with Snowmass clocking in at 1.09 Earth G, the feeling of pressure on his feet and a balanced equilibrium more than made up for any discomfort. It didn't help that the sky was a clear, vibrant blue and the crisp morning air bit gently into his lungs. Winter was certainly near, but the day promised to be warm and bright and infinitely better than another day spent in orbit doing anything else but walking on solid ground. He and Vannix had disembarked from one of the smaller shuttles from *Taal's Fury* over two hours ahead of Gray and Whirr aboard the larger of the transports. While not combat-capable dropships, the large shuttles could hold a squad of four CASPers each and could make four or five trips to orbit and back without running out of fuel. The MinSha were nothing short of efficient in their approach to transportation, and as long as the cover of Guild Master Rsach's concern held true, those same transports wouldn't have to be used to get them the hell out of Dodge anytime soon.

Not that Rains wanted to go anywhere else. For the first time, he and Vannix were dressed in their dark blue coveralls with the Peacemaker patches on either shoulder, their bright platinum badges on their chests, and sidearms holstered at their hips. He resisted the urge to swagger, but he had to admit it felt good to be noticed. The colonists barely covered their stares and shock as they moved through the streets and thoroughfares. From the moment they'd walked away from the starport, bags in hand, it had taken exactly two minutes for the first Zuul mercenary to tap frantically on a wrist slate. They'd seen him and commented to each other about it, but he'd kept his face impassive. A young Human and two of his Zuparti friends collected their bags for a quarter credit and took them into town, promising that the Hotel Rève was the best accommodations for Peacemakers. If they lied, they'd have quite a surprise with the tracking device Vannix had hidden inside their bags. If they were honest, doctrine said they had potential friends who could be leaned on more and more. Building trust was everything.

"Contact," Vannix said. "Two o'clock, about a hundred meters up. See the gray and white Zuul with the bandolier?"

Rains stared on the azimuth his partner indicated. "The one leaning by the wall?"

"Yeah, he's been talking into a throat mike since we turned onto this street," Vannix replied with a snort. "Amateurs."

"They've only had this one contract for like forty years, Vannix. They're not amateurs, they're just lazy," Rains replied. "How long you want to bet before we're approached by the Knights?"

"Less than ten minutes." Vannix chuckled, but the sound was muffled as if she'd done so out of the side of her maw. "Especially once we make our way toward the mayor's office. That should just about send their entire governmental section into…what's that thing called again?"

"A tizzy?" Rains said. "That's what you're thinking?"

"I guess so. Though I think I like Colonel Ibson's three-meter-hover comment better for a state of intense agitation," Vannix said. "Target's moving."

"I see him. He still thinks he's being smooth," Rains said. He swept his gaze around the thoroughfare and what looked like an old town square ahead. For a moment, he thought of the square in Troy, Alabama, where he'd spent a few years in and out of foster homes before ending up on the street.

Missus Green, I wish you could see me now.

He shook the thought away and noticed the Zuul mercenaries attempting to play it cool by window shopping along the perimeter of the square itself. Save that the store they were intensely interested in was a Human woman's clothing store, they would never have been noticed by an untrained eye.

"Two more on the west side."

"I've got them. Target is moving directly toward us now," Vannix said. "Are you ready for this, Jackson? You know he'll ignore you."

Rains didn't respond, save to clear his throat. "His funeral."

Vannix tittered. "Lighten up, Rains."

He was about to say something when he caught sight of a Veetanho perusing the produce in what appeared to be a farmers' market on the far side of the square. "Is that Veeka?"

Vannix's head snapped around. "Yes. The leader is moving toward us, but the other two are on her."

Rains watched them for a moment. They were certainly watching every move Veeka made. The crowd parted enough that he could see both Zuul were armed and trying carefully to keep watch on both

Veeka and him and Vannix. "Yeah, they're waiting to move. You think this is going down? Right now?"

Vannix was already quickening her pace. "I think so, partner. Stay with me."

He was about to argue that they should split up to cover the entire square itself when he realized she was right. They needed to intervene. Now. The only way to do that was to do it together.

"I'm with you." Movement off to his right caught his eye. He glanced that direction and saw a very familiar Equiri also moving toward Veeka. At his side was a gray-white Zuul carrying a sniper rifle at the low-ready. "Fuck. That's Qur'atta."

"Move!" Vannix barked and darted toward Veeka. "Get down! Get down! Peacemaker! Peacemaker!"

The crowd didn't seem to either hear or move. Rains drew his pistol and fired twice into the air. Panic spread through the square as the colonists scattered quickly; some hit the ground where they stood. Across the square, Veeka looked up as the two Zuul at the storefront moved her way. Honoring their perceived threat, Rains ran. Behind Veeka, the Zuul raised his rifle and centered his focus on the target just twenty meters in front of him.

"Veeka! Veeka! Get down!" Vannix screamed and fired twice at the Zuul. The first round tore a swatch of cloth from his gold and black vest. His head snapped toward her. By the look on his face, he'd received the message. He brought the rifle barrel toward Vannix, but she'd closed the distance and launched into his chest. Rains looked up, sighting for Qur'atta, and saw the large Equiri turn his way and sneer.

"Rains!" the horse-like alien bellowed above the screaming of the crowd in the square. Without taking his eyes from Rains, the Equiri leveled his pistol at Veeka. In a fraction of a second, Rains identified it as a Marauder PK-35. The kind of weapon meant for overkill.

"Get down! Veeka, get—"

Qur'atta fired once and tossed the pistol aside. Veeka went down, blood spraying from a head wound. In that moment of shock, he didn't hesitate. Rains brought up his pistol and fired all twelve rounds at Qur'atta. Several hit the mark, but the big Equiri screamed and charged straight toward Rains. His rounds spent and with no time to reload, Rains holstered the pistol, grabbed the knife tucked into his left boot, and came up in a fighting position, intent on beating the alien to death with his own fucking hands.

* * *

At the Peacemaker Academy, they organized sports as intramural events that served two critical purposes: the first was, while Peacemakers would act alone in almost all their interactions once commissioned, they needed to understand teamwork. Sports did that to a certain extent, forging friendships that would carry each of the candidates well past their education. The second and more vital reason for the organized sports was as an outlet for all the vast emotions felt during their formative years. The Academy required Peacemaker Candidates to play at least two different sports. The more individual focused sports, everything from fencing and swordplay to the Human sport tennis, were required one semester of every year. The other semester was for team sports with quasi-violent action. Vannix relished the Human sport of Australian-Rules Football. There were many alien races with similar sports, including the Oogar's particularly violent Kr'aat'kala, but the Human version consolidated all the rules—what few there actually were.

Vannix's Veetanho stature always drew smirks from the other players, until she charged in, lowered her shoulder, and knocked the wind from their bodies. For her, there was nothing more satisfying than delivering a thunderous hit. While she carried herself as a calm, quiet professional in every instance off the field, inside those lines she was a ferocious athlete unafraid to break arms, ribs, or thoraxes to get what she needed.

As she lowered her shoulder, ducking under the barrel of the Zuul's sniper rifle, there was almost time for her to smile. Shoulder down and legs pushing off the ground for speed and power, she came up into the Zuul's side under his forearms with a resounding crunch. Air shot from the Zuul's lungs in an explosive gasp. His feet came off the ground. For a moment they flew through the air, until gravity took over and they arced toward the ground. She kicked her right leg at the rifle and knocked it free. It clattered to the cobblestones and broke into three pieces as it hit.

The Zuul swung hard with his right paw, but she saw it coming from the twist of effort in his face. Her left hand came up and deflected the blow with ease, but the Zuul's other paw came up from under her and connected with her lower jaw, slamming it shut with a *click* that rang through her skull. She spun, whipping the pistol across the Zuul's exposed face, where it connected with an equally hard *thud.* His legs came up, frantically scratching, but she was already moving up his chest and standing in one motion. Her left foot kicked the Zuul's face as she stood. Dark blood sprayed across the cobblestones, but the Zuul moved and twisted to his own standing position facing her.

He stooped to remove a knife from a lower leg sheath. She'd never understood why the Human Peacemakers loved to carry a knife there, but it totally made sense now. From a downed position, it would be a viable weapon. The Zuul slashed at her face, stepping into the strike as he did. Vannix flinched backward and felt the blade slice the whiskers on the left side of her face. She took another step back, expecting the next attack. The Zuul hacked down at her, and she blocked it with both arms locked together.

"Damned rat," the Zuul wheezed. He lunged again, but his knife was too wide, and Vannix saw her opportunity.

Move only when you see it.

At the Academy, that mantra had been the core instruction of their hand-to-hand combat teachers for three years. They'd said a split-second mistake could be a huge opening. The Zuul's lazy attack gave her a door, and she stepped into the attack, closing the distance, and kicked the Zuul hard in the notch between its lower legs. Unlike a Human's, Zuul anatomy easily deflected her attack, but that was the point. Her left leg stepped up onto the soft inner thigh tissue, and she climbed up the shocked Zuul, twisted in mid-air, and grabbed its neck with her hands. As his momentum carried him forward clumsily, she felt his balance give way, and she tossed him over one shoulder and flat onto his back in the street. As she followed through, she snatched her pistol from the ground and turned back to see the Zuul moving. The impact should have stunned the assassin, yet he rolled and came up facing her with the knife at the ready.

She leveled her pistol at his chest. "Lay the knife down."

"Fuck you, rat," the Zuul hissed.

She frowned and lowered her aim in a millisecond, then fired twice, one round at each of the Zuul's upper thighs. He howled and went down again in the street. Flat on his back, his paws came up to his face, and she realized what he'd done, but it was too late. Pistol in his face, she stepped forward to see his pupils fixate and a thick, orange foam erupt from his slack maw.

"Dammit." She stepped back to avoid contamination from the poison. As she did, she turned and froze.

"Jackson! No!"

* * *

Qur'atta charged. Rains shifted his weight and remembered, oddly, a lesson from the first semester at the Academy, Species 101. The Equiri had a physical weakness he'd thought was funny. Like the wild horses of Earth, they could run fast as hell in a generally straight line. Also like the horses of Earth, they couldn't turn for shit. At the last possible second Rains juked to his right, and Qur'atta barreled past. As he did, Rains spun the combat knife in his hand so the blade pointed down from his fist and rammed it up to the hilt in Qur'atta's lower back.

His gluteal muscles severed, the Equiri's powerful left leg crumpled under him. As he fell, Rains swung away, drew his pistol, ejected the magazine, slapped another into the weapon, and prepared it to fire. He turned to find Qur'atta lying face-down in the street, laughing.

Pistol pointed at the Equiri's face, Rains steadied himself and asked, "Where's your boss?"

"Why don't you come arrest me, Peacemaker?"

"I asked you a fucking question, Qur'atta." Rains clenched his jaw and focused on not doing the only thing he wanted to do at that moment: pull the trigger. "Where's Kr'et'Socae?"

"Somewhere you won't find him." Qur'atta raised his head a few centimeters above the street.

"Don't move another inch."

Qur'atta laughed. "You Humans expect to rule the galaxy, yet you cannot define a unit of measurement for your singular, pitiful planet."

"Why was Kr'et'Socae following me on Araf?"

Qur'atta's laughter stopped, and he snorted once. "You assume too much, Rains."

"Bullshit. If he's not after me, he's after Force 25. That makes it about me, whether or not you want to admit it."

"You killed Sa'texia, Peacemaker. My sister. Kr'et'Socae's chosen mate." Qur'atta's smile returned, but it was almost feral and vicious. "He wants you dead, yes, but there are others he wants to share your fate."

"That's why he attacked Victoria?" Rains asked. "Or is that why he funded the mining outpost at Parmick?"

A ripple of uncertainty flickered across the Equiri's face. Rains stepped forward once and kept up the questioning.

"He's moving to do something big, Qur'atta. Why don't you tell me all about it?"

Qur'atta laughed. "So you can cut me a deal, or whatever that stupid Human phrase is? Please, Peacemaker. Take your deals and shove them where only entropy remains."

"I said keep talking."

"You're an idiot, Rains." Qur'atta set his face down on the ground. "You can't stop what's already begun."

"Why were you after Veeka?"

"She's like you. In the way," Qur'atta said. "Kr'et'Socae will clear that path soon enough. I'm done speaking with you. Take me into custody, Peacemaker. I demand legal assistance."

While not technically protected under the limited laws of the Galactic Union, a citizen suspected of a crime could ask for legal assistance. While barristers were somewhat scarce, especially on the distant planets of the various galactic arms, the only recourse for a Peacemaker in that situation was to summon a second Peacemaker.

Rains nodded. "I've heard your request, citizen. Show me your hands."

There was a gruff laugh. "I don't have hands, Peacemaker."

"You know what I mean."

"I'm injured. My left arm is broken from the fall you caused," Qur'atta said with a lilting tone that was almost insubordinate. "I may have to pursue personal damages against you."

"Shut up," Rains barked and took a step closer. "Get your limbs where I can see them."

The Equiri moved his right forearm free, but the left remained pinned under his body. "I cannot comply, Peacemaker. I require your assistance to do so."

"Then you're just going to lay there."

"You're required to provide me with medical assistance in a timely manner." Qur'atta chuckled. "That time is up. From here, I'll place a complaint with the regional barracks."

"There isn't one here, asshole." Rains lowered the pistol and holstered it. "My partner and I are the only Peacemakers in the region, and that means I let you lie there until you tell me what I want to know."

"You want Kr'et'Socae?"

"Yeah, I do," Rains replied. Two meters away he squatted down to stare into the injured Equiri's face. "Where is he?"

"Everywhere."

Rains laughed. "Nice try. Maybe I should get my knife and carve a few more muscles away?"

"Torture wouldn't be beneath you. You murdered my sister just to try and arrest Kr'et'Socae. That won't be printed in the Peacemaker record, will it?" Qur'atta sneered. "A high and mighty Peacemaker who's a murderer?"

"Shut up and tell me what I want to know."

"Or you'll what? Toss me in a maximum-security Peacemaker prison? We've proven we can breach even those impregnable fortresses with ease. Throw me in your jail. Kr'et'Socae will break me out, and you'll lose again."

He's right. That's exactly what we'll do.

Rains reached into a pocket of the bandolier across his chest and withdrew a pair of restraints powerful enough to contain Qur'atta. "Fine, asshole. You're under arrest. You'll be held until such time as we can place you before a Peacemaker tribunal. Your rights of redress and citizenship are suspended until released or acquitted. You're entitled to obtain said representation, if possible. Credit will be extended to you if you cannot afford said representation. Do you have any questions?"

"How will you restrain an injured Equiri with dignity?"

Rains stood and shuffled one foot slightly forward but did not step. He opened the restraints. "Put your free limb out to the side and we'll start there. You're way beyond dignity, Qur'atta."

"Jackson! No!" Vannix screamed from across the square.

Qur'atta squirmed as if trying to free his trapped limb, and that was enough. Rains drew his pistol faster than he'd done since his days at the Academy and sighted on the Equiri's head. Without a second thought he pulled the trigger three times in rapid succession and spread Qur'atta's brain matter across the street.

The oldest trick in the book. Good thing we studied it.

Without looking, he holstered his pistol and tapped his earpiece. "You okay, partner?"

"Veeka's critical, Jackson," Vannix replied. "Don't go near Qur'atta or the Zuul's bodies. I'm sure they're rigged to explode. This Zuul poisoned himself."

"Qur'atta was almost certainly wearing an explosive. I wasn't going anywhere near him. He wouldn't be taken alive, either."

"I think they were simply here to kill Veeka."

"I'm not sure it was just Veeka," Rains said. "Qur'atta said she was in Kr'et'Socae's way. Like I am, apparently."

"Well, then, we won't have to wait long for him, will we?"

Rains walked back toward his partner. "He won't come here. What we need to do is find out why Qur'atta was really here. Assassination isn't his thing."

"A target of opportunity, right? Someone wanted Veeka dead."

"True, but you know Qur'atta wouldn't be here just for that. The Zuul maybe, but not him. We'll need his slate."

"What about his ship? I'll bet he came on the *Strong Arm*."

"You're right."

Rains snorted, and there was a touch of a smile on his lips. The headset chirped twice as a new connection established. "Jackson? It's Tara. What's going on down there? Lucille reported shots fired."

"Veeka's hurt bad. They had a hit out on her. The fucker who shot her is an old friend of Kr'et'Socae's. Equiri named Qur'atta. He and a Zuul assassin attacked her in the marketplace. We put them down, and security forces will be here any second."

"Oh, shit."

"Yeah," Rains replied. "We got a situation down here, Tara. And it ain't a good one. We need to stop the *Strong Arm*, too."

<<The *Strong Arm* has just shunted away,>> Lucille chimed in over the shared and encrypted mission frequency.

Godsdammit.

"Jackson!" Vannix yelled, breaking his frustration like a dry twig. "Get over here! She's talking!"

*****

Chapter Thirteen

Central Square Market

New Perth

Snowmass

In their multi-species lifesaving courses at the Academy, Peacemakers learned the skills necessary to evaluate and treat the known races of the Galactic Union. They identified a small percentage of Peacemaker Candidates to serve as medical officers based on their scores in their coursework. Most of the others suffered through quick overviews of alien anatomy and physiology and hoped they'd never have to use their skills. While their slates were preloaded with the basic steps for every known race, Vannix never thought to consult hers. Instead she tore a combat dressing from one of her vest pouches, opened it, and pressed it against Veeka's head.

The location of the wound, thankfully, wasn't immediately fatal, but given the curvature and length of the Veetanho skull, there was undoubtedly some damage to the skull and the brain underneath. Without immediate surgery, Veeka wouldn't survive.

The older Veetanho stiffened and looked up at her face. Vannix leaned over her. "Honored Veeka, be still. Help is on the way."

"You…" Veeka's eye flitted down to the badge on Vannix's chest. "Peacemaker?"

"That's right." Vannix pressed one paw to the elder's face and was surprised when Veeka's paw reached up to clasp hers. "We've got you. We'll take care of you."

"You know my nest-daughter…Jessica."

Vannix nodded. "Yes. Yes, I do, Veeka."

"Has she found Snowman?"

Vannix shook her head. "She's looking…we're looking. Trying to help her find him."

Veeka drew a shuddering breath, and her eyes threatened to roll up in their sockets before they snapped back to Vannix. Her paw tightened on Vannix's and drew her closer. Vannix leaned over, her face hovering close enough to the injured female she could feel Veeka's ragged breath against her face.

"Reecha."

Vannix nodded. "Yes, I know her name. From Snowman's files."

Veeka drew another breath, and her eyes unfocused again before regaining their clarity. The older Veetanho was losing her grasp on life.

"Easy, Veeka."

Rains appeared at Vannix's side. She looked up and saw the commotion around them as a crowd gathered in the marketplace. He looked down at her. "I got this, partner."

She watched him raise his badge and heard him yell from the depths of his diaphragm like they'd been taught at the Academy. Armed mercenaries were entering the market, as were shoddily-equipped security forces.

"Peacemaker! Peacemaker!" Rains pointed at the oncoming security forces. "Establish a perimeter around the marketplace, now! You! Get my weapon and bring it here."

"Right away, Peacemaker," she heard one of the Humans chirp as the security team scattered. The mercs kept coming. She readied herself to stand as she watched Jackson Rains reload his pistol and stomp toward the Zuul with his badge raised above his head in one hand and the other pointing his pistol at the mercenary leader's narrow chest. "Stand the fuck down! This is a Peacemaker investigation. Disband and return to your commander. Tell him to report to me right fucking now. Is that understood?"

The lead Zuul grumbled something she couldn't hear. Rains stepped closer.

"You want to repeat that, motherfucker?"

"No, Peacemaker."

"Damned right," Rains said. "Get your asses out of this marketplace and don't come back. I want your commander here, alone or accompanied by his legal officer, before the next hour is out. Am I clear?"

"Perfectly." The Zuul sighed and turned to his squad. With a few silent gestures he motioned the squad to sling their weapons and reverse their march out of the marketplace.

Vannix looked down at Veeka again. Her face was calm and almost slack. She blinked rapidly, and her eyes focused on Vannix again.

"Reecha is alive. Here." Veeka's voice was little more than a whisper. Vannix leaned closer. "North. Beyond the glacier."

Vannix saw the elder's face slacken, and her eyes rolled up into her head. "Veeka! Veeka! Stay with us!"

"Hmmm," Veeka moaned, but her eyes blinked again, and she focused on Vannix. "North, Peacemaker. The caves."

"What's to the north, Veeka? What's in the caves?"

Veeka squeezed her paw fiercely and strained upward to whisper in her ear, "Snowman."

Vannix flinched even as the elder Veetanho sagged in her arms. "Veeka!"

Vannix heard Rains calling for a medic, but none came. She laid Veeka on the ground and cradled her face with both paws. Emotion tightened her throat as she tried to recall the prayer for the dead. Her face quivering in sudden, unexplainable grief, Vannix lowered her head to touch her forehead to Veeka's and held herself there, oblivious to the chaos emerging around them. She heard Rains shouting, and Tara's voice was in her ears, but there was nothing Vannix could do in her anger but weep.

* * *

Taal's Fury

Maarg sat forward at her console. Her elongated head in her massive hands, she closed her eyes and tried to quell the sudden rage in her hearts. Through her headset she'd heard everything from the square via the Peacemakers' linked slates, the security camera system, and every slate or system she could reach with an audio feed. With Lucille's help, all of it was at her fingertips, and there was still nothing she could do.

<<Is something wrong, Maarg? I am detecting elevated pulse and respiration consistent with emotional distress.>>

She didn't respond. Lucille was trying to be helpful, which she understood. Yet no one else on the mission seemed to be willing to actually help anyone. All they practiced was killing other beings. Mission readiness, they called it. They studied and rehearsed combat actions more than they enjoyed life. There hadn't been a conversation about music or holofilms in weeks. All the Humans and the MinSha wanted to do was kill and kill again.

Even the Peacemakers.

Since they'd come into her life, the Peacemakers had hardly been peaceful. In fact, they'd been as violent as the surrounding mercenaries. As much as they were working together, Maarg couldn't help but wonder if the passion for death and destruction had tainted the Peacemakers.

She shook off the train of thought. *Jessica isn't violent.*

The hells she isn't. Everything you've seen about her paints her as a perfect Peacemaker—making friends and all that. The reality is she's responsible for the deaths of far too many lives to count. Even some Human ones.

She snorted and shook her head.

<<Maarg? Are you okay?>>

"No."

She cast her headset aside and slumped all the way forward to the console. There was silence on the bridge, enough that all Maarg could hear was the air handling units circulating the surrounding atmosphere. Her hands found the edges of the console and wrapped over them, squeezing as hard as she dared, and then harder still. No release came.

All they do is kill!

Innocents are dying because of the Peacemakers!

They will kill off my people. All of them.

She rocked backward, raised one fist, and slammed it against the Tri-V in front of her. As the holographic image flickered and died, and sparks emitted from its housing, a new voice came from behind her.

"You okay?"

Maarg spun and met the concerned expression of Tara Mason. She looked back at the damaged panel and curled one side of her mouth under. "It's not obvious that I'm not?"

"What's wrong?"

Maarg shook her head. "They couldn't save Veeka."

"Lucille told me." Tara propelled herself through the microgravity and bypassed her command chair. Instead, she angled for the navigation station immediately to Maarg's right. "That's not what's bothering you."

Maarg snorted and turned back to her console. "They didn't even try to save her."

Tara frowned. "What are you implying, Maarg?"

"The Peacemakers. They don't care about anything but showing off how great they are. They didn't bother trying to protect Veeka. They only sprang into action after she'd been shot. They're baiting a war to my home planet. All of this is madness, Tara."

"That's not true," Tara said. "You watched the whole thing, Maarg. They were aware of the situation and were moving to intercept when the situation changed."

"Changed?" Maarg spun to glare at her commander. "It didn't fucking *change*, Tara. Veeka was gunned down in cold blood, and instead of trying to arrest the shooters, Vannix and Rains charged in and killed them. What happened to investigating? What happened to learning about the situation? What happened to blending in? Is that peaceful to you?"

"They made a judgment call, Maarg. The Zuul shooter killed himself. I'd imagine the Equiri would have done the same thing."

"They were carrying explosive devices," Maarg sighed, "but that's not my point, Tara. The Peacemakers aren't supposed to charge into a situation with violence. They're supposed to broker *peace*."

"They're not called Peace*keepers* or Peace*brokers*, Maarg. They have to *make* the peace. Sometimes, that means violently. When that happens, good and innocent beings can also die. It's not what they want to do, but they honored the threat. You heard them, right?"

"I did." Maarg buried her face in her hands. "You don't understand. All they do is kill, Tara."

"Maarg?"

Maarg unbuckled her restraint and pushed her bulk up and free of the console. She spun in mid-flight and reached up for an angular rung. With a finger, she pushed herself toward the hatch.

"All we do is kill, Tara. I don't know if I can do this anymore."

"Where are you going? You have the watch."

Maarg chuffed. "No I don't. Not today, and maybe never again. When you can guarantee a mission where no one dies, I'll sit at that console again. Until then, I'll be in my quarters."

Total calm filled her mind as the words came from her mouth. Her father's desire for her to be far away from conflict and remain with friends didn't matter. He'd never told her he was a Peacemaker until the days after her rescue on Weqq. That he'd killed other beings in pursuing his duty was a certainty. She'd never asked for a violent life. All she wanted to do was explore the jungles of Weqq and live a quiet one.

"You know I can't promise that, Maarg."

"I do," she replied as she caught a rung by the hatch and turned to smile at Tara Mason. "And I—"

The words froze in her throat. Tara Mason was floating above the navigation console with one hand on a ceiling rung and the other leveling a pistol at her chest.

"You want a break? Fine. Get off this ship. You have seventy-two hours leave on Snowmass to collect your thoughts and get your shit together. Push that time by more than a minute and I'll leave you down there on your own."

"You…you can't do that!" she stammered. "You have an agreement with my father. A Peacemaker captain."

"My agreement was for a viable and employed crewmember, not a passenger. And the irony of you badmouthing the Peacemakers and then pulling your father's rank on me is duly noted and will be filed in my official report."

"Fine," Maarg replied with as much spite as she could muster, but the word fell flat. Shoulders hunched forward, she pushed away from the bridge toward her quarters without looking back. "Seventy-two hours."

"Not one minute more," Tara called after her.

* * *

Godsdammit.

"Track her every move, Lucille. She's an albino TriRusk, and someone down there will figure that out and figure out why she's important. Where there's one of Kr'et'Socae's minions, there has to be at least one more."

<<You are using her as bait? Her father would not approve of that course of action, Tara.>>

"I know, and honestly, Lucille? I don't care." Tara made her way to the commander's console and sat down. She tapped out a series of instructions. "When will *Mako 15* return?"

<<One hour twenty-six minutes and thirty-two seconds.>>

"Loading status of Demon 16?"

<<Ninety-one percent. There are four CASPers remaining. They are the ones requiring extended maintenance, which is estimated at four hours.>>

"Call Gray and ask for landing permissions. If Pryce and the government really want us to negotiate, they'll see our hefty bill of goods and provide us space. Once you've done that, have Major Vuong get those CASPers loaded, and prepare for departure. When *Mako 15* returns, I want it loaded as fast as possible. Establish a ready ten posture. I want us out the door in ten minutes or less."

<<Acknowledged. Major Vuong reports he is moving to comply now and expects to meet the timeline. Are you expecting some kind of action, Tara?>>

Her eyebrows rose. "You tell me, Lucille."

<<The probability for an uptick in resistance maneuvers, given the friendship between Veeka and Reecha, is a near certainty. As she was a friend to the outer colonies, I would imagine their rough winters, if proven a result of the Dream World Consortium, will foster hostilities.>>

"All that's true. What else?"

<<You're expecting the government to have Captain Gray start a dialogue for possible contract negotiations. This will inflame the mercenaries already on the planet, and they will probably defend themselves. As the resistance rises, the mercenaries will blame the violence on the Goblins. That is what you are hoping for, is it not?"

Tara smiled. "Yes. We'll hold off on combat operations as long as possible, but the whole idea is to determine both what Reecha has of Snowman's in the caves to the north and what the Dream World Consortium is up to. That's your job, Lucille. After you find us a landing zone at least a terrain feature away from New Perth."

<<I have a landing site identified, Tara. May I rewind our conversation a bit? You're expecting Maarg to further confuse the situation how? >>

Tara leaned back against the chair. "If Kr'et'Socae has another asset on the planet, they'll be very interested in her. Maarg, though, won't be able to stop herself from trying to figure out what's going on. She might be fifty years old, but she's a kid. As she's poking her snout into things, you're going to be watching her."

<<What if she tries to block my access to her systems?>>

"Can she?" Tara asked, surprised.

<<She is savvy with systems engineering. It would be difficult, but it is possible.>>

"We'll cross that bridge when we get there, Lucille. Right now we'll let the situation develop. Jessica would be proud." Tara blinked. "Veeka called her a nest-daughter. What does that mean?"

<<It's an honorific. The closest attributable Human custom would be a godparent.>>

"Snowman was that close to Reecha and Veeka?" Even as she asked the question, she recalled the audio transcript of the first time James Francis had been on Snowmass and met his future wife. Both Reecha and Veeka had played a prominent role in their story.

Of course they were close.

Tara gasped. As if a series of locks had clicked open in her mind, she pieced the puzzle together a little further.

"A Human couple and Veetanho having a familial relationship pissed off the Mercenary Guild—specifically Peepo, who was related to Reecha. That's why she targeted Snowman at Shaw Outpost. All she had to do was recruit someone from the Haulers' organization. That's where DuPont came in—but he's just one employee. How many did Intergalactic Haulers have at that point? Employees?"

<<Six hundred and thirteen, counting Jessica, though she never received a wage. She was not reported as a mercenary for their clandestine efforts, either. Why are you asking about employees?>>

"It's the most obvious source of intelligence, but we're fairly certain he only told a few people what he was up to. Have there been any reports of harassment by Haulers' employees, past or present?"

<<None that I am aware of. The Haulers' board of directors shuttered the organization and froze the assets and files accordingly. Their offices throughout the galaxy have been closed. Only Jessica has direct access.>>

"But those former employees are out there, right?" Tara scratched her temple and ran her hand down her cheek to her chin. "They might be worth looking into."

<<For intelligence?>>

"Maybe. Depending on who they were and their relationship with Snowman, they might be assets we hadn't counted on. The kind who could save the day."

<<Tara? I have analyzed some data from the Dream World Consortium's servers and would like to recommend a change in strategy.>>

Tara made a 'come on' gesture with her hands. "Let's hear it."

<<There is a DWC science station at Lake Pryce that is far larger and more advanced than the other stations or PCMU devices across

the planet. While I haven't been able to break the encryption yet, there is clearly an activity underway there that bears reconnaissance. The distance from New Perth could prove problematic without air support, however. The landing site I've chosen is roughly at the mid-point of that transit.>>

"Got it. Good suggestion. Has there been any word from Ibson?"

<<Negative. I will continue monitoring communications channels as ships emerge. Are there any outgoing messages?>>

"Just one," Tara replied with a sigh. "Send a request for status to Xander, and copy Ibson. Tell them we're condition yellow and need support as soon as possible."

<<I have sent the message via a Besquith Thrustcore carrying produce bound for Ghosa. They shunt in six minutes.>>

Tara nodded to herself. Twelve days at the earliest. It would have to do. She touched her slate and connected the intercom to her headset. "Quin'taa? Meet me in the main hangar complex with the Misfits. I'm changing your mission."

"For the better or the worse, Colonel?" The Oogar's gravelly laugh brought a smile to her face. Her team were all cut from the same cloth. Her cloth.

"For the better." *I think.*

"Roger that, Deathangel. We're moving now."

<<Anything else, Tara?>>

She nodded to herself, then looked up at the nearest speaker and camera system. "Find Reecha, Lucille. Find her before anyone on Snowmass does. That's our priority now. If she's as special as we think she is, she knows where Snowman is, and what he's up to.

We're going to get her out of there. Gods help anyone who opposes us."

*****

Chapter Fourteen

Central Square Market

New Perth

Snowmass

"I said *move*!" Rains brought up his pistol and pointed the barrel at two of the Trenta Knights who'd been following Veeka. "Get over here."

Neither moved.

"What? You fuckers can't understand a Human? Or you want me to add disrespect to a Peacemaker to my official charges against your company?"

The two Zuul glanced at each other and walked forward. One sported a coat that was black and white, and the other was a brindle color. Both carried pistols in holsters on their thighs and, more importantly, Rains noticed both of them were wearing earpieces and carried mini-slates mounted to the inside of their forearms.

"Get your paws up where I can see them. Go for a weapon, and I will drop you where you stand. Am I clear?" Rains called.

The two mercs continued forward. They were ten meters from Rains when he called over his shoulder.

"Partner?"

There wasn't an immediate response.

"Vannix? I need you up here."

"I'm here," she said from his left. Her weapon wasn't drawn, but her eyes were clear and focused on the two Zuul. "You okay?"

"Me?" Rains snorted. "Are *you* okay?"

"We'll talk later," Vannix replied. Her voice was low and clipped. The two Zuul approaching would be best served by the respectful following of her orders and commands.

"Did you get her slate?"

"What?" Her eyes flashed to his. "Did I get her slate?"

"Yeah. Did you get her slate?"

Vannix hesitated. "I haven't searched her body, Jackson. There'll be time for that."

"Crime scene 101. Secure everything, partner. There are too many shitheads here."

"Don't you quote regs to me, Jackson Rains." Vannix stomped forward to the two Zuul. She looked over her shoulder, and the cold glint of her eyes froze his reply on his tongue. She snarled, "You leave these shitheads to me."

Rains stepped to his right to create a better angle on the two Zuul should they attempt anything against his partner. It wasn't established Peacemaker standard operating procedure, but he'd always argued that a better angle on a potential attacker gave him an advantage. Many of the instructors at the Academy said nothing—the equivalent of tacit approval without disrupting the time-honored traditions of the Academy and the guild itself.

The Zuul were three meters away when he heard Vannix growl, "That's far enough."

The tone of her voice almost made him laugh. He'd only heard it a few times in their years at the Academy and their young service in the guild. She'd growled like that before hauling him out of a Memphis bar and kicking his ass to get him back into the Peacemakers. One day he'd have to thank her appropriately for that, too. But that memory wasn't what almost forced the laugh.

Vannix was an incredible athlete, and during their first weeks at the Academy, she'd made quite a name for herself on the obstacle course. At over three kilometers long and filled with obstacles requiring climbing, swimming, lifting, and balancing, Rains equated it to at least an hour of hell every day. For Vannix, it was a warmup. The little Veetanho flew through the course, and on the third day she came within eight tenths of a second of beating a record that had stood for almost five years. Vannix's time was the best since, and unprecedented for a first-year candidate.

At the end of that day's formation, Guild Master Rsach himself had been present at the announcement of the proximity of Vannix's attempt. The proud guild master read a statement about the current record holder, another Veetanho named Grexx, and her constant attempts for two years to better the record. He'd been lauding Grexx's accomplishments when Vannix had growled loudly enough that her candidate platoon heard her.

"Grexx? I'll bury that bitch with my dust tomorrow and every day after."

And she had, by more than fourteen seconds.

As she confronted the Zuul, Rains called out, "I'll have the dust ready."

"You do that, partner," Vannix said and turned to the Zuul. "I'm Peacemaker Vannix, and you're submitting to a lawful search of your beings according to the laws of the Galactic Union. We will seize no property unless directly tied to the crime at hand. Your property will, however, be searched and categorized for evidence prior to being returned to you. If you don't submit to this request, as this is a criminal case of homicide of an unarmed victim, you'll be held until a Peacemaker tribunal can be convened. Do you understand this request?"

The two Zuul mumbled their responses, but based on their actions, they'd heard the litany before. Forepaws came up slowly, and their eyes were downcast at the ground in front of them.

"Yacks," Vannix commanded. "Slowly."

With careful movements, the two mercenaries handed over their cards. Vannix scanned them in her wrist slate, more from habit than actual necessity. They knew they were mercenaries and which unit counted them as members.

"What unit are you with?" Rains asked anyway. Sometimes keeping a potential arrestee on edge worked to a Peacemakers advantage.

"The Trenta Knights." The brindle-colored one brought his eyes up to Rains.

Rains harrumphed, and the confident eyes of the mercenary dropped back to the ground.

Take the wind out of their sails with words before actions. Damned if that didn't work.

"Who is your commanding officer?"

"Colonel Krukk," the darker Zuul replied. Unlike his partner, he didn't look up confidently. Reality had set in. If they weren't arrested by the Peacemakers, they would likely face discipline from their commander—which could be worse.

"We'll summon them shortly," Vannix said as she pocketed their cards in her vest. "Why were you following this Veetanho?"

If a dog-like alien could look sheepish, the two Zuul would have defined the image. Rains bit the inside of his cheek, trying not to laugh. Most mercenaries displayed a confidence and air of experience with an impenetrable facade. These two Zuul were both young and inexperienced, which spoke both to their company's multi-decade mission on the planet and a lack of any real threats.

"Orders," the brindle grumbled.

"Orders, what?" Vannix barked.

The brindle's head snapped up. "Orders, Peacemaker."

Vannix held the Zuul's gaze for a long moment before it dropped its eyes again to the ground.

Damn, she's good.

"Surrender your weapons," Vannix said. She pointed at the brindle. "You first. Nice and slow, or my partner will drop you."

The brindle removed the pistol from the holster on its leg slowly and handed it to Vannix. A breeze freshened across the vacant plaza. It was enough to carry the slightest sound of a whimper to Rains.

"You next," Vannix said to the other Zuul, and the ritual was repeated. Weapons on the ground and their yacks in the possession of the Peacemakers, the two Zuul stood powerless. Rains couldn't help but think it was a feeling he'd love to immerse himself in for a long time.

Finally, doing some real Peacemaker shit.

"You," Vannix pointed at the brindle, "did you summon your commander or not?"

"Yes, Peacemaker." The Zuul reached for its wrist slate and hesitated. Vannix's head came up and pivoted toward the west.

"What is it, Vannix?" Rains asked.

"They're coming. Several motorized vehicles. Unknown number of dismounted infantry."

His face screwed up. "I don't hear anything."

"Better hearing," Vannix chittered. "Keep your eyes on these two. I'll handle them."

She withdrew her platinum badge from the inside of her vest and walked across the square along the street where she'd heard the activity. Rains admired her calm. His own heart thumped wildly in his chest. Keeping his weapon trained on the two Zuul, he was already looking for cover positions and withdrawal routes in the event the Trenta Knights came in with weapons blazing.

Vannix stopped about twenty meters away and stood in the street with her face in the breeze. Rains could hear the approaching vehicles now. Based on their high revs, the vehicles were small tactical vehicles with small capacity engines.

They almost sound like motorcycles.

Sure enough, the lead vehicles came into view and were indeed familiar designs. While not the traditional motorcycle, the Zuul-designed conveyances had a similar effect. Given the dress of their occupants and the loud rumble of their unmuffled internal combustion engines, Rains desperately wanted to shake his head and laugh out loud.

Biker dogs. Are you fucking serious?

In a rush, the hair on the back of his neck bristled. They were being watched, and not by the Trenta Knights or any local security forces. Something else. Rains glanced back at the corpse of Qur'atta laying in the street with its brain matter spread across the cobblestones. The Equiri still wore a wrist slate, and there was no doubt the vest it wore was impregnated with explosives. Any attempt to get the slate would detonate the vest and everything around it.

Nice try, Rains thought with a slight grin. *Lucille can get the slate as long as it's still connected to the AetherNet here in the square. When that happens, I'll find you, Thraff.*

Rains looked at the two Zuul. "Take five steps back and sit down on the ground. Do it slowly."

They did so, and Rains adjusted his angle so he could see both the disarmed and dejected Zuul and their approaching counterparts.

You and Qur'atta never went anywhere without each other, Thraff. I know you're here. You're not gonna make it out of here alive, motherfucker.

* * *

Mayor's Chambers

New Perth

The door to his chambers burst open, startling Citsym from the never-ending deluge of paperwork on his slate. He flinched in his specially designed couch and stared at the door into the furious face of Sophie Pryce.

"What is it, Sophie?"

"Veeka!" Pryce shook her head. "She's dead in the city square. There are two Peacemakers holding members of the Trenta Knights. What have you done?"

Citsym shook his head. "What? There are Peacemakers on the planet?"

"What have you *done*?" Pryce demanded again, stepping closer.

"I have done nothing!" he blurted. Sudden anger took him to his feet. "Veeka is dead?"

"That's what I said," Pryce replied. "Tri-V four, on Channel New Perth Charlie One."

The wall-mounted Tri-V to Citsym's right, across the room from the floor to ceiling windows, flickered to life and turned to the planetary camera system. New Perth City Square came into view. There were three bodies lying in the square, and he could easily identify the Peacemakers by their distinctive dark blue uniforms.

A Human male?

Citsym studied the image more. He saw the body of a Veetanho lying in the street near both a Zuul and an Equiri.

"I don't understand."

"Those two were supposed to follow Veeka and find Reecha, not gun her down in the street!" Pryce pointed at him with one finger. "You've endangered everything we've been working for, Citsym."

His anger boiled over. "I've done nothing!"

"You hired them. They gunned down Veeka in the city square. This points back to your contract with them."

Citsym rubbed his forepaws together, twisting them against each other. "I hired them to find Reecha! They acted outside their contract. Why are there Peacemakers here?"

"I don't know yet," Pryce said. "The *Taal's Fury* reported them aboard as ferried passengers en route to Ocono. They must have debarked the ship for fresh air. I'll find out why."

Citsym shook his head. "No. I will meet with them. Fetch my security team, and I will go to the square myself."

Pryce blinked. "You really think that's a good idea?"

"No," Citsym said. His anger ebbed, and he took a deep breath. "There is more to this situation. My job is to get ahead of it. I am the public face of the Dream World Consortium and the leader of this colony. I will go to the square myself."

"I'll try to figure out why they killed her. There has to be a way to access their slates and files," Pryce said, typing away on her slate. "The Trenta Knights have arrived in the square. Are you certain going there is a good idea?"

Citsym studied the scene. On their motorized tricycles, the Trenta Knights deployed in a semicircle around the Veetanho Peacemaker. "Can we hear what they are saying?"

"No," Pryce replied.

"Then I will go there myself. With all possible speed."

* * *

Central Square Market

Vannix watched the mercenaries ride in on their motorized cycles and tricycles. In her bemusement, she quickly identified those who were leaders of some type, and those who were simply soldiers. The lowest echelon leaders—say, squad leaders—rode on the back of bikes driven by other Zuul. Platoon leaders, keeping the framework, rode larger bikes carrying a heavy weapon platform either mounted with rockets or machine guns. The weapons looked menacing, but appearances didn't necessarily indicate operability. Two of the missile-bearing systems she recognized as having been removed from service while she was in the Academy. In both cases, the cheaply made weapons misfired or prematurely detonated in their launchers.

What is it Jackson says? They walk the walk, but can they talk the talk? Something like that?

The mercenaries fanned out on either side of her, arranging the lower section leaders with the intermediate platoon leaders every second vehicle. Engines shut down one by one. In the center, the Zuul left a wide gap for their leader, Colonel Krukk. There was no mistaking him as he rode up in a brand-new cycle adorned with several small and exotic weapon platforms. His darker coat was hidden mostly under a ballistic vest that looked conspicuously new and pristine compared to the ones his troops wore. His stern face locked eyes on hers as he approached, parked the bike, and dismounted in the sudden silence of the square.

Vannix held her ground. Truth be told, she enjoyed their nervous eyes following her every move. "You must be Colonel Krukk."

"And who might you be?" His voice was deep and raspy. Given his lack of combat experience, she wondered if his tone was from drink.

"I'm Peacemaker Vannix. This is my partner, Peacemaker Rains. Your mercenaries appear to be part of a plot against the Veetanho, Veeka." She gestured back to the corpse of the older female lying on the ground. "We observed them following her just before another Zuul not wearing the colors of your unit appeared with a sniper rifle and an Equiri accomplice."

"You said yourself the Zuul was not one of my troops. As for his accomplice, I have never seen that being before in my life. Well, what's left of him."

Vannix considered that for a moment. Without glancing back at their captives, she remembered their conduct at the moment of arrest. Neither of them wanted to look at the dead body lying in the square. The very real possibility that the two groups and their missions were unrelated existed.

"What were your troops doing?"

Krukk stiffened. "That information is classified. It is protected by contract with the leadership of this colony world."

Vannix laughed. "You recognize I'm a Peacemaker, yes?"

"You are dressed for the part, but given recent events, how can I take you seriously, rat?"

Her eyes narrowed and for a moment she considered clawing the Zuul's eyes out and dancing on his blinded corpse no matter the steps his troops would take to protect him. She took a calculated breath, a method learned at the Academy, and kept her voice low. "Colonel Krukk, I understand the reason for your veiled insult, but make no mistake about my loyalties and my duty to the Peacemaker Guild. My partner and I watched a murder take place in this square. Your mercenaries are both young and inexperienced. They were ordered to follow Veeka and did so clumsily. Now I will ask one more time. Who gave them the order to follow Veeka?"

"I did." Krukk ground his lower jaw for a moment. "They were not ordered to engage her, much less kill her in broad daylight."

Vannix considered his words carefully. He wasn't lying, at least not about everything. His mercenaries had acted stupidly, and would likely pay a price for it, but that was not her concern. What mattered was determining why the Equiri and the Zuul had brazenly walked into the square to commit homicide.

If he doesn't know the other Zuul and the Equiri, someone else does. That's what we get to find out next once the crime scene is secured.

Vannix turned to Rains. "You can lower your weapon, partner. We will release these two mercenaries to their commander on their own recognizance. Colonel Krukk will make them available to us should we need to question them further."

Rains holstered his weapon. "I'm clear, Peacemaker."

The words were both a reminder and standard operating procedure. By announcing he was clear, Rains let her know his weapon was safe and safely stored away. But it also reminded her the scene itself wasn't clear. There were several things that needed to be accomplished in a very short amount of time.

"Colonel Krukk," Vannix said, "we will need your assistance. Our guild paid for passage for the two of us from Sraka to Ocono via the MinSha cruiser *Taal's Fury*. We're without our operational gear, beyond what you see on our persons. We believe the two deceased suspects are wearing some type of explosive garment. Would your unit happen to have an ordnance disposal robot we could use to safely remove and detonate those devices?"

"Would it not be easier to simply detonate the bodies in place?"

Vannix shook her head. "No. Both appear to be wearing wrist slates that may be tied to accounts and other privileged information we deem necessary for this investigation. Unlike your mercenaries, we can't release them in good faith. We need every shred of evidence we can get to determine exactly what happened here."

Krukk seem to consider that for a moment. Given the implication of two of his soldiers and the crime, the smart move would be to cooperate. "I will see to it immediately, Peacemaker Vannix."

"We are in your debt, Colonel Krukk," Vannix replied. The mercenary commander nodded and stomped across the square toward his waiting troops. She watched him for a moment before turning to Rains. Vannix let one corner of her mouth twitch upward in a quick smile.

"You really think he'll give us a robot?"

She shrugged. "Does it really matter at this point? We've got two of his mercenaries at the scene of the crime as it happened. Do you see all the camera emplacements? There's no doubt whoever has those cameras has a full record of what happened."

"Unless they've already erased the footage," Rains stated and smiled at her, his lips making a thin line across his face.

"If there is one benefit of working with Force 25, it's riding into battle with an unseen and very capable ally watching from my wrist slate." Vannix allowed herself to grin.

"You brought Lucille to the fight?" Rains asked. "Do you really think that's smart, partner?"

"It's beyond smart, Jackson. It's necessary."

*****

Chapter Fifteen

Watering Hole

New Perth

The sudden warbling of emergency sirens made Harmon Gray almost consider moving. Something had happened in the city square, that much was obvious. And while there was nothing more he wanted to do than see what it was, a seasoned mercenary would do no such thing without provocation or the promise of credits. Likewise, his counterpart Whirr barely twitched an antenna at the rising sirens around them. Several shocked patrons shared scared glances and tried to go on about their business. Most of them failed to cover their fear. The intelligence workups Lucille had compiled discussed rising unrest among the populace, given recent apparent terrorist attacks. While the attacks seemed focused primarily on Dream World Consortium assets, it was clear the citizens were afraid. It was equally clear that the mercenaries hired to protect them enjoyed a less than stellar reputation among the planet's citizens.

Gray reached for his beer, a local brand that tasted like a combination of honey and nuts, and took a deep swig. After hyperspace transit in the required alcohol-free environment provided by the MinSha, any beer was a good beer. Gray flagged down the bartender and ordered another as Whirr looked up from her slate.

"I've been unable to access the camera system to see what's happened." Her antennae were relaxed, and her voice, even through the translator, was laconic and disinterested. She was playing the role better than he was. "Our secure communications with our friends haven't been activated, so I'm reasonably sure nothing has happened to them."

Gray harrumphed and waited until the bartender delivered his second beer, taking a long drink before replying. He wiped his mouth with the back of one hand and said, "It's not our problem anyway. We have our mission, and they have theirs. Our instructions were to stay out of their way, keep our heads down, and see what we can see."

"I'm not sure where getting an alcoholic beverage fits into this equation," Whirr chittered. "Though I must admit, it is quite tasty."

"What's the deal with not having alcohol in transit?" Gray asked. "Is this some kind of local rule or regulation the ship's captain initiates?"

Her antennae bobbed in amusement. "Something like that."

Gray made a 'come on' gesture with his hands. "You're not telling me everything. I'm very curious why I couldn't have a beer onboard the ship. It's certainly not a rule from our new commander. I bet she has a private stash."

Whirr ground her lower maw. "I would imagine most of it relates back to the perception of Humans across the greater galaxy. It's well known once the Humans get into the booze, bad things tend to happen. I mean, how many bar fights have you seen over the course of your career, Harmon?"

Gray harrumphed again. "Survived more than a few, my friend."

Face down on the table between them, Gray's slate chimed to life. He reached for it, turned it over, and slid two fingers across the screen to activate it. He read for a moment, and his eyebrows slid upward in surprise.

"What is it?" Whirr asked.

"Permission for us to land the bulk of the force. They've given us a landing spot on the opposite side of the town, that wide clearing we saw tucked up against the hills? We have about six acres of space. Should be more than enough to land all the CASPers and the tanks." Gray studied the message again just to make sure he wasn't missing anything. He didn't bother telling his partner about the personal touch at the bottom of the message.

"What else is in that message, Harmon?"

"What do you mean?" Gray asked incredulously. "Do you think I'm lying?"

Whirr laughed. "Not at all. I'm willing to guess the message is from a certain Sophie Pryce, and you likely have some sort of interlude planned."

"Interlude?" Gray laughed. "I wouldn't call it an interlude. How about a necessary meeting?"

"Necessary meeting? You Humans will say just about anything to cover your romantic interests, won't you?" Whirr shook her head and chittered a long laugh.

There wasn't really anything he could say. He had thought it possible. Sophie Pryce appeared to be a woman on a mission, and the only reason she would accept his offer of dinner would be to pry for additional information about his own company's capabilities. Or maybe she was serious about removing the Knights from their current contract? Either way, he'd have to make sure, even if it meant a pleasant dinner with a beautiful woman.

Oh, the sacrifices we make.

He tapped quickly on the screen of the slate. Composing the message took a moment, and running it through the encryption to transmit via the available local Aethernet connection took a moment more. When he was finished, Gray looked over the message one more time.

Commander sends. Landing privileges granted at zone six. We have the entire clearing for our disposal. Recommend moving down all vehicles requiring maintenance and refit. Recommend station one ship on the planet to shuttle resources as required. Recommend low posture, security personnel, and systems being placed. Inform me when all forces are ready to depart, and we will meet them at the landing site. Commander out.

The subterfuge for the message almost made him laugh. First, he wasn't the commander of Force 25, but the leadership of New Perth had no idea Force 25 was even in orbit. The only forces they knew about were Gray's Goblins. Second, by couching the request as moving disabled vehicles and those needing significant repair work, anyone able to intercept the message locally would make an assumption that his Goblins couldn't fight if confronted. Likewise, stationing one dropship on the surface gave the pretense they expected to move resources frequently. Which would mean, to an adversary, an opportunity to attack without air support being available to the Goblins. Finally, requesting the low posture, security personnel, and systems wasn't what he'd actually done at all. Tara Mason and the others on board wouldn't be sending minimal security for this mission, but the locals didn't need to know that.

Gray passed the slate to Whirr. "Tell me what you think about this."

Whirr looked at it for a few moments, reading the message carefully. "My English is getting better. I can almost read this untranslated." She laughed at him, her antennae bouncing from side to side.

Gray rolled his eyes. "I'm sorry, I forgot to switch to translate."

"It's okay." Whirr leaned back and sipped her beer from the specially made cup and straw. "Are you going to send it?"

"Right now," Gray said.

From the time they sent the message until it would actually get into Tara Mason's hands would be a minute or two at most, but they had hours to kill until his face-to-face meeting with Sophie Pryce. The landing of the entire force had to take time, too, if for no other reason than to ensure the Trenta Knights, and any other interested eyes, didn't see through their gambit. Performing a reconnaissance on the landing zones to the east of town would be the most profitable expenditure of their time, but Gray decided he really wanted another beer and perhaps something to eat.

He motioned one more time to the bartender, a pleasant-looking woman a little older than him.

She approached the table with a half-smile on her face. "Can I get you something else?"

Gray replied with a smile, "What's good to eat around here?"

"I'm sure I can rustle something up for you." She inched closer to the table, and as she continued, her voice softened, as if trying not to be heard. "But I have a question. Are you mercenaries?"

Gray nodded. "Yes, ma'am. Gray's Goblins, at your service."

The woman's friendly smile vanished, and she leaned forward, her ice-blue eyes blazing with intensity. "If I were you," she replied, her voice barely above a whisper, "I'd get out of here as fast as you can. Those Knights can't be trusted, and neither can the government. If something isn't done about them, they're going to kill us all."

* * *

Central Square Market

Much to his surprise, Jackson Rains saw the Trenta Knights slowly perform a security perimeter check and carefully search the surrounding buildings for additional explosive devices. Their work was shoddy and methodical, the work of those who've seen too many training iterations and not enough natural situations. Rains watched them for a few moments, then turned his attention back to the recovery and decryption of Veeka's wrist slate.

His partner Vannix gingerly removed the slate from the dead Veetanho's wrist and gently laid her forearm back on the ground. He watched his partner's paw gently stroke the fur on Veeka's forearm before she collected herself and stood to face him. With the slate cradled in her hands, Vannix moved to a simple table under a species of pine tree Rains hadn't known existed until that moment. They looked similar to the long-needled pines he remembered from a foster home in the Appalachian Mountains, but the smell was different, more pungent. As he watched the Knights finish their perfunctory sweep of the square, Vannix sat down, tapped on the slate, and waited.

"Dammit." Vannix frowned. "It's encrypted. Even with the tricks and backdoors we learned in the Academy, I can't get around this security system. It's nothing I've ever seen before."

"Not a showstopper, though." Rains turned toward her. "We do have a few tricks up our sleeves, partner." His voice carried the tiniest bit of inflection, and when she looked up at him, he rolled his eyes skyward toward orbit. Lucille was much more than a trick up their sleeve, and they both knew it.

"You're right," Vannix said, "but I don't want to let that particular cat out of the bag just yet. That is the expression, isn't it?"

Rains blinked. "What do you mean?"

"What I mean is pretty simple. Let's see what kind of support we get from the locals." Vannix unconsciously rubbed her front paws together. "Remember, Jackson, we're two Peacemakers in the wrong place at the wrong time. Playing into supporting the locals, government or mercenary, will help us get what we need."

Rains knew she was right. A major portion of the plan they'd collectively developed revolved around interactions with the local populace. Whether it was making friends where friends seemed impossible, or working on the goodness of people's hearts, it didn't matter. They could find a way to get what they needed without bringing out their big guns until it was necessary. If anything, the security of the entire mission counted on their discretion. Should they forget that, finding Snowman would be the least of their troubles.

A brief commotion in the southeastern corner of the square caught their attention. Voices were raised suddenly. Along the security perimeter, the line of mercenaries on their ridiculously motorized tricycles suddenly parted. A resplendent vehicle, a weird hybrid between a terrestrial golf cart and an ornate sled with rails, pushed through their perimeter and into the square itself.

Rain chuckled. "Betting that's the mayor."

"No bet, Jackson."

"What we do now?" he asked, keeping his eyes and attention firmly on the approaching mayor and his entourage.

He heard her sigh behind him, and when she spoke, her voice was both suddenly strong and tired. "This is a tragic situation, Jackson. Especially for me on a personal level. To be here to witness this crime has a special meaning with my species. If she has no immediate family in the local area, the rituals for her end-of-life fall to me. It's my responsibility to see that her effects and...estate are taken care of. My position as a Peacemaker is equally unique and honored because it allows me to make an inroad with the mayor and his administration. I doubt they've had to deal with something like this in the colony's history. Right now, the best thing we can do is play on that responsibility and your sterling sense of duty."

"My sterling sense of duty?" Rains asked. "You've gotta be kidding, right?"

Vannix laughed quietly. "I'm not kidding at all, Jackson. You've said you wanted to do more Peacemaker shit since you left the Academy. Now's your chance."

Rains frowned. He knew what she meant, and he wasn't sure whether he'd like it or not. In situations where a local government official was involved, the standard operating procedure for a Peacemaker was to avail themselves to the official in an official capacity. He understood it to be a gesture of goodwill, but the Peacemaker Archives were full of instances where government officials manipulated such a professional relationship in an attempt to cover crimes and other misgivings within their governments. Rains realized Vannix wanted him to take the lead in this particular case, and that meant he would be the one availing himself to the mayor for the duration of the mission.

Godsdammit. There's gotta be a better way.

Yet as soon as the thought crossed his mind, he knew it was the right answer. He knew about the responsibility Vannix would undertake, having seen Veeka's murder and knowing Veeka had no family on the planet. Just as surely, the sudden appearance of a Human Peacemaker, one who wasn't Jessica Francis or Nikki Sinclair, would catch the local government by surprise. They would undoubtedly check his credentials and such, which served to let the guild know both where he and Vannix were and what they might be doing. Then another thought came to mind.

"I'm guessing that means you'll follow standard burial procedures for the Veetanho?" He turned to see her look up from Veeka's slate.

"Yes." She sighed. "Unless I find anything in her—what do you call that? Last will and testament? If there's something there that defines a different wish, then I'll follow that. If not, I'll ensure she's buried within the requisite four days."

And that means I get the mayor. Great.

Stop it, Jackson. It's the right thing to do and you know it.

The mayor's vehicle ground to a stop about twenty meters away. The driver dismounted from the front of the vehicle, spun theatrically toward the passenger compartment, and opened a small door, allowing the mayor to step down to the ground.

Gods, I hate politicians.

At the Peacemaker Academy, candidates learned a basic introduction to political sciences across the galaxy. Like many of his counterparts, Rains hadn't believed the class would be helpful at all in his role as a Peacemaker in the Galactic Union. However, in the relatively short time he'd actually been on duty, he realized they were dealing with politicians at almost every turn. Whether it was Governor Watson on Victoria Bravo, or the different gate masters in charge of their specific sectors for the Cartography Guild, it didn't seem to matter. Politics was everywhere. As he watched Mayor Citsym approach, Rains tried to remember the words of his instructors. Politicians fell into two groups: the ones who'd tell a lie while smiling, and those capable of stabbing a victim in the back while smiling. As the Zuparti approached with a measured, jovial look on its face, Rains knew which one Citsym was at his core.

The mayor approached and stopped two meters away, clasped its forehands in front of its waist, and nodded solemnly. "Well met, Peacemakers."

Rains turned to the Zuparti, nodded slightly, and replied, "Well met. You must be Mayor Citsym, is that correct?"

"Indeed. I am most surprised to discover there are Peacemakers patrolling my colony. Are you here on a specific mission? Why was there no official communication regarding your presence?"

Rains shook his head. "No, Honored Mayor. We're transiting aboard the MinSha cruiser *Taal's Fury*, currently in orbit. Given the cruiser, and the mercenary company it ferries, needed supplies and would be here for several days, we assumed it would be acceptable for us to get some fresh air. It appears we happened to be in the right place at the right time."

Vannix spoke up from her seat at the table, "This appears to have been an assassination. Two perpetrators, one a Zuul and the other an Equiri, stalked this Veetanho and shot her in cold blood. We'd like to know why and, more importantly, who they are. Would you be willing to help us identify the bodies?"

The measured look of joviality on Citsym's face faded quickly. "You would like my assistance? How can the office of the mayor serve the Peacemakers in this tragedy?"

Oh, please. Stop wallowing in the drama, man.

Rains bit back the comment and said, "Yes, as the mayor of this colony, you and your staff undoubtedly know its inhabitants much better than we could, and until we have access to the GalNet through your local servers, our slates are little more than calculators."

Citsym's whiskers twitched slightly. "Well, we can certainly provide you access to the networks, and I will be happy to assist in any way possible with your investigation. I hope by doing so you may assist me in pressing matters of significant importance."

There it is. Not even two minutes into our conversation, you're already asking for help.

"What kind of assistance do you need, Mayor?" Vannix asked.

"We've had some…incidents of late. As you are aware, Snowmass is a Dream World Consortium planet. There is expensive, proprietary equipment located at various sites around the globe. Some sites have recently been attacked by terrorists."

Rains allowed his eyebrows to rise slightly. "Terrorists?"

"We're uncertain whom, but someone is trying to disrupt our peaceful daily lives here on this planet," Citsym replied.

"What types of equipment are being attacked?" Rains asked.

"As I said, it's proprietary information, but they are units designed to monitor and adjust the climate of the planet."

"I see," Rains said. "I'd imagine that's a serious concern on a planet whose winter lasts over eight months. Is that right?"

Citsym nodded again, even more solemnly than before. "Most definitely, Peacemaker. But until we can determine who is responsible for these attacks, and stop them, there is nothing we can do to further adjust the climate of the planet. The system only works if all the individual units are performing nominally. This hasn't been the case for some time."

Every Dream World planet I've been on has issues with its climate. That tells me that either your equipment sucks or that some things, like nature for example, shouldn't be messed with at all. Either way, you morons never seem to learn that lesson, Citsym.

Still, this is the in Vannix was talking about. Gods help me.

"Mayor Citsym, we'll be glad to assist with your investigations. However, as you may know, there are specific rights and duties regarding the victim and my partner. Having seen this attack firsthand, my partner is responsible for the burial rights of the victim. According to their custom, we'll bury the victim within ninety-six local hours. Once that's complete, you have my assurance that our attention will turn to your investigations, and we'll try to help understand these attacks. At least until our ship is ready to depart."

"I understand, Peacemaker. Thank you for your assistance."

Vannix asked, "Now, can you help us identify the victim? And help provide us access to her slate?

"Certainly. Her name is…was Veeka. One of the original Veetanho colony group on this planet more than fifty years ago. She held a spot on the local governing board. As for who these other two beings are, I am afraid I cannot help you."

Bullshit.

"You'll ensure we have access to your customs and clearing documents? As well as permit us to ask questions of citizens who may have come into contact with them?" Rains asked.

"Of course." The Zuparti mayor danced from one foot to the other. At the Academy they'd learned such movements were impulsive reactions to a controlled fight-or-flight response. To his credit, Mayor Citsym simply asked, "Is there anything else you require?"

"Colonel Krukk is providing an autonomous robot to deactivate what we believe are explosive vests on the perpetrators." He pointed at the two bodies. "Those lumps on their sides and backs indicate something under the vest material itself, and we're not taking any chances. Once we have those secured, we can finish securing the crime scene, clear the bodies, and reopen your square for business."

Mayor Citsym sighed. "I cannot imagine why our luck and fortune continues to turn against us. But there is at least a bright spot; we have Peacemakers. Though I was unaware of a third Human Peacemaker."

Rains smiled. "My name is Jackson Rains. I am the third Human Peacemaker, but I won't be the last."

A peal of thunder rumbled through the western sky. The attention of everyone in the square turned to the approaching charcoal gray squall line. Rains turned to his partner.

"We ain't got much time."

From behind them, the mercenaries brought forward the robot to disarm the explosive devices on the assailants' bodies. Rains turned his attention to those preparations while Vannix approached the mayor.

"Mayor Citsym, may I have your help in activating the victim's slate? Is there anything more you can tell me about her?"

The mayor sighed again, this time more heavily. "I am heartsick over this tragedy. We had hoped she could finish an initial investigation into the attacks on the Dream World equipment, but that seems impossible now."

Vannix replied calmly. "My partner has already told you we would assist, but there are more pressing matters at hand. We need to clear this crime scene and ensure the bodies are properly cared for according to the requisite customs of their species."

"I understand, Peacemaker. You will have my assistance and that of my board for the duration of your stay, no matter how long that may be."

"Thank you, Honored Mayor. Am I to understand there's no Peacemaker office on this world?"

His back to the conversation, Rains allowed himself a small smile at his partner's not-so-innocent question. Dream World Consortium planets never had a Peacemaker assigned. The guild master wouldn't allow it. For whatever reason, he'd never trusted them, and since their continued proliferation across the Union, they'd been nothing but trouble. Keeping Peacemakers at their regional barracks, far enough away to observe but not be affected by DWC incompetence, was a prudent move.

Maybe it would be worth having a permanent office here.

He shook off the thought. Having grown up in rural Mississippi, the idea of snow on the ground at any depth above his ankles chilled him to the bone. Most locations on Snowmass received up to five meters of snow every year. There was no way in hell he'd be on Snowmass any longer than he had to be.

* * * * *

Chapter Sixteen

Snowmass

Through the forward view screen's cameras, Irene Mata saw the approaching storm clouds were unlike anything she'd experienced as a girl on Victoria Bravo. Around *Mako 15*—the new number to honor the deaths of two original crew members—ground crews moved to secure everything that could be secured. Autumn storms on Snowmass approached hurricane force, as they'd learned from the ground crews frantically tying things down outside.

"Drop bay is clear," Carter called. "Maarg is safely at the customs and immigration portal, and the supplies for Captain Gray are secured on the ground."

"Then we're out of here." Mata smiled. "All ports closed. *Mako 15* ready for launch."

"Kinda miss the old girl," Carter replied, "but a state-of-the-art MinSha drop shuttle as a replacement? I could get used to it. Well, except for the angled rungs everywhere."

"They help you move in microgravity. I like them."

"Then they can stay." Carter laughed. He reached forward and activated the communications platform. "Perth Departure Control, this is *Mako 15* at the central landing facility. Request clearance to orbit, bearing three four five."

A bored alien voice growled. "*Mako 15*, vector approved. Heavy weather on your bearing at sixty kilometers. Thanks for visiting."

Mata snorted. *It's not like we won't be back in a few hours.*

Carter replied smoothly, "Copy all, Perth Departure. *Mako 15* is light on the skids in two minutes."

"PDC, cleared and switching." They were done talking, with several other ships preparing to depart before the storm.

"Understood. *Mako 15* out."

Mata glanced across the cockpit to Carter in the command pilot's seat. He smiled at her and gently shook the flight controls.

"Your aircraft, chief."

"What?" A bolt of adrenaline shot through her system.

"Yeah, I think you're ready for this. So why not a little bit of on-the-job training? Your aircraft." He shook the flight controls one more time.

Fighting the butterflies in her stomach, Mata reached for the flight controls, grasped them tightly, and then forced herself to relax. She jiggled them in return.

"My aircraft."

She saw Carter lean back in his seat. Flying approaches through atmospheric interface and countless combat situations via the simulators on board the cruiser was different. She couldn't help but feel a little nervous holding the controls of a viable ship for the very first time. She sighed once and lowered her chin slightly to focus on the aircraft itself. Well, it was an aircraft, not a spacecraft. As soon as she guided them through atmospheric interface, the descriptions blurred into one.

"Hey, remember what I told you. You can fly anything meant to fly. Just stay ahead of the aircraft and you'll be fine."

"Thanks for the vote of confidence." She laughed, but cut it short as she applied power to the maneuvering thrusters, and *Mako 15* took to the sky. With a delicate touch, she pivoted the ship to bearing three four five as it rose to one hundred meters above the pad area then accelerated away. "What was scarier, your first boost to orbit, or atmospheric interface?"

"Interface, hands down," Carter replied. "You'll do that one later, when the atmosphere calms down a bit."

"Tell me about it. You remember it, right?"

Carter laughed. "Gods, yes I do. We were on fast approach to Earth over the southern hemisphere. Somewhere around Fiji, I think, and headed for the Hawaii starport. I'd been sitting right seat for so long, I thought I'd never get an opportunity to fly, so I hadn't bothered to even go to the restroom before getting into the cockpit for de-orbit. So there I am, with a very full bladder, already dreading the pressure of G forces. When all of a sudden, my command pilot, Captain Peeples, flicks the controls and says, 'Your aircraft.' I think when I replied my voice was about two octaves higher than normal. Honestly, I've never been so scared in my life."

"That's supposed to make me calm and composed? You being scared to death the first time you flew an atmospheric interface?"

"Yes, because you're a better pilot than I ever was."

Mata stared at him for a long moment. He'd been the copilot of a dropship for Victoria Forces for as long as she'd been a CASPer pilot. Their paths had never crossed until after she went down on the battlefield in the midst of the attack. Seeing that her vital signs were weak and fading, Carter and others had risked everything to get her out. His pilot and their pararescue man had died in the attempt. In the months that followed, she couldn't help but feel guilty about her role in their demise. But Carter set her mind to rest. He told her repeatedly that dropship pilots and combat rescue pilots understood what their role was. And if the roles were reversed, they'd want to know everyone around them would do the same for them. Simply put, do everything possible to get them home safely. "That others may live" was more than a motto.

"I can't stop thinking about Victoria," she said with a sigh. "What would they think of this now?"

Carter reached over and touched her on the left shoulder lightly. "Well, Becky would tell you you're grabbing the controls too tight. Alphabet? Gods love that guy; he'd probably be too scared to say anything knowing he had a rookie pilot on the stick."

"Bastard!" She laughed.

He cleared his throat. "You know, I've been thinking a lot about the cabins on the upper rim back home."

"Oh, really?"

"Yeah, I think it might be fun to, I don't know, maybe buy one."

Mata blinked and realized she was holding her breath. "Does that mean what I think it means?"

Carter shrugged. "I think we go pretty well together. So I thought it might be an opportunity for us to maybe move in together. That's still a thing?"

She smiled. "Anything would be better than the barracks."

"Do you think Colonel Mason will approve that?"

"Approve what?" the new voice called from where the passageway met the cockpit. Mata turned and saw Tara Mason climbing into their space with a smile on her face. "Now what am I approving?"

"A change of location for personal reasons. Once we complete this mission, of course," Carter said.

Mason nodded, still smiling. "We'll see. Right now, it's time for Phase Two of this mission."

"Maarg didn't see them?" Mata asked.

"No, the Misfits were aboard long before she loaded Gray's initial landing package. Lucille made sure she had no idea they were aboard," Mason replied. "Did departure control approve your vectors?"

Carter grinned. "Yes, ma'am. We'll be over the eastern edge of Lake Pryce in about six minutes. We have a drop zone identified."

"Perfect." She patted Mata on the shoulder. "Put us on altitude and speed, and we'll do the rest."

"We?" she said. "I thought you were going back to *Taal's Fury*?"

"No. Major Vuong will lead the landing party and refit operations at New Perth. The *Fury* is on orders to defend themselves as necessary, and I've already requested support from headquarters. There are a lot of things happening with this mission, and it's better that I'm on the ground. Out here, unless something really shitty happens, I won't be recognized."

Carter caught Mata's eye for a moment and then looked over her shoulder at Mason. "But how are you going to get air support if you…oh, us?"

"That's right," Mason said. "You're the best aircrew I have. Don't get me wrong, the MinSha flight crews are good, but you two have experience in combat operations, and I'm expecting things to go south at New Perth, and likely at Lake Pryce, too. Your job is to stay flying. Lucille will help you do just that and maintain silent, encrypted communications. Think of her as a third crew member."

<<There is an S-band radar set powering up at Lake Pryce. It matches a Zuul weapons platform known to be in the Trenta

Knights' inventory. They are sweeping but have not locked onto us.>>

Did she just say us?

"Copy, Lucille," Carter said. He glanced at Tara. "Orders, ma'am? If you're going to jump, you'd better get going."

"Keep flying the route. Keep yourselves safe at all costs." Tara touched Mata on the shoulder. "I knew we made the right choice. Nice flying, Renee. We'll see you when we see you."

* * *

The return of gravity made moving from the tight cockpit of the dropship to the matching, belly-mounted cargo bays much easier than floating. Tara scrambled down a ladder-like set of rungs and ran. She passed the first bay where she'd stashed Maarg and the gear for Harmon Gray on the first part of the mission. Further toward the engine compartments she dropped into the lower, second bay.

Through the hatch she saw the two CASPers, one closed and ready for departure, and the other with its cockpit door open for boarding. The rest of the team sat rigged in their high-altitude, low deployment parachute assemblies.

The Oogar, Quin'taa, stared at her. "Cutting it a little close aren't we, ma'am?"

Tara grunted but didn't reply. She made her way to Deathangel 25 and climbed aboard. Climbing into the suit, she slipped her legs into their familiar positions and engaged the cockpit close switch. As it swung down and clamped over her, the cockpit systems flickered to life, and she initiated the start-up sequence from memory.

Lucille chimed in her ears. <<Sixty seconds to drop.>>

"Copy, Lucille. Let the flight crew know we're doors open in thirty seconds."

<<Acknowledged.>>

As her external camera systems came to life, and the last of her sensors powered on in standby mode, she engaged the communications system to the squad.

"Okay, Misfits, check in," Tara called.

"Misfit 1," Quin'taa replied.

"Misfit 2," Each replied. His Tortantula mount Ladow raised one of her legs and tapped it against the hull in response.

"Misfit 3," Ladow whispered.

They were ready to go.

"Misfit 4," the Pushtal Homartaga replied. They called him Homer, both for brevity and because of his fondness for obscure twentieth century television programs.

"Misfit 5," the other Human in the group called from inside her newly-refurbished Mk 6 CASPer. Araceli Cignes had distinguished herself on the battlefield at Victoria Bravo and found herself without a unit because of her age and Major Vuong's aversion to taking a teenager on combat missions. Tara had no such reservations. The young woman had enormous potential and no family. Tara could sympathize.

"Ma'am? Does that make you Misfit 6?" Homer asked.

Tara laughed. "I hadn't thought of that. Given the state of our entire organization, maybe?"

There was a chuckle across the group frequency. Releasing her CASPer from its moorings, Tara saw the bay doors on the side of the ship open. On cue the drop status light illuminated, glowing red on the right side of the door.

<<Fifteen seconds to jump,>> Lucille said.

Tara pointed at Misfit 5. "You're jumping the door position, Araceli."

"Say again?" the teenager said incredulously. "I'm not even qualified for this in the first place, Colonel Mason."

Tara pointed at the door with one mighty hand. "Five seconds. Get ready."

She watched with pride as the young girl pivoted her CASPer and took three quick steps toward the open doors. At the moment they crossed into the drop zone, the light flicked to green. Araceli stepped forward and leapt into the storm. Quin'taa and the others followed without hesitation, though she noted Ladow's cautious approach to the ramp and powerful lunge into the slipstream. The other Misfits followed in rapid succession, with Tara bringing up the rear.

As she left the door in her CASPer, Tara called to the flight crew, "*Mako 15*, Deathangel 25. We're out the door. Nice flying. Stay in touch, you guys."

"Roger, Deathangel 25. Good hunting."

Tara turned her attention back to the ground and the accelerating cloud deck pouring over their position. Her CASPer was buffeted in the fall. From an altitude of just over 10,000 meters, the group would collectively follow a low deployment procedure for their parachutes. With heavy weather inbound, the last thing they wanted was to be at a significant altitude when the wind shear took effect. As it looked from up here, the storm would be a doozy, and the faster they got to the ground the better.

<<I have engaged with Araceli's systems,>> Lucille said. <<She is in positive control of the drop, but I know you were worried about her ability to deploy on time.>>

"As usual, Lucille, you're dead on. Stay engaged, let me know if she has any trouble."

<<Acknowledged.>>

Confident that all was well, Tara did her best to relax and enjoy the feeling of flying, even if she couldn't feel the breeze on her face as her CASPer shot towards the ground.

There were far too many variables still in play for her to completely relax. The two Peacemakers seemed to have their mission well in hand, except for the assassination of their primary subject right before their eyes. Still, Lucille reported there had at least been some communication from the dying Veetanho, though until the Peacemaker slates could engage a GalNet connection, there was no way to get that information in an encrypted format. Whatever had been said would hopefully be worth the cost.

The same could be said for Gray and Whirr and their mission to get the rest of Force 25 on the ground without incident. Undoubtedly the Trenta Knights were well aware of what was going on, and their suspicions would prove fruitful in more ways than one. All Gray and his team had to do was ensure the Knights attacked and put themselves in a position to lose their contract. If they did, and a replacement contract could be negotiated with the Goblins, they could eliminate one of their major threats. But Tara didn't believe that would happen. If anything, she expected the feisty little bastards to attack without such provocation, and soon.

Of all the plans in play, placing Maarg as bait didn't sit very well with Tara. Even with Lucille and all the other assets watching over the young one, there was still too much danger given her abilities. Yet if Rains and the others were right, there could be a direct line to their hidden adversaries on the planet. All they had to do was flush them out. Who could resist a young albino TriRusk?

Stuck inside the cockpit of her CASPer, falling under radio silence, Tara Mason was alone with her thoughts for the first time in a very long time. Try as she might, focusing on the mission only amplified her anxiety. She thought of Jessica Francis and where she was in the galaxy at that moment and said a quick, silent promise to find her friend's father before it was too late.

Falling through 8000 meters with nothing more to do than watch the altimeter, Tara allowed herself to think all the way back to her family on Earth. It was early February, and the snowy ground near Omaha was slowly being prepared for an abundant spring. Maybe there would be time to go home someday. Maybe if she did, it wouldn't hurt so bad to think about it.

* * * * *

Chapter Seventeen

Headquarters, Trenta Knights

New Perth

The storm broke over New Perth with unbridled rage. For its citizens, the experience was nothing new, as the short spring and autumn seasons were pleasant days punctuated by stormy nights. The surprisingly torrential rains, however, were welcomed. As long as the carefully controlled climatic conditions produced actual liquid water, and not the snows that would blanket the planet in a few weeks, it was a resource to be gathered and set aside for the long, cold winter.

Colonel Krukk cradled a mug of warm tea, gazed out the small window of his headquarters, and watched the rains and winds bathe the landscape so thoroughly he couldn't see the fence line of his company's property. They'd finished the cleanup operation in the central square, under the supervision of the two Peacemakers, only a short time before the storm broke. He'd ordered everyone back to the relative safety of headquarters and their barracks and received word through an accountability check that everyone was safe as the gusty front slammed into New Perth, scattering leaves, branches, and debris across the town. Even mercenaries needed to be safe.

"Colonel? Are you well?"

The voice came from behind him near his office door, and Krukk realized it was his executive officer, Tolem.

Without turning, Krukk said, "I'm fine. What is it, XO?"

"Sir, we've completed the after-action review with the teams present in the square. None of them were familiar with either the Zuul or the Equiri. No one had seen them before. All our soldiers knew Lmott by reputation only, but none admitted to working with him."

Krukk nodded. "And we have assurances from their subordinate leaders of their individual loyalty?"

"Of course, sir. Are you concerned about loyalties beyond the Trenta?"

Krukk sighed so hard the sides of his mouth fluttered. The code of the Trenta Knights spoke of loyalty to the company above all else. For generations that foundation had served them well, through good times and virtual famine. There were cracks developing in the foundation, though. He'd suspected it for a very long time, and it had started with those above him. "I am. We have entered a place where I don't know who to trust in our own leadership. I have always considered the Dream World Consortium to have our best interest in mind. I no longer feel that way."

"Why is that, sir?" Tolem asked. "I thought we were performing a mission assigned to us?"

"As did I. Mayor Citsym's orders to follow her with no serious engagement were crystal clear. Veeka was not to be threatened. If our personnel did as they were told, which it sounds like they did, she should be alive. I believe they set us up to fail. I cannot stop thinking the order to kill Veeka came from his office as well."

Tolem gasped. "What do you mean, sir? That Mayor Citsym was duplicitous?"

Krukk turned and locked eyes with his long-time assistant. "No. I don't believe that order came from him."

"You believe it was Miss Pryce?"

Krukk nodded. "I suspect that to be the case, yes. I can't help but think that woman is making a run on the mayor's office itself. Certain decisions she has made have an inherent amount of risk that the mayor would never accept. Are you aware that she has ordered us to reinstall the remote defense turrets?"

Tolem looked surprised. "Does she not know or understand that the software controlling those turrets is obsolete? That they would likely malfunction and cause another incident?"

"I don't believe she cares, Tolem." Krukk set his mug of tea on the desk. "This is why I am concerned."

A storm of emotions crossed Tolem's face. The younger Zuul had never been good at covering his emotions. He knew something that needed to be said.

"What is it, Tolem?"

"Sir, if your suspicions are correct, then why is Miss Pryce meeting with a Human mercenary commander this evening?"

"What?" Krukk erupted. "Why in the name of the gods did I not know about this?

"Sir, our intelligence personnel learned that she made dinner reservations for herself and another Human guest at the Southgate. The name on the reservation for the guest is Harmon Gray. He is the commander of Gray's Goblins."

Krukk nodded. "They are a reputable company, for a bunch of Humans, if my memory serves correctly."

"We observed them discussing the eminent landing of the bulk of his forces at the industrial areas across town. Once we established his identity, we dug deeper into their current status and projected capabilities. They suffered significant defeats in their last several campaigns and barely escaped being captured in totality by General Peepo's forces at the start of the Omega War. Since then they've been in hiding. They appeared at several random stations over the last several months but hadn't been spotted recently until today. They have a cruiser in a high-altitude, but not geosynchronous orbit.

In any case, they are in no shape to either take over our contract or mount a defense against us, should we exert our combat power against them."

Krukk allowed a smile to form on his maw. His XO had clearly identified who the enemy was, and the opportunity to strike was close at hand. If they could determine what Sophie Pryce and Harmon Gray were meeting to discuss, it could certainly provide justification for an attack. As much as he wanted to believe that Pryce wasn't interested in dissolving his contract or negotiating a new one with a replacement company, he couldn't be sure. He'd learned from his father that some situations, especially ones where motives and facts seemed hazy and unclear, needed to simply play out under the watchful and attentive eyes of a good commander. Krukk believed he had the assets in place to do just that, but he also knew it was best to prepare for conflict as a good mercenary leader should.

"In the last fifty years, Tolem, there have been two serious challenges to our contract. You are aware of what happened to those challengers, yes?"

"I am, sir. Which is why stationing this company in the industrial areas plays to our advantage. When last a challenger landed there, they could not repel our attack because of superior firepower and lack of maneuverability. We have them in a position to take advantage of the tactical situation and end any threat to us before it develops."

Krukk nodded vigorously. "We are in agreement then. Where is this dinner taking place tonight again? Southgate?"

"That's correct, sir. The reservation begins in two hours, at 1800 local."

Krukk growled a low chuckle. "That seems awfully late for a dinner meeting. Especially for Humans."

Tolem grinned. "I believe she may have other intentions. She has quite the appetite, as you are aware."

"We'll see about that, won't we?" Krukk laughed. "In the meantime, what can you tell me about these Goblins?"

"Not much, sir. Most of the unclassified records from the Mercenary Guild Archives state they are a capable company, for Humans. They have some good capabilities and a good combat record, but like all Human companies, they have suffered when it comes to the business of being a mercenary company."

"Humans like to spend their credits, don't they?"

"Indeed, sir. What is interesting is that Gray's executive officer appears to be a MinSha."

"You're joking?" The Humans and the MinSha weren't allies. They'd enjoyed no type of peaceful coexistence. The Humans blamed the MinSha for their entry into the Galactic Union and the decimation of their original mercenary forces. Most Humans couldn't stand the sight of a MinSha, much less work with them. Similarly, the MinSha were almost entirely female warrior caste. Their disdain for Humans approached legendary. So why would they be working together?

"Where are they staying with their company on planet?"

"They are in the Garden Temporary Lodging facility, sir," Tolem replied with a glint in his eyes.

"I see. Keep them under observation. We will see about an intervention into their negotiations if necessary." He paused for a moment and scratched behind his right ear as an idea formed. "Though it might be worth an opportunity to confront this Human."

"I can have a team ready in as little as an hour, sir."

Krukk shook his head. "No, I think this meeting should be with you and me. We'll bring backup, as I don't trust his MinSha and the rest of his company not to intervene. But I believe leaders speak with leaders in this case. We can, perhaps, buy his company out of consideration. They've asked for landing privileges to resupply, am I correct?"

Tolem nodded. "We have the best maintenance facilities in this sector, sir. It certainly fits, given their recent defeats. I can search for a supply manifest, if you'd like."

"Do that. If they are in need of materiel and supplies, I believe we can use that to our advantage as we state our case.

"Yes, sir. I shall be ready," Tolem said. "Shall we bring weapons?"

Krukk grinned ever wider. "Of course, my friend. If Gray is as good as we think he is, he'll have at least one weapon, if not more. We'll make certain to have more firepower on ourselves and our associates in the shadows. I will not lose the opportunity to make a point. Even to a damned unpredictable Human."

* * *

The Misfits fell toward Snowmass as the sun slipped beyond the western horizon. Below them, the roiling deck of storm clouds resembled a dark, angry sea. Tara checked their position via the heads-up display overlaid across the camera view from outside her CASPer. At altitude, the calm relative wind appeared to cause little drift or effect as the team's icons fell toward the center of the drop zone.

<<Araceli will enter the storm's gust front in thirty seconds.>>

"Copy, Lucille." Tara could see the information for each of the team by zooming into the display's information. "Any update on Maarg?"

They'd debarked the young TriRusk at the customs station before leaving. She'd never traveled by herself, and while Tara considered it a huge risk to leave the young albino on the surface to fend for herself for a couple of days, it was necessary. Maarg needed to see the hidden mechanisms of the universe at play—that everything wasn't pleasant all the time. Bad things happened for reasons. While Force 25 fought for good, they fought for a reason beyond credits. Maarg needed to understand her worldview, and that the actions of others didn't always measure up to her internal standards. Good people sometimes did morally bad things for good reasons.

Tara chewed the inside of her bottom lip. Leaving Maarg as bait to draw out those behind the scenes on Snowmass met those criteria. Any threat to her was enough to trigger Gray and the others to drop their mission to protect Maarg. Despite their assurances, Tara wasn't sure it was enough.

There's nothing else I can do.

<<Ten seconds.>>

"Is Maarg connected to the GalNet yet?"

<<Affirmative. She is actively tunneling into the local servers under the guise of an initial connection test.>>

"Impressive."

<<It is. She is very capable, Tara and—>>

A warning buzzer sounded. Tara's eyes flashed to her screen. Instead of six green boxes indicating the position of her team, two of them were yellow, and one flashed a bright, ominous red.

"Misfit 5, Deathangel 25. Status?"

The response from the young girl, significantly lower than the rest of the formation based on the weight of her CASPer and her trajectory, was garbled and filled with static. "Zzzzzz...heavy weather...winds are zzzz..."

Another warning buzzer, this one louder and more insistent than the first, sounded.

<<Loss of signal, Misfit 5. Her systems reported fluctuations in atmospheric pressure within a few seconds of entering the cloud

deck. Nothing approaching warning levels for her CASPer, but an anomaly nonetheless.>>

"What do you mean?"

<<Atmospheric pressure readings are scrambled on all the sensors across the unit.>>

"Misfit 5? Araceli, do you read?"

There was nothing but static on the laser link.

"Lucille, go full spectrum radio and data."

<<Acknowledged. There is no return from connection attempts, and her beacon appears inoperative. I cannot verify that her auto-parachute deployment system is active.>>

Dammit.

"Keep trying, Lucille. Get us connected."

"Deathangel 25, Misfit 2. Ten seconds to the clouds, and your auto-deployment system is flashing."

<<Concur. Warnings on Misfit 2 and 3. The sensors for Misfits 1 and 4 are also indicating fluctuations approaching deployment criteria.>>

"Lucille, can you link and take control of the deploy—"

The icons for the Flatar and Tortantula pair flickered to yellow and flashed intermittently. Before she could speak, the parachute deployed above them fully inflated and ripped away in the space of one heartbeat.

There was a high-pitched screech of feedback across the frequency. Two more icons flashed to red and disappeared. As the Flatar and Tortantula fell into the clouds, silence fell across the frequency.

"Set your reserve chutes! Set your chutes, Each!"

<<Loss of signal, Misfits 2 and 3.>>

"Misfits, disengage your auto-deployment systems. Connect them to your altimeters as the primary. Maintain deployment at two hundred meters. Acknowledge."

"One."

"Four."

That's all we've got now. She shook her head. *Stop thinking like that. You don't know Araceli and the others aren't okay down there. Get on the ground and figure it out.*

Just get down, Tara.

Lucille's voice snapped her thoughts like a dry twig. <<I am boosting signal strength to laser connections. It may enable us to maintain communications with Quin'taa and Homer as we fall through the cloud deck.>>

"It might?"

<<I am working to boost signal transmissions and reception, Tara.>>

Tara glanced at her mission timer and altimeter on the heads-up display. They were about twenty seconds from the top of the cloud deck. There wasn't time to fix everything. Only the most important.

Tara watched her camera displays intently as the Oogar disappeared into the cloud deck. Unlike before, the square icon around him didn't disappear. Its color flickered from green to yellow, but the lock appeared strong enough to hold.

"Misfit 1, can you hear me?" she called.

"Loud and clear, 25," he replied. "Can't see anything, and it's really…rough, but I can hear you."

Homer's icon disappeared into the cloud deck next—and it remained a nice, steady yellow. She would have preferred green, but it wasn't a time or a place to be picky.

"I've got you, boss," Homer called. "Damn, I'm flying all over the sky."

Tara breathed a sigh of relief as her CASPer descended into the wispy tendrils of vapor along the top of the clouds before dropping into the maelstrom itself.

Immediately her CASPer rocked from side to side and departed controlled flight. With multiple high-altitude, low-deployment insertions under her belt, she'd never seen anything as turbulent as the storm she was falling through. With careful movements of her arms and legs, combined with gentle taps on her jump jets, she righted herself into a stable, face-down falling position.

At 8,000 meters, with the vibrant yellow icons below her, Tara focused on the center of the wide, marshy plain below they'd marked as the primary drop zone. She couldn't see it, but the map overlay showed they were on course for the center of their preferred spot.

"Lucille, set my deployment at five hundred feet by radar altimeter."

<<Acknowledged. Your systems differ from the ones on the Misfits' harnesses.>>

Which means Araceli might be okay.

Focus, Tara.

She pushed the transmit button for the team frequency. "Get ready for a little jolt on deployment."

"It's going to be worse than falling through this blender?" Homer asked with a chuckle.

Tara allowed herself to smile. "Keep the chatter down. Engage your forward sensors. We've got three Misfits down there somewhere. We need to locate them and make contact."

"Deathangel 25, Misfit 1," Quin'taa called, "I've got a weak signal from Misfit 3's top platform. Bearing is 035 at six thousand meters from ground level."

A section of Tara's display switched to a map overlay of the ground below, which Lucille augmented by creating a three-dimensional topographic map using radar data from her own sensors. Using the relayed position from Misfit 1, Lucille placed the signal on the map, and Tara sucked in a shocked breath. The platform appeared to have dropped on the side of the escarpment six kilometers from the intended landing point.

Gods. We'll never make it up there.

<<There appears to be significant terrain in the area, both steep and restrictive. The distance from the drop zone seems to suggest reserve chute deployment might have been successful, but the mid-level winds likely shredded the system.>>

"I understand, Lucille. Set a nav beacon on that spot. We might be able to get back there, or we can have the dropships check it out on their next sortie. Unless we get definitive life signs or establish positive communications, we may have to press on with the mission without them. Based on that location, I'm not sure anyone survived."

<<I concur with that assessment, Tara. I am…sorry.>>

Nowhere near as sorry as I am.

* * * * *

Chapter Eighteen

Central Square Market

Snowmass

Clearing the bodies of explosive devices and weapons took the better part of an hour. Had one detonated, the powerful devices could have destroyed the better part of the city square and most of the surrounding buildings. The Trenta Knights' demolition specialists worked quickly and carefully, which Rains and Vannix noted for their credit statements to funnel through guild headquarters. As they disarmed the devices and carried them away to be detonated safely, their commander, Colonel Krukk, met Rains' gaze and nodded solemnly before removing his forces in a roar of engines and a cloud of dust the freshening wind carried across the entire square. Rains turned to his partner as they collected the weapons and personal effects of both the victim and the assailants. Seeing the pile they'd collected, they were lucky to have both put down the attackers and minimized collateral damage.

"Storm's coming," Vannix said as she gathered the slates and placed them into a large pocket on her Peacemaker vest. "We need to get this stuff out of the square and secure it."

Rains knelt to help her. "This is when we need a Peacemaker office."

She grunted in response and then glanced around the square. "There has to be a local business we can use in the meantime. At least until the storm passes."

Rains turned and saw the local coroner collecting Qur'atta's body. They'd been given assurances they could investigate the bodies further, and while it was possible they'd need to inspect them further, standard operating procedure dictated they secure all personal effects and investigate them separately. There was much to learn and not only from their slates. Weapons told a tale, too. Communications devices could be inspected, and their connections explored. All of it would take time.

He looked up into the darkening sky. "We don't have much time, Vannix."

"I know, Jackson." She stood and wiped her paws on her vest. "I'm going to find a store we can use."

No sooner were the words out of her mouth than the gust front whipped into the town like the hyper trains he'd heard crisscrossing the humid fields of Mississippi as a child.

Vannix turned to her right. "There!"

Rains made sure the coroner had his own situation in hand, collecting the body of the Zuul assassin last, before turning and grabbing an armload of weapons. He followed her pointing paw and saw a Human woman waving them toward her storefront.

As the storm broke upon them with a fury he'd never experienced before, they ran across the square and onto a wide, covered veranda. The storefront appeared to specialize in exotic crystals and jewelry. Its name was Joy, Rains noted as he pushed past the door held by a pleasant-looking woman with her dark hair tied up on the back of her head.

"In here! Hurry!" The woman slapped at a control panel and lowered a rolling metal shield over the windows and doors.

The interior of the shop was tiny compared to the other shops on the square, but there was a wide table, freshly cleared, in the center. He carefully laid the weapons down and left a place for the load Vannix carried.

"Anything else out there?"

Vannix ducked into the shop. "No, I got it all. The coroner just left, and the square is clear. Gods! What a storm!"

The door to the shop closed, and the woman wiped at the rain glossing her face. Outside, the storm lashed the steel coverings, slapping them against the frame of the building with loud, reverberating bangs that covered all other sounds.

The woman approached them, her eyes on Jackson. "My name is Kay, Peacemakers. This is my store. Welcome."

"Well met," Vannix replied.

Rains nodded. "Thank you, Kay. I'm Jackson Rains."

"You're a Peacemaker? A full one?" Kay's brow furrowed. "There've only been two Humans as Peacemakers."

Rains smiled and shook his head. "I'm the third. First man, too."

Kay's face softened. "We don't get much news out here. At least not from Earth. When did you commission?"

He paused. "A while ago. I think it was about—"

"Thirteen Earth months ago," Vannix interrupted. "We've been on mission ever since, so there's been no official announcement of Jackson's graduation and commissioning. I can assure you, he's a full Peacemaker and more trouble than he's worth."

"Is your GalNet that bad out here?" Rains asked.

"No," Kay replied. "It's just not what the DWC wants us to see."

He stared at her for a long moment. While it wasn't uncommon for beings of all species to be immediately trusting of Peacemakers, the woman's comments seemed almost rushed, as if she wanted to get something off her chest.

Vannix spoke up, "You're saying the Dream World Consortium controls your information and news sources?"

"Oh, they control more than that, Peacemaker. Everything we can see, what we can and cannot talk about, and what news we get over their official broadcast channels. They hate discord or discontent of any type, and they'll squash it if they find it."

"Can you elaborate?" Vannix asked.

Kay laughed. "Things are never as good as they make it sound here. We're bombarded with information telling us how great the world is and the amazing things they're doing for us on Snowmass. Advertisements. News stories. They design all of them to divert our thoughts from anything bad, or anything approaching the truth. Our rights don't seem to matter."

"They're subverting your rights?" Rains asked. "How? All the original colonists signed legal contracts. How are they restricting your freedoms? Your livelihoods?"

"It's a conglomeration of things, Peacemaker. They don't want us to complain. They expect us to pay their taxes while we eke out our livings because we've had to over-insulate our homes because of the winter extremes. They promised long growing seasons for the farms up north, and we don't get them. The booming tourism industry they promised for the mountain cities hasn't materialized."

"Taxes?" Vannix asked. "The Dream World Consortium is a fee-based organization."

"Semantics," Kay replied with a frown. "They limit our sales and export capabilities and restrict our imports. They want a percentage of profits to support infrastructure and security. I believe the definition of taxation is very similar, is it not?"

"Their contracts never stipulated that," Vannix replied.

"The contracts are old and may never expire. We haven't been able to negotiate anything, either. The DWC board stipulated those 'fees' to support their operations on top of all the money they make from new colonists and settlements," Kay replied. "They've done whatever they want, knowing we'll pay. Most of our colonists can't pay the fees to leave the planet. Whatever goods and services we provide aren't enough. This isn't a dream anymore. It's a nightmare."

"They've set up the fees as a cooperative cost-sharing." Vannix nodded. "It's not illegal, but it's a terrible practice."

"They should share their profits with us," Kay said. With her hands on her hips, she stood staring at them for a long moment. Taller than Vannix, but shorter than Rains, the dark-haired woman seemed to be in her forties. Her eyes and face appeared weathered and hardened. He glanced at her hands and saw they were calloused and strong. She'd likely dug and clawed the gems surrounding them from the ground herself.

"Forgive me for asking, Kay, but are you telling us this just because we're here? Did you wave us inside to vent about the situation, or do you expect us to do something on your behalf?"

"I brought you inside, Peacemakers, to get you out of the storm. If you were out there now, you'd be prostrate on the ground, soaked to the bone, and unable to stand in the wind. Exposure to those elements, and the slight acidity of the rainfall, could damage your components and equipment. Everything they've promised us about this planet has failed to materialize. If you think *I* have discontent, Peacemaker Rains, talk to my friends up north."

He saw Vannix's face grow troubled. They'd entered a situation they knew to be less than ideal, only to learn it was a worst-case scenario. Still, discontent on the part of colonists played into Tara Mason's plans.

"I think we'll have to meet some of those folks from the north, partner. Right now, we need to get to work on this equipment and learn about the victim. Why did our two assailants target and kill this Veetanho? Who was she? We need a little more than what we know now."

The comment was a leading one, the type he'd learned at the Academy that could draw more information from bystanders who wanted nothing more than to talk. Kay seemed to be that person, and he didn't have to wait long.

"Her name was Veeka," Kay said with a trembling sigh in her voice. "She was the best of us. I've known all measure of beings in my time out here, from Goka to Besquith and everything in between, but Veeka was the best of them all. She was a warrior in her youth, and a leader everyone here respected. I can't imagine who could be behind such a tragic event. It will devastate the Veetanho community and push them to the breaking point. They could leave us once and for all."

"There's not a large contingent of them here," Rains said. "I thought most of them left years ago."

Kay nodded. "There are less than fifty of them on the planet now. Talking about the erosion of rights, when Reecha and the others left, the DWC board placed Veeka as their sole representative and made the other dedicated slot into a rotating position between a

Zuul and a Human. The Veetanho are always outnumbered in such decision-making. Without Veeka, the Veetanho have no representation anymore. You might look into the board's actions, too."

"Tell me about the board?" Vannix asked.

"The positions were supposed to be equal across the founding communities—Zuul, Veetanho, and Human. We elected them until about ten years ago. Now the seats are filled by appointees for life and easily controlled by the board's initiatives and promise of profits. Their limitations on us line their pockets. Except for Veeka, that is. She asked why the manufacturing sector we have only supplies the needs of the Trenta Knights—those godsdamned mercenaries."

Rains saw Vannix staring at him. "They're as bad as the board?"

"Worse." Kay sighed. "They promise us security, and I guess they provide it, but they take much more than they give. If they spent half the credits they earned on the local economy instead of traveling to Karma and the other shitholes of the Union to spend them on prostitutes and drugs, things could be different here. Businesses could have a greater voice. As it is, shops like mine survive purely on tourist trade. Given our short seasons, that's only a few months per year."

"The mountain resorts and those sports don't have the draw the Dream World Consortium reports?" Snowmass enjoyed a reputation as a winter sports paradise. The Human sport of skiing had an exceptional draw for the other bipedal species and was currently enjoying a Renaissance of sorts.

"Hardly." Kay shook her head. "The storms are too bad. Once it gets colder outside, a storm like this happens every few days and can drop up to five meters of snow in the north. The 'carefully controlled weather patterns' are anything but. Forecasting is impossible.

All we can do is dig in and wait out the storms. It just keeps getting worse. With Veeka's death, we have no one to look out for us and deal with the incompetence of the DWC Board."

Kay fell silent, and the fury of the storm against the shutters filled the room with sound for a long moment. Rains couldn't help but think they'd stepped into a much bigger, and much worse, situation than they'd originally assumed.

Finding Snowman may be the least of our problems.

Kay gasped and shook her head. "Where are my manners? Can I get either of you some tea?"

Vannix stepped forward and clasped Kay's hands with her paws. "We'll do everything we can do, Kay. I for one would love some tea. How long do these storms last?"

"At this time of year? Days."

* * *

Garden Temporary Lodging Facility
New Perth

Harmon Gray decided to sleep through the onslaught of the storm. He believed there was no way the storms could be anywhere as potent as the ones during his childhood on Earth. Living in the southeastern United States, he'd dealt with thunderstorms and tornadic activity for most of his life. He even remembered a few hurricanes strong enough to make their way inland, dumping rain and heavy winds in all directions.

He lay down on his bed in the small quarters approximating a hotel and expected to gently nap with the rain pelting the building outside. He hadn't been prepared for the extreme wind gusts and the rain falling so hard the entire building shook. Sleep, therefore, had been out of the question.

Instead, he turned on the Tri-V and scrolled through the available channels until he found a sport something like rugby and volleyball played by the millipede-like Jeha. After a while, bored with the sports and the unintelligible language of the sportscasters, he turned off the screen system and pulled up a book on his slate. The classics of Ernest Hemingway filled the doldrums of the late afternoon, and he relished the opportunity to simply sit quietly and read.

It was still raining, though not as hard, when it was time for his meeting with Sophie Pryce. About an hour prior to their meeting, just as the sun set, she sent him a message via the hotel's system, giving him the name and location of a small restaurant she'd picked out. Southgate's GalNet site described it as a proper steakhouse with a laid-back, rural atmosphere specializing in farm-to-table foods for all species. Curious about their menu, Gray looked it over and decided it had been far too long since he'd eaten anything approximating a good steak. Though, he noted with a grin, they claimed Rocky Mountain oysters as one of their house specialties; one of Snowmass' major export crops turned out to be beef. Studying the rest of their menu down through the numerous dessert listings, his stomach rumbled. With credits from Force 25 flush in his account, there was no question the finest cut of steak on the planet would be his that evening. Perhaps even something called apple pan dowdy that vaguely tickled his memory.

So at the appropriate point of time he dressed in clean coveralls, cleaned the mud off his boots, and headed out the door to the small restaurant about five blocks south of the city square.

As he walked, he could see the perimeter of the square was still blocked by Trenta Knights who looked positively miserable manning their security positions in the pouring rain. As curious as he was to know what had happened, he knew his best course of action was to stay as far away from the Peacemakers as possible. While there was little doubt in their ability, or his own, to treat each other as strangers, it was better not to take any chances whatsoever. He could find nothing about the confrontation in the square and the subsequent cleanup actions on any of the local news programs. Then again, every single program he watched was full of advertisements for the Dream World Consortium. There was little doubt they throttled and controlled the media.

Some dream world.

But New Perth seemed like a nice little town. There were plenty of shops and small businesses in the downtown area. To the east sprawled an industrial area, the same area where Force 25 would land come sunrise. The city seemed well laid out in equal space and portions throughout the pastoral, rolling hills. There were certain areas, like on Araf and other DWC planets, where groups and species lived together. It was easy to see where the Humans lived. Their homes and businesses reflected pretty much any similar-size community on Earth. Likewise, those establishments that catered to the Zuul mercenaries were easy to find, and during their fifty years on the planet the mercenaries and their families had become a viable part of the society. Conspicuously absent was a substantial showing of the Veetanho. Having been one of the primary settlers, and even with a small complement staying on after the major schism fifty years before, it was surprising to see so few of them as he made his way through the streets, busy again as the rain turned steady with a near constant breeze; all he saw were Humans and Zuul.

Strange, it's almost like the Veetanho are non-citizens.

Shuttling between the wide covered porches on nearly all the buildings, he made his way across the main thoroughfares toward the restaurant much faster than he thought. The realization that distance in a Dream World Consortium colony was different dawned on him. A city block here was no more than two hundred meters. Their spacing gave the center of New Perth a close, comfortable feel, with no structures—save for the government offices—taller than three stories so they could have views in all directions. Gray smirked. From the government building, the entire city of twenty-five thousand people could be seen, too.

All things being equal, what better way to observe your people when they don't expect it?

His gut twisted in on itself. Something wasn't right. Tara Mason had made sure the entire unit knew about the history of the Dream World Consortium and their shady dealings—particularly on the planet Araf. Enabling proxy conflicts was nothing new. The whole reason behind having mercenary forces fight in the first place came from organizations and individuals who didn't want to get their…appendages dirty.

As he walked, a line from his mentor surfaced from his memories. *What is ground truth, Harm? When you discover that, you'll know how to proceed.*

He drew a breath of the moist, cool air and exhaled.

"You're right, Top," he said to himself. "Until then, stick to the damned plan, right?"

At the door to Southgate, he pushed through and stepped into a different world. Country music from the early twentieth century played softly in the background.

Is that Dolly Cline? Or Patsy Parton?

A long bar dominated most of the back wall, and a scattered collection of booths and tables filled the floor space. There were no Zuul or Veetanho in the restaurant, and the cynical part of Gray's mind wondered if that was by design, or the coincidental choice of menu and atmosphere. He'd expect something like this restaurant in rural Kansas or Oklahoma, not on an engineered planet in the Tolo region of the galaxy.

Sophie Pryce subtly waved to him from the booth in the far, dim corner. He half-raised his hand in return and made his way between the tables. Curious eyes darted to him and his clean Gray's Goblins' uniform. Conversations lulled and restarted in his wake, almost making him smile.

Nothing spreads faster than rumor. Perfect.

He reached the booth. "Good evening, Miss Pryce."

"Commander Gray," she smiled.

"May I join you?"

"I thought that was the plan." She laughed softly. He liked the sound of her voice. Her eyes glittered in the dim light of the restaurant and cast a golden glow on her hair.

"One can never be too sure," he said and slid into the booth opposite her. "Thank you for the invitation. I haven't had a good steak in years."

"Then you've come to the right place." She pointed to matching goblets of red wine. "I ordered the perfect pairing for steak. It is, after all, Southgate's specialty. Our chef is from Kansas City and really knows how to prepare steak."

Gray picked up the goblet. "And what's this? A cabernet? A merlot?"

"Neither." She grinned. "Nebbiolo. From Italy. I have a case flown out here every year. It's my favorite vintage by far."

He sipped the wine and noticed nothing different from any other wine he'd ever tasted. Beer would have been preferable; it had been too long since he'd had a good Earth-made beer, too.

When in Rome, right? That's from Italy, too.

He smiled involuntarily and covered it with another sip of wine.

"What do you think?"

"I like it," he replied. "Something tells me you've ordered the steak already, too."

"Would that bother you?" Pryce smiled. "Letting someone you've hardly met choose for you?"

"You seem like the kind of woman who likes to take charge. Who am I to argue with that?"

Pryce sipped her wine and leaned closer as she set the glass carefully on the bare wooden surface. "Then I'll get right to the point. Are Gray's Goblins interested in being considered to take over the planetary security contract for Snowmass?"

Gray allowed himself to look surprised. He'd expected this question since their first discussion on the landing pad. "I appreciate the consideration, Sophie. You'll forgive me if I'm not able to give you a certain answer. Once we land our folks and take stock of our situation, I'll have a better answer for you. How well your colony can refit and replenish our needs is also something I have to take into consideration."

She nodded. "I expected that answer, Harm. You don't seem to be a rash decision-maker."

"You can't be a good leader without considering all the possible outcomes of your decisions." He smiled at her and took a slow sip of his wine. "That being said, if we can reach a readiness condition appropriate for consideration, I believe we'd entertain the bidding process."

"What if there wasn't a bidding process?"

His eyebrows rose again, this time without calculation. "Are you terminating a current contract?"

"We're in a period of renegotiation and, in all honesty, the Trenta Knights are late with their proposal. Until your chance arrival, there was a real discussion that we might have to enter a financially prohibitive deal with them. We already have to charge our colonists fees far above our founders' thresholds just to maintain the planetary economy."

"I imagine your colonists don't appreciate that at all."

Pryce shrugged. "They understand it's a necessary evil. I want to get away from that, but I'm unsure what your company would charge."

"I believe we could beat the Trenta Knights' contract, but I'd know for sure if I knew the Earth-year cost."

The question carefully toed an uncrossable line. Contracts, particularly Mercenary Guild–approved ones, dealt with costs over the course of the contract or by certain defined terms. None of those terms, particularly for contracts involving non-Human companies, broke down the terms of service into Earth-years. The specified terms of service for every contract were protected information. A non-specified term, however, was not.

"I'll see what I can do." Pryce smiled. The mischievous look in her eyes made him smile and sent a ripple of excitement down his spine. As they served the salad with warm pumpernickel bread and hand-churned butter, Harmon Gray realized he was looking forward to more than the steak being prepared in the kitchen.

Much more.

* * * * *

Chapter Nineteen

20km SE of Lake Pryce

Snowmass

At the first sign of trouble, Araceli Cignes disengaged the atmospheric sensor inside the auto-parachute deployment system and programmed it to deploy using data from her terrain-following radar. Her technique wasn't standard operating procedure, but it made the most sense. Storm systems created significant differences in atmospheric pressure. Even on Victoria Bravo where she'd grown up, the occasional summer thunderstorm made her ears pop and gave her headaches until it passed. Atmospheric pressure was no joke. With the wild fluctuations approaching the threshold for system deployment happening over twenty-five thousand feet in the air, it made the most sense to disengage the system completely and tie parachute deployment to the reliable onboard radar system.

She'd always loved studying the weather. Her mother's passion for the environment carried over through to her schooling. Araceli's favorite memories were of checking the numerous weather stations around Lovell City and helping her mother learn the Victorian atmosphere and climatic conditions. Meteorologists were a dying breed with the development of learning algorithms on Earth, and exometeorology was something only Humans seemed to be really invested in. Nature was nature to most species. It was a series of conditions that had to be dealt with. Humans ultimately dealt with the weather conditions, too, but having a meteorologist to bitch and moan at made them feel better while doing so.

With the explosive wind shear inside the storm, she also recognized deploying her parachutes higher than about a thousand feet or more could be catastrophic. Lower was better.

With a series of taps on the instrument panel, she queued her jump jets and focused on maintaining a stable falling position. Rocking from side to side with the occasional gust of wind threatening to make her tumble made that difficult. Still, she did the best she could, watching the altimeter tick down quickly. Flashes of lightning around the CASPer didn't distract her once she registered the shock of a bolt of lightning hitting the mech's external skin, and she was thankful the engineers had figured out a long time ago how to make the CASPer impervious to such strikes. Only engineering didn't state there couldn't be problems, so she quickly ran her eyes over the electrical system to make sure none of the buses or circuits had failed. All seemed right with the world.

She smiled.

All things being right with the world had been one of her father's favorite sayings. During the first battle of Victoria Bravo, both he and her mother had perished fighting with the tanks near the Sentinels under the command of their good friend Colonel Ibson. In some ways, she couldn't believe they were gone. Everything about her life had changed in the blink of an eye. Now only a few months past her sixteenth birthday, here she was in a CASPer dropping into a combat situation. She knew her parents hadn't wanted her to become a mercenary, and they were even less receptive to the idea of her serving in the Victoria Forces. She was certain they wouldn't like what they saw. But somehow she knew they would understand. What else could she do?

At one thousand meters above the planet's surface, she readied the CASPer systems for parachute deployment and fired the jump jets to cushion her landing. Given the wind strength, speed, and direction across the drop zone, there was a substantial chance it could throw her mech off course, or worse, should the jump jets or her onboard laser ring gyros fail to stabilize her fall. At three hundred meters altitude, the parachute deployment warning sounded in her ears, and a millisecond later she felt the thumps as the explosive hatch for her chute blew away. In less than two seconds, the parachute fully inflated and snapped every muscle and bone violently inside the CASPer's tight cockpit.

Under the parachute, the mech oscillated hard to the left and then snapped violently back to the right. She focused on the ground approaching quickly through the torrential rain. Within seconds, her jump jets auto-fired and stabilized the fall. Her CASPer hit the marshy ground with a wet *thump* and settled into the mud over the vehicle's feet and ankles.

Her eyes swept the cockpit quickly, determining that multiple control systems appeared to be affected along with the communications problems. There was no datalink to the rest of her team. Through the radio, all she heard was static on every frequency. Indicator lights told her the primary antenna on the back of her CASPer appeared to be malfunctioning, and she wondered idly if it had taken the brunt of the lightning strike earlier.

Under her graphic overlay function, Araceli pulled up the mission plan and saw that she'd fallen more than three thousand meters from the center of the drop zone. She'd fallen in some type of deciduous forest below the escarpment on one side of the valley. Even in the rainfall, she saw a thick blanket of fog develop over the surrounding ground.

She let her passive sensors penetrate the environment and saw a faint reading for Misfit 3's landing platform more than three thousand meters away on significantly higher terrain. Without the datalink to the rest of her squad, standard operating procedures from her old unit served as a backup. Her priority was to make contact with whatever unit she could find. In this case that meant Misfit 3, the Tortantula known as Ladow.

Her mind set on a course of action, Araceli made a step forward with her left leg. The CASPer whined and groaned, its servos complaining in the lower leg joints, and wouldn't budge. The marshy soil grasped at her machine as if not wanting to let go. She tried the other way, being careful not to strain the machine in any way, shape, form, or fashion. When it didn't move in that direction either, she determined it was time to fire her jump jets. Stealth had been a primary mission objective, so the sound of the jump jets firing might not be acceptable in the situation, but with the storm raging around her, she decided it was worth the risk. It only took seconds to program the jump for both legs, with a duration of three and a half seconds and a five-degree forward angle. While the surrounding mud and sloppy terrain threatened to mire her every move, she believed if she could get the CASPer moving, it would stay moving until she reached more stable ground.

The escarpment was only three clicks away, and the terrain leading up to it appeared hilly and rocky. All she had to do was cross about eight hundred meters of marsh and wetlands. Even if she was forced to use her jump jets, she could use them sparingly and still have plenty of fuel to complete the mission.

She took a deep breath and waited. The surrounding storm appeared no different from a thunderstorm on Earth or Victoria Bravo. She waited for a bright flash of lightning followed by a cannonade of thunder to engage her jump jets. She didn't have to wait long.

WH-WH-WHAM!

She flexed her knees and pressed down on the jump jet pedals. Her CASPer rocketed upward about five meters and cleared the mud around her impact point. Preparing for landing, she moved her legs into a running stance and prepared to hit the ground moving. The CASPer settled back toward the marshy ground. As soon as she felt her right leg make contact, she pushed forward, and the CASPer's mighty legs responded. She kept up the pace, moving each leg rhythmically and tapping the jump key pedal for each at the moment of impact. As a result, Araceli pushed quickly through the marshland. After about thirty seconds, she risked a glance through her rear facing cameras to see if she was leaving a discernible trail across the marsh. She was, but the mud and the rain quickly filled in those areas. Within minutes, there would be almost no trace indicating her CASPer had ever been there.

Running became easier the farther she moved away from the escarpment. As the ground under her became more stable, she moved the big machine with uncanny grace and agility. Above her the terrain grew exceedingly steep and more restrictive. The exposed rock formations ascended almost vertically from her. The signal from Misfit 3 was stronger, but her systems still couldn't lock it in. She had a basic azimuth and elevation for its location, but nothing else. As she reached the top of a small rocky knoll, Araceli paused and took in the view of the wide valley through the storm. She could see nothing beyond about four hundred meters from her position. To her right the escarpment rose more than eight hundred meters above a wide grassy plain. To her left, down into the valley, only the marshland along the tributaries of a major river ran toward the sea. Her heads-up display showed the temperature dropping, but still above freezing. There was no doubt when the weather turned cold enough Snowmass would become a veritable frozen hellhole.

As she continued her solitary climb, Araceli depressed her transmit button. "Deathangel 25, this is Misfit 5, do you read?"

There was no reply in the static.

She sighed and kept moving. Her immediate target was to rendezvous with Misfit 3. From there she'd try to get a visual on the others and move in their direction, or find an easier path to their rally point at Lake Pryce. Until then, all she could do was keep moving. Movement kept hope alive. While not a method, hope was all Araceli Cignes had as the rains fell.

More than six hours after landing in the marsh, Araceli closed the final distance to Misfit 3's signal to within a couple hundred meters. The location appeared to be high on a cliff wall above her, and she made her way into areas she wasn't sure a CASPer was meant to go. She moved forward relentlessly.

The weak beacon on Misfit 3's landing platform was clear and vibrant on her heads-up display. However, there were no life signs. After the fall of darkness she'd been unable to visually identify anything about the crash site. The beacon showed the platform to be another thirty meters higher than her current position, among some rocky spires not unlike the Sentinels back home on Victoria Bravo. Rain continued to fall. Torrential downpours and the occasional collapsing blast of a microburst from the storms above had replaced the heavy gusts of the earlier storm. As she studied the rock wall for a way forward, she slumped in the CASPer's harness. Exhaustion pulled at her limbs and clouded her thoughts. She found a ledge wide enough to turn the CASPer sideways, its back against the rock wall. Again she tried the radio, to no avail.

If I could just jump up there and see it, I'd at least have an idea what was going on.

With her parachute already deployed and gone, all she could do to stop her fall would be to use her jump jets. If she did so, her ability to cross the marshland would be compromised. Even if the jump was successful, the drenching rain and much colder temperatures could hamper the effectiveness of her infrared systems by keeping everything cold. There might be nothing to see at all. So she closed her eyes, listened to the gentle hum of the CASPer around her and the rain thumping across the mech's skin, and allowed herself to rest.

An hour later, Araceli opened her eyes and consulted her map one last time. From her present location, there was no way she would get anywhere near Misfit 3's beacon unless she climbed down the wall and found another way up the escarpment. As she zoomed out the map display, she found what looked like a narrow pass twenty kilometers to the south. There really wasn't much choice. Her CASPer had enough fuel and personal rations on board to make the trip. The only thing she'd have to replenish would be water, and with the near constant rainfall, that would be easy enough.

Once I get on top of this thing, maybe I can reach Tara. If I'm not too late.

With careful and calculated steps, she made her way down the slick rock wall as darkness fell.

* * *

Customs and Immigration
Snowmass

Word must have spread fast through the galaxy. That was the only way Maarg could explain it. The customs officer, a bored brown- and white-faced Zuul, reviewed her card, handed her a small pamphlet on Snowmass, and wished her a good evening. The entirety of her customs experience had taken less than two minutes.

"Can you direct me to a place to stay?" she asked.

The guard looked at her and pointed to the pamphlet in her big hand. "That will tell you everything you need to know. Enjoy your stay on Snowmass."

With that, the guard pulled down the security gate and closed the immigration office for the night. Twenty seconds later the exterior lights for the customs office area also clicked off. Maarg made her way through the dim hallway to a set of wide glass double doors and pushed through onto the covered porch outside. Rain continued to fall, but not as hard as it had been when she first offloaded from the ship. She didn't mind the heavy precipitation. Her thick coat kept her dry and warm no matter what. She'd seen stronger storms, she was certain, on Weqq.

Looking around in the fading light, Maarg consulted the pamphlet in her hand and found that while there was nothing in her language, she could read a few bits. There were several hotels and lodging facilities in the city, and the closest was only a few blocks away. With her bag slung over her wide shoulders, she made her way toward the hotel in the rain. The streets weren't empty like she thought they might be during a rainstorm. The earlier gust front had slammed into the city with violent winds and rainfall so hard she could barely see through it. By comparison, the evening had an almost calm, pleasant feel with the steady, gentle rain and light, cool breeze. Humans moved in all directions. As did the Zuul, and a very few Veetanho. None of them appeared to look at her for more than a couple of seconds. A part of her had assumed her presence would cause a little more curiosity than it appeared to. While slightly disappointed that no one seemed interested in her, she was thankful. Blending in was difficult for a TriRusk.

At the edge of the porch, Maarg connected her slate to the local GalNet connections and downloaded an interactive map of the city from their visitor's bureau. From there, she found better directions to the closest all-inclusive hotel. She turned away from the town center and made her way to the south through a slightly more forested area. Under the wide-branched trees, the rain didn't fall in a constant downpour, but with large, spattering drops. Some were large enough she felt them under her fur. As she moved past a set of one-story buildings that appeared to be some type of restaurant and bar—whatever that was—she noticed a couple of figures sitting on the dark porch, but paid them no mind.

All the buildings possessed wide porches. Given the rain and snowstorms they endured, the wide porches and walkways provided the citizens an easy way to get from place to place without getting wet or having to trudge through the snow soon to fall for the remainder of their year. She kept walking, head down and focused solely on the path in front of her, while trying not to look around like a tourist. Her father had warned her about such telling behavior only a few months before.

Always walk like you know exactly where you're going. Don't look up at the skyline. Don't look up at the tall buildings. If something flies overhead, give it a cursory, annoyed glance, but that's about it. There's no faster way for anyone to know you're someplace you're not supposed to be than to have too much curiosity. Enjoy your time, but don't make yourself an easy target.

With the memory of her father's words, Maarg suddenly missed his company. She'd grown up in relative peace and quiet only to have her entire world overturned in the last several months by conflict and unexpected interstellar travel. As a child she'd never thought she'd end up leaving the cavern system on Weqq. Now she was untold light years from her home planet and the whole rest of her species could be in danger.

Try she might, she couldn't help but believe the danger was in part because of the Peacemakers. While Jessica Francis was her friend, Maarg couldn't help but think others inside the guild had other motivations. Jessica's actions had been very simple. She'd saved Maarg and her people from a band of pirates. But in the days after, the guild master and others had appeared on the planet. Their seemingly good intentions gently pulled Maarg and her people out of their caverns with the promises of a return to the Galactic Union. The same Union who'd burned them hundreds of years before when the Veetanho had attempted to kill them off. Ever since Jessica had shown up, things had gone downhill, as her Human friends said.

But are they really my friends, or are they just after my abilities? Am I just a synthetic diamond making machine to them?

Maarg sighed and kept walking. She needed a break, and somehow Tara had relented. The sudden rashness of Tara's decision made her question the intentions behind her commander's actions, but Tara Mason had given her no reason to be suspicious. She'd asked for a break and received one. Maarg had a couple of days to enjoy herself and see what the rest of the Union was all about. Even with night falling, it appeared there were places she could find food, shop, or just sit and rest if she wanted. After weeks of semi-privacy, the idea of going to a hotel and renting a private suite for herself with GalNet access called to her. From there, she could easily start looking around until sleep came. The same could be said for the morning time prior to actual daylight. There would always be something she could find.

Just don't poke your snout too deep, Maarg.

Her father always said things like that. He knew she was overly curious, but given her abilities with computers and technology, he knew very well she could get herself deep inside a network within minutes, if not faster. Given Force 25's mission, both finding Snowman and now determining what was going on with the Dream World Consortium, she figured the local networks were a good place to start. While the connections onboard the ship were great, nothing beat being on the ground. From here she could plug in directly to the infrastructure itself.

As she rounded the final corner with her head down, Maarg barely saw the two Zuul beyond their boots suddenly in her line of sight. She carefully dodged to the right with uncanny grace for her size. Maarg raised her long head to look at the two Zuul, noting their mercenary uniforms, and nodded. "My apologies. Well met."

The taller of the two Zuul nodded respectfully. "Well met. We hope you have a pleasant evening."

"You, too," she replied.

The Zuul kept walking toward the city center, and she glanced around to find the hotel. While it didn't immediately seem to meet the luxurious expectation she had in mind, it appeared to be clean and quiet. As a bonus, it advertised GalNet access and private suites. That was enough for her. She could get a decent meal and have a warm, dry bed to sleep in. That would be enough for now, at least until her curiosity got the better of her.

* * *

"Was that what I think it was, sir?" Tolem whispered as they made for their planned rendezvous.

Krukk nodded. "Yes. We'll determine what that little one might be up to after we deal with the situation at hand." His mind worked quickly through the last moment or so of interaction. While it was not uncommon to occasionally find new species visiting Snowmass, he certainly hadn't expected to find a TriRusk. His own sense of skepticism had kept him from believing the long-disappeared species had been seen again even after seeing the GalNet videos of one on the airfield at Araf. That one had been a Peacemaker, too. For a TriRusk to simply appear on Snowmass was one curious thing, but her choice of language was another.

"Well met" was an expression commonly used by the Peacemakers. The words were as much a part of their lexicon as contracts and agreements. The obvious answer was that the TriRusk and the two Peacemakers had come into the system via the same ship. Maybe they'd even interacted on board during their hyperspace transits.

Or maybe it was something else. Tolem's question broke Krukk's sudden unease.

"You saw the others, right? In the shadow of the bar over there?" Tolem walked and kept his head and eyes forward.

"Yes," Krukk replied. "A Zuparti and an Equiri, though the Equiri was hard to see in the shadows. Something tells me they might have some insight into what happened in the square today."

"Should I order our people to engage them?" Tolem asked.

Krukk considered his answer carefully. "No, I'm assuming they're armed and very dangerous. Order our intelligence operatives to observe them, and the little one, until we can determine a plan of action based on our conversation with Commander Gray this evening."

"There are a lot of things happening suddenly, Colonel."

Krukk nodded. Try as he might, he couldn't help but feel they were unprepared. The last several months of training had focused the Knights on mission readiness. They'd sacrificed many things, including intelligence analysis. Assuming they knew the planet they operated on appeared to have put them at a disadvantage. One he intended to correct directly.

"There are, Tolem. But we focus on the greatest threats first. If this Human and his mercenary company are being courted by the government behind our tails, we must address them. What better way than by a civil discussion with their commanding officer?"

"Commander Gray will most certainly get the points we make." Tolem smiled softly. "I believe it will be a most profitable conversation."

Krukk grinned savagely. "As do I, Tolem. As do I."

*****

Chapter Twenty

Force 25 Headquarters

Victoria Bravo

Jamie Ibson wanted a third cup of coffee. Despite hating paperwork and the administration of a mercenary company, the comfort of his desk chair was enough to keep him in place for a while longer. When he left the desk, he'd search for good coffee, not the barely passable dark liquid the young lieutenants made in the command post. Something strong enough to burn the paint off a CASPer would be in order for the morning. Suppressing a groan, he rubbed his temples and vowed for the fourteenth time not to go drinking with Xander Alison ever again.

The door to the headquarters opened, and a young soldier Ibson didn't know poked his head inside.

"Sir? The Honorable Governor Watson is here to see you."

Ibson didn't immediately look up from his desk. *Sonuvabitch.*

He glanced at the Tri-V displaying his calendar for the day and a slew of additional paperwork unit commanders typically churned through in the course of their duty. There was nothing showing a meeting with anyone, including the governor.

Ibson looked up at the young soldier and considered his words carefully. The last thing he wanted was an audience of any type, official or not, with Brian Watson. Since ascending to the governorship, his old friend had proven to be a less than stellar politician. The pursuit of profit, Ibson knew, had destroyed leaders throughout history.

"Let me secure some classified information, and I'll be right with Governor Watson. Tell him two minutes at the most."

"Yes, sir."

Ibson tapped the controls for his monitor and turned his attention back to the door before placing both palms on his desk and drumming his fingers idly. Mentally he counted as he watched the door. Brian Watson never liked to wait for anyone, especially someone he viewed as a subordinate. Making him wait was more than sticking it to his former friend. Ibson believed it to be a not-so-subtle reminder that the governor had no jurisdiction or influence inside Force 25's headquarters. Watson wouldn't see it that way, even with his checkered past regarding Force 25 and his accidental shooting of a Peacemaker.

Being persona non grata *isn't anything new for Brian, though.*

Ibson reached twenty-two seconds in his mental count before the door was pushed open.

"What's this making me wait, Ibson?" Brian Watson scowled as he stomped into the room. "You realize I'm the governor of Victoria Bravo now, yes?"

Ibson forced a smile across his face. "I know that, Governor Watson. You're awfully fond of saying it. Need I remind you this is a private mercenary corporation? Though we're flagged as a mercenary force under the auspices of Victoria Bravo, we don't fall under your legal jurisdiction. As such, my request to secure *classified* and *proprietary* information from your prying eyes was valid. Had I not done so, it might've been necessary to report you to your own security forces for violating a sovereign company's security procedures. Don't you think?"

Watson stopped two meters from Ibson's desk and put his hands on his hips. For the first time, Ibson noticed that his old friend had gained weight. The sedentary lifestyle of a politician, always sitting behind a desk and having fancy, catered meals hadn't been good for Brian Watson. He'd always been slender—almost freakishly skinny. Seeing his friend with a more rounded face and equally rounded belly amused him almost to the point of laughing. Ibson said nothing and kept his face calm.

"Look, Governor. You can't just waltz in here and expect to affect this mercenary company's operations. It just doesn't work like that."

Watson smiled in return, but it stopped at his eyes. "Oh, this is beyond even the auspices of my office, Jamie. As a matter of fact, it's the entire board of the free-trade zone. They're very concerned that your company has continuously disrupted production for the metallurgical facility and several other critical infrastructure providers in your frantic attempt to rebuild the starport."

"You contracted us to rebuild the starport, Brian. As for the infrastructure providers and the foundry itself?" Ibson laughed and noted the color creeping into Watson's face. "Interrupting their production schedule? Based on what we saw, the foundry is running at about twenty-five percent of capacity right now. I can't help but wonder if it's because the free-trade zone has taxed them into submission or merely over-regulated the amount they can produce daily as if to manipulate the local economy in your favor."

Watson shook his head. "That's not fair. But you know what? How about I bring in the rest of the board and they can explain how they see your activities, Jamie? Then you'll see this situation for what it really is and not just sour grapes on my part."

Watson turned and walked to the door, leaving Ibson to frown and stab a button on his desk; a heartbeat later Xander Alison replied.

"What's up boss?"

"I want you guys to come up ASAP. The free-trade zone board apparently has issues with us again, and want an official audience with me. I want back up present for the record."

He heard Xander's sigh. "Great. We'll be up there in a minute."

The free-trade zone developed on Victoria Bravo was the product of four separate species and their involvement with several key guilds and sub-guilds. Given Victoria Bravo's unique location, climate, and abundant natural resources, the interest in it as a commercial zone was obvious. After the adoption of the zone, the local government had served to represent the guilds to the local populace and their respective objectives. Ibson believed Watson had been frantically treading in shark-infested waters from the moment the guilds approached the planet's governing board. Humans were still a new and curious presence in the Galactic Union. There were many species with which Humans had less than friendly relationships. There were still others that openly viewed human beings as targets. Given the recent history of attacks, Force 25 had secured a defensive agreement with the local government. Calling it a contract wasn't fair. Contracts were the legal writ in the Galactic Union, and both protected and enforced by the Peacemaker Guild. While it was undoubtedly a fact that Force 25 had significant friendly contacts within the Peacemakers, they couldn't say the same for their involvement with the government of Victoria Bravo.

Brian Watson wanted them out. The first time elements of Force 25 had left their base for commercial involvement with their normal suppliers within Lovell City limits, Watson and his cronies had raged and protested. They stated having mercenaries living on the local economy presented a security threat while ignoring that those same mercenaries had defeated two separate attacks within the last year. A competent and well-informed enemy would want nothing to do with Victoria Bravo, given the troops and capabilities present on the planet. The first disagreements concluded with Force 25 agreeing to pay a small but nominal fee for transactions with their normal suppliers in the city as part of a rebuilding initiative for the destroyed portions of the city itself, and not the starport property now owned by the company. The fee structure seemed to appease Watson for a short period until the Merchant Guild asked to double their customs and port of entry holding areas at the starport. Doubling the available land opportunities meant reducing the footprint allotted to Force 25 agreed upon with Colonel Mason's signature several months prior. The planetary government appeared ready to throw that agreement out, along with countless others. Ibson couldn't help but wonder what exactly Watson was making on the side.

Watson returned to the office with three very different representatives tagging behind. All of them wore a cultured and careful countenance. Their presence in the headquarters surprised Ibson because normally the masters of the free-trade zone sent lower level emissaries for such discussions and negotiations. This time the heads of the respective zone councils presented themselves. He watched them enter the room.

There was a Jivool wearing an interesting combination of clothes resembling something between a Human three-piece suit and overalls. His name was Torf, and he represented the sub-guild for mining. His first order of business had been to hire the Flatar battalion who'd served alongside Victoria Forces to guard mining operations to the south. Ibson wasn't surprised the Flatar had taken the contract, either. The miners had a lot of credits to throw around.

Behind Torf was a Midderall whom Ibson had never seen before, nor did he know the parrot-like alien's name. Bright and colorful, the Midderall were typically secretive and best known for their abilities as pilots. The unique and eclectic species represented a particular faction within the Cartography Guild at Victoria Bravo. They sought to limit interstellar freight along certain routes and sub-routes they either controlled or collected tolls and tariffs on for their use. Perhaps limit was a bad word, because what they wanted to do was to regulate the shipping industries with high fees and reduced traffic. Such had been the same for pretty much every business Ibson had ever known.

The last representative was a Cochkala. He bounded into the room with a wide, maniacal smile on his tiny face. The regional director for the Merchant Guild was a shrewd and capable negotiator with a mean streak several kilometers wide. Named Thcko, he openly criticized the government and Force 25 for what he called unsanctioned and unprecedented attacks on his brethren during the second battle of Victoria Bravo. The facts didn't seem to matter, considering his brethren had been behind the attacks. When he approached them claiming the disgraced Enforcer Kr'et'Socae was the mastermind behind the attack, which they knew, Thcko cast all blame aside from his brothers and tried at once to proclaim their innocence and collect upon the payments the disgraced Enforcer owed them. For Ibson, the Cochkala's actions stank of greed.

They sauntered into the office and stood behind Watson. There was no question what the three aliens wanted. Each of the guilds taking part in the free-trade zone kept the ability to hire their own security forces. Undoubtedly they believed they could negotiate a much better deal than the tax breaks and incentives the government had provided for Force 25 to remain in place.

It all comes down to money. Some things never change.

Ibson knew all too well that was the case, so he figured either they wanted to hire their own security forces, or they wanted to take more money out of the coffers of Force 25. It didn't matter what had happened in the recent past, nor did the danger of future attacks appear to matter. His team had done the intelligence analysis and knew any mercenary forces brought in by the guilds as private security forces would have much less capability than Force 25. He'd tried to appeal to Watson and the board with that data, and it had appeared to work during the early negotiations, but with the continued application of fees amounting to taxes levied under a supposedly tax-free society, the writing was on the proverbial wall.

"Lieutenant Colonel Ibson. We'll come quickly to the point," Torf said. His voice was deep and gruff through his translation pendant. "Force 25 has enjoyed a sterling reputation amongst the colonists. However, the recent interruptions of production in the metallurgical facility and the push for increased space infringing upon the commercial trade zone at the starport have left us with quite the conundrum. I am afraid either Force 25 must pay for the expanded space and the recent disruptions in production or be required to leave the planet."

Ibson blinked. It took every effort to keep his face straight and persuade himself not to either laugh or leap onto his desk and scream at them.

"I'm sorry, what?"

Watson stepped forward. "Either you must pay for the disruptions to infrastructure and metallurgy, or we will be forced to evict you and your company from the planet entirely."

Ibson looked up into his friend's—make that former friend's—eyes. "Let me get this straight. The only reason you're standing there as governor is because we repelled two separate attacks. The forces behind one of those attacks are dead because of the intervention of Force 25 augmenting Victoria Forces. The forces behind the second attack on this colony are still alive and could be planning another attack which, to me, would constitute a clear and present danger to this planet. First you dissolve Victoria Forces, and now you're willing to evict Force 25 from this planet under the guise that the security forces hired by your guild representatives can do the job?"

The Jivool rumbled. "We are more than confident in the forces we have engaged to protect this planet, Lieutenant Colonel Ibson. Please do not make this any more difficult than it is."

Watch out for anyone who consistently uses lieutenant in front of colonel, Jamie, he remembered Tara Mason telling him from her experience. *Those who understand its significance will never use it in a condescending manner.*

Ibson thought about it for a second and played a different tactic for fun. Watching Watson slowly erupt would be worth it. "So the fee, then? What are we talking? I mean, if we're really disrupting things so badly, what reparations are you seeking for interrupting infrastructure and metallurgy and anybody else we need to do business with daily?"

The Midderall spoke up, its head bobbing up and down in time with its words. "Two million, I say, two million credits. Two million. That's what we deem necessary. Necessary."

For the second time in the conversation, Jamie fought the urge to laugh. Instead he turned his eyes back to Brian Watson and frowned. "I can't believe you. I really, really hope you think you're making the right decision here, because this time you won't have me or anyone else to bail your sorry ass out of making another bad one."

Watson laughed. "What can I say? I seem to always land on two feet."

"Really?" Ibson blurted. "That's what you call it? You and your squad owe your life to Peacemaker Francis, not to mention your daughter's life after Chinayl attacked her. Does that ring a bell? Or how about the time you almost killed a Peacemaker in the performance of her duties? More than anything in our friendship over the last twenty years, your actions in recent combat proved to me you're a fucking idiot."

Ibson stood and faced the three representatives. The Cochkala had been silent, but in its eyes, Ibson could see the little bastard mentally wringing his paws together in anticipation.

Fine.

"As the duly noted representative of Force 25—"

The side door to the office opened abruptly, and Xander Alison stepped inside. He asked, "What's going on?"

Ibson met his friend's eyes and nodded respectfully at the entourage in front of his desk. "The esteemed representatives of the board for the free-trade zone and his honor, the governor, have asked that we pay a fee of either two million credits for interrupting production of their critical facilities or that we evacuate the planet."

Xander looked at Watson. "Two million credits? For six hours' worth of work in a plant operating at less than thirty percent of its capability at the time? Sorry, Governor, but that sounds a little like highway robbery to me."

Watson shrugged. "Fees are fees, Mr. Alison. The price of doing business for Force 25 has grown fairly steep on this planet, I'm afraid."

Xander laughed. "Meaning Force 25 cuts into your profits. You want to cut us away and hire a cheaper and less capable mercenary force for your private security. We've suspected you'd try something like this for quite some time. Honestly, we all thought you were smarter than that, but I guess we're wrong. Again."

Ibson saw color creeping into Watson's face. The governor turned to the representatives and then back to him. "I think we've been more than judicious in our determination and application of these fees, and it pains me to do so, given your company's reputation and history of protecting this planet from outsiders. But as I stated, the cost of doing business here has grown. Hence, the fees."

Ibson shook his head. "By calling them fees instead of taxes, you're inferring that we'll pay them every single time we do business with anyone outside our compound. That also means the way Tara constructed us as a unit and how we occupy the depots and facilities at the starport mean we have no access to the free-trade zone itself. Because you won't allow us to have outsiders immediately dock at our locations, we're screwed into paying a fee every single time we have any transaction."

The Cochkala chittered. "That's exactly what we want, Colonel Ibson."

There was a knock on the outside door, and the fourth representative of the board, an Altar, stepped in. "My apologies, my esteemed colleagues. I was detained in a most unfortunate meeting regarding the sewage system repairs. Am I to understand that you have presented a fee schedule to this mercenary company?"

The Cochkala grinned ever wider. "That's correct, Rilik. The colonel was just about to give us his decision."

In more than fifteen years of active military service, fighting different aliens with both mercenary and provincial security forces at his side, Ibson had never had the urge to walk up and stomp an alien being to death, until now. The power of the image shocked him, but not more than the sudden appearance of his friend Bukk.

Bukk stepped in through the side office door. Immediately the other Altar in the room noticeably flinched. Bukk nodded at Jamie and Xander, and then to the board representatives. "My apologies. How can I be of assistance?"

The Cochkala spoke but was cut off in an instant by the Altar. "I must confess, my colleagues, I do not believe we have thought this through. While I realize my decision will not affect the course of the board's direction, I must go on the record as changing my vote on this punitive matter to a demonstrative no."

Watson whirled around on the Altar. "What do you mean? You pushed for this as hard as the rest of us."

The Altar nodded at Watson and then turned to peer across the room at Bukk. "I was mistaken."

"The board's vote is now four to one," the Midderall chirped. "Four to one. The action stands. Stands."

Watson turned back to Jamie. "What's it going to be?"

Ibson glanced at Xander and Bukk, who both nodded, Xander with a sly smile trying to spread across his face.

Fuck you, Brian.

"Governor Watson and esteemed members of the board of the Victoria Free Trade Zone. As the duly noted representative of Force 25, in the absence of our commander, Colonel Tara Mason, I hereby declare that Force 25 will evacuate Victoria Bravo. Our facilities, barracks, and depots will be emptied, and our materials and supplies evacuated within forty-eight hours. Our agreement to provide security forces and planetary defense ends right now. Does this meet your stipulations?"

Watson shook his head. "Twenty-four hours. Not one fucking second more."

Xander stepped forward to argue, but Ibson caught his arm. He'd expected as much from Watson. The company's emergency load plans required them to be capable of evacuation within six hours. Given a 24-hour deadline, it was his intent to complete the evacuation at twenty-three hours fifty-nine minutes and fifty-nine seconds out of sheer spite.

Done.

"Twenty-four hours," Ibson nodded.

"Don't wreck the place," Watson said. "You damage anything further, and I'll report you to both the Peacemaker and Mercenary Guilds."

Ibson smiled. "We're professionals, Governor Watson. Only a politician would do something like that out of spite."

Watson spun on his heels and gestured to the rest of the board. They quickly exited the room, save the Altar. The ant-like alien being hesitated, and they could see his eyes were on Bukk.

"My apologies, Lightbringer. I was unaware you were still on this planet and not evacuated home. Sometimes our friends do not fully understand what they do," Rilik said and solemnly bowed forward from deep in his abdomen.

Bukk silently returned the gesture. As the Altar exited the room, followed by Brian Watson, the two Humans looked up at their friend with incredulous faces.

Xander asked, "That Altar changed his mind the second he saw you. Why?"

"And why did he call you Lightbringer?" Ibson asked.

*****

Chapter Twenty-One

Southgate Restaurant

New Perth

The automated car service appeared under the wide, scalloped awning of the restaurant. A gullwing door swung up and revealed the passenger compartment to be empty. Gray stepped forward and stuck his head inside for a second look. While it was an unnecessary gesture, he did so more out of habit than a desire to impress Sophie Pryce.

He withdrew from the passenger compartment and stood straight. She stood next to him, and he couldn't help but smile as he looked at her eyes. "Everything checks out."

Pryce smiled up at him. "I appreciate your checking, Harm. Are you certain I can't offer you a ride?"

Gray shook his head. "No, thanks. My folks are supposed to pick me up here in a few minutes."

After their pleasant conversation, he felt bad for lying to her, but it was necessary for two reasons. The first was that he didn't need to get his hopes up. On the surface, Sophie Pryce seemed like everything he would ever want in a relationship. But he also knew they couldn't trust her. His immediate commander had a plan requiring both vigilance and discretion, and Gray knew his role, even if playing it felt worse by the moment.

Standing in the rain under the awning, he couldn't see their observers, but Gray knew they were there. They'd followed him at a distance during his walk from the hotel. Throughout the delicious and decadent meal, there was little doubt in his mind the same observers were watching everything he and Sophie Pryce did and listening to everything they said. At least twice she'd all but made an official offer to the Goblins for the planetary security contract. He remained professional and neutral. Despite how he felt about her and his desire to see her again, Harmon Gray recognized the situation was worse than they'd thought. As such, his goals were very simple. If Pryce wanted out of the contract with the Trenta Knights, she'd do almost anything. Part of him wondered if she'd already started by sowing the seeds of discontent. He also wondered if he was playing a part in her own production.

"Thank you again for a very pleasant evening, Harm. You'll review your readiness and supply reports this evening and get back to me tomorrow? I'd really like to continue our conversation." Pryce smiled up at him.

Gray nodded. "Once I see how far we've come with our supply requests, I'll know how long our maintenance period here will have to last. The weather is also a concern for me. I want to get all my forces down to our landing area tomorrow. Even if we're able to do that, getting everything set up and prepared to enter that maintenance cycle will take a couple of days. We can certainly continue the conversation, Sophie, but I really don't have any idea of timeline yet."

"That's fair," she said. The smile on her face faltered slightly, and he realized it wasn't fair to her. "If you're able to land your forces tomorrow, please let me know. I'd like to be there to see them."

Which means you'd like to be there to inspect them. To see if they're worthy of defeating the Trenta Knights. And here I didn't think we'd be looking for a fight just yet.

"I'll let you know. Good night, Sophie."

"Good night, Harm." She pushed herself onto her toes and let her lips brush his left cheek.

Harm felt a slight thrill run down his spine, but the sensation was cold. *She knows we're being watched. She's really setting the bait.*

Too bad.

Without another word, Pryce turned and climbed into the automated car. The door swung shut, and with the slight hum of an electric motor, the vehicle accelerated into the night. Gray slowly stepped back toward the foyer of the restaurant. He watched and patiently waited until her car disappeared from sight.

A young Human valet, no more than eighteen years old, appeared at his shoulder. "Can we arrange transport for you, sir?"

Gray shrugged and looked at the kid's name tag. "No, thanks, Duncan. I'm gonna walk and enjoy the evening."

The young man smiled. "Keep to the porches and you'll stay dry, sir."

"I'll do just that." Gray stepped out from under the awning and into the cool mist. The interconnected porches and walkways of the town would provide shelter from the rain, but Gray didn't want that. Neither could he walk in the middle of the street, given the automated cars, so keeping to the side streets and the darker roads made the most sense. Especially if he was really going to be the bait and pull the observers out to confront him.

Three blocks from the restaurant his wait ended. He turned the corner of an apothecary building and came face-to-face with two armed Zuul. In the mist, he couldn't see if there were any others, but his sense of caution told him there were definitely more nearby.

"What can I do for you?" Gray asked.

"You're Gray, right?" the larger one said. "Commander of Gray's Goblins?"

"That's right. Who's asking?"

The larger Zuul chuckled. "My name is Krukk and I command the Trenta Knights. I thought it best we speak privately."

Gray looked to the other mercenary. "Privately means a one-on-one conversation, Colonel Krukk. You've brought backup. How am I supposed to converse privately like that?"

"I never travel anywhere without my executive officer. Perhaps that is a technique you should learn."

Gray shrugged and forced a smile onto his face. With a laconic drawl, he said, "Well, my executive officer ain't exactly the kind of being invited to dinner parties very much."

The smaller of the two mercenaries, the executive officer, spoke, "I suppose that's what you get for having a MinSha at your side."

Gray erased the smile from his face in a heartbeat. "Now what is it exactly you're proposing?"

"Did Miss Pryce explicitly offer you our contract?"

Gray paused for dramatic effect. "No. She asked if we would place a competing bid against yours. She insinuated that your contract was in a period of negotiation. That your proposal was due to her within the next several days, and with that being the case, our arrival here could prove fruitful if we decided to bid against you."

"I would advise you not to do so."

"Why's that? Would that happen to have anything to do with your track record? I mean, it's fairly well known your company's had the same contract for more than 50 years. You've never wanted to do anything else. So anyone being asked to compete against you threatens to take you off the gravy train, doesn't it?" Gray watched his words having their desired effect.

"I don't understand your Human idioms. I'm warning you not to bid against us or there will be consequences," Krukk growled.

"What if I decide to ignore your warnings and see those consequences? What then?" Gray resisted the temptation to put his hands on his hips. Any sudden move would provoke them.

"We prevent you from accepting that contract."

Gray snorted. "That sounds an awful lot like a threat to me. Are you certain that's something you want to do? Especially with your contract in a negotiation phase? An unnecessary conflict might turn the government of this planet against you."

Krukk laughed. "There is much more to this planet than the government, Human. Should I choose to eradicate a threat, and do so with extreme prejudice, our benefactors will richly reward my company and me. Should any of your forces survive, I would ensure they never served as mercenaries again."

Gray stood as tall as he could and pushed his shoulders back. "There it is. You want me to leave?"

"That would deescalate the situation." Krukk half-smiled.

"What's in it for me? I mean, if you want me to leave and not get the supplies or the maintenance I need to have done on my equipment, I should be paid for that."

Krukk grunted. "Your payment will be keeping your life."

Gray chuckled. "You have no idea who or what you're dealing with."

The executive officer spoke up. "We know all about you, Harmon Gray. Your company is less than twenty percent combat effective. Whatever vehicles and personnel you land tomorrow could not survive the brunt of an attack from the Trenta Knights."

Krukk added, "If you land your forces tomorrow, we will attack. There will be no further negotiation. This is our planet, and you and your company are not welcome here."

"Sounds to me like you're afraid we'll take your contract. That goes back to my comment about your track record earlier. I mean, killing innocent civilians with out-of-date equipment is pretty heinous. It's no wonder they're unhappy with you."

The commander stepped forward and brought up a long knife with his left forepaw. He brandished it in the light, turning it slightly as he did. "Another word, Human, and your life will end right now. Get off this planet before I change my mind. Tolem? Get his slate."

The executive officer stepped forward. "Hand it over, Human."

I really hate the way they say that.

Gray reached for the small slate strapped to the inside of his left wrist.

"No. The other one." Tolem pointed at the slate pocket hanging from the utility belt he wore over his coveralls.

Keeping his eyes on the two mercenaries, Gray carefully opened the pouch mounted to his left hip and withdrew his slate. He handed it over and stepped back. "I don't know what you think you can get from that. You seem to know a lot about me already."

"Think of it as payment for your life. With this I know all your creditors, your business associates, and your entire employment history. I assure you, you will never work again," Krukk said.

Gray watched as the executive officer attached a cable from its slate to his. He frowned, wondering why it was so important to the manufacturers to have a universal connection and transfer port. He'd never seen one forcibly transferred before, and he was certain in that moment the Knights could break the encryption and get to the data they wanted.

After a few moments the mercenary disconnected the transfer cable and threw Gray's slate to the ground, where it shattered. For good measure, the mercenary stomped it into the wet pavement several times with his heavy boots. He stepped back and grinned at Gray.

Krukk raised the knife slightly higher, pointing it at Gray's throat. "Land your forces and we will attack you. We will crush you. Leave now, and I will transmit your files back to your ship."

"I don't think so."

If there was one sound in the universe Harmon Gray liked more than the racking action of a shotgun, it was the similar sound of the MT-1901X5 chain gun spooling up to fire. Seeing the massive twenty-millimeter multi-barreled cannon swing out of the darkness and aim at the two Zuul brought a smile to his face. Whirr stepped into the light as a flash of distant lightning illuminated her full form.

The two mercenaries flinched. The commander slowly lowered the knife back to a holster mounted to his thigh and slipped it inside. His forepaws came up slowly.

Gray stepped forward. "Kinda changes the narrative, doesn't it? And to your point, I never leave home without my executive officer either. This conversation is over."

The commander turned his eyes back to Gray. "My warning stands. Land your forces, and we will crush you."

"It's your funeral, Krukk. I might only have twenty percent of my forces, but my twenty percent is a hell of a lot better than your band of idiots. You can keep my old files, too. I'll just start over again after the Goblins stomp your asses into the mud."

The two mercenaries backed away. When they reached a distance of about fifteen meters, they turned their backs and walked faster until they disappeared into the night. Gray ran his hands through his short black hair and felt the mist that had collected running through his fingers. He stepped across the alley to Whirr and shook his head.

"I was thinking you weren't going to make it."

"You told me to stay in the shadows, Harm. If you haven't noticed, the porches and walkways in this town make it hard to do that."

Gray couldn't help but smile. He looked up at the mantis and for the first time truly felt a kinship with the female warrior. "Thanks, my friend."

Whirr's antennae rocked back and forth in satisfaction. "It pleases me to be called your friend, Harm. I think of you in the same manner, and as a warrior. I'm honored to be part of your formation."

Gray looked in the direction the two mercenaries had fled. "I get the feeling we're going to test that formation soon. As soon as we can land our forces, we will. Alert Major Vuong to be prepared to drop in combat ready status."

"You really think they'll attack while we land?"

"No, given their history and their belief in their own capabilities, Zuul attack in the night. But in case they get any ideas about a daytime attack, we have an insurance policy. Sophie Pryce wants to meet our team. I figure several hours of the dog-and-pony-show, pun intended, will keep Krukk and his idiots from attacking until we're ready to face them."

"And then what?"

"Well, they took the package with them. That pretty much puts us ready to start Phase Two. Until everyone else is ready, we look like a mercenary company in disarray."

"That'll be hard for me to do, Harm."

He laughed. "You and me both, Whirr."

* * *

Two Days Later

New Perth

Maarg spent two days in her quarters sleeping, eating, and tunneling into available networks. She determined quickly that the Trenta Knights possessed an outdated and easily defeated security system. She established a foothold there in less than two hours. Once inside, she'd gathered in-depth information and intelligence on their capabilities out of habit more than direction. Her "vacation" threatened to become work. Yet the heavy rains continued unabated, and much heavier, for another twelve hours. When she'd woken at 1300 local on her first day, the fog and rain obscured everything in sight. Even transports to and from the starport reported difficulties with visibility. So she'd ordered food from the hotel's service and returned to work, in between watching Tri-V holoprograms from all manner of species.

By that evening, the bulk of what the media called Gray's Goblins landed in an abandoned industrial area on the east side of town. The Trenta Knights' networks lit up with intelligence reports and observations, but no definitive action. They appeared to be entertaining a "wait and see" tactic, and most of their communications seemed routine and, frankly, bored.

Speaking of bored, she found where the Peacemakers had worked on the assassination. Details from the government media sites portrayed the attack as a tragic, unexplained event. Maarg decided against digging into the government system Vannix and Rains appeared to be using. They'd moved from a small shop downtown to a lower level of what the locals called Government Center. From what she could gather, they appeared to be working slowly through the personal effects of those involved in the attack on the square. Watching the footage of her friends working, she couldn't help but think they were killing time.

At least they aren't killing anything else.

Yet.

Maarg sat back and stretched before reaching for her tea. She glanced outside, noticing the rains had ended, and the fog was dissipating. Blue sky appeared overhead, and the promise of a much nicer day, made her smile.

From her position, Maarg determined there were a couple of things she needed to do. One was to get out of her room and explore New Perth, since the morning was clear and bright, if cool. There were several things she wanted to see around the town, and her ulterior motive was to get close enough to the infrastructure around Government Center to tap into their connections.

Since the completion of their landings, there were no updates on Gray's Goblins. She'd browsed the available connections for ships in orbit and had been surprised not to find *Taal's Fury*. She knew where the ship was, and the gate's control systems confirmed its presence, but the ship was running silent. While it wasn't their standard operating procedure, Maarg didn't think it made sense. Having everyone trying to get information to or from the ship would cause problems. An intelligent enemy recognized patterns and could assume that all the different pieces of the operation, including her, could be connected.

The fascinating aspect she'd discovered was the current state of things on Snowmass.

After deciding to dig deeper, she found there was significant unrest in the colonies to the north. Climate predictions had been wildly off since the first days of the settlement. The areas expected to get only a meter of snow per year regularly expected more than five times that amount. Growing cycles planet-wide were shortened. The massive domed colonies of the north, built to withstand the harsh winters and take advantage of rich volcanic soils, weren't as well insulated as the colonists had hoped. As a result, crop yields from those colonies had been down the last two years. The Dream World Consortium blamed the colder than normal temperatures and a return of the planet's natural ecosystem with all the attacks on their PCMU units around the globe.

Marge extrapolated the data and knew that wasn't the case. The planet's natural ecosystem hadn't returned, it had never been fully quelled by the Dream World Consortium. Which fit their track record perfectly, and her research confirmed it to the letter.

These guys really don't seem to care about anything other than profit.

The history of the planet was equally checkered, and while the research was tempting, Marge decided it was time to get out of her room. She had about six hours until she was supposed to rendezvous with the dropship and return to *Taal's Fury*. There was enough time to explore the town and see a little of the sights. There weren't that many broadcast programs worth watching. She grew tired of sports, and the melodramas, everything from Human productions to strange Tortantula love triangles, really didn't sit well with her either.

Prior to checking out, Maarg took one last shower in the oversized all-species-capable bathing facility. Since leaving the cavern system on Weqq, she'd grown fond of the experience, and spent more than twenty minutes scrubbing and cleaning and singing along to the entertainment pod. Soon after she exited the shower, there was a tap on her door.

"Yes?" she answered.

"Housekeeping." She checked the video display from the security camera and saw a Zuparti wearing a hotel name tag and dressed in the uniform of a valet. "Clearing your dishes, if you please."

Maarg remembered her breakfast order sitting on the wide cart and unlocked the door without hesitation. She pulled it toward her, stuck her head around it to make eye contact with the server, and froze. Pressed against her face, on the wide part of her skull between her eyes, was a large pistol. Behind it was a coal black Equiri.

"Step back into the room and don't make a sound." The Equiri nudged the pistol against her face and scowled down at her.

Maarg did as she was ordered, and the Equiri stepped into the room, with the Zuparti pulling the door closed behind.

"Keep going." The horse-like alien tapped the pistol against her skull.

She inched back toward the wide bed and sat back on her haunches. "What you want?"

The Zuparti stepped forward with a laugh. "Let's see, an albino TriRusk who is still a child has certain abilities, yes?"

Maarg paused a moment, then said, "I can give you the diamonds I've passed this week. There's a bag of them in my luggage."

The Zuparti giggled. "Oh, we know that. We've been watching you since you landed on this planet. While your diamonds are valuable, your other talents have us intrigued, Maarg."

She glanced up. "Your name is Thraff. You're a friend of Kr'et'Socae, aren't you?"

The Equiri nodded. "If you want to survive this day, you'll do exactly what we tell you to do. Deviate from those instructions, and I will kill you where you stand. Is that clear?"

She nodded, suddenly realizing she was afraid. She hadn't felt that way since the mantis had locked her in the facility on Weqq. It wasn't a pleasant feeling. "I understand," she replied.

"Good," the Zuparti said as he collected her slate and belongings. "You seem to be good at finding things, so we're going to put that talent to use in another location on the planet. We're looking for something…someone, too. I think you will help us find them."

"I don't know who you think you are, but the only reason I'm doing anything is because I believe Thraff's threat against me. You'll understand if I'm not immediately wooed by your presence."

The Zuparti stared at her and then cackled. He stepped forward and reached one paw for her right shoulder as he laughed and fought to gain his breath. A half-second later, there was a blade pressed against the side of her long face.

"Let me be clear, Maarg. You'll do what I say just like Thraff is doing what I say. This matter is far beyond Kr'et'Socae, dear Tri-Rusk. It's my responsibility to ensure we do not fail. You will be a major part of that operation, or you will be dead. It's that simple."

Maarg clenched her lower jaw shut and studied the two of them. The Zuparti was in charge? In charge of what? With an Equiri assassin on a leash? Nothing made sense. The only thing she could do was something she'd learned from Tara—let the situation develop, no matter how difficult it was.

"Fine," she grunted. "I'll come with you even though I don't know your name. Or is that some big secret?"

The Zuparti brightened. "Oh, a TriRusk with an attitude. My name is Ch'tek. I'm quite sure you've heard of me. Tell me, Maarg, have you ever seen snow?"

* * * * *

Chapter Twenty-Two

3km Southeast of Lake Pryce

Snowmass

Tara Mason convinced herself the voice wasn't real. She was warm and dry, and there was nothing needing her attention.

"Hey, boss." The voice came again and jarred her awake and back to reality.

Without moving from her sleeping position, she asked, "What is it, Homer?"

"You wanted to know when the rain stopped and when there was activity at the facility. We've got both."

Tara sat up from her makeshift bed and reach for her wrist slate. She'd managed to sleep for all of four hours, her longest burst since they'd landed on the planet. "How long has it been going on?"

Homer shrugged. The gesture looked positively alien on the Pushtal's frame. "Quin'taa called in about five minutes ago. He reports a group of scientists are working outside for the first time in a few days."

"Any idea what they're doing?" Tara yawned and reached for a water bottle. The cool, crisp water had the faintest tinge of iodine in its aftertaste. They'd transitioned to using local water, suitably treated, twenty-four hours after landing.

"No, he says it looks like they're gathering samples. Since the fog lifted, he's been able to see they have several pools closed off from the rest of the lake."

Tara tapped her slate and activated her headset. "Lucille? Is your passive encrypted link running? Do we have a status report on all our units?"

<<Affirmative. Captain Gray has landed the bulk of our combat forces at New Perth. While there has been no active resistance, there is substantial intelligence reporting happening on behalf of the Trenta Knights. Peacemakers Rains and Vannix are working out of Government Center. I cannot establish a secure communications link with them. When possible, I would like your permission to do this despite the dangers inherent in open communications.>>

"Why, Lucille?"

<<Given the situation in the square almost forty-eight hours ago, and the pace of what they've reported to the government, I believe they found something and are unsure how to proceed.>>

Tara took a slow, deep breath. "I asked them to take their time if they decided the situation needed to develop further. If you can establish an encrypted direct connection, do it. We need to know what's going on with them. What about Maarg?"

<<She spent two nights at a business called the Restful Inn and checked out an hour ago. I could not determine her whereabouts. She is due to meet the dropship in five hours and 38 minutes.>>

"You can't determine her whereabouts because we lack a connection, right?"

<<Affirmative, Tara. Nor have I been able to see what she has found. I calculated her likelihood to infiltrate systems in New Perth at a virtual certainty.>>

"She's young and bored, Lucille. Something I've been very glad you're not."

At least she's moving and doing something.

Tara thought about it for a moment and recognized an opportunity. She tapped Homer on the shoulder. "Get in touch with Quin'taa and tell him to stay in place. We'll move to his position. We all need to see what's going on up there, and depending on how close we get, Lucille can tap their network connection, and we can update our folks on what's going on here."

The Pushtal nodded and rustled in his pack for some type of protein bar. "Sounds good to me, boss. I'll be ready to go in a couple of minutes," Homer replied. "What about the rest of the Misfits?"

Tara sighed. She'd been thinking about the ill-fated drop ever since they landed and found a concealed position. There'd been no data for Lucille to decipher. The team's radio frequencies were empty. All data links terminated. Without their coherent location data, there was no way for them to engage in direct laser comm link. Until there was some indication otherwise, it appeared the other Misfits were missing. Given what she'd witnessed during the jump, she presumed them dead. That wasn't entirely fair, because Araceli possessed a different parachute deployment system than Each and Ladow had on their jump platform, but there'd been no communications and, more importantly, no data from her CASPer at all.

They locked eyes for a moment. "We have to keep going, Homer. Once we identify what's going on at the Lake Pryce facility, maybe we'll have time to double back and find our folks. Right now, nobody knows we're here, and that's the biggest advantage we have."

"Understood, boss. You gonna be able to keep up with me?"

Tara smiled and worked her way out of the sleeping system. "Don't you worry about me, Homer. Just tell Q we're on our way."

Tara rolled up and compressed the sleep system into a pouch the size of a soccer ball. She moved to Deathangel 25, opened a cargo pod mounted on the inside of the left leg, and slipped the system inside before resealing the pod. She opened the cockpit from the outside and climbed aboard. With a glance behind her, she saw Homer was ready to move, and he'd gathered the extra gear Quin'taa had brought into a large, Oogar-size pack. Tara backed into the cockpit and worked her limbs into the CASPer's harness. She powered up the mech, closed the cockpit, and took a last deep breath of the cool, moist air as she reached one CASPer arm out for the Oogar's pack.

Lucille chimed in her ears. <<No further update from Quin'taa. Situation continues as described. We must disable the HF relay from the top of the hill, Tara.>>

They'd communicated via a positively ancient frequency using a simple relay antenna on a two-meter stake Homer had installed on the top of the hill between them and Quin'taa.

"We'll leave the stake. Give me the best route to Quin'taa's position," Tara said as she reached for a protein bar stowed in the food compartment near her left knee.

The multifunction Tri-V display pulled up a topographic map in three dimensions. A dotted line, orange against the green displayed terrain, outlined their trail to Quin'taa's position six kilometers away. She'd positioned them one terrain feature away from the facility at Lake Pryce. The hill above them was part of the ridge extending along the southwestern edge of the lake. They'd taken a position there to be able to either skirt the hilltop or use the natural cover of the draws on either side of the summit to get close to the facility without raising suspicions. Quin'taa occupied their overwatch position on the forward slope of the hill near a rock outcropping which provided excellent observation of the facility below.

"Lucille, do we have any more recent imagery of what's over there?"

<<The most recent public imagery taken of Lake Pryce is six months old.>>

"And what we're seeing matches that imagery?" Tara asked. She knew the answer but needed to know for certain.

<<Negative. The facility we're observing appears to have been built in that time. Would you like me to request a detailed report from Quin'taa?>>

"Can he send you an image over HF?"

<<He could, but the transmission and download time would be about the same as if we moved directly over the hilltop. He could use his laser link to the stake, but that could arouse suspicion if the facility is monitoring the laser bands in the electromagnetic spectrum.>>

"I understand." Tara sighed. For all their technology and all their capabilities, communications seemed to be the one thing continually hampering operations. It had probably been that way for several thousand years.

Tara activated the team intercom. "All right, Homer. Let's go."

The chosen route was easy. Despite the rocky ground, Lucille's analysis of the topography gave them a reasonably flat avenue of approach to the forward overwatch position. They made good time around the front slope of the hill. Homer slowed the pace until they were very close to the rock outcropping marking Quin'taa's position. At the base of the outcrop, Homer turned toward her and motioned with one hand for the CASPer to stop in place. Tara froze. Homer crept up onto the outcropping, ambling until he reached a position where he too froze in place. Using external amplifiers and receivers, Tara heard Quin'taa speak.

"Who goes there?"

"Homer and Tara."

There was a pause, and she heard the Oogar sniff the air with his powerful nose.

"So it is. And no one else with you."

Homer cackled softly. "You're supposed to use that challenge and password thing, remember?"

"My nose is better than any password sequence, buddy." Quin'taa grunted. "Come on up."

Satisfied that all was right, Quin'taa stood where Tara could see him and motioned her forward. Tara looked at the outcropping and decided it was too risky to move the CASPer, so she opened the cockpit.

"Lucille, keep the systems running. I've got a feeling we might have to make a mad dash out of here. Maintain comms relay with me."

<<Acknowledged.>>

Tara climbed out of the cockpit and down the CASPer's leg with practiced ease. She moved quickly across the rocks and up onto the outcrop. Near the top, she pushed into a small nook barely large enough for the three of them. Quin'taa took up most of the space.

"What have we got down there?" she asked.

Quin'taa shifted so she could see through the notch he'd used as an observation point. "You see the southern edge of the lake, right? On that corner, the southwestern one, there's five pools. They're rectangular and appear to be about five meters wide by thirty meters long. I have no idea how deep they are. I'm still trying to figure out what they might be."

"It almost looks like they're growing something," Homer said.

"Looks like a fish hatchery," Tara said. "It's something we do on Earth, use of a controlled pool to grow and populate fish to stock rivers or ponds so they can be fished sustainably."

"Maybe," Quin'taa said, "but from here we really can't tell, and there's no sensor I've got that can show me if there's anything in that water. You have any idea how to do that?"

Tara shook her head. "No. We'd be in the same boat with Lucille. Have you been able to observe them doing anything with those pools?"

"Not much, except for seeing them taking samples."

"What kind of samples?" Homer asked as he shifted to try to see more of the facility below.

"In the last few hours I watched them drain one pool and then refill it from the lake. Three Humans came out and tested the water with some large buckets and hand-held testing kits before they went back inside. Not long after that, a crew of Zuul and Zuparti came out and added different components to the water. Some looked like powder, and some was liquid. It's almost like they're trying to chemically adjust the water."

"That still doesn't rule out some form of hatchery," Tara said aloud. *Why would they be testing and retesting the lake water? And adding things to it? It makes no sense.*

"It's almost like they're trying to make the water something it's not," Homer said. "Maybe they adjusted it for some specific reason?"

"So they adjusted that pool, but have they put anything in it?" Tara turned to the Oogar.

"No," Quin'taa replied. "They haven't put anything living in there, no. Which means either they're not doing that, or they're adjusting for something else. Maybe something that doesn't live on this planet."

<<That is a logical, though unprovable, conclusion,>> Lucille said from Tara's slate. <<A lack of life forms in that water could indicate testing of some variety. Without getting closer, there is no way to know for certain.>>

"Do we risk getting any closer?" Tara asked of her counterparts.

Quin'taa pointed with one clawed digit down into the valley below. "I've seen more security patrols in the last two hours. They've been passing through in about thirty-minute increments. Usually one motorized skiff and a couple of infantry, all Zuul. They're guarding something. Interestingly enough, I haven't seen them cross that open space between the work area and the path they're patrolling. I've only seen them do that when there's some automated antipersonnel devices planted in the area. We know they have a missile radar system, too, though I can't see the missile launcher from here. Getting close at this point doesn't seem like a good idea. So my answer is no."

Tara glanced at Homer. His amber ringed eyes stared into hers for a moment. Even with him being a friend, she couldn't imagine being any closer to a Bengal tiger. He wasn't one, but his Pushtal features were close enough. "I'm with Q. Whatever they're doing is sensitive enough that they brought their own security forces. And they've likely got that whole place ringed with anti-personnel devices, and anti-aircraft stuff, too. Unless we're planning to go in there and take the compound, my vote is also no. I think we observe it and see a little more of what they're doing."

"If we try to take the compound," she said, "we'd need to bring the cavalry. I'm not ready to do that yet. That gives us two options: stay here and continue to observe, or work our way to the extraction point and get the cavalry ready in case we need to come back. The three of us aren't taking that compound by ourselves."

Lucille chimed. <<Tara? I have a weak laser lock on Misfit 5.>>

Tara's heart leapt. "What?"

<<I have a weak lock on Misfit 5 via laser. There is no radio connection, and the link connection on her end is not strong enough for voice. Her antenna has likely been compromised.>>

"Can you get a text message through?"

<<Unknown. As you would say, it's worth a shot.>>

Tara considered her options. If there was a way to get at least a text message to the young girl, there was hope she could rally the rest of the Misfits and get them together at the extraction point. Their mission to observe the DWC facility appeared to be over. Without approaching and risking a fight of some kind, there was no way to know exactly what was going on there. The facility, and whatever its objectives were, was something she might have to pass to the Peacemakers. Somehow, they'd figure out what was going on in those tanks. If they weren't hatching fish or anything else, why were they working so hard to adjust the water? None of it really made sense.

"Laser is our best chance to avoid detection. Send a text message to her and see if she can at least receive it. Tell her to move to the extraction point and we'll join her in six hours."

<<There's no way to determine if she'll be able to receive it. All we can hope is that she's able to move toward the extraction point.>>

"Unless we get to a position where the link is stronger," Homer said. "We do that, and we could link up faster."

<<That's correct,>> Lucille replied. <<Even then, there is still a concern that they could detect her.>>

"Where did you pick up the weak signal from Araceli?"

Tara's slate screen mirrored the multifunction display topographic map from her CASPer. Their current position was highlighted with a blue dot. The map zoomed outward and slid slightly to the south and west. A flashing red dot illuminated, showing where Araceli's auto-laser comm transmitter beacon had been found. By the map's scale, Araceli was more than twelve kilometers away and on top of the escarpment.

"Gods. What's she doing down there?" Quin'taa asked.

<<Unknown. I have transmitted a text-only message telling her to move to the extraction point as requested.>>

"Every time you get a ping from her beacon, resend that message, Lucille."

<<Understood, Tara.>>

Tara considered the map for a moment. The extraction point had been due east at the top of the escarpment. Araceli being so far south made getting to her position challenging. Still, it appeared there were areas where the terrain wasn't as steep or rocky to the south and east near Araceli's position.

Maybe she tried to move toward the extraction point and couldn't, so she changed her course to the south? That would make sense. She's a smart kid.

Tara tapped the share button and sent the information to Homer and Quin'taa via their slates.

"Okay, guys, check your slates. We're pulling out and heading for the extraction point, but we'll take a different route than originally planned. It looks like the escarpment is a bit too steep and exposed to the east where we thought we'd cross. You can see where Lucille picked up Araceli's signal. I'm betting she was trying to move to the extraction point, too. We're gonna move in the same direction she did and get up that escarpment. The route will add time, but it's easier terrain, and I really think it's the best way."

Both of the aliens nodded their heads in an all-too-Human gesture. Quin'taa responded, "I agree."

"Araceli couldn't make contact, and she's trying to get to the extraction point. Do we know if she has anyone else with her?" Homer asked.

Lucille replied, <<No. The signal is weak enough that there is no guarantee she'll be able to receive it, much less reply via text. All we can hope is as we get closer and get to the high ground, we'll be able to reestablish communications.>>

"Well, it's not much," Homer said, "but it's better than the alternative. Let's get moving."

Tara smiled at both of them. "Grab all your gear and leave the antenna stake. We need to make up some time."

Hang on, kid. We're on our way.

*****

Chapter Twenty-Three

Government Center

New Perth

During their initial year at the Peacemaker Academy, the "first years" faced a defined set of coursework designed to test their abilities and creativity. One of the most challenging, and the one they all remembered long after their time at the revered school on Ocono, was the Introduction to Cryptology. Part of the class required the students to construct and evolve their own encrypted language. It had surprised Jackson Rains to learn the impetus for the coursework at the Academy had a shockingly Human background.

Tap code, the instructors said, was developed by early Russian prisoners and adopted by Americans during their incarceration during the Vietnam War. Those men developed a way to communicate when everything around them was controlled and observed. The subtle tapping they produced using a quadratic table of letters, one set of taps up and the other to the right, enabled detailed communications when there was no other way. They'd created an opportunity where there'd been none, so the Peacemaker instructors demanded each class produce their own language.

After much gnashing of teeth and other chewing bits, each class formulated their own language. Over the course of the rest of their academic journey, the private language served as a way for the candidates to communicate, and a way for the cryptologists of the Peacemaker Guild to test their abilities. While no class had ever constructed a language the crypto-specialists couldn't decipher, their class had been good. So much so that in Government Center, Rains and Vannix tapped each other messages using the numerically based language their class had developed three years earlier.

They'd been at their workstations, decrypting the slates of Lmott and Qur'atta, for the better part of an hour when Vannix's tapped message chimed on his screen.

Rains looked at it and blinked in surprise. Just as quickly, his brain translated the question from the number and standard character sequence into workable text.

Did you see your slate connection reset a minute ago?

Rains tapped back. No.

They're monitoring everything we do, Jackson.

He took a deep breath and let it out slowly without raising his eyes to look at her. I thought so.

If we don't hear from Tara soon, we'll have to figure out a way to move north on our own. Find some reason without specifically naming Reecha. Have you gotten anywhere with Veeka's tablet?

No further than you got. I can't get past the seven-digit passcode, either. Lucille said that with all the characters in all the languages possible for that model of slate, it would take something like seventeen million years to crack it.

<<17,863,413.45, to be exact.>> Lucille's words appeared soundlessly on their slates. While she'd been able to penetrate the Government Center infrastructure and secure their slate-based communications, she couldn't vocalize her responses. Nor could she tunnel any further into the New Perth government network without

attracting attention. She'd hovered around their firewalls and security protocols, learning what she could, but hadn't attempted to get further inside.

Movement outside their work area caught his eyes and Rains looked up to see Sophie Pryce and Mayor Citsym walking toward them beyond the wide, clear doors.

Heads up, partner.

I can smell them. Vannix sniffed and looked up from her slate. "Let's get as much information as we can."

Rains sat up and stretched. As the mayor and his assistant entered the room, he stood. Vannix joined him. "Honored Mayor. Miss Pryce."

"Peacemakers," Citsym replied. "A fine morning to you, though much colder than we like."

Vannix nodded and rubbed at her sides with her paws. "It would seem winter approaches fast."

Sophie Pryce smiled. "The smell of snow is in the air, and it's wonderful. While we like our temperate seasons, Snowmass is really at its best when winter comes."

"Why's that?" Rains asked with a smile.

Pryce met his eyes. "Though our winters are strong and cold, our citizens embrace them. We make the most out of everything, Peacemaker Rains."

I bet you do.

Mayor Citsym clasped his forepaws in front of him. "With respect, Peacemakers, I have been asked to report to the board of directors this morning. Do you have any information we could share to put their fears at ease?"

Rains gestured to the table. "We've positively identified the two assailants. The Zuul's identity is Lmott. His twin brother attempted to kill Peacemaker Jessica Francis several months ago and was killed in the attempt. Their reputations as assassins were well documented."

"The other assailant, the Equiri, is known as Qur'atta. He's a known associate of Kr'et'Socae," Vannix said.

"What?" Citsym blurted. "Here?"

Rains nodded his head and focused on the mayor, but the calm, detached look on Sophie Pryce's face was far more telling. "We're trying to understand a motive now. We've been through their slates and have found nothing of value to the investigation. We were hoping to ask for access to local servers that might have been used for GalNet searches and communications to these slates."

Citsym nodded. "Yes, yes, of course."

"Honored Mayor," Pryce said.

"I know what you're going to say, Sophie, but no, I authorize the Peacemakers to use whatever they can. An honored member of our community was killed, and I want to know why. I want to know who hired these assassins. They've deeply wounded our reputation, and I will no longer stand for violence."

"Then we should officially denounce the terrorists," Pryce said. "Call them out to the entire community and have them arrested on sight."

Rains glanced at Vannix, who quickly met his eyes and turned back to the discussion in front of them. Neither of them said anything. One of their first lessons as candidates was to let those around them do all the talking. Especially when tempers flared.

"We don't know who they are, Sophie. We have no proof."

Pryce frowned. "We know one."

Sensing an opportunity, Rains stepped forward. "You have a lead related to your incidents?"

Pryce looked up at him and waved one hand. "Peacemaker, this is a local investigation and—"

"I'm sorry, Miss Pryce," Vannix interjected. "These incidents are potentially interrelated. Your lead may have a direct connection to this case."

Both Rains and Vannix suspected what the connection was, and watching Sophie Pryce's practiced visage cracking down the center was worth his interjection.

"We have reports of a Veetanho on the planet who was reported to have left more than fifty years ago. We suspect she's behind the other attacks," Pryce said. "We don't have proof, but Colonel Krukk's soldiers have reported attack scenes so clean only a Veetanho could pull it off. They're more practiced at stealth and sneak attacks than any other race." She glanced at Vannix. "Present company excluded, Peacemaker."

Rains almost laughed. *You don't know my partner too well.*

"What is their name?" Vannix asked.

"Reecha. She was the original founding member of the Veetanho community on this planet," Pryce said. "Her reputation as a leader was outstanding. But we have to determine if she's behind this."

Rains glanced at Vannix for a moment. His pause proved long enough that both Pryce and Citsym stared at him. He let his eyes dart between them. "We'll need everything you have on her."

Pryce and Citsym shared a look, and the mayor turned to him. "You'll have access to our government files within the hour, Peacemaker Rains."

"Thank you, Honored Mayor," Rains replied.

"Is there anything else we can get you?" Pryce asked, the practiced, easy smile of a politician returning to her face.

"No, thank you," Vannix replied. "Well, we may need some conveyance to your outlying colonies. There are several potential character witnesses we would like to interview regarding the deceased."

"Of course," Pryce said. "I'll ensure you have access to a charter whenever you require one."

"We appreciate your hospitality," Rains added. The dance of pleasantries was exhausting, but ultimately necessary.

"Your help in solving this case and letting us return to a peaceful and quiet winter is far more appreciated, Peacemakers," Citsym replied. "We must be going. The business of a burgeoning colony requires my utmost efforts."

With that, the two officials turned and moved through the door. Rains watched them go, then turned back to their workstation to see Vannix openly deploy an elSha-built scrambler.

"You sure about that?"

Vannix nodded. "Much faster than tapping, Jackson."

The device chirped and displayed three flashing green lights. The immediate area was secure, and any attempt to record their discussions was actively blocked.

"Lucille? Did you get inside?" Vannix asked.

<<Affirmative.>>

Rains blinked. "Inside what?"

<<Their slates, Jackson. Citsym has no security system, and there's nothing of value. Miss Pryce, however, has a vast secured file storage system.>>

"Which we probably can't crack any faster than Veeka's." Vannix frowned. "But an encrypted file system isn't enough to question her. That whole burden of proof thing, right?"

Rains grunted. "Yeah. They suspect Reecha is behind it, but I can't stop thinking they killed Veeka, too. One, to get at Reecha because they were old friends and two, because Veeka was probably in on the whole thing from the start."

Vannix nodded. "Lucille, as soon as they grant us access to their systems, you know what to do."

<<Affirmative,>> Lucille replied. <<Make an attempt on the government workstations here. There is no AetherNet connection to allow my access attempt. I am curious what they have on their system for public consumption.>>

Vannix raised her eyebrows, and her nose twitched. "I hadn't thought about that."

"I wouldn't have done it being afraid it would tip them off about Reecha."

Vannix chuckled. "Oh, they knew all right. And if you had, it would have made them curious. Speaking of curious, you saw the reaction on Pryce's face when we mentioned Kr'et'Socae, right?"

"Yeah." Rains smiled. "She knew about that, and the mayor didn't. Really makes me want to get to those encrypted files of hers."

"They were here looking for credits, Jackson. And probably wondering why we're searching for Jessica's father." Vannix tapped on the government workstation. "Well, let's see if there's anything here we can use."

Snowman.

Gods, man. Why does everybody want that motherfucker?

There really wasn't an answer. The Peacemaker Guild believed James Francis had been their friend and agent provocateur for the last twenty years by setting up and replenishing war stocks in various sites around the galaxy. The data didn't seem to support that theory, given what they'd been able to find in recent searches. With the assurance from a dying Veeka that Reecha, a close and personal contact of the elusive Human mercenary commander, was close by, and given the history of the planet where they now walked, there should have been something definitive. Like his partner, Rains believed the answers lay with Reecha in the communes to the north. With the approaching winter, the time for action was close at hand, but there'd been nothing from Tara Mason or the other elements of Force 25 to steer their collective course.

"There are a few references in the database. Her being part of the Veetanho Protest fifty years ago are the main ones. Then there's a bunch of frivolous stuff, like entries in food contests and such."

Rains leaned over and studied the screen. "Looks like an old-time county fair sort of thing."

"I have no idea what you're talking about, Jackson."

"It's a Human thing." Rains read the article. "Apparently Reecha is quite the cook. Has a famous aiticos soup recipe, whatever that is."

"Oh," Vannix blurted. "It's the best soup ever, Jackson. A Veetanho delicacy, and something we share with each other on special occasions."

Aiticos.

Seven letters.

Rains casually picked up Veeka's slate, opened the login screen, and handed the device to Vannix. "Type it in. *Aiticos.* In your language."

Vannix tapped and the slate's login screen opened to a file taxonomy.

"Holy shit," she said. "We're in."

Rains ran one hand over his face and rubbed his eyes for a long moment. They'd been too late to stop the assassination of Veeka, and as improbable as it seemed, Reecha had remained out of public view for decades. She had likely done that in the cavern systems to the north and west as Veeka said with her last words. As the Dream World Consortium continued to fumble their way through daily life and operations, and their promises fell flat, she'd been the one to take up arms. She knew they were up to something.

But what?

In the taxonomy, familiar words like "climate" and "storms" appeared numerous times. Documentation seemed to exist for every significant weather event on the planet for the last decade or more. As Vannix carefully scrolled, he pointed.

"Population. What's that about?"

Vannix plugged in a cable from her slate to Veeka's. "Lucille? You're up."

Three seconds passed. <<I have studied the data in the file you indicated, Jackson. The analysis is telling.>>

"Explain, Lucille. What did you find?"

Rains drummed his fingers on the desk and reached for his coffee mug. Snowmass left a lot to be desired, but the coffee they had was pretty damn good. Much better than what they had on board the ship.

Enjoy the little things. He smiled to himself. *I'm trying, Missus Green, I'm trying.*

<<My analysis is as follows: The current total population of Snowmass is 76,534. The population has decreased over the last twenty years from a high of 136,212. The immigration data follows a similar pattern. Over the last 20 years, more citizens have left Snowmass than those who have come here to live.>>

"What about over the last five years? Isn't that how long they've said the terrorist attacks have been happening?" Vannix asked

<<Over the last five years, 4,212 citizens have left the planet. By comparison, only 823 have immigrated to Snowmass.>>

"That's what they're doing. They're forcing people out," Vannix said.

"Lucille, of the citizens who've left the planet, how many of them were involved in agricultural pursuits?" Rains asked.

<<3,805. That number appears disproportionate to the other industries on this planet. It can be assumed that the constant environmental struggles have pushed out agricultural pursuits. When the growing system is not consistent or long enough, it's reasonable to assume the citizens would pursue their trades elsewhere.>>

Rains fumed. "Which is exactly what they're doing."

<<I would concur.>>

He stared off into space for a long moment. "Why would a successful Consortium run off paying customers? It doesn't make sense."

As he stared out the window, he saw a familiar shape in the distance. Lieutenant Whirr was making her way with two other MinSha warriors toward the Goblins' landing area. The citizens of New Perth gave them a wide passage. Seeing them sparked something. Before their hyperspace transit to Snowmass, the two Peacemakers received a message from the guild as part of the typical Stormwatch package.

He turned back to his slate and brought up the report from Lieutenant Colonel Tirr.

He'd found a list of planets and water sources at a Dream World Consortium expedition to Ngashia in the Aventa Region. There'd been several potential targets listed by the Dream World Consortium, but no one seemed to know what they were for. He scanned the list and found what he was looking for quickly.

Snowmass. Lake Pryce, eastern region, northern continent.

The pieces came together quickly. The Consortium seemed intent on pushing settlers out and was unconcerned about the failing climate. If they altered it further, embracing the dream world concept, there could be changes to the hydrology of the planet. Six months ago the facility at Lake Pryce hadn't existed.

He showed the list to Vannix and asked, "Lucille? Has there been any improvement made to the environment in the last six months?"

<<Negative. By all indicators, and the Dream World Consortium's own reports, there have been no significant changes to the atmosphere or the climate on this planet in two years.>>

They know something. Something about Lake Pryce. They want to play the long game. If this winter is half as hard as the previous ones, they'll lose farming communities in droves. Which is exactly what they want to do.

Veeka's slate pinged. A calendar reminder.

Dinner? Nathan Balyeat.

Vannix leaned over the slate. "Lucille, search Veeka's slate for contact information on Mr. Nathan Balyeat."

<<Nathan Balyeat is a farmer and amateur distiller who lives in Glacier Falls in the northlands.>>

"And how close is that to the caves Veeka mentioned?"

<<Twenty-four kilometers,>> Lucille replied. <<Access has been granted to the government system. I am inside and already hidden. According to transportation records, Balyeat and his family returned to Glacier Falls yesterday.>>

Vannix looked up and curled her maw in a smile. "I think it's time we go see him. We'll call it a character interview, but we can at least work the situation there, right? I'll let Tara know."

Rains sent a request for transportation to Sophie Pryce and managed to secure the gear they'd collected from Lmott and Qur'atta. Veeka's slate would go with them, more as a research asset than anything else. Lucille was a powerful asset, but it would take her time to really digest all the information available and be able to brief the rest of the team when the time inevitably came.

Given the situation, they hadn't had contact with anyone else from Force 25 since they'd landed. They needed to be someplace where they could talk more freely, and be around people they could trust. In New Perth there didn't seem to be anybody who could fit that bill.

"Got it, partner."

Lucille chimed. <<I established a connection and accessed recent security camera footage from New Perth as well.

<<We have a situation. It's Maarg.>>

* * * * *

Chapter Twenty-Four

12km ESE of Lake Pryce

Snowmass

The route to the south and east of her original landing position enabled Araceli to get to the top of the escarpment, but the climb was arduous. Instead of the sheer face she'd tried to negotiate in her CASPer, she moved through a boulder field. The vertical exposures where Misfit 3's platform appeared to have crash-landed were several thousand meters away, but it might as well have been millions of meters. Around her, boulders the size of her CASPer and greater slid and wobbled against each other on the unstable ground. The field matched nothing in her satellite imagery, and she realized it was likely a recent rockfall, which didn't make her climb any easier. There were too many tight spaces amid the unsteady rocks for her CASPer. So she moved atop them as best she could.

She remembered building dams as a kid in the many tributaries of the Swigert River at home on Victoria Bravo. Walking across those streams on her expedient rock dams had always been a tricky experience. More times than not, she'd fallen over and stepped into the ice-cold water. On top of the boulders inside her several ton mech, Araceli knew there was no chance of falling without being hurt. She focused her entire being on her balance and agility, though there still several times she stopped in somewhat stable positions to rest and drink water. Sometimes she paused just to consider her next move.

As she reached the top of an angular boulder standing much like a ship's prow overlooking the rest of the field, her communications equipment buzzed and flashed an "attempting to connect" message. Araceli spun her CASPer so the antenna platform on her back was pointed toward Lake Pryce. The signal had to be valid. Her gear wouldn't have bothered connecting if the signal hadn't been on the right frequency and with the right encryption. The other Misfits were reaching out.

The platform display flashed "connected." A text message typed across the screen, though it was hard for her to see them through the sudden tears filling her eyes.

Mission complete. Move to extraction point. Will join in six hours. Make…

There appeared to be another line of text, but something had garbled it. The laser link system had an effective range of about 10 kilometers, but given the terrain and the vegetation between them, there was no doubt in Araceli's mind that distance had affected the message. Still, it was a valid instruction, and one she intended to follow to the letter.

With a few taps on her instrument panel, Araceli reviewed her topographic map and saw she was only about four kilometers from the extraction point. Given the terrain and vegetation on the top of the escarpment, she could travel almost in a straight line and be there in less than an hour. Given the distance Tara and the rest of her team would have to cover, it would be some time before they arrived at the extraction point. From her current position, the saved beacon location for Misfit 3's platform was equally distant, but on significantly more dangerous terrain.

Tara would want me to find them. If they're alive, we have to get them off the field. Force 25 never leaves a friend behind.

Decision made, Araceli changed course and moved north and west along the top of the boulder field, back toward the edge of the escarpment. The boulders slowly transitioned to forest. The tall, gnarled pines blocking her way slowed her progress considerably. It took some time, and more than a few short jumps, but she was able to make her way to the edge and find a safe place to peer down into the wide valley. As it turned out, the platform was almost directly underneath her position. What was left of it, anyway.

The platform dangled from a column of rock more than 30 meters high. The gentle breeze thumped the mangled device against the formation and fluttered the remnants of both parachute and harness. Hanging from the platform, limp in the straps, was Ladow. There was little doubt the Tortantula was dead. A large, deep gouge across her bulbous abdomen revealed her insides with gross detail. At least three of her ten legs had been sheared off. Dark blood stained the rocks below it.

Araceli bit her lower lip hard enough to bring tears to her eyes. Since Victoria Bravo, she'd been unable to join the regular CASPer forces. Major Vuong wanted nothing to do with her. Despite her demonstrated prowess in her modified Mk 6 CASPer, Vuong wouldn't approve her to train, much less fight alongside any of his forces. She'd effectively been a soldier without a unit until the Misfits, as they called themselves, took her in. While she didn't know Each and Ladow very well, they were still teammates, and their loss stung.

Following the direction of the wind gently flapping the collapsed parachute and shredded harness, Araceli moved northeast along the rim, occasionally peering down over the edge. In the distance, only a few hundred meters away, appeared to be another collection of shredded white parachute cloth collapsed over the rocks. While she couldn't see Each's body, there was nothing to suggest the chipmunk had survived. Still, she knew she had to make sure.

Moving carefully, Araceli made her way to a position where she could look down on the second impact site. It appeared to be the shredded main parachute for the pair's platform. She assumed the primary parachutes for the pair had failed, and that had forced them to activate their reserve systems. By the looks of it, the reserve systems had fared about the same. Using her CASPer's sensors, what limited ones she had on board, Araceli searched for any sign of life in the area. There was nothing. To her right, some species of bird—three or four of them—circled lazily over the ground. They behaved almost like buzzards. She'd never seen them before, but her parents had often spoken about the flora and fauna of the desert Southwest where they'd lived as children.

There was something either dead or wounded nearby. Given where the birds were circling, though, that impact site was below the escarpment. Araceli decided not to investigate any further. If she could establish two-way communications with Tara, there might be a way to direct the other part of the team to the site before they made their way up the escarpment.

Inspiration struck. She turned back to Ladow's platform and located the communications equipment. She determined it was in better shape than her fried unit. If she could get down there and retrieve it, she might make an expedient repair to her own system.

She quickly walked the CASPer back to a stable position away from the rim and opened the cockpit. Without a second thought, she scrambled to the edge of the escarpment and studied the rocks for a way down to the platform about twenty meters below. It took more than thirty minutes to do so, but she made it. As her hands worked quickly to disengage the main antenna from its mount, she glanced over at Ladow's corpse. Araceli reached out and gently stroked the closest of the Tortantula's limp legs.

Sorry, my friend. I hope to see you again.

For the climb back up, there was nothing she could do to carry the communications device, except by clenching a length of its cable with her teeth. The heavy instrument package and antenna made the climb more difficult, but she was able to make her way up the rocks. Summers spent rock climbing on the spires of Victoria Bravo came in handy.

When she got back to the CASPer, Araceli carefully climbed up the rear of the vehicle and inspected the antenna mount. As she'd thought, it looked like it had been struck by lightning. Burn marks scorched the exterior, and the main antenna, a small nub designed to facilitate radio communications, had been completely sheared away. While the recovered antenna from Ladow's jump platform wasn't a perfect fit, she believed she could make it work. She'd spent too many hours messing around in the hangars of Victoria Forces, learning the maintainers' bad habits, to think otherwise. So that's what she did. Fingers flying through the cables, Araceli connected the antenna to the mount and used all-purpose combat tape to hold it down. She admired her work for a half-second and then climbed around the vehicle and into the cockpit.

Before she'd even moved her legs all the way into position, the radio set chirped to life.

<<Misfit 5, this is Lucille. Category 2 signal acquired. What is your current status?>>

Araceli worked herself into the straps and stabbed the speaker function. "Lucille, Misfit 5. I'm operational at this location. Misfit 2 is MIA and presumed KIA. Misfit 3 is KIA. Over."

<<Roger. Stand by.>>

Araceli completed getting herself strapped into the CASPer and closed the cockpit. A few seconds after it closed, Tara Mason's voice came through her speakers.

"Araceli? You're okay?"

"Yes, ma'am." A fresh round of tears threatened to spill over her eyelids. "I'm secure here. Misfit 2 and 3 are…"

"I know, honey." Tara's soothing tone brought forth her tears in giant, hot rivers down her cheeks. "There's nothing you could have done. Is that bucket of bolts operational?"

She half-snorted and smiled through her tears. For the last year she'd commandeered the half-cannibalized mech and learned its systems and processes intimately. She'd taken it from a base model Mk 6 to a scout model variant capable of operating like a Mk 7, potentially even a Mk 8. With increased fuel and lighter armor, the mech had proved to be both fast and resilient in combat situations.

"Yes, ma'am. I'm condition one. All systems nominal," Araceli replied. "The jump almost did a number on me."

"I'm glad you made it down, kid," Tara said. Her voice slowly lost its soothing tone and the calm, detached voice of her commander rang through and dried Araceli's tears in a heartbeat. "Listen up, 5, I need you moving now. Get to the extraction point and secure the area. We'll be there in about three hours, maybe less. Lucille says the ship will be overhead at your position in about twenty-six minutes. When they're over the horizon, make contact and get *Mako 15* down as soon after we link up as possible."

Araceli nodded to herself as the CASPer's displays fired up. "Roger that, Deathangel. Misfit 5 is moving."

"Good job, Master Sergeant Cignes."

Araceli beamed. A battlefield promotion hadn't been something she'd even considered, given her cool relationship with Major Vuong.

"Thank you, ma'am."

"No thanks necessary, Araceli. I need competent and experienced CASPer pilots. There's little doubt you're doubly qualified now. Get to the extraction point and report when on-station. Deathangel 25, out."

* * *

Headquarters
Trenta Knights

"You asked to see me, sir?" Tolem appeared in the commanding officer's door less than a minute after being summoned. Krukk appreciated the younger officer's diligence and promptness. He'd made a good choice to promote Tolem from the ranks to the executive officer's post. A good executive officer made or broke a mercenary company.

"I did, Tolem. Please come in." Krukk turned his desk and rotated it from a back-down and almost prone position to one where he stood and faced his fellow leader. "Ensure you close the door behind you. We have a personnel matter to discuss."

Tolem did as ordered while Krukk extracted himself from the desk. For the mountains of paperwork a commander endured, he'd saved the stress on his limbs by using the unique desk. Hanging from it was almost like traveling in hyperspace, something he'd done only twice in his thirty-four years. He stretched his back and shook gently. Finished, he looked to Tolem.

"Relax, Tolem. There is no personnel matter." Krukk beckoned the younger Zuul to approach his desk. He flipped a switch on the flat Tri-V screen mounted to the wall behind his desk, and an image of the industrial area occupied by Gray's Goblins appeared.

"Sir?" Tolem pointed at the screen.

"Yes, Tolem. We attack this evening. For the sake of security and the element of surprise, this cannot reach our forces until the end-of-day formation. I'm trusting you to have them prepared for combat."

Tolem nodded. "Preparing them for combat without them knowing combat is coming until it is imminent. I like the challenge."

"The fastest thing in any mercenary company is the speed of rumor." Krukk smiled. "They've drilled and prepared for weeks. An hour before sunset, order the recall and a full deployment. Vehicles and skiffs. The whole company detachment here. Do the same at the other barracks, too. No one escapes the preparations. That way our forces all prepare for combat."

Tolem turned to him. "Are you expecting combat in other places?"

"No, but our outlying stations must be ready," Krukk said.

"Why?" Tolem blurted. "Sir?"

"I expect trouble, Tolem," Krukk replied. "There is something I cannot—"

The Tri-V to Krukk's left displayed an incoming message icon from his starport security officer, Lieutenant Gnrra.

Krukk activated the connection and saw a golden brown Zuul fidgeting with his uniform tunic as the camera focused. "What is it, Gnrra?"

"Sir, reporting the departure of the Equiri and Zuparti you ordered observed by our forces. They departed for Glacier Falls with another being we had to use the GalNet to identify—an albino Tri-Rusk."

Krukk glanced at Tolem. "They haven't left the planet."

"Whoever they're working for isn't done with their services," Tolem said. "I'll alert the barracks at Glacier Falls."

Krukk nodded and turned to the Tri-V. "Good work, Gnrra."

"Sir, there's more. The mayor's office has contracted for a vehicle to transport the two Peacemakers on a series of interviews regarding the events in the square. They are also going to Glacier Falls."

Tolem opened his mouth and closed it again with a snap.

"Thank you, Gnrra. Keep me informed if anything changes." Krukk disconnected the message and glanced at Tolem. "You're thinking this is an opportunity?"

"I wouldn't mean to presume, sir," Tolem grinned, "but with the Peacemakers away from the city, there is nothing to stop our attack. I didn't want to say that with Gnrra listening. He is a good young officer, but his ability to keep details to himself is suspect."

"As with all young officers," Krukk replied. He leaned forward and stared down at the industrial area displayed on his working desktop. Changing the icon to a writing instrument in a dark red color, he drew on the map. "We will attack tonight. One hour after sunset, Tolem. Here's how we will deploy our forces and eliminate Gray's Goblins."

*****

Chapter Twenty-Five

Industrial Landing Area

Snowmass

Harmon Gray wiped his dirty hands on his flight suit. The move of the company's CASPers and maintenance racks into temporary shelters had taken far longer than they'd intended, given the sodden soil. With more weather expected, possibly even the first snow of the season, the erection of the temporary shelters and the stowage of the CASPers and their racks were the highest priority. Away from prying eyes the ruse of having sixteen CASPers in various states of disrepair was easier to control. Inside the shelters they loaded the CASPers with ammunition, checked their fuel, and gave them any servicing necessary. If needed, they were completely combat effective. The same couldn't be said for the four tanks they'd brought.

After the second battle of Victoria Bravo, they'd collected the remnants of the armored forces, intending to build at least a platoon of serviceable tanks. For their efforts, they got three hangar queens, and one barely moving shell. While Tara Mason had a history in tanks and wanted to have them as part of Force 25's inventory, Gray and Vuong, among others, had convinced her otherwise. The sixteen CASPers they possessed were Mk 6s and Mk 7s and were more than capable. Given the way the Cochkala armored skiffs had bludgeoned the Victoria Forces' tanks in short order, Force 25's table of organization and equipment needed to pivot to three-dimensional fire and maneuver.

Gray watched young Drew Morris move from tank to tank in their forward security positions. He'd given the young lieutenant orders to install remote firing mechanisms to the autoloading cannons in the event of an attack. By all appearances, the installation was complete. Morris wanted to conduct a dry-fire of each cannon using the mechanisms in the tubes without an actual round present. If satisfied, he'd load the cannon and prepare the system to fire. With power and fuel limits, though, they couldn't leave the vehicles running for an inordinate amount of time. The best they could do was power off the vehicles and override their master control systems to allow the gun tubes to be loaded with the autoloader in the mission ready configuration. Morris had worked all day on the three main tanks and looked exhausted.

On cue, the young lieutenant saw Gray watching him and waved before climbing into the third of four tanks to finish his tests and shut the vehicle down.

"He's doing good work," Whirr said as she approached from behind. "The systems in the command post are green across the board."

"The kid knows his stuff; that's for sure." Gray smiled. "Never underestimate a good mechanic."

"From what I understand, he's better than good," Whirr replied.

Gray nodded and glanced up at his executive officer's face. The MinSha's antennae wobbled slightly in the breeze. "What's going on?"

"The Trenta Knights have pulled back their manned observation post. The cameras are still in operation at three locations, though.

They're most certainly planning to attack. Perhaps as soon as this evening."

"Figures." Gray frowned. "Rains and Vannix caught a shuttle up north about two hours ago. They were going to Glacier Falls by way of Northingham. I got the word from Vuong. He had two pilots in town on a resupply request."

Whirr's antennae sagged. "It's unfortunate, but even with a Peacemaker present, a committed enemy will not pause their attack."

"True." Gray looked down at the damp ground and dragged the toe of his boot across it. He spat, frowned again, and put his hands on his hips. "Fine. They want to attack, we'll be ready for them. Can we get eyes on their assembly areas?"

"Yes," Whirr chittered. "We've accessed their closed-circuit security camera system with the help of Lucille. They're conducting inspections and drills."

"Rehearsals?"

Whirr sagged. "Perhaps. Looks more like…well, what you call chickenshit."

Gray laughed. "Oh, really?"

"According to my observation team, the Knights have repeated several drills and inspections at least three times," Whirr replied. "If they were actually conducting rehearsals, we could get actionable intelligence on how they fight, or what their order of battle might be. Right now we have little more than an opinion, Harm."

"What's that opinion, Whirr?"

She looked away from him for a moment, and the sunlight reflected across her multi-faceted ruby eyes. Her gaze returned to him. While the MinSha facial structure rarely gave a clue to their demeanor, nothing as perceptible as their antennae movements, her lower jaw worked from side to side. "They have a considerable amount of firepower at their disposal. Infantry forces, a high number of skiffs, and flyers, too. On a slate? They're a peer to our forces on the ground level. We have no idea what their flyers are capable of and without our own? I worry about that. If they attack, we must determine what can take down those flyers and knock out those skiffs. I don't believe their infantry to be a match for the CASPers. They're no match for *my* platoon."

He tried to smile at her comment, but he knew she was deadly serious. The MinSha infantry she'd brought with her were formidable. The last thing he'd want to see was a dozen of the MinSha female warriors rushing his position. For a split second, his memory flashed to his own mercenary training at a small former Army post on the island of Puerto Rico. They'd arrived on a transport aircraft, debarked and grabbed their gear, and found themselves holding two ice cold cans of Puerto Rican beer apiece. While they rode a bus to the camp, a safety officer stood in the front of the bus and went through a familiar litany for those in any mercenary outfit. When the officer got to one part, though, the collected mercenaries, veterans and newbies alike, listened.

"There are packs of feral dogs in the camp. They've been known to follow, chase, and even tree soldiers. If you walk anywhere after dark, make sure you have a weapon with you."

Most of them laughed at the admonition and instructions. They were soldiers of fortune. Why would they worry about a pack of feral dogs? What could be so terrifying about that? They chuckled, drank their beer, and focused on the training. One evening Harmon took a break to place a video call to a girlfriend in Alabama. Without a thought he walked in the dark from his barracks to the communications building about four blocks away. After the call was completed, he walked out of the building to find a stray dog lying on its side on the concrete walkway, literally blocking his way.

The dog had looked up at him with curiosity and then laid back down. He started walking, and the dog snapped upright, its head and eyes turned into the shadows at the end of the building not more than thirty meters away. He'd kept walking, passing the alert dog, heading back toward his barracks until the dog on the walkway started growling. Loudly. Twenty-four years of age and somewhat experienced, Harmon Gray broke into a run back to his barracks, convinced that a pack of feral dogs were going to tree him, or worse.

The Zuul, the Trenta Knights, weren't feral dogs. They were mercenaries. That they'd been part of a contract on Snowmass for the last however many years didn't matter. They were well-armed and seemingly well trained. Six hundred of them occupied different areas of the planet, with the main complement of three hundred on the other side of New Perth at their headquarters. His total forces of MinSha infantry, CASPer pilots, and support personnel numbered 98 on the ground, with another 45 in orbit on *Taal's Fury*.

Three-to-one odds. I'm supposed to be all confident and brave with those odds, right?

"Those skiffs and flyers could be a match for us," Gray said. He tapped his wrist slate and opened up a communication channel to his leaders: Whirr, Vuong, Morris, and Carter. "Prepare to defend the compound. I believe an attack is imminent. Set general quarters, and get pilots to their CASPers, but do it without urgency. We're being observed from multiple positions. You know what to do—get ready to protect what we've got. Gray, out."

The slate chimed. Vuong.

"Goblin 6, Avenger 6." The man was all business, all the time. "Incoming transmission from Deathangel 25. Relaying to you. Link window is fifty-three seconds."

"Copy."

Tara Mason's voice came through his slate with such clarity he thought she was standing right next to him. "Harm? What's the situation there?"

He told her. "What are your orders, Tara?"

"Get Carter to my position. Have them fly nap of the earth and avoid air traffic control problems. He'll know what to do. I want you out of there before they attack. I have coordinates for you. Execute a plan to get your CASPers where I need them."

A pang of disappointment—the desire for action for their forces—ran through him quickly and was almost instantly replaced by inspiration. "Roger that. I'm going old school with my plan. Like 1777."

"Trusting you, Harm. No more split ops after this. We stay together and accomplish…"

The connection faded. He tapped his slate, but a flashing icon reading SIGNAL LOST flashed multiple times and faded away.

Damn.

He glanced at Whirr. "I'm unfamiliar with 1777."

Gray smiled. "The boss wants us up north. We'll get there with a little historical, tactical influence, that's all."

His slate chimed again, this time with a simple text message. He looked at the slate with a grimace. "Man, the hits just keep on coming."

"What do you mean?"

"Sophie Pryce wants to meet. Officially."

Whirr's antennae bounced. "She's going to officially offer the contract we don't want."

"Which is undoubtedly the catalyst behind the Knight's attack." Gray frowned. "Here we go, kids. Fuck me."

* * *

Mako 15

Snowmass

Flight plans filed and clearance granted, *Mako 15* lifted off from the commercial pad at New Perth and turned north. Carter worked the controls, while Mata ensured their path was clear until they reached the departure corridor and outer marker beacons. Satisfied, she fine-tuned their course until it was headed precisely toward their objective, so when the time came to divert, they wouldn't have to move very far from their flight plan.

"Are you sure about this?" She glanced across the cockpit at Carter.

"Absolutely. All we have to do is play our cards right, and air traffic control will never know the difference. I'm willing to bet they haven't dealt with this kind of dropship inside their atmosphere, and their climatological reports discuss frequent thruster anomalies for space-capable ships in their atmosphere. We just have to follow that script."

"I don't feel right declaring an emergency when there isn't one."

"Well, if it'll make you feel any better, there really is an emergency. I mean, let's face it, Tara and the others are on the ground, and they need recovery. We have to do it clandestinely. Air controllers here or on any other planet realize mercenary forces can do whatever the hell they want to do. Here, we're just telling a little white lie regarding what we need to do. Hopefully the event doesn't call any attention to what we're actually trying to accomplish. We have to get them out of there and proceed north on the boss's orders. Kinda sets our priority," Carter said. The dropship buffeted as it passed five thousand meters altitude, and the forward thrusters fired.

Mata screwed up her face in disgust. "I don't know. I just don't like it. There are a lot of things on this planet I don't like."

Carter laughed. "Relax, honey. Everything will be fine. We're avoiding Lake Pryce, which seems to be their most sensitive area. All we have to do is maintain a course and speed that takes us close enough to Tara's position, then we slow down, declare an in-flight thruster anomaly, and emergency land. When we land, we just happen to pick up the Misfits, and then we proceed on to Glacier Falls under air traffic control radar capabilities."

"But Tara wants us to drop them short of Glacier Falls. That doesn't make any sense."

"Sure it does. All we have to do is get there." Carter took a deep breath. She thought he might be getting frustrated with her, but understanding the mission plan seemed to be a critical item they'd forgotten in the pre-flight briefing. "Look, the first part of the plan is pretty simple. We maintain course and speed at the altitudes they give us, and everything will be fine. When we reach our initial objective, we declare an in-flight anomaly and tell the air traffic controller we're going to emergency land and evaluate our situation. We land at the LZ where the Misfits are waiting. From there, everybody gets onboard, we have time to reset our cargo, then make sure everybody's in place before we're ready to lift off again. The critical factor is that once we lift off, we'll fly nap of the earth all the way to the landing zone outside Glacier Falls. We drop off our cargo, circle around, fly south maybe a hundred kilometers, and then we climb slowly to just short of our original altitude south of Glacier Falls. Air traffic control picks us up, we tell him we had some issues with thrusters and can we arrange a maintenance check at Glacier Falls. They'll agree. We land on their pad and examine our thrusters, only to find that everything is good. We file an anomalous thruster report, just like a hundred different ones in their database, and then we fly back to New Perth for another load. Simple."

Mata chuckled. "I wish I had your confidence about this. It seems like there are too many moving pieces for this little exercise to actually work."

"Spoken like a grunt." Carter snorted.

"Screw you." She laughed louder, and considerable tension left her body in response. "I just have a more cynical view of ground operations than you do, flyboy."

"Which is why you're gonna be a hell of a flyer pilot, honey. Right now all we gotta do is get our cargo to its required destination. Once we do that, everything will be fine."

And it was fine. Following their flight plan, Carter put them at the right altitude and speed for the journey north. About twenty kilometers shy of Tara Mason's requested drop zone, Carter took the controls from the autopilot and got to work. Retarding the throttle, Carter decelerated the ship and let the nose drift toward the ground. The key was not to do it too quickly and give air traffic control the impression they were going to crash land. A crash landing meant rescue teams could be sent and spoil the entire operation. Once the ship had descended more than three thousand feet below its required altitude, air traffic control radioed them on the planetary frequency.

"*Mako 15*, this is New Perth Center. Show you descending below altitude clearance and off speed. Do you have a situation on board?"

"New Perth Center, *Mako 15*. Experiencing some intermittent thruster problems. Requesting permission to set her down on clear terrain ahead and inspect our thrusters visually from the outside. How copy?"

"*Mako 15*, New Perth Center. Roger. You have clear terrain at fifteen kilometers bearing 008. Can you visually identify?"

Mata stared out the front displays and immediately saw where they were intending to put down. The heads-up display identified the clearing as Tara Mason's requested drop zone coordinates.

This is really gonna work.

"Copy, New Perth, I have visual on the site. Once we identify our situation, we'll let you know what our plans are. Please have a maintenance team on standby for deployment to Glacier Falls.

"Roger, *Mako 15*. Please advise on your situation within an hour. New Perth, out."

Carter turned to her and smiled impossibly wide. "See? They totally bought it. We'll put her down, load our cargo, then get off the ground. The only difference will be that once we take off, you're gonna hug the treetops all the way to the other landing zone."

Mata couldn't help but smile, even though she shook her head. "Still seems too easy."

"Like I said, spoken like a grunt."

* * *

Headquarters, Trenta Knights
New Perth

Inside the Trenta Knights Intelligence Center, Gnrra monitored the air traffic control frequencies regularly. Communication from *Mako 15*, the commercial ship registered to Gray's Goblins, caught his ears. The dropship was flying north to Glacier Falls for supplies and had experienced an in-flight anomaly. Instructions from New Perth Center directed the aircraft to land in clear mountainous terrain twenty kilometers to the east of Lake Pryce. Their particular situation wasn't unheard of on Snowmass. Dropships operating in atmosphere often had issues with the planet's unstable atmosphere. The differing pressure gradients and powerful storms could cause problems. So it wasn't unheard of for a dropship to want to stop mid-flight and check its systems before continuing on—no one wanted an incident to darken Snowmass's reputation. The problem in this case was the location of *Mako 15* and where it would land.

No more than an hour before, sensors from Lake Pryce indicated a possible low-power transmission in the same general area east of the facility. While weak, it was still enough to convince Gnrra that there might be something or someone operating in the area. The laser burst itself wasn't enough criteria to let Colonel Krukk know what was happening. There were several instances of unexplained weather phenomena across the planet. He'd learned a lesson as a very young lieutenant not to interrupt the boss, especially on a day when pre-combat inspections seemed to be the letter of the law. If he did interrupt, it needed to be good information. As an intelligence officer, there were many times he felt the necessity to act from his gut instincts. This was one of those times.

Gnrra engaged communications equipment that connected privately to Colonel Krukk. The response was gruff and direct.

"What is it?"

"Sir, I have two seemingly unrelated incidents in the same geographic area that might require consideration. Both would not be reportable events from your established collection guidance, but together they present a possibility I believe must be considered."

"What's the situation, Gnrra? Spit it out."

Gnrra related the detected laser burst near Lake Pryce and the in-flight emergency for *Mako 15*. He kept it short and to the point. Commanders usually liked receiving clear statements, especially with intelligence; state the facts, avoid conjecture, and be prepared to respond for analysis and further information.

The colonel's response surprised Gnrra. "Understood. Keep watching the situation and let me know if anything changes."

"Yes, sir." Gnrra covered his shock by maintaining his voice with a neutral monotone. In the past, intelligence like this had been actionable enough for the commander to deploy a team forward to check it out. That didn't appear to be the case this time.

I wonder what's different?

He consulted the closed-circuit television cameras hovering over the compound and watched the pre-combat checks and inspections continuing for the primary infantry and aerial forces. The realization came to him like a thunderbolt.

We're going to attack the Goblins. That could be the reason we spent three hours this afternoon preparing our gear into a ready one status.

Gnrra considered what the commander's logic might be. Yes, the commercial transport registered to the Goblins was having trouble in the area around Lake Pryce. They'd already overflown the facility there a couple of days earlier with no incident. While the Knights' missile batteries tracked the dropship via radar, they hadn't engaged or even attempted to lock the target.

What if that first flight was a sensing mission? Then an even more ominous thought came to him. *What if that first flight dropped a reconnaissance team? Our sensors aren't good enough to find them in the recent rain and fog. What if they've been watching what we're doing at Lake Pryce?*

Quickly, the virtual certainty came to him that the Goblins had done just that. Based on where *Mako 15* had been directed to land, it would make sense that a reconnaissance team would have had the time and the ability to cross twenty kilometers of terrain to get there. The escarpment and higher terrain would naturally shield them from the missile batteries at Lake Pryce.

The more he thought about it, Gnrra realized he might be correct. The problem was "might." Nothing was certain. Instead of interrupting the colonel one more time, he kept the assessment to himself. Colonel Krukk was clear that he didn't want to be interrupted. If he was truly in the final stages of planning an attack, he'd fine and penalize Gnrra for the interruption. Losing credits wasn't worth the risk. Depending upon what happened with *Mako 15*, which he believed would be to check their thrusters and find everything nominal, if it was a sensing mission, the dropship would return to New Perth for maintenance. If not, they would continue on to Glacier Falls.

Gnrra turned his attention to the sensors and cameras and saw that everything was normal, or as close to normal as possible around

New Perth. Satisfied, he let his eyes linger on the Tri-V as the local news program came on. He'd had a crush on the Human anchor for as long as he could remember. Watching the woman's long, golden hair shine in the studio lighting, he forgot everything else.

* * * * *

Chapter Twenty-Six

10km ESE of Lake Pryce

Snowmass

The sudden burst of emotion when her teammates appeared in the woods surprised Araceli. She'd assumed since she'd lost so many friends over the course of recent events that she was over feeling any attachment to anyone. With fresh tears in her eyes, the young woman let go a happy sob from her throat. As the remaining Misfits approached, she saw smiles on the faces of Q and Homer. Both seemed genuinely happy to see her. Behind them, tromping ominously through the forest, came Deathangel 25.

She snapped the controls to open the CASPer's cockpit. Immediately, fresh, cool air filled the cockpit, carrying with it the smell of the alien forest and recent rains. Before the clamshell had even opened fully, Araceli disengaged her harness and climbed through the front of the cockpit. She jumped to the ground as Quin'taa and Homer jogged toward her excitedly. Homer reached her first and scooped her up into an embrace that thrilled and terrified her at the same time.

"I'm so happy to see you!" Homer said. "We were worried you didn't make it."

Araceli didn't respond as another happy sob threatened to choke her words. Instead, she squeezed the Pushtal tighter until he set her gently on the ground.

Quin'taa walked up and greeted her in the Oogar way. Lowering his face to a few inches from hers, he closed his eyes and sniffed both sides of her neck. Foolishly, she felt like she should do the same thing. Quin'taa snorted, a rumble of thunder sounding from his chest.

"I, too, am thrilled to see you, little one." He grinned at her. "We've always suspected you are resilient, but you've proven it today. I am proud to call you my friend."

More tears came. She wiped them away with a laugh and tried to smile. The Oogar's face screwed in sudden confusion.

"Have I upset you further, little one?"

"No," she blurted out and then threw her arms around the surprised Oogar's neck. "I'm happy, Quin'taa. Happy to be your friend and teammate. Just happy as hell you're all alive."

"We feel the same way," Homer replied. Quin'taa released her embrace and peered closely at her as if checking her for wounds.

"You are unhurt?"

"Not a scratch," Araceli said.

She heard the cockpit opening sequence of the other CASPer nearby and knew Tara Mason was dismounting her mech. Quin'taa stood erect and half turned. Her unlikely teammates faced her as Tara walked up. Her commander's face had always seemed stern and unforgiving, until that moment. Tara smiled down at Araceli and wordlessly opened her arms for an embrace. Araceli stepped forward and wrapped her arms around Tara, who reciprocated the gesture. In silence, they stood there holding each other for a good two minutes.

Fresh tears came fast, much faster than she expected. Standing in Tara's arms, the crushing loneliness she'd felt since the death of her parents finally overwhelmed her, and there was no choice but to let it out, which she did in great, heaving sobs.

"It's okay, honey," Tara whispered into her ear. "Let it out, Araceli. I'm here for you."

"*We're* here for you," Quin'taa rumbled and stepped closer. She heard the distinctive slap of one of the Oogar's paws against the shoulder armor of the Pushtal.

Homer yelped. "We're here, kid. We've got you."

"I'm sorry," she choked out as her normal breathing returned slowly around double breaths.

"For what?" Quin'taa asked. "The rivers of emotion we carry must flow, Araceli. Damming them does no good."

"Crying like this isn't what a CASPer pilot does," Araceli said as she stepped back from Tara's arms.

The older woman's hands were still on her shoulders, and her commander smiled. "It's okay, Araceli. I understand. Probably more than you know."

Araceli only nodded. "This company is all I have now."

Quin'taa rumbled. "We are your family, cub."

"We're not gonna let you down," Homer added. The Pushtal smiled, and his eyes glimmered with mischief. "Not so bad for a Human, present company excluded, Colonel Mason."

As usual, the Pushtal had broken the tension. Araceli wiped her eyes and dried her cheeks. "I'm so glad to see you all," she said.

Tara's smile faltered slightly. "Tell us what happened, and what you found."

Araceli shrugged. "My auto-deployment sequence appeared as if it would fire prematurely, so I disengaged it while I fell through the cloud deck. I lost radio with you all instantly in the soup and took a lightning strike to my antenna package. Scared me pretty good. I went to manual deployment and used the radar altimeter, then fired the chute at about five hundred feet. The wind was awful. I think I swung once to the left, and the jump jets fired to land me upright."

She took a deep breath and continued, "After landing, I got a weak beacon signal from Misfit 3—Ladow's—platform. With no contact with you, I followed the old standard operating procedure we used in the Victoria Forces: I doubled back to find the teammate I could locate. When I got there, Ladow was dead. It looks like the secondary parachutes failed during the descent, and she crashed into a rock outcropping. The harness tore her to bits."

"What about Each?" Tara asked. "Did you find any trace of him?"

"No, ma'am. I found his reserve parachute, but there was nothing else to see. I found some…well, they looked like buzzards flying over the area, but I couldn't see anything in the forest below. I'd imagine he's dead, but the terrain was too steep to investigate any further."

Tara frowned. "I don't like leaving them on the field, but there's nothing we can do about it now. I'll have *Mako 15* scan for him when they fly back to New Perth. Their sensors are better than what's on board the CASPer. Thank you for looking for them."

Araceli nodded. "Yes, ma'am."

Tara checked her wrist slate. "They should be here anytime now. As much as I think we're out of danger, let's post security and be ready. Mount up, Araceli. Quin'taa, you have point when we move to the dropship. Let's hustle and make sure we don't look like our namesake suggests."

"Does that mean you're going to let us keep it, ma'am?" Homer asked.

Tara nodded. "I think so. Now if I can just figure out what to do with you all."

* * *

Goblins' Cantonment Area
Snowmass

When the security guard at their front gate called, there was little doubt in Harmon Gray's mind who their visitor could be. Instead of dispatching one of the younger officers like Morris to fetch the visitor, he left his makeshift office and stepped out into the cooler afternoon. Heavy gray clouds swallowed the western horizon, and in the crisp air there was the unmistakable smell of snow. He'd heard stories from the locals about the sudden approach of winter. Seasons changing as if autumn never existed, and they transitioned from warm, sunny days to frigid, icy winters in the blink of an eye. Every culture complained about the weather, that much was a given across even the expanse of the Galactic Union. However, on Snowmass, he had more than ample reason to believe the gloomy predictions of the locals. The long, cold winter was upon them, and as much as he'd hoped to be off the planet and on to the next in the search for Snowman, there was nowhere to go because business remained unfinished.

His headset buzzed, and he tapped it as he stepped outside. "Yeah?"

"She's here, yes?"

"Yeah, Whirr. She's here," Gray said. "Keep everybody working, but don't make it look like we're in the process of evacuation, will you?"

"That may be difficult, Harm. Perhaps a wise course of action is for you to keep her at the security perimeter and not allow her inside."

Gray couldn't help but smile. "Well, I wasn't planning on her coming inside. But she's not the only one we have to keep up the charade for, you know."

"The Knights have vacated their positions," Whirr replied. "I've got eyes on their empty manned positions, and Lucille has connected to the closed-circuit system, and can, if we need her to, move them to cover our movement. She's also recording remotely."

"Copy, that." Gray walked toward the front security gate. He saw Sophie Pryce standing outside the gate in her impeccably fitting teal business suit and perfect hair. She looked the part of the professional businesswoman, and as much as he didn't want to admit her apparent role in the unraveling of Snowmass, he accepted the very real possibility that it was she who'd ordered the assassination of Veeka. If that was the case, there was also little doubt in his mind she'd planned to play the Knights against the Goblins. Her appearance at the compound, now, with the Knights engaged in pre-combat checks and drills, was undoubtedly to deliver the *coup de grâce*. If it was indeed the full contract to take over the Knights' contract for the security of Snowmass, there was little doubt of two outcomes.

First, the Trenta Knights would attack as Tara Mason had forecast. He had to wonder how she'd known that would be the case, but ultimately it wouldn't matter. Second, and possibly the more concerning, was the collapse of the local government and the Dream World Consortium presence on Snowmass. While they'd been sporadic guardians, they were the government. Amid a heavy winter, the outlying farming communities could fail and destabilize everything. Aside from Snowmass' export market, lives were at risk. Tara Mason seemed to have a plan for the Knights' imminent attack, hence his movement north, but what could she possibly have worked out to stabilize the government?

Maybe that's the Peacemakers' job, Harm.

And maybe pigs will fly out my ass.

He took a deep breath and kept walking. Around him, maintenance crews moved two separate Mk 6 CASPers into their maintenance racks across the tight thoroughfare they'd constructed with shipping containers, more for security than actual use. Even with the distance between them, he could see Sophie follow the CASPers with her eyes and take in every detail she could.

Sophie Pryce was beautiful, but her heart was cold.

Gray sighed. *Dammit, Marsha. Why couldn't it have been you?*

Before he'd gone to the CASPer course at Camp Benning right out of high school, Gray had known a country girl from western North Carolina named Marsha. They'd worked at the local supermarket together. He'd been a stock boy, and she'd found a job as a register attendant right after she and her mother moved into town. He'd never asked about the situation, but it was clear they'd fled from something or someone. Her mother was nice when she was sober, but Marsha was unlike any woman he'd met in his short life.

They'd both been athletes. She played basketball, and he was starting linebacker for Asheville High School. Her physicality drew him in, and before either of them had known what they were doing, they'd made love in her mother's trailer. A few months later, he'd looked down into her eyes after they'd made love and said, "I love you."

Her brown eyes widened slightly, but she hadn't said the words back to him. They'd embraced a last time before he caught the bus to Camp Benning. After the year-long course, he'd come home and found her running an aquatics program in town. He stopped by the pool, and they had a shitty lunch from the concession stand and went their separate ways. While she didn't pervade his thoughts daily, she represented a road not taken, and he knew when his thoughts turned to her, he'd really fucked up the present.

Come on, Harm. Not now.

He tried another deep breath with no palpable relief. *What's that crazy shit the Peacemakers do? How the fuck does that calm them—*

"Hello, Commander Gray," Sophie Pryce called out as he approached. "Sorry to bother you. I know you're very busy refitting your company, but I wanted to…discuss something with you. Privately, if we may?"

Gray shrugged. "I really don't have a place, Miss Pryce. My apologies, but I think we can speak here if that would be fine with you?"

She smiled, but the glint in her eyes said she was far from happy about being kept at the security gate. "Certainly. I understand. You must be very busy."

Probing, huh?

Gray nodded. "The parts we've been able to gather, unfortunately, aren't filling some of our more critical needs. We're making do, but it requires longer hours and lots of unnecessary stress."

That ought to be enough for you.

Pryce nodded and consulted her slate. "I'm not sure how to tell you this…"

Gray shifted his weight and kept his face neutral. "What do you mean?"

"I think the Trenta Knights are considering an attack on your forces, Harmon." She looked up at him. "I worry they may do something before you can defend yourselves."

"I see," Gray replied. "Doesn't the government have any restraint they could enforce?"

Pryce shook her head. "Not right now. The Knights are within their renegotiation period, and there are some vagaries as to what we can and cannot do during this time."

Bullshit. I've read that contract, Sophie. You could shut them down if you wanted. The problem is you're afraid they'd turn on you.

Gray twisted the knife, so to speak. "Aren't there two Peacemakers on the planet? Couldn't you ask them to intervene? I mean, if you have concerns about the contract, they'd be able to assist."

"The Peacemakers are handling the attack in the square at the insistence of the mayor's office. They've moved to Glacier Falls to interview possible suspects. We've been unable to contact them."

Again, bullshit.

"Well, you know the Knights better than anyone. How soon do you think they'll attack?"

"As little as six hours." Pryce grimaced. "I'm here to offer you the complete Snowmass defense contract, Captain Gray. Will you be able to review and sign it as soon as possible?"

Gray nodded. "I'll review it, certainly. Provided the Knights don't attack, I expect we can negotiate the final contract this evening, then? Perhaps over dinner?"

Pryce smiled, and then her grin widened a bit. "That sounds perfect. I'll make reservations for us. Is Southgate acceptable?"

"Best steak I ever had," he lied. If the Knights were going to attack in six hours, just before dinner, and she wanted the Goblins to have the contract, dinner would be out of the question. She wanted him away from the compound under the assumption his subordinate commanders would fold in combat.

"Great. I'll let you know as soon as I can. You'll do the same?"

"Of course," Gray replied.

Pryce stepped forward on her tiptoes and kissed his cheek before she turned and walked purposefully toward Government Center.

"Is that normal for Human duplicity?" Whirr's voice chittered in his headset.

Gray watched Pryce walk away. "Pretty much. Lucille got all that recorded?"

"Video and audio," Whirr replied. "I'd ask how Miss Pryce knows the Knights are planning an attack versus drilling themselves stupid right now."

"That's one question." Gray turned and walked back into the center of the compound. "The other question is how much does she know about what we're really doing? Did you catch her comment about the Peacemakers and the mayor's office?"

"I did. Her intent may be to usurp the office."

Gray laughed. "Oh, I think that's her goal. What bothers me is she's willing to risk collateral damage between two mercenary companies at the edge of the city to get what she wants. What's our status right now?"

"The second load is at eighty percent. We'll have everything but the tanks moved. We can't risk another flight to get them out."

Gray spat in the mud. *Dammit.*

An idea formed. "Whirr? Get Morris and meet me at the tanks. Five minutes. I've got an idea."

Whirr chittered. "We'll be there, Harmon. What did you mean about 1777? Is that a reference to Human history?"

"A hell of a story." Gray chuckled. "One we're going to replicate tonight when the Knights attack us."

* * *

Aboard Commercial Transport

Snowmass

As a child, Jackson Rains hadn't flown in an aircraft until he was twelve. Moving between the foster programs of Georgia and Mississippi, they'd placed him on an airplane in the Hartsfield-Atlanta International Airport bound for Jackson, Mississippi. The airport was a crowded, chaotic place for a child. The shiny airplanes and the glossy advertisements for everything from jewelry to food he'd never known existed called to his senses. As much as he'd wanted to observe everything around him, the handlers from the foster agency had dragged him by the arms to his gate. They'd sat him in the first row of a small, propeller-driven aircraft that smelled of oil and disinfectant. In contrast to the shiny airport, the aircraft itself was dirty and old.

The plane was full and hot during the entire trip. A man seated near him complained about the air conditioning system and kept twisting small vents above his head. When the propellers roared to life, Jackson had pulled his knees up to his chest and tucked his chin to his chest in abject fear. No one consoled him. No one bothered him at all. From the time the plane leapt into the air until the wheels bounced onto the destination's runway, his eyes were closed, and he was oblivious to the outside world.

Interstellar travel, and the displeasure of the hyperspace transition on the Human equilibrium, cured his fear of flying to a certain point. Flying over the northern continent of Snowmass with another massive storm approaching caused turbulence like he'd never seen before. The urge to close his eyes overwhelmed him several times, and one particular jolt felt like the aircraft had dropped through a hole in the sky. Jackson grasped for the armrests.

"You okay?" Vannix turned to look up at him from her seat.

"Yeah," he grunted, but he was far from okay. "How much longer?"

Vannix consulted her slate. "We land in thirty-eight minutes. For what it's worth, the weather forecast at Northingham is much calmer. We should see smoother air soon."

Rains nodded and looked for the hundredth time toward the fuselage wall. "Would be better if there was a window."

"Trust your balance, Jackson. You remember all those tricks, yes?"

He did, but the last thing on his mind was trying a breathing routine or some mental exercise. Rains wanted the fuck off the roller coaster flight. He closed his eyes, pressed his head back against the seat, and tried to relax between bursts of turbulence.

His peace only lasted for a couple of minutes. A familiar and distinct chime sounded from his slate. It was the notification that duty had to be addressed right then and there. When the guild called, a Peacemaker wasn't to look away. He opened his eyes and saw Vannix studying her slate as well. He tapped the screen and saw the incoming message from Stormwatch. With another series of taps, he activated the slate's decryption package.

Stormwatch was a combination of official report and clandestine message service specifically used by the Peacemaker Guild. He opened the message and immediately saw it wasn't an authentic Stormwatch message, despite having the same appearance, syntax, and internal coding. On inspection, the message appeared to have been constructed by Lucille. There were certain matters of legality to be considered, given the Stormwatch coding, and its clandestine capabilities were restricted to authorized members of the guild. That being said, they'd needed a secure way to talk with Force 25 during the mission on Snowmass, and hadn't had any other way to do so without attracting unwanted attention to themselves or to the others playing their roles. A Stormwatch messaging was a viable option, and given the tactical situation, there was little doubt Guild Master Rsach would have approved the use of the message structure.

Rains watched the message appear in code and then resolve itself on his screen.

<<Message follows. Believe an attack on Force 25 imminent at New Perth. Trenta Knights conducting pre-combat inspections and preparing vehicles. Local government concerned, but likely manipulating the situation via proxy. Force 25 assets under evacuation order and moving north for assembly area thirty kilometers outside Glacier Falls. Commander and Misfit elements are already in place and maintaining surveillance of the target area.>>

Rains glanced up and saw his partner looking at him intently. He could almost read her mind. *They're moving north. Why?*

The next frame of the new message loaded. <<Working to locate next subject. Hopeful to find her based on intelligence you received.>>

His brow furrowed in confusion. *How do they know we gained intelligence from Veeka? We haven't reported anything.*

He mentally slapped himself. *Lucille. Dumbass. She's on both sides of this and is much more than a message service. Get it through your thick head, Jackson.*

The final frame of the message read, <<Understand the situation with Maarg. Advise on any action or intelligence via this platform.>>

The aircraft seemed to have found calmer air. With the ride smooth, Rains wanted to consult with Vannix about what they'd read, but he didn't trust the privately arranged aircraft or its crew. Critical intelligence like this could be easily compromised. Instead, he used the GalNet connection from aircraft to terrestrial servers there on Snowmass.

The Knights always planned like Zuparti. They've never executed a combat operation without a significant amount of planning.

As he considered his thoughts, Rains connected to a server at Government Center with the login information Citsym had given them. Mayor Citsym was a Zuparti and, were he typical of his species, he'd have notes for just about everything he did. Even as a Dream World Consortium planet, the mayor's office and all governmental entities were required to have open files for routine business. While the mayor himself had done nothing to suggest impropriety, Rains couldn't help but wonder if they'd missed an opportunity to investigate his routine dealings on a more thorough basis. Rains found and selected an information site for the mayor's office. There wasn't much available to the public without a separate login credential, but there was access to the mayor's office calendar. He looked into the mayor's activities for the last several months to see if there was anything that could shed some light on the current situation. He didn't have to search long.

Three days ago. A calendar entry doesn't list the attendees by name and says it was a matter of critical importance and was secured for those reasons.

Digging farther into the information, Rains found a similar meeting note from the Office of Immigration for the same time and location. There was more information in their unsecured meeting notes. The appointment between the head of immigration and the mayor was to provide an update on undocumented individuals. A total of 30 subjects were reviewed, but they struck six from the docket at the mayor's request. He needed to see who the mayor didn't want to count for the official report to the DWC. Rains tapped the screen information and sent it over the private connection he and his partner had with Lucille. The response was immediate.

<<There's no information on the subjects discussed in this meeting. There is however visual evidence that was presented to the mayor left on an under-classified system. Would you like me to access it?>>

Rains quickly tapped, "Yes."

Several images appeared, and it was fairly obvious that the government of Snowmass was now aware Reecha was both alive and still on the planet. There were also pictures of her and smaller Veetanho who were undoubtedly her family. Further down in the information, though, were images from the closed-circuit security cameras across Snowmass. There were two figures, easily identifiable by their species. A Zuparti with brown fur and a large, coal black Equiri. The latter Rains knew on sight.

Knew I'd find you here, Thraff.

Lucille ran a facial recognition scan on the Zuparti from the Peacemaker files and found the official criminal record of Ch'tek.

The little bastard who tried to ship a Canavar egg to Earth. Jessica stopped his ass cold, too.

Rains smiled.

There was also little doubt the two of them had captured Maarg. The complicating factor to her disappearance was that the contracted aircraft supposedly flying them to Glacier Falls had disappeared from radar a few hours earlier. With a massive snow squall approaching, and their own operation underway in New Perth, the rescue assets from the Trenta Knights had decided not to pursue a search. The last known position of the aircraft was three hundred miles north of New Perth at a location equidistant between the two cities.

Easy to fake a crash when nobody gives a shit about you.

He surmised they landed somewhere near the caverns. Dropping off radar on Snowmass was easy to do because of the mountainous terrain on the northern continent. Likewise, there was very little doubt in his mind they were going out to do the same thing. Reecha knew something, or she had something, and she'd been able to keep her presence on Snowmass quiet for decades. No one had found her until recently. While Maarg had great capabilities with networks and information, he doubted she had the knowledge or the skills Thraff wanted from her to find Reecha.

We have an advantage with Lucille. All we have to do is get there in time.

Rains sat back in his seat as the aircraft started its initial descent into Northingham. They'd have a hefty layover until their next flight to Glacier Falls, but that was okay. He'd be off the aircraft on stable ground, and that was enough for him.

* * * * *

Chapter Twenty-Seven

Snowmass

Whether it was common sense or an intense desire for self-preservation, Maarg decided to largely remain quiet during her captivity. Part of her wanted to observe her two captors as closely as possible. She recognized their names, more from reputations than her own research, and understanding their motives seemed like the thing to do. Ch'tek was the one she knew the least about, having only skimmed the files provided by Jessica Francis several months before. His name was familiar enough that she associated him with the Dream World Consortium, but at the same time she didn't understand who he was or why he'd chosen the side he'd apparently chosen.

Thraff had much clearer motives and allegiances. Everything Peacemaker Rains had reported about the Equiri thug resonated true. His every word, every steely glance, and every movement was both sinister and powerful. He was the chief associate of Kr'et'Socae, and it showed.

In the first moments of her captivity, Maarg believed them to be fairly docile, wanting only to find Reecha. They'd gone to the airfield and hired a private commercial aircraft to take them on the four-hundred-kilometer journey north to Glacier Falls. They were cleared for departure when Thraff stood from his seat and walked aft toward the cargo compartments. It might have been for the lavatory, so she paid it no mind as the aircraft took off, turned north, and climbed. As soon as they leveled off, the flight crew indicated the aircraft was at a safe altitude for them to get up and move around. No sooner had their announcement ended than Thraff walked past, and she saw the large pistol in his hand. He deactivated the cockpit door, stepped inside, and there were two quick shots. He dragged the dead Humans into the passageway and stepped over them into the cockpit. He glanced at Ch'tek and slammed the door behind him. Maarg watched in rapt fascination, her mouth agape.

Ch'tek laughed. "What's the matter? You look like you've seen a ghost. That's funny, because to the rest of the galaxy, you and your species *are* ghosts. All two hundred and twelve of you."

Marge snapped her eyes to him. "There's over three hundred in my colony."

"I'll be sure to update my intelligence."

Dammit. Don't give them anything, Maarg!

She tried to salvage the situation. "Then again, my colony is only one of several."

Ch'tek was having nothing of it. "Please, young one. I know better."

"Well, if you know better, then why am I here? What do you want from me? You said it's not about my physical capabilities, so what is it?"

"Not your physical capabilities, no. If we wanted to, I'm certain we could process our own with an even greater, shall we say, purity than recent attempts showed. We've tried a few procedures here and there, even some you've probably heard about recently. No, your biosynthetic diamonds are not my concern. We've watched you from the moment you hit the ground here, and it's fairly obvious you have a talent for getting into computer systems you're not supposed to. That's why you're here now."

"Why couldn't we have done this from New Perth?"

"For what we need, it's best to be on site and right at the terminal. Breaking into a secure compound isn't something easily done. Realizing you're not our best option, but a good one nonetheless, we want you to have every opportunity to succeed. After all, your life depends on it." Ch'tek grinned at her.

Maarg paused and let her thoughts work for a moment. Her talents for infiltrating computer networks notwithstanding, they wanted her to get into a secure compound. What kind of secure compound? There were a million technical details she wanted to ask about, and watching how Thraff had dealt with the two Human pilots, she wondered how much leeway she had.

"You seem pensive," Ch'tek said. "I would imagine right now you're wondering what it is exactly we want you to do. Is that the case?"

Maarg nodded. "I am, but I'm also wondering exactly how much I can ask before your friend puts a bullet in my head."

"The only way my friend will put a bullet in your head is if you can't do what we need you to do. That should provide you some incentive."

"It does, but it doesn't answer the other question. What's my target?"

Ch'tek looked away for a moment and stroked his chin with one clawed hand. He looked back at her, and an icy, sinister grin crossed his features. "I'm sure you're aware of my history."

Maarg shook her head. "I don't know a thing about you, Ch'tek."

It was mostly the truth. Aside from the mention in Jessica's file, and his ill-advised attempt to send a Canavar egg to Earth, she didn't know a thing about him.

"Don't lie. Your father is a Peacemaker. Your whole species is potentially returning to the Galactic Union because of Jessica Francis. She and I have a particular history. Inasmuch as I'd like my personal revenge upon her, my target is much bigger. As a matter fact, it's the same target she shares. Her father is wanted by the Mercenary Guild, and by several other entities, for information and potentially stolen goods. He has something the rest of the galaxy wants, and I'm determined to figure out what it is."

"So this facility you want me to break into, it belongs to Intergalactic Haulers?"

"We believe so. There are five such compounds on this continent, but this is the one with the additional prize of the Veetanho Reecha. She and Snowman are quite close, and if we find her, she'll tell us where James Francis is so he can be dealt with accordingly."

Maarg shook her head. "You realize all the Intergalactic Haulers' systems and hardware I've dealt with had encryption much more complicated and resilient than anything I can crack with my slate?"

Ch'tek nodded. "We're aware. However, we also think we can provide you a few tools of our own that might be able to do the trick."

The nose of the aircraft pitched down suddenly, and conversation ceased. Maarg thought that was a good thing because it gave her an opportunity to think through some things Ch'tek had said.

They'd give her tools to accomplish the job at hand. They told her that her life would depend upon success. Both couldn't be the case. If they really wanted whatever was in this facility and would stop at nothing to attain it, there was nothing to prevent them from killing her the moment they gained access. They wouldn't want their precious tools captured, either, especially if they proved capable of doing the job. She was in a no-win situation. Exactly the situation her father had warned her about—one requiring her sense of trust.

Your trust is the most important and most precious thing you have. Given to the wrong people, it will cost you dearly. Given to the right people, it will save your life.

She wondered who really had her trust. Clearly it wasn't Ch'tek and his friend, and while she'd originally been concerned that the Peacemakers did anything but instill peace and harmony, she recognized that they had her best interests in hand. And while Tara Mason wasn't a Peacemaker, she did, too.

The speaker in her seat clicked on, and she heard the rumbling, deep voice of Thraff. "Going to drop off their radar. Stay in your seats for the rest of this flight. Given the terrain and what I'll have to do to keep our signature low enough, I can't ensure your safety."

Ch'tek turned and looked at her. "How quaint. He wants you safe? Well, that's only because we need you. For now."

She looked away, and her eyes lingered on the dead bodies of the two Human pilots in the forward passageway. They needed her. There was little doubt in her mind that when they didn't, she would suffer the same fate as the pilots. While hope seemed to be such a Human response, she realized with a certain amount of disdain that hope was all she had. Hope someone had discovered her missing. Hope someone was on their way to save her. Hope they got there in time.

As the aircraft prepared to land, a gust of wind rolled the vehicle thirty degrees hard to the left. Ch'tek reached for the armrest on his seat and pressed with all his might. Maarg thought it was funny until she realized she'd involuntarily done the same thing. The descent was dicey. Buffeting winds moved the aircraft seemingly all over the sky. When the landing gear finally touched the ground, Maarg realized she'd been holding her breath and let it out slowly. She glanced across the aisle at Ch'tek to see if he'd done the same thing.

The cockpit door opened, and Thraff stepped forward. He didn't look at Maarg, instead turning his coal black eyes to Ch'tek. "We didn't make it here in time. The gust front is right over us. We won't be climbing down the ice fall today."

Ch'tek opened an extensive communication suite folded in a small case and sat tapping quietly for a moment. "You've put us right on top of it. The caverns are below us, roughly eight hundred meters. I can tell they're there by comparing our position with the geographic survey from when the planet was terraformed. However, I'm not picking up anything in the electromagnetic spectrum. I'm not seeing any power system, nuclear or geothermal. It's like there's nothing there."

Thraff grunted. "That's exactly what she wants. With this being an Intergalactic Haulers' site, you must understand that it's hardened and protected. Nothing gets in or out that doesn't either have the proper coding or clearance tokens. Francis was smart about how he built these caches."

Ch'tek turned and glanced at Maarg. After a moment, he looked back up at his large partner. "Well, I guess we'll just have to wait until tomorrow. Perhaps we should do a little housekeeping?"

Thraff looked behind him at the dead Humans. He turned back to Ch'tek. "I'll ditch the bodies. Why don't you get out the food we purchased and see about preparing it? Then I'll make sure the gear for our traverse down the mountain is accessible and ready."

"Understood." Ch'tek turned to her. "Not only do you get to see snow for the first time, but you get to climb on ice, too, Maarg. If you survive that, we'll see just how good you are, young one. We'll see."

* * *

Goblins Landing Pad

Snowmass

Loading was complete, and Mata made sure *Mako 15*'s doors and hatches were secured. She checked with the ground crew for clearance before she pushed the throttles forward and took the dropship into the air. Pivoting the craft, she swung the nose toward the northwest for the initial departure vectors they'd given her from ground control. Satisfied all was well, she pushed the throttles forward slightly and accelerated over the city.

Carter was looking out the window. "Do you see what they've done over there?"

Mata risked a glance out Carter's side of the dropship cockpit, and she could see where the Goblins had constructed a defensive perimeter at their initial landing point. "What? The perimeter? Is that what you're talking about?"

Carter kept staring out the window. "It looks like Captain Gray moved all those shipping containers into a hexagonal shape. At four points of the hexagon he's got one of each of the tanks in some kind of elevated firing position."

"I thought we were supposed to bring everything, including the tanks?" Mata asked.

A new voice came from behind them. Harmon Gray climbed up the ladder into the cockpit and stood holding onto handholds along the ceiling. "We couldn't get everything. We got eighty percent, with the remaining twenty percent being the tanks. They're too heavy based on the load plans. We'd have to make at least one more run, and we don't have that kind of time with the storm approaching and the Knights' imminent attack."

Mata turned her view to the opposite side of the cockpit and the right side view screens. The atmosphere above them appeared dark gray, almost green, and frothy and wild in nature. "Looks like it's gonna be a hell of a storm."

Gray replied, "I think that's putting it mildly, Lieutenant. If you guys are good here, I'm going to make sure everyone is strapped in position in the back. What's our ETA to the landing zone outside Glacier Falls?"

Mata glanced at the heads-up display. "Sixty-eight minutes, sir."

"Copy that," Gray said before he turned to the ladder and descended again. Mata and Carter were alone in the cockpit again.

Carter glanced at her. "The boss won't be happy about leaving the tanks behind."

Mata said nothing. She knew Tara Mason had been a tanker in her previous life, and there was undoubtedly a standard operating procedure for Force 25 to have as much combat power as possible at any given time. Tara definitely didn't enjoy leaving anything behind.

"I didn't ask, but are those tanks manned? Do you think he left crews there, too?" she asked.

"No way," Carter replied. "If the Knights are going to attack, we had to at least give them something that looked like a defense perimeter. I'm willing to bet Captain Gray understands that. Maybe he used some programming to make the tanks move and stuff, but I'm reasonably sure he wouldn't leave anybody behind."

As she swung the dropship's nose to the north, she felt the wind gain in intensity from the west. The dropship yawed slightly to the northeast, and she brought it back to center quickly.

"Contact departure, get us a higher altitude. That storm looks vicious," she directed Carter.

Carter smiled. "You got it, boss."

Even in her concentration at flying the dropship, she couldn't suppress the giggle of laughter that came from her throat. They were a good team. She'd never thought about pursuing a relationship while being a mercenary, but with Carter it just felt right. Maybe it was the idea that she wasn't fighting a CASPer all alone anymore. Instead she had an air crew, someone to spend considerable time with for conversation and teamwork. Whatever the cause, she realized she was happy with the relationship and her job for the first time in months. Her time with Carter had been wonderful. Her time learning to be a pilot, not so much.

With a deft touch on the controls, Mata kept *Mako 15* on course and ascending as Carter talked to departure control.

"New Perth Departure, this is *Mako 15*. Request altitude change. Winds at flight level gaining in intensity from the west. Please advise."

The response was immediate. "*Mako 15*, New Perth Departure, proceed to flight level fifteen, report when on station."

Carter replied, "Flight level fifteen. *Mako 15*, out."

Mata was already changing her thrust vectors and climbing to fifteen thousand meters. Above ten thousand meters, the air calmed significantly.

She took a deep breath and let it out in an explosive sigh. Carter told her a pilot always maintained control of their emotions. Even in the worst situations, the best pilots kept their feelings suppressed and really tried to stay in front of the aircraft. She guessed she still had a long way to go, but her relief at the calmer sky was palpable.

"Good job, honey," Carter said next to her. "I'm glad we don't have to make another fully loaded run in this soup."

Mata nodded and relaxed her fingers on the controls of the dropship. The climb to fifteen thousand meters was uneventful, and as they ascended, she glanced over at the approaching storm and marveled at the dark gray blanket rolling across the entire expanse of the northern continent.

"They say the first snowfall around here is pretty significant."

Carter nodded. "Looks like it'll be that way. I'm gonna go check on everybody in the back. Are you good here for a few minutes?"

She nodded. "I got it. Just hurry back."

"I always do."

She watched him unstrap and head back to the ladder quickly. On his way by he gently squeezed her left shoulder, and she smiled in response. For the moment she worried only about flying the aircraft at the present speed and altitude required. They'd be on the ground at Glacier Falls in an hour, and then she could relax. At least for a little while.

Carter returned to the cockpit fifteen minutes later with a frown on his face. Mata could tell something was very wrong. "What is it?"

"We don't have everyone on board. Gray left several people behind."

"What?" Mata's mouth dropped open. "How many did he leave behind?"

"Five. Major Vuong and Lieutenant Morris are in command. They have automated defenses, and they tried to get ready in the event the Knights attack, but he left them there to die."

"The boss isn't going to like that." Mata stated.

"No, she isn't."

One of the longest standing orders for Force 25 was that no one was left behind. Here, Tara Mason's evacuation order was rock solid. She wanted the entire unit moved north. While Captain Gray's idea to automate defenses was good in theory, practice told them that wouldn't be the case.

They flew in silence for the rest of the mission before touching down at the landing zone outside Glacier Falls. They'd had no contact with air traffic control for the last half hour. The storm, and the unique ionizing properties of the precipitation, had blanked out pretty much all their scopes. Communications was solely by voice, and only if necessary. The idea being to keep all channels clear in case someone needed help. There'd been a broadcast twenty minutes before that had said, if necessary, ships were authorized to set down in the nearest clear terrain they could find. The first time around they'd set *Mako 15* down for a maintenance check before going on to Glacier Falls and declaring everything was nominal. This time around, the weather was on their side.

"Landing checklist," Carter said.

Mata tapped her Tri-V displays, and the checklists populated automatically. They ran through the litany of commands to switch positions and readied the dropship for landing just as the position icon identified they were over the designated landing site. On cue, the radio link opened.

"*Mako 15*, this is Deathangel 25. Have you over our position. The landing zone is clear. Winds at the surface are all over the place, but primarily from the west and heavy. How copy?"

Carter replied, "Deathangel 25, Roger all. We've initiated landing. Be on the ground soon. Out."

Mata wiggled in her seat and flexed her hands on the dropship controls. "Here we go."

"You want me to take this?" Carter asked

Mata glared at him. "No. I've got this."

Carter smiled. "Damn right you do."

She focused her efforts on total control of the aircraft, and through the buffeting winds and swirling low clouds, the landing zone appeared below marked with several flares held in the hands of Mk 6 CASPers. Seeing the center of the area, Mata put the dropship down perfectly. As they opened the outer doors and started the shutdown sequence, she saw through the aft cameras both the offloading process begin and Tara Mason approach the rear of the vehicle.

Harmon Gray appeared behind them, climbing up the ladder with a smile on his face. "Hey, just wanted to say thanks for the great ride. You guys are incredible pilots."

Carter jerked his head toward Mata. "That was all her, sir. I'm just happy to be along for the ride."

A new voice called from below. "Gray, is that you?"

They all recognized the voice of Tara Mason.

"Yes, ma'am."

"Move over and let me up there. I can brief all of you at once."

Gray did as ordered and stepped aside. As Tara climbed up in the cockpit, she smiled at Mata and Carter. As her eyes turned to Gray, Mata saw her commander's smile falter and drop away.

"Where are the tanks?"

Gray took a breath. "Ma'am, we got eighty percent of the load plan. I made a judgment call that the tanks were too heavy to carry, so we left them there with minimal personnel to—"

"You did *what*?"

Gray stiffened and put his hands on his hips. "I made a judgment call. With the storm coming, and not wanting to attempt to either lift them or delay our evacuation, I loaded everything but the tanks and one CASPer to man the automated defenses."

Tara's face flushed. "You left Major Vuong there, along with Lieutenant Morris and how many other people?"

"Three others, ma'am. They all volunteered. It was Major Vuong's idea. Well, that's not exactly true. My intent was to pull off something like Washington's retreat from Trenton in 1777."

The color of Tara Mason's face slowly returned to normal. "Now I get your reference. But I'm still not entirely sure of the method."

Gray shrugged. "When Washington left Trenton, his intent was to make the entire British Army believe his forces were still in place across the river. When the redcoats crossed and entered the camp, everything was gone. He had a few soldiers stay behind and make as much noise as they could while tending fires, making it sound like the Army, in its entirety, was bedding down for the night. In reality, there were only a few people there while he evacuated the army further north toward Valley Forge."

Tara took a deep breath, and to Carter's surprise, she nodded. "I understand. I'm not happy about this, and were anyone else planning this action besides Major Vuong, I'd be tempted to suggest mutiny. But I know what he's doing." She paused and turned to look at Mata and Carter. "You two are going to have to go back."

Carter replied immediately. "Yes, ma'am."

Mata added, "We'll get them out of there, ma'am. Request permission to take infantry support? They might benefit from having a gunship overhead."

"I think that's a great idea, Mata." Tara smiled. "Make sure you get two full squads of infantry with two CASPers in the cargo doors. That way you have one CASPer on either side, along with whatever small arms we can generate, but you can cover the retreat into the rear base by firepower."

"Yes, ma'am," Mata said

Tara nodded at them. "See to that while I discuss the next phase of our operation here with Captain Gray. The weather is positively shitty outside. You sure you have everything you need?"

Mata nodded. "We do, ma'am. We'll go get our guys."

"You do that. We'll see you when you get back here."

* * * * *

Chapter Twenty-Eight

Trenta Knights Compound

New Perth

Snowmass

By sunset, the massive storm front had rolled through New Perth and was headed east to points beyond. Satisfied the weather conditions met his minimums for attack, Colonel Krukk assembled his intermediate leaders and gave them the attack briefing. Shortly after sunset, they boarded their skiffs and positioned the infantry for the short march to the industrial area. At the same time, Krukk broke from his own standard operating procedure to dispatch a forward intelligence team to observe the Goblins' assembly area. He'd always relied on previously gathered intelligence, believing that an enemy sufficiently capable of defending would never change the bulk of their organization or position beyond their established norms.

Still, the establishment of a new observation post overlooking the Goblins' compound was ultimately useful, because the Humans had been hard at work. Gone were the long, parallel rows of shipping containers. In their place, the Goblins had moved the containers into fortifications resembling a hexagon with each side being three containers wide and stacked at least three tall. On four points of the hexagon, the ones forming a central rectangle in the compound, tanks rested on top of shipping containers and swept their fields of fire methodically. They were ready to defend.

The site of the sudden fortifications made Krukk smile with glee. It had been far too long since they'd fought a prepared enemy. Yet the fortifications and changes to the defensive structure in the area clearly indicated the Goblins had been tipped off to the attack. Krukk went through a quick mental litany of factors that could have influenced their actions and decisions before quickly settling on a few and deciding he would act upon them later.

Their last-minute fortifications were a sign of weakness. The Goblins knew they were over matched, as did whoever had tipped them off to the Knights' planned actions. He would make them all pay.

At five minutes before the appointed attack, Krukk left his office in the assembly area and mounted the command skiff. The crew of six came to attention and saluted as he approached. The driver disappeared into his hatch while four others mounted their machine gun positions. The fifth, his communications operator, prepared the radios and communications devices for the attack. At one minute prior, Krukk slipped on his headset and tapped the transmit button.

"Knights, tonight we fight for our future. Tonight we show the government of New Perth our value. We show them why they should pay for our protection. Tonight we show the Humans and their MinSha counterparts we mean business, and no one takes our contract from underneath us. We storm. We win."

He organized his maneuver force in a simple and familiar way. In the lead was a reconnaissance element of two skiffs and one company of infantry forces on wheeled platforms. They would quickly determine and report on the enemy's position and draw early indirect fire if any were present. The second echelon was entirely skiffs, fourteen of them, each mounted with four mercenaries on their direct fire weapon systems—mainly rockets and chain guns. They would quickly establish a base of fire and determine the next place for the maneuver forces to hit the compound. That would be the third echelon, his infantry. Holding down the enemy with suppressive fire from the skiffs, the infantry could close with and breach the obstacles to pour into the objective. As the Goblins would undoubtedly focus on the close attack of his infantry, his skiffs would then have the ability to maneuver to the far flank and potentially rout the enemy defenses in short order from the rear. Behind the infantry, Krukk and the rest of his command platoon would operate and control the battle space.

Given the residual winds from the storm, he decided at the last moment to ground his flyer forces. While the Goblins didn't appear to have any air support capability, he knew air superiority was already in his favor simply by the threat of launching his winged assets. The risk of loss for the flyers wasn't something Krukk was willing to accept, except for any opportunity that might be provided by the Goblins' retreat from their positions. If they did so, he could order the flyers to strafe and bomb them to the point of submission.

The movement across town would only take a few minutes. As his maneuver forces spread out and prepared to conduct operations, Krukk enjoyed the thrill of battle for the first time in a very long time. His father had been an exemplary commander, but a terrible garrison leader. As a result, the Knights had experienced many problems with discipline over the course of his young life. Since his assumption of command, Krukk had done things differently. Now, rolling the company into battle for the first time in a couple of years, he wondered if he'd done all that was necessary to assure success. As the first echelon—his reconnaissance element—entered the industrial area, Krukk watched the displays from the lead vehicle. The tank closest to the avenue of approach slewed its barrel and locked onto the vehicles, but didn't fire.

They know we're here. Why aren't they firing?

Human tactics—well, that concept seemed a little strange, because Humans never seemed to actually fight with tactics—seemed to have dictated a wait-and-see approach. While he'd only brought four vehicles for the lead component, the Humans might be merely watching to see their intent. As the vehicles rolled to within one thousand meters of the tank, there was still no sign of activity from the Human position.

Krukk tapped his radio. "Continue to move forward until the Humans engage."

On his display, the reconnaissance pressed forward. But at eight hundred meters from the forward position, there was still no response from the Humans. Only at five hundred meters from the first tank did the Human position finally respond by direct fire. The tank fired several rounds in rapid succession, and one of the forward reconnaissance skiffs exploded spectacularly, taking four mercenaries with it. The other three found somewhat defendable positions and returned fire with seemingly minimal effect.

Krukk waited to see if the Humans would engage any indirect fire. They loved their artillery, but nothing came. Likewise, there had been no type of maneuver force dispatched outside their makeshift compound. They seemed to be holding their own.

As the first of his combat echelons rolled into the industrial area, there was no sense in waiting. He turned to his communications officer. "Shut down the entire city. Communications, AetherNet, Gal-

Net. Everything. I want everything down. Hold all messages and disable everything under the emergency action controls from the mayor's office. You have the codes. Execute them now."

"Yes, Colonel."

Krukk turned his gaze to his control screens and tapped his radio controls. "All Knight forces, engage and destroy the Human position. No prisoners, no quarter, no surrender."

He heard the cheer from his forces beyond the radio. The roar was strong and ready. They, too, were relishing the opportunity to fight.

Krukk watched his combat forces split into two echelons, one taking on each of the two tank positions closest to them. They closed the distance quickly, and the Human tanks roared to life, spewing fire at his approaching forces. Several vehicles took damage, some catastrophically, but they continued through the attack until they almost reached the Human tanks on the squared sides of the strongpoint. The closest tank, the first one his forces had engaged, suddenly erupted in a spectacular fireball. From its position at the top layer of shipping containers, the blast ripped open several containers nearby, but there was no evidence of anyone around the vehicles. Krukk waited to see if Humans would appear on the roof of the position to maintain direct fire, but they didn't.

Sensing an opportunity, Krukk diverted his second combat echelon to hit the hole the assault forces had breached in the Human position. As they thundered down upon the gap, Krukk knew they'd be successful. The second Human tank erupted on the far side of the hexagon. As his forces roared up against the position, a new source of fire suddenly appeared at the tip of the hexagon between them, behind his forces. A single CASPer, the indomitable Human fighting machine, appeared on top of the containers with two magnetic accelerator cannons in its hands, and started to lay waste to his forces.

Krukk stabbed his radio controls. "There's a CASPer behind you! On top of the Human position. The forward point of their hexagon."

But it was too late for a sizable portion of his attack forces. The sole CASPer quickly mowed down the skiffs through their nonexistent rear armor. In no time, five skiffs on either side of the CASPer's position had detonated and were burning in place. As the infantry charged forward, taking aim at the CASPer, their small arms and small lasers couldn't stop the mech from doing its damage. Silhouetted against the flames from the two Human tanks atop the containers, the CASPer appeared like an ominous vision in the distance.

Krukk pushed the radio button again. "All forces, center your fires on that—"

No sooner had the words exited his maw than the area around the CASPer detonated with thousands of impacts. The remaining skiffs and the infantry had all sighted their weapons on the position of the lone Human vehicle. By all appearances, the CASPer detonated in place. Debris showered across his forces, who, in their bloodlust, continued to scream and charge the Human position.

Krukk was furious. Not only had the Humans suckered his forces in, they'd cowardly struck the unprotected portions of his vehicles. Krukk mashed his intercom button. "Driver. Get me to that position. I want Harmon Gray's head on a platter."

"Right away, sir."

His vehicle shot forward, racing through the industrial area until he found himself amongst the infantry forces scaling the container system. When he got there, he watched his forces dropping over the containers into the center of the Human position, but there was a surprising lack of weapons fire. Krukk saw one of his lieutenants in the distance as he made his way through the sea of infantry.

"Lieutenant Gnrra. What is the status?"

Gnrra turned and looked at him with surprise in his wide eyes. "Sir, the Humans are not here."

"What do you mean?"

"Sir, there are no Humans in the position. It appears they programmed the tanks to auto-fire."

"But that CASPer... Surely there are Humans here? They can't have vanished."

Gnrra held a hand to his headset and looked away for a split second before turning back to his commander. "Sir, there are a few Humans trying to escape from the far side of the objective. A dropship is approaching from the north."

Krukk roared in frustration and slapped Gnrra across his long face. "Get your forces into the attack. Keep them from retreating. Don't take my victory from me!"

* * *

From his position in the command post, Drew Morris didn't immediately see the last explosion. He consulted the camera system and discovered that the forward position, where Major Vuong had positioned himself, was gone. His destruction set the final protective fire standard for the unit. Morris turned to the three other operators for the tanks and rose from his own console.

"Grab your weapons and gear, flip your consoles to automatic, and get to the extraction point." He reached across the terminal, grabbed his communications headset, and slipped the radio into the combat vest he wore on the back of his coveralls. No sooner had he inserted the earpiece than he heard a familiar voice.

"Avenger 6, this is *Mako 15*. On station and prepared for close air support."

Morris tapped his headset. "*Mako 15*, be advised, Avenger 6 is down. I repeat, Avenger 6 is down. We're evacuating to the extraction point now. Provide us what cover you can."

"Morris? It's Carter. We've got your back. Get your guys to the extraction point, and we'll cover your move. Just hurry the hell up."

"Roger that." Morris tapped his headset to the off position and turned to the operators still fumbling with their gear. "I said get your shit together. We've got to go, right fucking now!"

The soldiers quickly gathered their gear, slung it across their shoulders, and moved toward the rear exit of the compound. As they pushed through the door, Morris reached for the remote detonation device for the command center complex and activated it. He pocketed the detonator and followed the three soldiers into the night, making sure to stay opposite the position of the Knights' attack.

Above the breeze, he heard *Mako 15*'s engines. He looked up into the thin clouds above the compound and saw the silhouette of an aircraft appear with weapons fire coming from both sides. As the dropship descended into view, he saw the side doors were open, and it appeared CASPers were standing with one hand grasping the doorjamb and the other firing magnetic accelerator cannon rounds into the swarming Knights below. Ahead of him, the first of the Zuul soldiers entered the rows of containers marking the outer boundary of the compound. The moist earth around them rippled with countless impacts as the Knights fired down at them from the front of the compound.

"Take cover!" Morris yelled, but the lead soldier couldn't hear him. The young woman went down in a hail of rifle fire. The trailing two darted to one of the empty, broken CASPer racks and cowered behind them. Morris moved toward them, noting the automatic cannons emplaced to cover any retreat weren't firing.

"Get up! Get up and follow me!"

Neither of the young men moved, nor did they bother to bring their weapons to the ready. Out of the line of fire, they sat frozen with fear. Morris closed the distance to them, but a burst of laser fire cut off his route. Instead, he angled toward a motionless auto cannon thirty meters away. Darting behind a collection of detritus from CASPer maintenance, mostly damaged parts unable to be salvaged, he stopped about ten meters from the cannon. An idea formed.

"Morris! Get your asses to the LZ, now!" Carter yelled in his ear.

Morris looked at the soldiers, still frozen. "Negative, *Mako 15*. I've got two soldiers pinned down. Going to get them out by fire."

"Where are they?"

Morris shook his head. "Cover us, *15*. We're taking fire from all sides."

"Copy. Get to the LZ and we'll get you out of there."

"We'll be there directly," Morris replied. Without hesitation, he jumped up from his position and sprinted to the auto cannon. To his surprise, the Knights either didn't see him moving or they couldn't bring their weapons to bear. Behind the cannon and its wide shield plating, Morris allowed himself a few deep breaths as he slowly turned the gun with its manual traverse mechanisms. With the cannon aimed at where they'd taken the most fire, he bypassed the automatic system and unlocked the cannon. Morris pivoted the barrel and opened fire on the Knights' hasty positions along the top of the container wall.

As he walked rounds along the containers, he stared over at the two soldiers. Both of them watched him with wide eyes. He drew a great, deep breath and bellowed. "Get your asses up and moving! Now!"

The cannon bucked as he kept depressing the firing switch. Not wanting the barrel to overheat, he limited himself to short, staccato bursts. When the soldiers got up and moved toward the extraction point, Morris laid on the trigger longer to give them time to get out of the way.

They didn't make it.

Morris screamed as he fired on the Knights. Impacts from his left and right fell around the cannon. A glance to the left told him the Knights were flanking him. There wasn't anything he could see coming from the right. Fire poured down onto his position.

"Morris! Get moving. We're taking heavy fire."

He swung the cannon up and fired again. The Knights just kept coming over and through the walls. If he ran and made it to the extraction point, there was no guarantee he'd get safely aboard.

"*Mako 15*, break off." He licked his lips and realized his hands were trembling violently as he reached for the firing handles and the thumb-activated triggers again. "I say again, break off. The LZ is compromised. Get out of here."

A missile roared up from the Knights attacking the compound at Morris' front. He sighted on the Zuul soldier and the shoulder-launched missile and fired. The Zuul went down, but there were several behind him carrying similar weapons. Another missile narrowly missed *Mako 15*.

"We've got you, Drew. Get out of there."

Morris shook his head. "Negative, *15*. Missile carriers approaching; am engaging them now. Get out of there before they fire one up your ass."

As if the Knights heard him, four missiles streaked up. Two of them slammed into the side of the dropship. *Mako 15* swung violently to the right and boosted thrust. In seconds, the ship was away from the compound. Tracer rounds and missiles continued to follow the ship, but none appeared to do any significant damage.

"We're coming around, Morris."

Drew Morris laughed and shook his head before laying on the triggers again. The Knights turned as one and filled the surrounding air with fire. A steady thrum of lasers and ballistic rounds struck the armored protector plate. A missile roared overhead and exploded against the container wall forty meters behind him. Morris kept firing.

"Negative, *15*. LZ is comprised. Stand Victoria!" Morris said. His trembling ceased as the last vestiges of fear ebbed. He felt calm, strangely composed, and more determined than ever. "Tell Araceli and the others I died a hero, will ya?"

"Drew, we can get you out of there," Carter pleaded. "Just hold on and we'll drop CASPers to—"

"No!" Morris yelled on the frequency. Silence filled his earpiece. "I said I've got this, Carter. All due respect, sir, get that ship out of here and back to Colonel Mason up north. These fuckers will figure out where everyone went and come bringing fire. You have to be there. Copy?"

Carter's voice came back slowly, thick with emotion. "Roger, Drew. You done good, kid."

"Not bad for a maintenance puke, huh?" Morris grinned. The surrounding fire paused, and he brought the cannons up again and kept firing. He grabbed the remote detonator and set the command complex to detonate in thirty seconds. "I'll hold the line. Get out of here!"

For a brief moment, he thought of the warm summer sun on Victoria Bravo and day-long rafting trips on the Swigert River. He'd had his first beer and his first kiss on that river. There was no place he'd rather be. Even as he'd lost too many friends and family to count, he'd sought solace in the wide, cool water. Eyes closed, he kept firing at the Knights and pulled the blanket of memories around him tight enough that he could feel the cool water on his feet and hear the laughter of long dead friends welcoming him home.

He simultaneously felt heat and nothing at all.

*****

Chapter Twenty-Nine

Government Center

New Perth

Sophie Pryce poured herself another glass of expensive cabernet and leaned back against the chaise lounge in her office to watch the battle. From the moment the Trenta Knights attacked, the skies above the industrial area reminded her of the fireworks demonstrations her parents had overseen for landing day celebrations throughout her childhood. When it was discovered the fireworks scared the Veetanho, the yearly ritual turned into a multicultural festival without excessive noise or explosions. She'd always missed that.

There was a considerable irony in learning the Veetanho ran the Mercenary Guild and had been responsible for all-out war across the Galactic Union on numerous occasions. The fireworks were forgotten amidst the many troubles of the Dream World Consortium. Now, watching the certain destruction of the Knights and the elimination of so many of her problems in one fell swoop, Sophie couldn't help but feel the same level of frivolity she used to as a child. Maybe when she became the mayor of New Perth, they could reinstate such things. But there was much to do before then.

Everything she'd been able to observe about Gray's Goblins pointed to the fact they'd be prepared for such an attack. Her warning was likely unnecessary, but it still provided some insurance for their success. If all went well in the next hour, the Knights would be defeated, and it would leave Mayor Citsym looking for answers he couldn't find at the election polls. Her ascendance to his office was all but assured.

An orange glow lit the low cloud deck over the industrial area, the result of many fires burning nearby. In the clouds, she caught the shadow of a dropship circling the compound. Bursts of laser fire and streams of tracer fire arced down into the area where the Knights were attacking. From the sides of the dropship, streams of tracer fire were concentrated in a way she didn't believe was possible. More impressive was undoubtedly the effect the ship's rate of fire was having against the Knights. But something appeared to be missing. Flyers were a critical part of the Knights' inventory, and they didn't even appear to be nearby, given the complex winds in the swirling storm. The appearance of the armed dropship performing close air support pushed the advantage in favor of the Goblins. Sophie Pryce couldn't help but smile. The dropship continued to circle and descend to where she knew it intended to land.

Reinforcements. This will go much faster than I expected.

She looked across her office at the small bar and considered grabbing another glass of wine and pouring it for Harmon Gray, but she didn't want to be presumptive. At the same time, there was no way the Knights were going to win the day. Sophie sat back, made herself more comfortable, and prepared to watch the end of their mercenary problem.

Several spectacular explosions lit up the night sky over the industrial area. She couldn't help but wonder if one of them meant the destruction of Krukk or any of his leadership. There was no way of knowing. She reached for her slate, intending to manipulate every security camera in the colony to view the battle space. Some of them she couldn't move, but there were a few she could manipulate, though they didn't really provide her with any significant detail. Likewise, the colony's communications network appeared to be down, but she couldn't determine the scope of the outage. For a moment, she considered contacting Colonel Krukk directly. If they'd won the field, she'd need to continue to play both sides.

No, that's not what happened. I just need to have faith.

Over the next few minutes, the weapons fire she saw diminished to nearly nothing at all. The dropship appeared to have either landed or disappeared.

At the complex, a tremendous flash forced her eyes shut. A millisecond later the massive explosion shook the building.

Gods!

A minute later, as she took a deep sip of her wine, the dropship lifted off and rocketed into the sky with a curtain of tracer fire trailing behind. The ship was clearly out of range of the weaponry on the ground, but the Knights continued to fire. After a moment, they ceased as well, and the entire industrial side of the town grew quiet. What was happening? Why did the dropship leave? There wasn't an immediate answer to her questions.

Unable to contain her sudden curiosity, she tapped a private message to Harmon Gray.

Please advise on the situation at your earliest convenience. I'm in my office observing.

She waited for a couple of moments, but there was no immediate reply. She checked the outgoing message folder, saw the message had been sent, but there was no confirmation of delivery. Mentally she shook her head and recognized her error. Krukk would've jammed communications in the local area. It was a standard operating procedure for the Knights when dealing with threats. She didn't fret, though, because as soon as they restored the network, the message would bounce through and be delivered to Harmon Gray. All would be well, and her plan could continue. Since her ascension to the deputy mayor's position, she'd sought a way to remove the mercenaries from their contract. This attack had proven Krukk and his collection of miscreants didn't have the planet's best interests in mind.

Her office door opened, and she sat up from the chaise longue and turned with a smile on her face. "I've been expecting you."

As the figure entered, her smile froze on her face and faded away. "Something tells me you weren't expecting to see me here, Miss Pryce," Krukk replied.

"I expected a report, yes," she lied. "Have you eradicated the Goblins?"

Krukk's face was impassive, but his eyes blazed. "After you warned them of our attack?"

"I did no such thing."

"I beg to differ, Miss Pryce. I have the audio and visual records from the security cameras at the Goblins' perimeter. I had my people install it several days ago because I did not trust you." Krukk's maw curled slightly.

She'd observed his crews working in the area, but they hadn't been installing the typical and familiar communications package. His intelligence section often bordered on incompetence, so she'd paid no attention to his dealings after the arrival of the Goblins. She'd hoped for a different outcome instead of planning for it. Pryce didn't really consider him as an adversary because she knew like most mercenaries, his interests were best served by credits. Those credits were something the local government didn't have unless the Dream World Consortium came through on their promises.

But even those promises were daunting. Over the last several years, their carefully calculated efforts to slow population growth by not completely adjusting the environment had proven viable. With crop yields going down, the agricultural draw of the northern continents had weakened significantly. There was ample opportunity for other resource development, especially in the stormy southern half of the planet, but she knew the DWC's goals were focused on the north. In those areas, all the colonists had to go. She'd made it her goal not only to meet the Consortium's expectations, but also to rid the planet of the Trenta Knights. She believed they could hire a better mercenary force to secure the colonies before the Dream World Consortium presented their final phase of operations.

Pryce frowned and put steel in her voice. "I was there on official government business."

Krukk laughed in her face. "That's what you call it? Official business when you're trying to pass a contract to them without fully adjudicating it? You know, there are Peacemakers on the planet. I'm sure we could bring them in to settle this dispute."

"There is no dispute," she spat. "I was doing what Mayor Citsym wanted me to do."

"The mayor had no intention of offering anyone but me that contract, Miss Pryce. And while my forces attacked and dispatched Captain Gray's forces from the field, you sent him a message and said you were here observing, and then you said you were expecting him. You were not expecting me."

Sophie Pryce shook her head. "I'm afraid there's been a big misunderstanding—"

Krukk drew the pistol strapped to his thigh and pointed it at the center of her face. "No, Miss Price. I understood you perfectly, Human."

The last thing she saw was a flash of light from the pistol's barrel.

* * *

Objective White

2km East of Cavern Complex

There wouldn't be time for an ass chewing. She knew it needed to happen, but time appeared to be against them. Tara Mason realized Harmon Gray was a solid commander, but she understood what had happened at New Perth couldn't happen again. Force 25 never left a man or woman on the field. While his decision had been tactically sound, it had cost the lives of good people. Major Vuong wasn't easily, if ever, replaceable. Neither was Lieutenant Morris. The young man had come to their rescue on Victoria Bravo and helped pull Force 25's proverbial asses out of the fire. She'd left him under the care of Captain Gray, and he died on her watch. The facts didn't make her happy, and she took very little solace in knowing that Drew Morris had saved much more than the dropship *Mako 15*. If she ever got back to New Perth, she hoped to at least be able to give the young man a proper burial.

Tara also wanted the time for burying others to be over sooner rather than later, but there was still work to do.

Since his return, Gray had given Tara a wide berth. He knew he'd screwed up, and while she wanted nothing more than to jump into his ass with both feet and start kicking, it wasn't the time or the place. The Knights were on the move, and based on what they'd learned from the closed-circuit televisions and monitoring the departure control frequencies in New Perth, they would arrive soon.

Around them, a blizzard raged. She'd emplaced Force 25 in a dense pine forest on the edge of a shallow valley only two kilometers wide. On the far side, the terrain rose more than thirty meters above their present elevation. At the top of that small rise, a sparse line of forest separated the lower terrain from the higher, more mountainous area where the glaciers ran. Under that higher ground was their target.

Using the survey maps from the original terraforming initiative, she recognized the area where the caverns existed under the rocky escarpment. Finding the actual door would take more effort, but it wasn't the kind of effort that required the entire team. Maintaining their hidden position would be critical, so Tara planned a solo action. Plans, though, required her elements to actually follow them to the letter.

Harmon Gray entered the temporary headquarters, a heavy-framed tent designed to slough the snow off and not compromise its internal structure. He nodded at her and approached with a straight, serious face.

"The company is in position and radio silent, ma'am. Our energy signatures are zero, given the amount of snow falling."

Tara glanced up at him from her slate. "And the Misfits?"

"I put them in the position you wanted. They had to move farther than I wanted to keep them undercover, but they're coming up through the forest on the other side of the valley right now. They'll be able to provide overwatch within thirty minutes."

"Within thirty minutes? Do we have an exact time?"

Gray frowned. "Ma'am, they've estimated their time of arrival to be in seventeen minutes."

Tara leaned back on the ammunition crate she was using as a stool and took a slow breath. "Captain Gray, I think it's time you understand something about me. And not just me, but how we do leadership and command in Force 25. I don't like estimates. I know real life moves faster than reports. You don't have to quote von Clausewitz to me; I understand. That being said, I can't have you not getting to the point. You need to tell me precisely what's going on in as few words as possible. If you put a thirty-minute estimate on something that's supposed to take them seventeen minutes, that's thirteen minutes they could be on-station and at risk. I would much rather know what they expect; they expect to be there in seventeen minutes. That means I can expect to be in position in seventeen minutes. There's plenty of time before I get mounted up to change my mind or for them to radio in with any issues they might be facing. In the meantime? Tell me what the facts are. Do you understand?"

Gray nodded, but his eyes weren't on Tara. He'd picked out a spot above her head on the tent wall and continued to stare. "Yes, ma'am."

"Bullshit. Look me in the eyes, Gray. Do you understand?"

The captain met her gaze with his blazing, narrowed eyes. "I understand, ma'am. You want the facts."

"I want more than the facts, Harm, but that's a good place to start. When you can provide those to me in a timely matter, you'll have my trust again. I'm very close to sitting you out because of what happened at New Perth. I gave you an order, and you failed to execute that order to my standards. While I appreciate the initiative you took, and it undoubtedly bought us some time, it also cost us five good soldiers. Five men and women I can't take home to Victoria Bravo. That's unacceptable."

Gray sputtered, "But, ma'am, we're a mercenary company. Losses are to be expected."

Tara stomped toward him. She raised a finger and pointed it at his face, leaving her extended digit only a couple of inches from the end of his nose. "You don't have to lecture me about combat losses, Gray. Never think I don't understand the gravity of what we're dealing with. Now I want you on the line and ready to provide security as dictated in the plan. The minute the Misfits are stationed across the valley, I'm walking over there. If we've done this right, the Knights will buy off on our subterfuge and attack the wrong spot on the other side of the valley. When they do, your orders are to hit them fast, hard, and keep right on hitting. Do you understand that?"

"Yes, ma'am."

"Good. You're dismissed." She watched him exit the tent with his shoulders rounded forward, and while she couldn't see it, she imagined steam coming from the young captain's ears. Every young officer she'd ever known sometimes needed to learn not only exactly what the commander wanted, but how they needed to better themselves for the next fight. Leaving him in command of the field with three platoons of CASPers at his disposal was risky. She had little doubt he would seize the initiative, for better or worse. Given the mission at hand, she would've preferred to remain in command of the situation herself, but there was only one way they were going to get inside the cavern complex. She would have to directly engage Lucille.

* * *

Araceli moved as quietly as she could behind her two teammates. With Quin'taa in the lead, and Homer trailing ten meters behind him, she focused on keeping a similar distance while allowing the CASPer's sensors to scan the local area for threats. Amidst the swirling snow, there were no threats visible, and realistically, her ability to see anything at some points was minimal.

"This snow is something else," Quin'taa growled over the frequency. "Always hated the stuff."

"I don't know," Homer whispered. "I think it's kind of pretty."

Araceli couldn't help but smile. She'd dealt with snow in Victoria Bravo's mountain ranges for most of her life. In the northlands, there always seemed to be some snow on the high mountains. Her parents told her they looked like the Himalayas back on Earth, but she'd never seen them. She'd studied Everest in one of her classes, mainly discussing the Human folly of exploration in the 21st century, but she'd never been there. While the snow was pretty, she was thankful she didn't have to walk in it with her boots. Her CASPer was warm and toasty. More importantly, it was dry.

"I love the snow, too," she said. "I'm just glad I don't have to walk in it."

Quin'taa grunted. "One of your few shortcomings, kid. Not having big, furry feet that don't get cold."

"That's fair," she said with a smile on her face. "You gotta understand; I don't forget the shortcoming. I mean, we know you're just jealous that you're not sitting in a nice warm cockpit like this."

Quin'taa laughed. "Sorry, kid. Even if they built one of those things for my fat ass, you wouldn't catch me dead inside one. I'd rather be out here in the clear than cooped up in a can."

"Look, it's a can with fantastic weapons," Homer added. "And she can jump a lot higher than you can, Quin'taa."

"What happens if it runs out of fuel?" the Oogar asked with a grunt. "Okay, let's cut the chatter. We're getting close to the objective. Araceli? See anything out here?"

She reviewed her sensor spread once more. "I've got nothing. Even the biological signatures are low in this snowstorm. Temperature is really falling out there, too. I don't think I've ever seen snow this hard anywhere."

"That's perfect for us Misfits," Quin'taa replied. "Let's close up to five meters. Delta formation."

"Copy," both she and Homer answered at almost the same time over the frequency.

Homer stepped to the left side of the route of march, so Araceli moved her CASPer to the right. The intent was to widen out their security to the front and still be able to keep track of things on their sides. Araceli set her sensors to focus more on their rear so she could maintain watch as the CASPer walked forward. The forest floor was littered with branches and fallen trees. Weapons in hand, her focus remained on moving as quietly as possible. In a thousand-kilogram machine, that sometimes proved more difficult than others. Yet the muting effect of the snow falling combined with the howling winds made her reasonably certain no one would hear them coming. Which was the entire point. Her laser link communication system chimed, and Araceli engaged the connection with the touch of a button. A text message typed across her screen.

Misfits, Deathangel 25. What's your status?

Araceli engage the voice-to-text function. "Deathangel 25, Misfit 5. Two hundred meters from our objective. Negative sensor sweeps in all directions. ETA is three minutes."

The response was almost immediate. Understand. I'm moving now. Set overwatch position and let me know when you have visibility on me.

Rather than send a message, Araceli simply tapped the screen twice in reply. The two taps, a common brevity code for acknowledgement used by pilots, would get the point across.

"I have eyes on the objective," Quin'taa said.

The coniferous trees had been impossibly thick along the escarpment for most of their traverse. As they neared the cavern complex, the trees were sparser. Only one grove appeared to be thick enough to provide them cover. They set their objective for that small grove of trees where they could overwatch Tara's move across the valley.

Moving took only another minute or two. As they set their positions, they found that with one side of the cliff against them, they could focus their attention on the remaining one hundred and eighty degrees of visibility. The inaccessibility of the cliffs overhead and the ice fall behind them gave the Misfits a reasonable sense of security. But if a determined enemy popped up there, they could easily rake fire across the team's position and render them dead in minutes. It was a risk they'd have to take.

Araceli engaged her laser comm system. "Deathangel 25, Misfit 5. In position. Negative visibility on you at this time."

A few seconds later the response appeared. Moving out. About one third of the way across the valley. Keep looking.

Araceli went back to the team's frequency. "The boss is moving. We should see her soon."

"Going to be hard to see anything in this shit," Homer said.

"I thought you said the snow was pretty." Quin'taa grunted. "Now it's shit?"

* * *

Airfield
Glacier Falls

Rains and Vannix debarked the commercial transport as the first appearance of light broke over the eastern horizon. Getting to Glacier Falls had been a nightmare. Stuck overnight in a tiny terminal at Northingham, they'd finally wrangled a ride on a supply aircraft by showing their badges and asking for help. The crew had been more than happy to oblige. After thanking the pilots, they collected their gear and stepped into the frigid air. Snow fell in a steady blanket of huge flakes. In a short time, the storm had covered the ground and everything in sight with several inches of the white precipitation. The tarmac itself remained remarkably clear, thanks to both automated clearing machines and what could only be heated surfaces. Making their way anywhere was a challenging prospect.

"It's beautiful," Vannix gasped as they walked down the boarding ramp.

He glanced at her. "You've never seen snow?"

"No. It's incredible." The soft, almost innocent smile at the corners of her maw made Rains smile. "You've seen this before?"

"Yeah," Rains replied. "Well, not like *this*. I mean, where I'm from we get snow, but it's never this bad. Except for one year." His voice trailed off as the memory swam up. He'd been fourteen and on his own. The storm rolled across southern Alabama with great sheets of ice, followed by six inches of heavy, wet snow. The entire state had shut down. He'd tried to find a place to hole up in Troy, Alabama, when he'd found Mrs. Greene by accident. The older woman took him in with the other orphans she housed. Cold and wet, his tattered shoes crusted with ice, he'd wandered past, and she'd called to him and brought him inside. Her chicken soup was the first real meal he'd had in several days. The warmth of her fireplace as it slowly dried his clothes and warmed his chilled feet was something he'd always remember.

"You okay?" Vannix asked.

He nodded. "Memories. That's all."

Vannix didn't reply immediately. She fixed her eyes on something in the distance, and he turned his attention that way. A large man stood next to a tracked vehicle. Rains thought about it for a moment and believed it was called a snowcat, or something like that. The man waved them in his direction.

As they approached, Rains realized the man's face was familiar. Vannix, however, was the first to speak.

"Nathan Balyeat?" she asked.

A grin appeared under the man's fur-ringed hood. "Peacemakers. Well met."

"Well met," Rains and Vannix replied in unison.

Vannix continued. "We were looking for you."

"We know." Balyeat stepped forward. The bear of a man shook Rains' hand in the traditional Human way. He offered his hand to Vannix, who took it with practiced ease.

"You said we," Vannix said. "Meaning who exactly?"

Balyeat glanced around them quickly. The tarmac was empty, but he still whispered. His voice was barely audible against the swirling wind. "Reecha, Peacemaker. She hoped you'd come north."

Neither Peacemaker responded for a moment. "We weren't certain she was alive, or even on the planet anymore."

"She never left," Balyeat replied with a wide shrug. "She's looked out for the entire planet for years. Longer than I've been alive. There's no one we trust more."

"She's behind the terrorist attacks?" Vannix asked.

Balyeat's grin faded. "Peacemaker Vannix, would a terrorist act for the betterment of society, or to instill fear in the general public?"

Rains answered. "That depends on whose side you're defending."

"And things are never that clear," Vannix finished. "The betterment of society? How?"

"By showing the DWC that their equipment and promises are inadequate. By attempting to force them to adjust the climate to help facilitate growth and not shrink the populace alongside the growing seasons."

Rains frowned. "Why now? Why has all of this come to a head now?"

"Because timelines and situations have changed. You're here looking for someone Reecha knows. My job is to get you to her location, and sooner rather than later, I might add." Balyeat leaned forward. "I believe our common enemies know where she is, and they're coming for her."

"That's what we were afraid of," Rains said. "Some may already be here."

"Please, let's get your gear loaded on the snowcat. There are friends and enemies nearby."

Vannix hefted her bag into Balyeat's outstretched hands. "Friends?"

"The mercenaries? You filed them under the name of Gray's Goblins." Balyeat grinned. "We know who they really are and where they're massing now. Thankfully, they're close by. We may need them."

"What do you mean?"

"There was an attack last night in New Perth. The Trenta Knights attacked the compound where your Goblins, actually Force 25, were conducting refit operations. The Knights found nothing there. We tracked a dropship moving nap of the earth—several times, I might add—moving to a position near the glaciers and high ground outside town here. But they weren't the only ones."

Rains nodded and loaded his gear. "We were following another aircraft that dropped off the radar. I'm assuming it didn't land here?"

"No," Balyeat said, "but we know exactly where they are. There's not much time, Peacemakers. Let's get you aboard before all hell breaks loose. The enemy's eyes are everywhere."

"You don't seem all that worried, Mister Balyeat," Vannix observed.

"I'm terrified, Peacemaker. Unless your friends are really damned good, Reecha and the rest of us willing to save this planet won't survive the day."

They heard a soft chime. The big man rolled his left wrist over and consulted the slate mounted on the outside of his heavy parka.

"We have to get moving. Someone's very close to Reecha."

"Is she in a safe place?" Vannix asked.

"Or can she barricade herself in wherever she is?" Rains added.

A soft, sly grin crossed Nathan's face. "They may be close, but they won't get in. Still, we haven't much time. Please get aboard, Peacemakers."

*****

Chapter Thirty

Trenta Knights Headquarters

New Perth

The terminations began with his intelligence section. Krukk's anger was unlike anything he'd ever felt before. From the moment Harmon Gray and his Goblins had landed on Snowmass, the information he'd believed he should get never matched the information he actually received. When they stormed the Goblins' compound in the industrial area, his forces found one thoroughly destroyed CASPer, three tanks set up to auto load and fire, one tank that was completely inoperable, and exactly four dead Human bodies. The rest of the Goblins had gotten away. Their battlefield deception was dishonorable, even for a bunch of Human mercenaries. He would take great pleasure in killing Harmon Gray. Yet he recognized the problems he faced were those of his own creation.

Killing Sophie Pryce had only been the start. Had he been able to locate Mayor Citsym, Krukk would've already killed the rest of the colony leadership, taken control of the government, and declared martial law. Citsym appeared to be missing, so the only remaining course of action he could see was to attack and destroy his greatest threat once and for all. That meant Harmon Gray and all those helping him.

That had been his first discovery. The dropship responsible for dropping off the Goblins several days before had overflown the facility near Lake Pryce. Satellite imagery collected by the various agriculture-focused systems showed evidence that something, or someone, had jumped into the area near the Dream World Consortium's facility there. The imagery wasn't clear enough to see exactly what it was, and the sudden change in weather made sending a team to visually identify the debris counterproductive. What mattered was prior to the arrival of the Goblins, the debris near Lake Pryce hadn't been there. So the Goblins had apparently jumped into the area. He didn't know why, and their objectives seemed unclear, but he knew the Dream World Consortium would be very interested in knowing whether someone, or something, had observed their facility. But that wasn't the only discovery he'd made.

Try as he might, Krukk couldn't get the idea out of his head that the very ship that had brought in the Goblins—a MinSha cruiser—had also carried the two Peacemakers. There'd also been at least one other being of a species he'd never seen before. The TriRusk had presumably also arrived on Harmon Gray's ship. All of it seemed convenient. Though the Peacemakers had been busy with the investigation of Veeka's death, as part of their investigation, they'd traveled north to Glacier Falls to interview witnesses who knew the respected leader. That meant they were nearby. The other young being had been shown on security cameras being escorted by two known mercenaries to a ship also hired to go north to Glacier Falls.

Krukk wasn't stupid.

He undertook a quick research project himself. His query wasn't something he would give to his lieutenants or underlings. He studied the areas around Glacier Falls and consulted original topographic maps and all the records for landings and transits in that region over the course of Snowmass' history. What he found was surprising. Near Glacier Falls, the renowned shipping company called Intergalactic Haulers had several facilities they'd established and used over the course of the last thirty years. Some of them appeared to be nothing more than container farms, including one at least that seemed to be a remnant from some container mishap during the early days of colonization. Still, that wasn't enough reason to launch an attack. While he believed Gray and all the others would be in the same area and looking for the same things, he didn't quite understand why. Nor could he figure out what it was worth to him, until he discovered that James Francis, the man commonly known as Snowman, was not only missing, but had a price placed on his head by the Mercenary Guild for more than five million credits, the equivalent of the annual salaries for the entire company for their Dream World Consortium contract on Snowmass. If Gray and all the others were looking for Francis, they would have to fight him for the man.

He turned to his executive officer, Tolem. "What is our status?"

"Sir, we are about one hundred kilometers southeast of Glacier Falls. The weather at the surface is bad enough we cannot get direct sensor readings until we're almost on top of our objective. If we maintain our speed and altitude, we should be able to surprise anything there. We can overwhelm them by force and speed. I've readied our skiffs and two full companies of flyers for operations."

Krukk nodded in appreciation. The night before, during the storm, he'd been unable to launch his flyers, as he deemed the risk to them too great. While he was more than confident in the ability of his ground forces to fight, his flyers provided a distinct advantage. Harmon Gray had no flyers. The dropship the Goblins had converted for close air support was too big and slow. Had his forces been able to adjust their direct fire, the dropship would never have made it anywhere near the compound. They wouldn't have been able to rescue the remnants of the Goblins before their total domination.

"Excellent. Have them ready to deploy the moment we break the lower cloud deck. Will the weather continue to hold? Or will we find some lull in the winds?"

"We're forecasting a lull, sir. The snow will still be heavy, but the winds will die down enough to mitigate any risk to our flyers and enable a complete aerial attack profile," Tolem said.

"Very well," Krukk replied. "Increase our approach speed and lower our altitude to the treetops. Gray has a head start on us, and he gets no more advantages. We have the airpower, the firepower, and the ability to maneuver better than his measly forces can. It is time we take the Human and his company down. We will tear the flesh from their bones and leave their bits scattered across the snow. We own the storm."

* * *

At the exact moment the cockpit of her CASPer closed, Tara left the concealed positions of Force 25 and headed across the small valley. Her loadout differed from that of a typical combat operation. On each shoulder Deathangel 25 carried a magnetic accelerator cannon. There were extra hand cannons bolted to exterior hard points on each thigh, and in the event she was faced with a particular problem set involving hacking or slicing, she'd also bolted a prototype combat machete to the hull.

<<All sensors are operational. No immediate contacts,>> Lucille reported.

"Thanks, Lucille. Have you been able to tap into anything nearby? Is GalNet available?"

<<Negative. I'm scanning all known adversary frequencies and air traffic control, but I've heard nothing of significance. The heavy weather is hampering our detection capabilities. That plays well both ways.>>

Tara didn't respond, instead focusing on bringing the CASPer up to a run as she cleared the edge of the tree line and started her traverse across the wide, snowy valley. Swirling winds tore at her from all sides, but she couldn't shake the elation she felt at being alone in her CASPer for the first time in a very long time. As happy as it made her, she knew she needed to temper that response, given what was about to happen. There was no doubt the Trenta Knights were on their way. Harmon Gray and the rest of the CASPer elements of Force 25 lay in wait for them at the position Tara had just left. In their powered down states, combined with the use of the snow and wind of the blizzard conditions, the mechs should be able to avoid detection. Tara hoped it was enough to keep them hidden until it was too late for the Knights.

Across the valley, however, were the remainder of the Misfits. Working hard to establish their position, the Misfits created one larger and seemingly more populated than it actually was. Tara knew that deceptive operations were a critical aspect of combat operations. It was a force multiplier. As such, she knew a successfully executed deception plan could have a massive effect on the battle to come.

Tara scanned the far wood line with Deathangel 25's onboard sensors. She could see the heat signatures clearly. While she couldn't make out the number of personnel, the seven or eight different signatures she saw gave the impression of at least a company-sized element operating in the area. Given the Trenta Knights' inability to gather actionable intelligence, it was a logical assumption they had no real idea how many CASPers remained in the Goblins'/Force 25's inventory. While it was tempting to bring down all their additional forces from orbit, Tara had decided not to. She believed they could win the fight with what they had. That belief was critical to their own subterfuge.

<<I have a telemetry laser lock on Misfit 5,>> Lucille reported. <<I am estimating they are eighty percent complete for the setup of their operation. Is there anything you want me to relay to them?>>

Tara shook her head. "No, Lucille. I trust them."

Her brief experience working alongside Quin'taa, Homer, and Araceli had more than bolstered her trust in them. The Misfits were shaping up to be an important facet of Force 25. While she'd never been a fan of irregular forces, Tara realized the traditional line units of CASPers and tanks wouldn't cut it much longer in the Galactic Union. The more mercenary companies united different species and capabilities, the more difficult it would be for a straight line Human CASPer unit to combat them effectively.

"Maintain contact with them as long as possible," Tara said. "Have you identified our primary target?"

<<Affirmative. There is a cavern entrance I've marked on your heads-up display at bearing zero five four which appears to have some artificial components just inside the entrance. I cannot determine exactly what it is at this distance. I believe closer inspection will reveal a door or vault structure. The electromagnetic spectrum is quiet. There are also no appreciable heat sources in that area.>>

"Anything else I should know?"

<<Glacier Falls air traffic control center reported an anomalous contact roughly four minutes ago. They issued weather guidance to all aircraft to either fly above the storm system or to seek emergency landing until the storm passed. This is apparently standard operating procedure for storms like this. In this case, an aircraft flying above the storm suddenly cut their engines and dropped into the storm at a rate much faster than considered safe for that maneuver. It was roughly forty kilometers south of here at the time.>>

Tara chewed on the inside of her cheek. "What's the probability it's part of the Knights' attack or reconnaissance elements?"

<<I calculate a near certainty,>> Lucille replied. <<I believe the weather is a strong enough variable, but not understanding what their capabilities or fighting history are in the snow, I think it's a possibility they are on the attack. Or at the very least, like you suggested, they are performing a reconnaissance. Either way, they are coming.>>

"Contact both Gray and the Misfits via laser text. Maintain radio silence. Tell them to upgrade their readiness posture and stand by for enemy contact. I think an attack is imminent."

<<Information relayed and accepted at both stations. You are four hundred meters from your objective. Do you wish to maintain this speed?>>

Tara smirked. "It feels good to run, Lucille. It's been a while."

Tara activated her terrain-following radar to see the ground underneath the rapidly accumulating snow. The heavy snow made judging where to plant each step difficult, but as she ran, the CASPer responded to her every move.

Gods, I needed this.

Lucille chimed. <<We are two hundred meters from the objective.>>

"Copy, Lucille." Tara adjusted her course slightly to her right and made for the cavern mouth. Through the snow she could see the outline of the higher terrain and the tree line nearby. What she saw concerned her.

"Lucille? How tall is that entrance?"

<<The cavern's entrance appears to only be one point two meters tall. This vehicle will not fit through.>>

No shit, dammit.

Tara slowed to a jog, and then to a walk just outside the cavern's mouth. With uncanny grace, Tara executed a pirouette and backed the CASPer up against the cavern's mouth, off to one side. She unbuckled her harness and verified her sidearm was loaded and holstered on her thigh before she opened the cockpit and let the freezing air swirl inside.

"Lucille? I authorize you to fight Deathangel 25. Do whatever you have to do to make sure nobody gets into the entrance."

<<Understood. I have control of Deathangel 25.>>

Tara pushed up from the CASPer's cockpit and swung her legs outside to climb down the external handles. She stepped into snow already above her ankles before she turned and ducked into the mouth of the cavern. Bent over with her back parallel to the ground, she moved into the space and stood up carefully, trying to let her eyes adjust to the dim light. From her left thigh pocket she pulled a mini torch and flicked the switch to the "on" position. The space surprised her. She could see the cavern was only about ten meters deep and twenty meters wide. At its highest point, the cavern was easily a few meters. On either side of the entrance were large boulders strewn in all directions. Amongst them she could see maintenance pallets and other piles of detritus—some of it bearing the emblem of Intergalactic Haulers.

Jackpot.

At the far end of the cavern was a steel door. Tara tapped her headset. "Lucille, I've got the door. I'm moving in. What's the situation outside?"

<<I copied your last transmission. I am tracking air traffic inbound from the south and east. Based on their speed and course, I believe them to be the Trenta Knights preparing to attack.>>

"Have you estimated their landing point?"

<<Negative. I am relaying my data feeds to Captain Gray and Misfit 5 as directed.>>

"Roger, Lucille. Keep me informed. I'm going to directly connect you into the door controller. You're going to be able monitor both things at once, aren't you?"

Tara grinned. Lucille had once fought a major space battle and autonomously controlled a fleet of her own ships. Given the variables there, she knew her near-AI would have no trouble monitoring the situation outside the cavern and be able to run whatever programs needed to get into the door.

Lucille replied, <<You should know better than that, Tara.>>

"Of course you can, Lucille. I was just joking."

<<While I am familiar with humor, I'm not sure your statement actually qualified.>>

Tara snorted and walked deeper into the cavern. Lucille had figured out bad humor. Tara wondered what would be next. Bad knock-knock jokes? Puns? Only time would tell.

The inside of the cave was considerably warmer than outside. Whether it was protection from the wind or other natural phenomenon, the caves held a current temperature somewhere around fifty degrees Fahrenheit, and she was glad for it. Her green fire-retardant flight suit wasn't thick enough to shed the chill from outside for very long. Being at least a little warmer helped considerably.

"Lucille? Run a routine sensor sweep with my slate, please."

<<Initiated. I am detecting nothing out of the ordinary, except for echoes from the rock structure itself. These are unlike any sedimentary rock I have seen before. There is very little data available about it, and it's likely a reason Intergalactic Haulers chose this as a cache location.>>

Tara didn't reply, but she was thinking exactly the same thing. Having a secure location like this made sense. She made her way to the door and found it was a massive blast door. It reminded her of something she'd seen in an old movie or documentary about a once classified military base on Earth. The door was easily three meters wide by a little more than three meters tall. By appearances alone, it looked to weigh several tons. To the left of the door was a small control panel that appeared to be powered down. Tara made her way there and touched the darkened screen. The small panel, no larger than her spread hand, flickered to life. There was no text of any type, but at the bottom left-hand corner was a command prompt. Below the screen, though, was a small protective cover which she removed carefully. Underneath were standard connection points for the many standard cables across the Galactic Union, including one for Human slates. She withdrew her own cable and plugged it in first to the slate on her wrist before plugging it into the control panel.

Let's see if this works.

All at once the display came to life. Lines of green, monochromatic text filled the screen line by line and rippled fast as the screen scrolled and continued to populate.

<<I am connected. The encryption system is old, so I'm working through the Haulers' database to find the relevant coding and hope to find—>>

With a heavy *clank*, the massive blast door unlocked. Tara reached up to grab the door and found it was already swinging toward her. On the other side she barely caught sight of a Veetanho reaching at her in the near darkness before she felt herself grabbed by her flight suit and yanked forward.

"Get in here!" a high-pitched voice squealed.

She felt the instant heat from a laser blast at her left shoulder. As they pulled her through the door, she recognized that the shot hadn't been aimed at her, but at the display panel itself. Now destroyed and with the door unlocked, it might not lock again. Inside the small space beyond the door, Tara found herself in a dimly lit foyer area with three Veetanho. All carried weapons at the ready.

"Who are you?" the one who'd grabbed her by the suit demanded.

"My name is Tara Mason, and I'm commanding Force 25. We're looking for James Francis. You're Reecha, aren't you?"

"I am, but I've never heard of any Force 25. How did you get in here?"

Tara pointed to her slate with the cable still dangling from it after the rapid disconnection. "Lucille."

The older female's eyes widened slightly, and her tiny maw opened and closed without a sound. She turned to the others. "Manually lock the door. If whatever's out there comes in—"

The heavy door was flung open, no small task given its mass, but in that split-second Tara recognized Thraff standing outside. The massive Equiri snatched one of the Veetanho through the door and tore off one of its arms in a snarling fit of rage. Reecha fired her small pistol at point blank range into the thug's wide chest plate. Thraff staggered backward but grabbed the door with one forehand and caught his balance quickly. The second Veetanho jumped forward, and Tara drew her pistol. Firing at the center of the Equiri's chest, she pushed him back with shot after shot. The other Veetanho aimed its fire at Thraff's relatively unprotected legs. He crumpled to the ground and crawled fast for the mouth of the cavern.

"Lucille! Threat inbound! Threat—"

She heard the Equiri roar as Deathangel 25 stepped toward the opening, grabbed the Equiri by the combat harness, and flung him into the snow.

* * * * *

Chapter Thirty-One

As the Knights' dropships descended through the storm, Krukk heard his sensor operator call out.

"Sir, I have thermal signatures near the objective."

Krukk turned to the Tri-V display between him and his executive officer. "On screen."

His executive officer toggled the controls, and a real-time visual image of the valley they'd identified as their target appeared. To their left, the high ground extended above the narrow valley. He recognized that the expansive cavern systems in the area were likely the Goblins' target. For a moment, he scrolled through his munitions stores to see if he had anything capable of knocking down the hilltop and its underlying caverns in totality. There was nothing capable, as they'd never imagined having to drop enough ordnance to alter the landscape on Snowmass.

He leaned forward and studied the image. A half dozen thermal signatures of varying strengths dotted the area around the end of the tree line near the cavern entrance. He estimated the distance between the forces in the wood line and the cavern entrance at a couple of hundred meters. In other words, well within the range to support by fire.

"Switch to thermals. I mean thermals only, no visuals," Krukk directed. He wanted to see if his hunch was right.

"Yes, sir."

The image changed to green monochromatic display, where the hottest signatures appeared black, and the cooler surfaces appeared a very light shade of green. He clearly saw the enemy positions along the tree line. What he could see indicated a company of infantry, though there might be more Humans if their discipline with heat and light was up to mercenary standards. Those positions, and their units, didn't bother him. What he saw in the valley itself did. A single heat source, likely that of a Human CASPer, made its way to the cavern entrance and stopped. With the remote sensors, he watched it back up against the hill by the cavern's mouth, and a lone Human figure climbed out. He couldn't see who it was, but his gut churned with sudden certainty.

I know that's you, Harmon Gray. I'm coming for you.

Krukk tapped on the display and withdrew a stylus to quickly draw his attack plan for transmission to his troops.

"We'll land in the center of the valley and orient on those heat signatures. First section will move left into the tree line and take out those targets. Second and third sections will make for the cavern entrance to secure it and hold off any additional forces. I don't believe all of Gray's forces are in the tree line, but they're not far away. I've scanned the hilltop and the boulders on the other side of the cavern entrance. They're close by, and they favor high terrain, so we're going to hold the flyers back until the infantry and the skiffs have identified the enemy and pinned them down by fire. Gray will play into our hands. All we have to do is pressure his forces."

Krukk didn't wait on the frequency for questions. In his mind, a commander's intent was always clear. The graphics he'd drawn on the display helped orient his forces on the situation at hand, and he knew by their training they would do exactly as he ordered.

Krukk turned to his executive officer. "I want you on the ground with the skiffs."

"Will you be taking the flyers, sir?"

"We'll scout the high terrain for Gray's forces. Humans love their hilltops. I'm going to give him the chance to die upon one."

* * *

Through the heavy snow, Harmon Gray heard the rumble of dropship engines approaching from the south and east. The Knights had arrived. With his forces hunkered down and under complete radio silence, including having their power levels at the barest minimum, Gray wanted to believe their signatures were low enough to avoid detection. Part of that relied on how well the Knights employed their sensors, and another part of it relied pretty heavily on blind luck. So far on this mission, he believed, luck hadn't been on their side. Watching the Tri-V display inside his cockpit, Gray held his breath as the first ship approached right at the center of the valley and prepared to land. He recognized the Zuul dropship and its capabilities. That particular model with an unpronounceable name could carry only four skiffs and two companies of infantry, which made up exactly half of the combat forces the Knights had garrisoned at New Perth. There would be at least one more ship.

Given his CASPers and the state of the overall force under his command, he had to believe the numerical advantage went to the Knights. The best he could do was surprise the living hell out of their rear. Sensors indicated at least one more dropship above, but it didn't land, at least not immediately. As the first ship deployed skiffs and infantry, Gray watched them gather in an orderly manner and form up into a marching formation. The four skiffs had the lead and moved in a line abreast formation by twos. A company of Zuul infantry, wearing white and gray camouflage jumpsuits over their loadouts, fell behind each of the sections of skiffs. One section of skiffs and infantry went to the left of the landed dropship, and the other section moved to the right. They were on the attack.

His fingers hovered over the radio controls for the company. Radio silence had been the order of the day, and while he wanted desperately to take out the Knights and their dropship, his gut told him to wait.

An incoming text message from Lucille caught his eye. Knights' forces have paused three hundred meters in front of the dropship. They are holding a beachhead for the rest of their forces. Watch for air deployment.

Sure enough, the second dropship landed approximately two hundred meters to the right of the first ship. Just as quickly as the first, the second ship offloaded a similarly comprised force. As they moved to the front to assume their own attack position, the two dropships spun up their engines and lifted off. Gray watched them ascend and turn back to the south. They continued to gain altitude and speed and were soon out of the area.

He turned back to the field in time to see the first missiles streak from the skiffs toward the Misfits' positions in the far tree line.

Come on, Quin'taa. Fire up that auto cannon and—

On cue, the automated cannon let off a burst of rounds at the forward line of skiffs. The Knights pivoted their attack slightly toward the cannon's position at what Gray saw as the far left of the Misfit's location. He knew the Oogar and his teammates were hunkered down at the opposite edge of the tree line, waiting for orders to attack.

The Knights' skiffs proceeded across the center of the small valley and climbed the sloping terrain toward the cavern entrance. As the infantry crossed the shallow ditch in the middle, their formation slowed slightly. He counted to ten, and while the skiffs continued to move at a steady pace, the infantry nearly crawled by comparison through the semi-frozen mud.

He pushed his transmit button. "Mantis 6. Go!"

Gray stood from his protected position and zoomed his optical cameras in to the valley floor. Bursting through the snow from small dug-in positions, Lieutenant Whirr and six of her female MinSha warriors erupted into the fray with heavy weapons, tearing the closest Zuul infantry to bits.

"We're on the attack," Whirr called over the frequency. "Ready, Misfit 1?"

The Oogar's growl filled the channel. "Standing by. The minute we engage them, the charge is yours, Gray. We're counting on you to take the skiffs out."

He nodded to himself and felt his throat tighten with emotion. There was no way in hell he intended to leave the Misfits or any of the others on the field. He'd learned his lesson. Just as he touched the transmit button, Harmon Gray thought not about the mercenaries from his own company he'd lost over the last two years, but about Lieutenant Drew Morris. The young officer had turned back from certain rescue to provide cover for the dropship and the others to escape. He'd known precisely what it took to win the field that day, much as Gray knew what it would take in the snowy valley.

The MinSha swarmed toward the infantry, and the skiffs slowed until the tree line in front of them erupted with heavy weapons fire and held their attention.

"Reapers and Hammers up!" Gray called. "Hold that line and follow me!"

He pressed the jump pedals, and his CASPer tore through the snow-covered boughs above him and into the sky above the valley. His heads-up display populated with both infantry and mechanized targets. He selected the MAC and oriented on the closest of the Zuul skiffs. Gray made a fist and dispatched fifteen rounds. The results were catastrophic, and the skiff erupted with a massive secondary explosion. Around him a curtain of MAC rounds and small arms fire tore down on the Trenta Knights.

"Here we come, assholes!" He whooped in his cockpit and prepared to land for his next bound forward. "Misfits! Phase Two, go! Mantis 6, hold your position until Hammer elements close on your flank, and then gut those bastards. This is for Lieutenant Morris and those lost at New Perth. We hold the line!"

* * *

The snowcat tore through the falling snow on a trail no wider than its treads. Rains tried to see where they were going, but couldn't. Only the trees framing both sides of the trail gave any indication of its location. The wind and snowfall blanketed everything. He'd never seen true "whiteout" conditions before, and losing his visual senses was disconcerting, to say the least. Crowded into the tight cockpit with Vannix and Balyeat added to his discomfort. The larger man drove the snowcat deftly. The basic vehicle didn't feature Tri-V displays or topographical mapping or anything to provide them situational awareness of the approaching valley.

"How much longer?" Rains asked, trying not to sound like an impatient child.

Vannix chittered. He realized he'd lost his attempt. "We're close. I am seeing intermittent laser connections from Lucille and unknown contacts on the Force 25 frequencies. I believe they're nearby. Once she locks on, we'll know for sure."

Rains nodded. "Sorry."

"Don't apologize, Jackson. Our friends are in danger."

Balyeat rumbled, "All our friends. I know Reecha would want me to apologize for her subterfuge, but it was necessary, Peacemakers."

Vannix placed a forepaw on his wide shoulder. "There will be a time for apologies, Mister Balyeat. For now, we must do what is right."

"And just," Rains added.

Balyeat nodded. "I would be honored if you would call me Nathan, Peacemakers."

Rains and Vannix glanced at each other for a moment. Each of them tried not to smile. In the literature advertising the Peacemaker Academy to potential candidates, one of the most entertaining phrases was translated often as "earning the trust of a Peacemaker is difficult." The reality they'd discovered was that they were taught not to trust anyone for the most part. For Peacemakers, though, they'd studied the giving of trust and respect diligently during their first year at the Academy. Of the species they worked with, Humans were often the most trusting, and one indicator of that given trust from Humans was the use of their first name. Nathan Balyeat was an ally, and his apologetic take on Reecha's activities spoke volumes about his own character. Rains knew in the eyes of the colony leadership, their activities bordered on illegal, but he also understood the intent behind their actions.

Things on this planet didn't add up. The Dream World Consortium's reputation, and recent history, didn't entitle them to determine what was right and wrong on Snowmass. When the dust settled from this conflict, the Consortium and their governing board would have much to answer for—especially if Tara Mason and the others discovered anything more substantive. For now, Reecha was the key.

Ahead of them, the narrow vehicle path widened, and the trees gave way to the valley below. The swirling storm abated. In front of the snowcat, Rains realized he could see several hundred meters downslope and almost completely across the widest portions of the valley. As they shot through the opening, both the cavern entrance and the waiting CASPer positioned outside were easy to see through the moderate snowfall. There was no doubt whose CASPer it was.

She's already inside.

He glanced at Vannix. "Can you reach Lucille?"

Vannix tapped on her slate furiously. "I've got her. Tara is inside the cavern, and Lucille is auto-fighting Deathangel 25 against any threats."

"Ask her to look for us and disengage when we're in range. We need to get down there."

"Copy that," Vannix replied. She tapped the driver on his wide shoulder. "Nathan, find a place to park the snowcat, preferably somewhere in the wood line and out of the line of fire. I have a feeling we're about to see a real shit storm in the valley."

Nathan wasn't looking at either of them, but instead appeared fixated on something in the clouds above them. "You can say that again, Peacemaker."

Rains followed Nathan's gaze and felt bile rise in the back of his throat. A dropship descended through the low gray clouds. It bore the familiar paint scheme of the Trenta Knights.

Dammit.

He was moving in a flash. Rains opened the door and vaulted into the ankle-deep snow without bothering to slip on additional cold-weather protection. He turned and looked over his shoulder at his stunned partner and their equally stunned driver. "Tell Lucille I'm on my way. Get down here and provide backup."

He barely saw Vannix scramble from her position in the cockpit before he turned and resumed his frantic sprint the across the face of the hill, past the cavern's mouth, and up to Deathangel 25 as the dropship settled in the valley in a swirling white cloud of blowing snow and offloaded troops and equipment.

"Lucille? Lucille, open up. It's Peacemaker Rains. I need inside that CASPer."

At first he wondered if she either hadn't heard him or had ignored him. He drew another lungful of air, prepared to yell louder, when he heard a rush of air and saw the cockpit of the CASPer open slowly while the external handholds deployed. When he reached the mech, Rains climbed aboard the CASPer with practiced ease and slid into the cockpit. That he could easily do so struck him as both odd and mildly funny at the same time. He'd never dreamed of being a CASPer pilot, much less a Peacemaker, and somehow he'd found a way to do both.

"I don't have a headset, Lucille. On speakers. Let's get the show on the—"

From outside and behind the CASPer, muffled by the rocky hill covering the cavern's entrance, came the sound of laser fire. One sharp blast followed by several smaller ones.

The fight is inside.

<<Threat warning. Inside the cavern. Contact is unknown. Observable vital signs on the adversary indicate an Equiri.>>

Thraff.

Rains closed the cockpit and strapped himself in while making sure its systems and weapons were operational. Lucille continued to relay sounds from the outside. A fusillade of rounds of different types echoed out of the cavern's mouth. He established positive control of the CASPer and stepped forward with his right leg, twisting toward the entrance in time to see a familiar black Equiri scramble out amidst a flurry of laser fire. Thraff's combat vest smoked from numerous places. He'd taken a beating from whoever Tara had inside with her.

Without thinking, Rains lunged forward and grasped Thraff's armored combat vest with the CASPer's left hand. In sudden anger, the realization of the capture of his quarry being within his literal grasp, Rains violently flung the Equiri as far as he could into the snow. Rains spun toward the tumbling figured and stalked forward.

As he did, he glanced at the side cameras and looked for his partner. She'd taken up a covered position in the boulders outside the cavern's mouth. He snapped on Deathangel 25's external speakers. "Get your ass in there, Vannix!"

"Moving." His rear cameras showed her scampering through the boulders toward the cavern's entrance. Weapon drawn, she ducked into the ragged entrance.

PING! PING!

Multiple laser impacts on the CASPer's external frame and armor shifted his attention. A warning klaxon sounded in his ears and indicated the magnetic accelerator cannon on his right shoulder and the external hand cannon on his right side had been sheared away. He drew the left-hand cannon and turned toward Thraff to see the Equiri, his black coat thick with snow, standing with a large rifle in his hands, the barrel pointed directly at Rains. Thraff aimed and fired again, and Deathangel 25 bucked backward after several impacts in the left shoulder area. Fresh warning signals alerted him that the left MAC was now gone. Rains brought up the hand cannon and squeezed a burst which appeared to have little effect as Thraff started forward. A new burst of rounds tore the hand cannon away from Rains' fist.

Fuck!

"You're mine, Mason!"

Jackson depressed the external speaker switch. "Bring it, motherfucker."

Recognition flash across the Equiri's face. He snarled and screamed as he charged with his head down, his massive legs churning through the snow. "Rains!"

Rains attempted to put the CASPer into a fighting stance with one foot forward and the other braced behind him. He brought both hands up to deflect the charging horse. While not a great course of action, it was all he could think of because he'd excelled in hand-to-hand combat at the Peacemaker Academy. While this wasn't a training exercise, he believed the CASPer's agility and power would allow him to fight effectively.

Lucille chimed. <<There is a machete on hard point six—back of the right leg.>>

There was a slight thump on the back of his right leg, and Rains reached instinctively for it. He found the handle easily and he drew the machete from its holster, and his weapons indicator connected to show its current status. It also showed the weapon was a prototype.

No better time to test it.

As he drew the weapon, time slowed appreciably. The Equiri was almost upon him. Rage boiled through his adversary's dark eyes and curled his foam-flecked mouth as Thraff screamed an inhuman scream of death. There was little doubt of his intentions. Rains wanted the perfect moment to—

<<Override.>>

Before he could ask what Lucille meant, the right arm rocketed forward. With a mighty swing outside his control, the CASPer's arm swung the heavy machete in an arc that cleaved into the space between the Equiri's neck and his armored combat vest. Rains felt the impact as the blade dug deeply, tearing bone and tissue, and rendering the pure white snow red with blood. Thraff's momentum carried him forward, and the machete's handle was torn from Rains' hand. He spun gracefully out of the way and positioned himself to shove Thraff hard into the rock wall behind them. With any luck, the impact would stun Thraff long enough that Rains could get him into restraints for questioning. His hands easily found purchase on the Equiri's wide shoulders, and Rains shoved with all the power Deathangel 25 could manifest. Through the cockpit Rains heard the dull, wet thump of the Equiri's skull as it shattered on impact. Rains realized he was holding his breath and let it out slowly as Thraff's lifeless body crumpled to the snow.

<<Threat warning. Multiple skiffs and two companies of infantry are attacking this position, Jackson.>>

"Why did you kill him?"

<<I calculated you had a thirteen percent chance of even injuring him, Peacemaker. No offense, but you're not a fully trained CASPer pilot, and I'm much more than a virtual assistant. No one knows Deathangel 25 better than me. Not even Tara.>>

Rains laughed. "Thanks, and fair enough. Show me the inbounds."

Across his view screens, dozens of red icons appeared. He could barely make some of them out as the snowfall increased. On his screen, a tsunami of red appeared headed his direction, intent on killing him and stopping Tara.

No hand cannons. No MACs. Rains grinned. *Just a machete. Might be doable with Lucille swinging away.*

To his right, the sparse tree line lit up in the snow with intense weapons fire from several auto cannons and other weapons.

"Deathangel 25, this is Misfit 5. We've got the Knights covered. You have flyers vectoring on your position. At least four of them and maybe more. They're obscured in the clouds. We're not out of this fight yet!"

<<I have sensor readings from the two hand cannons damaged in the attack. Both are still usable and would double the amount of ammunition we have aboard.>>

Rains scanned the snowy ground and located them with Lucille's assistance. Both hand cannons were serviceable. He was lucky. Again.

<<Cannons ready. Force 25 CASPers are attacking the rear of the Knights' formation now. I have the flyers located. They are preparing for an attack run.>>

"Let's get in the fight, Lucille," Rains said with a grin. "Do I have a better than thirteen percent chance of making it through this fight?"

<<Only with me as your wingman, Peacemaker.>>

*****

Chapter Thirty-Two

The CASPers raced into the valley. Stunned Zuul mercenaries froze and gawked as the two platoons bounded and jumped through the blinding snowstorm toward them. Gray took position at the center of the formation as they descended on the Knights.

"Mantis 6, we're moving in. Prepare to charge."

The response from Whirr was immediate. "With pleasure, Avenger 6."

He blinked in recognition. Whirr had bestowed the callsign of the field commander on him. Tara Mason might have something to say about it, but she'd left him in charge of the attack. There was little doubt in his mind that she wasn't sure about her decision. Truth be told, after his screwup in New Perth, he wondered if he'd made any correct decisions in her eyes during the first phase of the operation. He bit the inside of his cheek and tasted blood. The pain focused him.

"Charge, Mantis 6."

In front of him from the left of his camera feed, the MinSha warriors charged into the Zuul infantry, where they'd attempted, with some success, to dig themselves into hasty fighting positions after the ambush. The charging MinSha frightened them into a full-fledged panic. Their panic spread to the second infantry company, which stopped their march and hesitated for five glorious seconds.

There we go!

"Reapers and Hammers, put rounds on target!" he called and brought his MAC to bear on the collection of infantry stalled in the middle of the valley. Their skiffs continued marching toward the Misfits' positions, seemingly oblivious to the chaos behind them.

As he watched, the Zuul infantry reformed and pushed toward the MinSha. Suddenly steeled, they appeared ready to attempt an envelopment of their greatest threat in order to establish a defensive perimeter. Gray wouldn't let that happen. He touched his jump pedals and bounded sharply toward the center of the Zuul formation.

"Mantis 6, they're moving to envelop you. Hasty perimeter. We'll clean them off you." He fired three MAC rounds in quick succession and took down two of the Zuul at the maximum range of his weapon. "Force 25, your instructions are BUSTER. I say again, BUSTER. Move your asses and let's clear the field!"

"Copy," Whirr replied. "Avenger 6, we're halted and forming up. We're taking losses."

Gray bounded again and risked looking away from the collection of targets in front of him. Two of Whirr's eight warriors were down. Both were still fighting, however. The MinSha females were fearsome creatures, and he couldn't help feeling lucky to have them on his side. They weren't going down without a serious fight.

Neither are we.

At the apex of his jump, Gray activated his hand cannons and set his MAC to track his visual movements. He squeezed his right hand into a fist to fire the MAC while he kept his index finger ready to squeeze off bursts from the cannons. Falling toward the center of the Zuul formation, he brought his weapons to bear. The rest of the CASPers did the same, and the snow around the Knights erupted with weapons fire, slinging mud and flesh into the air.

"Misfits, phase three is active. Good hunting!"

* * *

"Contact front!" Homer called from his defilade position. Slightly forward of the tree line and hidden in a depression just large enough for his Pushtal frame, Araceli had to look twice in his direction to actually see him. As she did, her camera feeds showed the approaching Zuul skiffs.

"I count four," Quin'taa growled. "I like those odds."

Araceli couldn't help but grin. She felt much the same as her Oogar friend, and inside her CASPer she believed herself just as capable in a fight. "They're tracking on the auto cannons."

"Ready to engage them instead of the infantry?" Homer asked.

Quin'taa didn't immediately reply. "No. They think they're advancing under the cover of the weather. We'll let them get a little closer."

Araceli remembered something she'd learned from her history courses in school on Victoria Bravo. Human schools focused on Human history no matter their location in the galaxy, and her school in particular carried a fondness for North American history. She couldn't remember the battle, or who said it, but the intent of the statement had been clear.

"Don't fire until we see the whites of their eyes."

There was a deep chuckle on the frequency. Quin'taa whispered. "Little sister, you honor us."

Araceli blushed in the cockpit of her CASPer. From what she knew of the Oogar, Quin'taa's statement was as close to a declaration of love and acceptance as anything ever said in any language. Her eyes filled with fresh tears. They were her family now, and there was no way in hell she would let them down.

"I have my first shot opportunity," Homer called. "Not wanting to break up the love fest, but I can hit the first skiff commanders. They're heads-up out of the skiff and directing movement."

Araceli zoomed in her camera feed as far as it could go. Sure enough, the heads of the Zuul vehicle commanders were plainly visible. "In this wind? That's a tough shot."

"Doubting me again?" Homer laughed. "Guarantee I get one of them, at least."

"In one shot?" Quin'taa bantered. "I'll buy drinks for a month if you do. Hold off, though. I'm activating the final two cannon positions now. I expect them to turn broadside to you. When they do, you're cleared to fire. Be prepared to move, Araceli."

She flexed her fingers and toes. Adrenaline flashed through her body. "Misfit 5 is ready to move."

"When you do, little sister, rain fire on them. We'll be right behind you."

Intelligence from the battle at Victoria Bravo suggested the skiffs were much more susceptible to damage from the rear than their heavily armored front and side skirts. If she could get into position and jump over them, she could pump MAC rounds into their rear decks. The goal would be to get the first two skiffs in one bound. The remaining two would pivot again toward her and Homer's side of the position and leave their flank and rear open to Quin'taa on the opposite edge of the position. All they had to do was hold the skiffs' attention long enough to disorient them from the real threats. With the rest of Force 25 decimating the infantry down the slope, victory was within their grasp.

This is for Drew Morris, assholes.

"Homer?" Quin'taa's voice was a low grumble. "Ready to fire, Homer. Standby to jump, little sister."

Araceli placed her toes against the jump pedals. The system indicated ready to jump. She snapped the master arm switch to the fire position and heard Quin'taa growl once more.

"Send it."

Araceli couldn't hear the shot as she stomped down on the pedals for a max jump. As she cleared the snow-covered trees, she clearly saw all four skiffs. She targeted the one closest to her and squeezed her right hand into a fist. Twelve MAC rounds erupted from the cannon and tore through the thinner armor of the skiff's rear deck like a hot knife through butter. The skiff detonated with a spectacular secondary explosion that caused the others to swerve and attempt to evade both it and her. At the apex of her jump, she targeted the second skiff and let loose a similar barrage. There was little effect as the armored fairing protecting the deck from each side took the brunt of her shots. She adjusted slightly and fired five more rounds before turning her focus to landing the CASPer. One round tore into the skiff's engine compartment as another disabled one section of tracks beneath its skirts. The skiff lurched hard to one side. As it did, multiple rounds from the auto cannon positions tore into the skiff and set it ablaze. There appeared to be no survivors.

She fired the jets to slow her descent and saw the trailing two skiffs approaching her position. The shocked face of one commander disappeared in a cloud of blood and tissue. A second later the other commander joined his friend. As she landed, Araceli brought up the hand cannons and sprayed the skiffs, more to keep their attention than to inflict any real damage. When they turned to face her, she caught sight of Quin'taa with his heavy paws carrying the massive cannon. A tongue of orange fire at least a meter in length erupted from its barrel. The first skiff detonated under a hail of cannon fire. She watched it explode and followed the fireball as it rose into the sky.

"Missile! Araceli!" Homer yelped on the frequency.

She turned just as the missile slammed into her right shoulder and MAC cannon. There was an explosion, and she felt heat on her skin before a rush of frigid air filled the cockpit. In slow motion, she fell backward. Homer ran toward her, and a hail of bullets riddled his legs and the surrounding ground. He toppled forward in the snow as Araceli hit the ground on the CASPer's back. Unable to right it, she opened the cockpit and reached for her father's pistols strapped to the inside of the cockpit rail. As she climbed out of the cockpit, a Zuul bearing the rank insignia of an executive officer jumped from the burning track and stomped toward Homer lying face-down in the snow.

"No!" Araceli squeezed both triggers at the same time and rattled off four shots from each weapon. None seemed to hit their mark. The Zuul turned to her, and there was just enough time for Homer to leap up, claws and teeth bared, and ferociously end the Zuul's life.

Araceli did not turn away.

* * *

Valley Floor

Snowmass

Between Reaper and Hammer platoons, the CASPer forces routed the Zuul infantry. Whirr and her infantry could be used elsewhere, and with greater effect, so Gray cut them loose to support the Misfits at the cavern entrance.

The ten CASPers had little trouble with the infantry forces. Even with their strong combat armor, the Zuul couldn't fire and maneuver against the Humans.

"Avenger 6, this is Hammer 3," a voice Gray didn't recognize called over the frequency. "Sir, Hammer 6 is down."

Gray touched his Tri-V display and saw that the icon for Hammer 6 was black and motionless.

Damn you, Ordoñez. Your first command, and you buy the farm.

"Who's in command?" Gray replied. "Never mind. Take your orders from me. I've got eyes on you and am moving that direction. Stand by one."

"Yes, sir."

Gray leaped the CASPer into the air and adjusted his path to rendezvous with the leaderless Hammers. As he flew through the air, Gray noted the CASPers were about to completely encircle the Zuul. The sight brought back painful, recent memories. Try as he might, Gray couldn't immediately look away from the raging battle below, nor could he stop the tears that filled his eyes as he remembered the last minutes of his Goblins only a few months before.

* * *

"Goblin 6, this is 5. I've got eyes on you. Moving your way."

He'd been pinned down by Xiq'tal infantry forces after an amphibious raid and recovery mission had gone sour within minutes after hitting the beach. The one thing working in his favor was the combat trains with his maintenance, artillery, and logistical elements were several kilometers out to sea on a series of atmosphere-capable drop platforms modified to float. He'd left them under orders—implicit orders—that in the event of a tactical loss, they were to boost for orbit at the earliest launch window.

They'd disobeyed his orders. Worse, they were trying to come get him.

"XO, I told you to get off this planet. Cut our losses." Gray settled his back against the wet rocks. He'd been forced to leave his CASPer behind when it started taking on water. Turns out Xiq'tal claws could rend the metal hull pretty effectively.

"Cutting our losses doesn't mean we cut you, Harm," Hector Ordoñez replied. "Give me ten seconds of your recovery beacon. Should be enough to paint your location and keep the crabfuckers from dropping shells on you."

Gray bit his lip but argued no more. Hector wouldn't hear any of it. Worse, he'd keep coming regardless. They'd been friends too long for him to expect anything else.

"Beacon's on," Gray said into the radio headset. He snapped the simple HF recovery beacon switch to on and counted to ten before turning it off again. Over the crashing of the waves against the rocks he sheltered amongst, he listened for the sound of artillery shells falling. There was nothing for more than thirty agonizing seconds.

Out to sea he heard the buzzing of an engine, but it wasn't one of the fast boats he'd paid way too many credits to get from Earth. Six of those lay on the bottom of the surrounding cove. There were only two left at the assembly area, along with a smaller, much slower boat that could barely outrun a walking CASPer.

Oh gods, he's not doing that, is he?

To Gray's horror, the slower boat came trundling toward the cove. The dark gray hull rode low in the water because of the Mk 6

CASPer standing on the bow with MACs on both shoulders and cannons in hand. The boat turned and accelerated toward him.

The unmistakable whistling of Xiq'tal artillery rounds arced over Gray's head and impacted the water around the boat. Still, Ordoñez and whoever else was crewing the thing never wavered. When they were within range, the CASPer unleashed all its weapons in a methodical, targeted manner at the cliffs above him.

"You might want to start swimming, 6."

"Fuck you." Gray waded into the cool, murky water and wondered what creatures lurked beneath its surface as he dove forward. Surfacing, he drew a deep breath and saw the boat swinging to one side of him. The CASPer continued firing. Gray glanced back at the cliffs and saw six of the godsawful crabfuckers swarming and skittering across the place he'd hidden for the last several hours. Ordoñez and the other merc had saved his life.

At once the boat was there, and several sets of hands reached down to fish him out of the water. The boat lurched forward and sped up again. He watched Ordoñez in the CASPer firing his MAC until both barrels glowed a faint red at the bow of the ship.

"I'm the king of your world, motherfuckers!"

* * *

Gray landed next to the burning CASPer and kicked snow across it to douse the flames. There were no life signs from the CASPer, and while SOP said he should open the emergency retrieval hatch, Gray knew he should wait until the Zuul were completely contained and either surrendered or died in place.

You were the king of that world, buddy.

Gonna miss your sorry ass. "Sir, Hammer 3. The Knights have surrendered. Orders?"

Gray grunted. Hector had almost made it. While it was the life of a mercenary, there was nothing glamorous about it. "Standard operating procedures. Secure and silence them. We'll interrogate when they—"

A high-pitched scream filled the valley. Gray turned to the south and saw several dark shapes drop out of the low cloud deck. For a moment it felt like the wind stopped completely, and the temperature around him, even inside the CASPer, fell a good ten degrees.

"Red air! Red air! Weapons free!" Gray called and brought up his weapons as the first two flyers laid down strafing fire across the CASPers, and even their own soldiers.

What the fuck!

"Sir, Hammers 4 and 5 have two more inbound from the south. We're laying down fire." Gray noted Sergeants Avera and Zawahir had moved to the extreme southern edge of the position and were laying down coordinated hand cannon and MAC fire. One flyer exploded. The second almost waggled its wings as it turned toward them.

"Reloading!" Avera called. "Cover me!"

"I've got you, 4," he heard Zawahir reply. The two experienced CASPer pilots sounded like they were fishing or having a beer, not fighting for their lives. "Missiles in the air!"

"I'm up!" Avera yelled.

"Pour it on!" Zawahir replied. Tracers from their hand cannons tore through the sky around the flyer until both missiles hit their targets, wiping Hammers 4 and 5 from the map.

Gray followed the first two flyers as they looped to the east and banked back to the north. He smashed his transmit button. "Deathangel 25, Avenger 6. Two flyers inbound on your position. Over."

There was no response for a moment, and when the voice came back, it stopped Gray cold. "Avenger 6, Peacemaker Rains. We'll take it from here. Clear the field."

Unsure of what else to say, Gray licked his lips and replied, "Yes, sir."

*****

Chapter Thirty-Three

Cavern Complex

Snowmass

Reecha didn't move. The older Veetanho stood looking at the severed arm and remains of the other with a forlorn dread. Tara suspected it had belonged to one of Reecha's children or grandchildren; maybe it was remorse for having someone so young die under her care. It was a feeling Tara could relate to. Undoubtedly there were casualties on the field, as there had already been on the mission itself. The last thing she wanted to do was face them.

"We have to get moving," Tara said. Reecha remained frozen in place. "Honored Reecha? Please. We have to get you to safety."

"I was safe here," Reecha whispered. "At least I believed I was."

"That's why we have to go now," Tara urged.

There was a soft chitter as the Veetanho turned to face her. "Colonel Mason, they were always going to come for me. Like they've gone after Jimmy. They'll come after you, too."

Tara nodded. "I'm prepared for that, but right now I have to get you to safety. Nathan is standing by with the snowcat. We just have to get you there while Force 25 takes down the Trenta Knights once and for all. It's better if you aren't here."

For a long moment Reecha said nothing. Her dark, somber eyes never left Tara's face, and her nose twitched toward the door. "We can go. The Equiri is dead."

Tara tapped her headset. "Jackson?"

"I got Thraff, Tara. Gray's got the infantry pinned down, but there are flyers approaching. If you're moving, now's the time."

"Copy." She gazed at Reecha. "We need to go. Can this door be secured?"

"No. The damage to the control unit means it is open. You must win the field to protect it."

"Then we'll do just that." Tara motioned toward the door. "Stay behind me."

As they stepped through the door, Tara caught sight of Vannix approaching with a rifle in her paws.

"Oh, thank gods you're okay," Vannix said. "Jackson put down Thraff, but I wasn't sure if anyone here made it."

Tara caught sight of the other young Veetanho's body lying on the ground at their feet. "Just Reecha and I."

Vannix stepped around Tara and for a moment; she thought they'd initiate a full greeting ritual. Veetanho females often went through a complex sniff, touch, and groom display when first meeting. Instead, the two looked at each other with wide, dark eyes. Tara noted their ears slumped as well before they stepped forward and into each other's arms in a very Human embrace.

"You have my sympathies, Honored Reecha."

Reecha sniffled. "You have my respect and devoted honor, Peacemaker. Well met."

"Well met," Vannix replied with a catch of emotion in her voice. "Let's get you out of here. Follow me."

As they exited the cavern, Lucille's voice crackled over the frequency. <<Situation reports incoming. Are you ready to receive?>>

"Negative, Lucille. We've moving out of the cave." Tara tapped her headset twice to connect to Jackson Rains. "Jackson? You're in Deathangel?"

"I am, boss." He laughed. "Don't worry, I'll give her back."

"You'd better." Tara took up a position behind Reecha as rear security. Vannix stepped into the light of the valley beyond the cavern's mouth, and Reecha followed. Tara ducked, stepped through the opening behind them, and turned to see Deathangel 25 staring into the valley.

"Flyers!" Rains called. "Flyers! Take cover!"

Tara watched him bring up both hand cannons and scan the low clouds. "I've got something," Rains said.

<<Four flyers. Two sections of two. The first is three kilometers and closing,>> Lucille relayed to Tara. <<Twenty seconds.>>

Tara glanced at Reecha and Vannix before drawing her own weapon. "Go, Vannix. Get to cover. We'll hold them off."

The Peacemaker's mouth opened and closed without a sound. She tugged at Reecha's upper arm. "We must hurry."

The two Veetanho scampered toward the hidden snowcat. Tara watched them for a moment and turned to take up a firing position to one side of her CASPer and behind it, using it as cover. As she knelt, she heard the first flyers. Jackson opened up with Deathangel 25's hand cannons, and the first flyer took several rounds before spiraling out of control toward them. The flyer, however, kept firing as it spun. Rounds impacted the ground around Tara and arced over her head toward Reecha. Instinctively, Tara glanced behind her and saw Vannix push the older Veetanho to the snow and cover her. The little Peacemaker's weapon came up, and she fired at the approaching flyers.

Tara grinned, impressed. She turned and leveled her weapon at the second flyer as it fired a missile that tracked through the air and slammed into Deathangel 25's upper right shoulder. The explosion knocked Tara to the ground, and she rolled upright, expecting to see her mech burning. Instead, Jackson Rains continued to fire with the hand cannons.

Tara couldn't help but smile.

The second flyer exploded in mid-air and fell to the ground. When it slammed into the snow, Tara saw several figures move up behind it and realized they'd been responsible for knocking the Zuul craft out of the sky.

<<Connecting.>>

"Deathangel 25, Misfit 5. We're moving to you."

Tara raised up a hand palm out to them. "Stop and spread out. There're two more flyers."

"Copy," Araceli replied. As Tara watched, the three very different teammates did exactly as she asked. "Contact. My two o'clock at five kilometers."

"Give them everything you have," Tara called.

"We hold the line," Quin'taa growled. She recognized the phrase from something Drew Morris had said at New Perth, and she approved.

The first of the two flyers came out of the clouds low and fast. Araceli and the Misfits opened up first, and as the flyer got closer, Rains joined in. Tara watched, her eyes sweeping past the flyer to where its wingman should be, but there was nothing there.

"Lucille? The other flyer?"

<<In the cloud deck. Matched bearing and trailing the leader by a kilometer. Relaying targeting reticle to Deathangel 25.>>

"Get it to the rest of the team."

<<I cannot. Misfit 5's computer is incorrectly updated and connection is impossible.>>

"Jackson, light up the wingman," Tara called.

"Got it." Deathangel 25's hand cannons tracked the target and erupted with a steady stream of fire. The lead flyer rolled and slammed into the ground a few hundred meters in front of Araceli and the Misfits. She heard them yell and cheer over the frequency.

The second flyer careened out of the clouds and impacted very close to their position, but none of them moved. Instead, Tara lowered her head when the crashing aircraft detonated as it hit the ground. Tara felt the flash of heat from the explosion, and then debris and snow rained down around them.

"I've got a 'chute," Rains called.

Tara looked up and saw the round white parachute descending toward them with a single Zuul under the canopy. The soldier didn't move and appeared to be gravely wounded. Force 25's standard operating procedures went farther than the Mercenary Guild's expectations of combat. They'd recover and, if possible, treat the wounded pilot. No one fired. Instead, she saw Quin'taa and Homer move toward her and the parachute.

The soldier was about a hundred feet off the ground when it raised a weapon, but not at any of them. It fired once over their shoulders at Reecha and Vannix. Everyone froze. There was the *crack* from a single MAC round being fired. The Zuul dropped its weapon and hung listlessly in the parachute harness until it hit the ground.

"Nice shot, little sister," Quin'taa called to Araceli. The young woman marched her CASPer up the hill with her weapons on the Zuul. She'd come a long way in a very short time.

Mercenary life makes you grow up quick, Mason. Being a CASPer pilot, doubly so.

Sergeant Snyder's words gave her a little comfort as she made her way to the fallen Zuul. Quin'taa and Homer were already there with weapons trained on it. The soldier was alive, and his uniform bore the insignia of a commander.

<<It's Colonel Krukk. The Trenta Knights commander. I am cracking his slate now.>>

"Get everything you can, Lucille."

<<Acknowledged.>>

The Zuul coughed and lolled its head to look at her. "You're not Harmon Gray. I take pleasure in knowing we killed your commander."

Tara shook her head. "I'm Colonel Tara Mason, in command of Force 25. Harmon Gray is one of my company commanders. You're Colonel Krukk of the Trenta Knights. Let's discuss your surrender."

Krukk coughed again and a trickle of blood ran down his slack maw to the snow. "My forces have already surrendered. You'll give me amnesty and treatment."

"Treatment, yes. Amnesty? For what? Do you know what the Dream World Consortium is doing at Lake Pryce? With this planet?"

"Go fuck yourself, Mason." Krukk laughed.

<<Tara? Colonel Krukk murdered Sophie Pryce in her office. Her body was just discovered by Mayor Citsym. I have the office video files, and I've relayed them to Peacemaker Rains.>>

"Jackson?" Tara called over her shoulder. "Can you come out here for a moment?"

Deathangel 25's external speakers came to life. "Damned right I can. Dismounting."

Within a minute Rains was there at her side with his Peacemaker badge in hand. She looked up at him.

"You saw the video from Pryce's office?"

Rains nodded. "I did. I won't arrest him without pursuit of charges."

"I wasn't asking you to. I asked because I wanted to ensure you'd seen the video evidence that this mercenary killed an unarmed civilian in the performance of her duties."

"Pryce?" Krukk coughed. "That bitch was behind this whole thing. She was the reason the Dream World Consortium came here in the first place. She wanted power and credits. I did this world a favor."

Neither she nor Rains looked at him. Rains spoke slowly, "I saw the evidence, and the mercenary has pleaded guilty. Were I an Enforcer, the choice would be easy to make. Since I'm not one—"

BLAM!

Tara holstered her weapon without looking and turned back to the Peacemaker. "I think I served justice."

"Too good for that bastard," Rains replied. He looked over Tara's shoulder, and the thin smile on his face evaporated.

"Oh, no."

Rains sped past her, and Tara looked over her shoulder. Vannix appeared to be covered in blood, and Reecha lay motionless in the snow. Tara ran after the Peacemaker, and the Misfits followed. As she ran, Tara heard Lucille saying she was moving Deathangel on her own. She also saw Maarg and a snowcat approaching from the far tree line. Barely. Her eyes filled with sudden tears.

"Lucille? Medical emergency. Get me medics off the field. Primary target is down, and we need assistance."

<<Medics are across the valley in the assembly area. They are moving now. ETA is four minutes.>>

They're not going to make it.

"*Mako 15*, this is Deathangel 25. Critical casualty. I need you here. Now."

Carter's voice came back. "Descending from flight level now. ETA is one hundred and twenty seconds."

Shit. Just hang on, Reecha. We're so close. Just hang on.

* * *

Rains got to Vannix and Reecha first. He saw the blood all over Vannix's white fur and Reecha lying motionless behind her.

"She okay? What happened?"

Vannix blinked. "The flyers strafed us. That one under parachute shot at us. I thought I got her out of the way and—"

Vannix slumped forward and Rains caught her. "It's okay, partner. I'll check her."

He reached out and touched Reecha's lower leg. Blood covered her outer garment as he inspected her from head to toe. There was an immediate spasm, and the older Veetanho sat up quickly. "Reecha? Reecha, are you okay?"

"I think so." She sputtered and blinked several times. She turned to Vannix, and a squeal left her lips. "Vannix?"

Rains saw his partner look up at him and realized she *had* gotten Reecha out of the way. The blood on her chest wasn't from their quarry, but her own. Her nose twitched as she stared at him for a long moment.

"Oh, shit." He started checking her wounds. They were much worse than he thought. "No. No, no, no, no!"

Vannix nodded and glanced down at her bloodied paws. "It's not bad."

Rains stared into her eyes, and she tried to smile. A shiver coursed through her body. "Keep looking at me, Vannix. Focus on me. You're gonna be fine."

"In your language," she started and huffed several times to catch her breath, "there's a word that can be meant in so many ways. I haven't been…able to express it…and I'm sorry to do so now."

Rains scrambled to her and wrapped his arms around her. "Hey. Hey, it's okay."

She settled heavily in his arms. "Jackson…"

He looked up and saw Tara running toward him. "Medic! Tara, get a nanite kit! She's hit bad!"

Vannix's paw came up and touched his face. "It's too late, Jackson."

His vision blurred with tears. "No, it's not. It ain't too late, partner. Stay with me!"

"Jackson?"

A sob choked his throat. "I'm here, Vannix. I've got you, just stay with me."

"Hush," she said and patted his cheek with her forepaw. "Is Reecha okay?"

"She's fine. You saved her." Hot tears rolled down his face as the snowfall intensified around them. "Don't go."

Her tiny maw curled in a smile. "I did my duty. There's nothing I wanted more. When the time came, I mattered."

"You did more than that." Rains brought up a hand and tried to wipe his tears, but Vannix caught it and grasped it tightly. "Stay with me, partner. Help is on the way."

She chuckled. "I know better, Jackson."

Her head rolled, and he knew she was looking at Tara, Maarg, and the others who'd gathered around them at a respectful distance. Her eyes lingered on Tara for a long moment.

"I'm proud of you, Tara Mason."

Rains watched Tara's face screw up in sheer pain. "You honor me, Peacemaker. You're one of us. Now and forever."

Vannix took a deep, hitching breath and turned to Reecha. "Help them, Honored One. Help them find Snowman."

"I will, Peacemaker Vannix." She grasped her translation pendant and turned it off to chitter something in their own language. Vannix closed her eyes and took a deep breath he thought was her last.

"Hey!" He shook her gently. "Vannix, stay with me."

Her eyes fluttered open, and she smiled at him. "That word. That word was…that word was…love."

"What do you mean?"

Vannix touched his cheek again. "Not the love you Humans have for your mates and nestlings. The love you have for each other as beings. Friends. I have that for you."

He squinted his eyes shut. "I know you do, partner."

"It's important that you hear it, Jackson Rains." Vannix drew a shuddering breath. "I love you, Jackson. My friend. My partner. You brought out…the best in me."

"I love you, Vannix." He squeaked the words out around the sob in his throat. "You made me better. Please. I can't do this without you."

"Yes…you can." Her other paw found his hand, and she pressed her badge into his palm. "Remember me, Peacemaker."

He nodded and leaned his head forward to touch hers. He buried his face in her neck fur and sobbed. "I'll never forget you, Peacemaker."

There was the faintest touch of one claw against the back of his neck, and he felt her tiny body go limp. Anguish gripped his heart and squeezed. Rains struggled to breathe and pulled her tightly to him. Head buried in her lifeless fur, Jackson Rains cried hot tears like he'd never cried before. He'd never once heard the words before. He'd never told her or anyone, but in his life as an orphan, no one had ever said they loved *him*. Mrs. Green told all the boys in her home she loved them, but he never felt the words were directed at him. To his heart.

At once the pain in his heart turned to molten lava, and he raised his face into the cold, bright air and screamed from the depths of his very soul. His scream tapered off into sobs that wracked his body. For a long time, no one moved as he cradled Peacemaker Vannix's body in the quiet, peaceful valley. The only sound louder than his tears was the breaking of his heart.

*****

Chapter Thirty-Four

Snowmass

They secured Vannix's body in the hold of *Mako 15* and brought the rest of the company, along with more than forty Zuul prisoners, to the cavern's entrance. Security and the practice of maintaining situational awareness gave them a collective sense of purpose. There were no cheery congratulations to each other. No celebrations. Everyone was quiet. Their moods were muted, their faces stone. Several fought tears. Others let them come, not only for their friends and Peacemaker Vannix, but for those they'd lost at Victoria Bravo. Force 25 had never been given time to grieve. The day was a reminder that for the foreseeable future, they might not have other chances.

Tara saw Maarg approaching on all fours. The big TriRusk was still a child, and the pain in her large, dark eyes was unmistakable.

"I'm sorry, Tara," Maarg said as she came to a stop and sat back on her haunches. "For everything I said before. I understand now."

Tara clenched her jaw. "This galaxy is a fucking cesspool, Maarg. It'll steal the very best from you in a heartbeat. There might be a time when the peace can be kept, but right now, it has to be *made*. Vannix understood that. I think Jackson does now, too."

"I see it," Maarg said. "Was Ch'tek in the cave with you?"

Tara shook her head, and an icy bolt of fear shot down her spine. "No."

"He left me in the ship. I broke the security code. It took longer than I—"

Tara wasn't listening. She'd drawn her pistol and started running toward the cavern entrance. She saw movement from the corner of her eye. Reecha and Lieutenant Whirr appeared, moving with her.

"Stay here. If something happens to me, Whirr, take no quarter. There's a Zuparti inside."

"Yes, ma'am," Whirr replied.

"I am coming with you," Reecha said.

"Like hell."

Reecha sprinted alongside her. "You don't know how to open the door's secondary system. While you're figuring that out, you're at risk."

<<She is correct, Tara. I am scanning with your slate. Pause inside the cavern mouth if you can.>>

Tara shook her head. "No, Lucille. If that little fucker is inside, we're going to deal with him first and foremost."

Inside the cavern mouth there was nothing. She swept the boulders on both sides, as she'd failed to do before, and cleared the entire room. Reecha stayed with and behind her the entire time.

"The room is clear."

<<I concur.>>

Tara turned to Reecha. "Show me the secondary system."

"There are multiple ones, Colonel Mason. This one is the least secure, I'm afraid." Reecha made her way to a small boulder about five meters from the door. She bent down and rolled the stone over, revealing what looked like a small hand crank.

"Just a moment." Reecha cranked, and Tara heard the big door disengage.

Tara took a knee and pointed her pistol at the crack as the blast door swung ajar. There was only darkness on the far side of the opening. "Lucille? Can you connect to anything? Give us some light?"

<<Negative.>>

Reecha crossed to the edge of the door, careful to remain protected behind it. "There are emergency controls immediately inside and to your left."

Tara nodded. "Okay."

Before she could move forward, Reecha darted around the edge of the door and into the space. Dim emergency lights snapped on inside, illuminating what appeared to be a hexagon-shaped control room. On the far side of the room, the three walls she could see had large black screens. Everything appeared to be powered down.

Tara swept into the room, clearing it with her weapon, and keeping her eyes simultaneously on the exit, Reecha, and anything in her field of vision. There was nothing she could see. Near the blast door, the two walls she hadn't seen before opened onto passageways that appeared blocked by rockfalls and equipment. The main console bore only a single marking—a sticker belonging to Intergalactic Haulers.

"What is this place?" Tara asked.

"A master control station," Reecha said. She walked over to the central console on a small dais in the center of the room. "Jimmy built a few of them across the galaxy. After his disappearance, I found it and shut it down. Automated procedures collapsed the exterior passageways, and the computers appeared to have been wiped completely."

Reecha tapped on the console, and a single prompt appeared in white lettering against the black screen.

<<COMMAND?>>

There was a connection port for a slate, and Tara gathered a cord from a chest pocket and snapped one end to her slate and the other to the console.

"Okay, Lucille, you're up."

Reecha crept closer, watching the slate as Lucille engaged the computer system. Lines of data flashed and scrolled from top to bottom on as it scrolled faster than Tara could read them.

Come on, Lucille.

There was the *click* of a weapon arm switch. Tara froze and looked up. From one of the collapsed passageways, a Zuparti emerged with a tiny pistol in its paws.

"This ends here, Tara Mason." The Zuparti chittered a laugh. "Your fruitless pursuit robbed you of common sense and security. You've made this easy for me."

Tara watched Ch'tek, a businessman and confidence artist, handle the pistol in a cavalier manner and let her arms fall limp at her sides.

"Bring your hands up where I can see them."

Tara glanced toward the blast door for a split second. It was enough to distract the Zuparti. She drew her pistol and leveled it at the center of his head. "I don't think so, Ch'tek."

"Oh, how cute. A standoff!"

Tara shook her head. "One of us is prepared to pull their trigger, Ch'tek. It's not you."

The Zuparti sneered. "You think I fear you? You may be the Deathangel, Mason, but you can't stop this. Your friend Jessica

Francis couldn't stop it. She had too much restraint. You do, too. Where this Union is headed, there is no such thing as restraint. Action is all that matters. Now, drop your weapon before I kill you both where you stand."

Tara shook her head. "Jessica Francis is a Peacemaker, Ch'tek."

"Of course she is, do you think I'm stupid?"

"No." Tara curled in one corner of her mouth in a half-smile. "I was making sure you knew the difference."

"And what difference is that? What are you talking about?"

"I'm not a Peacemaker, Ch'tek." She pulled the trigger twice in rapid succession. Both rounds tore through the Zuparti's skull and exited in a cloud of brain matter and blood. Ch'tek was dead before he hit the ground.

"Tara?" Jackson Rains' voice came into her headset. "Everything all right in there?"

"I found Ch'tek. He's dead." She holstered her weapon. "Make sure we grab everything he and Thraff have."

"We're working on it." The young man's voice was soft and pained. He would need more time than most to grieve.

Tara tapped her headset to close the connection. "Anything, Lucille?"

<<This system is encrypted. All I have been able to determine is that the code is nine letters and must be entered physically on the console.>>

Tara flipped down the keyboard portion of the console and saw with relief a standard, though archaic, QWERTY-style keyboard. "Nine letters, huh?"

<<Affirmative. I believe the code is—>>

Tara quickly tapped the keys.

RESURGENS

At once the lights brightened, and Tara saw that the three screens weren't screens, but windows. Her breath caught in her throat as she crept to the windows and pressed her face against the cold glass. Beyond the control room was a massive lighted space. With a cursory scan, she noticed ammunition stores, food and water supplies, and twelve brand new CASPers—Mk 7s to boot—hanging in their maintenance racks.

"Sonuvabitch." Tara exclaimed. "He really built a cache."

<<I have access to the system, Tara.>>

"Excellent, Lucille. Standard scans and reports."

<<Acknowledged, Tara. You need to see the command screen.>>

Tara turned to see Reecha standing with both hands over her mouth in shock. She stared down at the command screen.

Jessica,

I'm fine. I know you're looking for me, but there's something I have to do. Something the whole damned galaxy needs to know. I can't tell you what it is. You'll have to trust me. Lucille has a star chart called Remote *in her database. From there, find Earth's position in the sky, and you can calculate the position of Uluru. See you soon, honey.*

"Lucille?"

<<The coordinates appear to be in the fourth arm of the galaxy in restricted space. Uluru is a moon in a system with at least two potentially habitable planets. Its very existence is classified by the Cartography Guild. Given what I can find in the files here, I may be able to crack their information if we can get close enough to a guild office. There is not one on Snowmass.>>

Tara shook her head. "Then we'll go find it. At least we have a theory on where he is."

<<Negative, Tara. This is a confirmation. Snowman went to Uluru. His note is specific enough to merit further investigation. We may not like it, but we're going to have to go to Uluru.>>

Tara looked at Reecha. "Is this true? You were closer to him than anyone except Jessica."

Reecha nodded. "I had hoped to see Jessica again and help her find her father. That you and she are friends is good enough for me. Snowman is at Uluru, Colonel Mason."

Tara drew a breath and stared out the control room windows. "He's given us his location and the stores we'll need to get there. When we go, we're taking the whole damned company and everything we can. We've got no other choice."

"I must warn you, he's likely no longer alone."

"What do you mean?"

Reecha shook her head. "I would imagine the Science Guild and the Dream World Consortium are both looking for him. Gods help us if they find him first."

* * *

Force 25 Temporary Headquarters

Snowmass

A Week Later

The full force of the raging Snowmass winter didn't stop their operations. With storms swirling, Tara made the executive decision to move Force 25 into the extensive Haulers' cavern system. Their new spaces were easily big enough to hold the entire complement of the company, which became urgent with the communications from Victoria Bravo regarding their expulsion from the planet. After the initial shock and anger, Tara realized it was a good thing. In the hours after the defeat of the Trenta Knights, the Dream World Consortium's local board of directors dissolved and fled to the stars. Their operations at Lake Pryce were stopped and the entire facility destroyed before it could be investigated further. Force 25 effectively had a clean slate and an entire planet glad to have them.

The outer garrisons of the Trenta Knights ceased their operations and sent emissaries to the Force 25 headquarters with full equipment and personnel lists. They'd deliberated for two days before Tara allowed the Zuul mercenaries to enlist *en masse* with Force 25. Working with newly appointed President Citsym, Tara removed the garrisons from the outlying communities and eased agricultural restrictions. The climate progression of the planet was still problematic, but Citsym and his advisors decided to let nature take its course.

All in all, Tara and the others believed it to be just another day in the life of Force 25. Nothing was ever routine. She'd called the key leaders together for a meeting to welcome the contingent from Victoria Bravo.

Xander Alison was the first into the wide hangar space in the cavern. He embraced Tara tightly and pulled back enough to kiss her cheek.

"Glad to see me?"

Tara laughed. "You know I am."

They released each other, and she embraced Lieutenant Colonel Ibson before doing the same to Bukk. The Altar stiffened, as usual.

He wasn't quite comfortable with the whole idea of Human embraces, but he'd come a long way in a short time.

"It is good to see you, Tara."

She smiled up at him. "You, too, Lightbringer. I want to know all about that when we have the time."

His antennae wobbled in sudden embarrassment. "I will brief you accordingly. You have my word."

"Thank you, my friend."

She stepped back and saw Ibson and Rains holding each other tight. There were tears again as the collected group silently watched them for a moment. Xander cried as he stepped up next to her and held her hand. The two big men cried together before stepping back. Ibson put his hand on the Peacemaker's upper arm and they shared a few words.

Tara released Xander's hand and stepped forward. She cleared her throat but didn't try to hide wiping her eyes. The Misfits, Gray, Lieutenant Whirr, Maarg, and the others turned to her as one. The Zuul lieutenant named Gnrra stood next to the Misfits, who'd already accepted him as one of their own. In their unity, she'd learned something about herself and her leadership, and it was time to share it with them all. She looked them over and took a deep breath.

"And then we were all together again."

Smiles broke out in the crowd. Ibson spoke for them, "And it was good, ma'am."

Tara smiled in response and let the emotion fade as her thoughts collected. "I wish I had better news, but we're not done. Yes, we lost a planet most of us considered home. We can't go back right now, and that's fine. There are plenty of things for us to do, not because we *should* do so, but because we *must* do so. Some of that starts right here on Snowmass.

"The Dream World Consortium was up to something, and no one seems to know what. Lieutenant Colonel Tirr and his team are on their way here to investigate Lake Pryce. Let's hope they figure out that piece of the puzzle sooner rather than later. Those corporate assholes have taken too many lives, and if given a chance, we're taking them down, too.

"The Peacemakers are worried about an attack on the TriRusk at Weqq. They think Kr'et'Socae is going after them, and they're bringing in Enforcers to defend. I'm not so sure, but what matters is we all do what we can to prepare.

"We have this facility now. We have other Haulers' assets out there fighting the good fight. I've been in touch with Captain Sloane from the *Stone Mountain*. When the time comes, he and his crew will be right there with us. They'll be part of us."

Tara shook her head and smoothed a lock of her blonde hair over her right ear. "Us. I've been thinking about that a lot over the last few days. We've lost so much along the way. I can't help feeling that as much as we need to grieve and heal, we're far from being done. As we're refitting and getting our collective shit into one sock, there are a few things I want you to keep in mind.

"First, we know where Snowman is. I've reported this to the Peacemaker Guild and directly to Jessica. We've been told to make ourselves as fully prepared as possible before we go. When we do, it's likely the Cartography and Science Guilds won't be too happy about it. We're going in armed to the teeth and prepared for war. Make no mistake, it won't be easy.

"Second, we're one effort of many in this conflict. Jessica will rejoin us soon, and there are others from the Peacemaker Guild conducting a highly risky mission right now that will help us execute our primary mission. When the time comes, we're all going in together. That's how big this is, people. I need you all focused on maintenance and readiness. Mainly that means you at the personal level."

She took a breath and felt the emotion rising in her voice. Disregarding everything she'd ever been taught about stoicism and leadership, she let it come.

"We're all hurting. Every single one of us. We've lost friends. We've lost partners. We've lost loved ones." She glanced at Rains and saw fresh tears flow from his eyes. Fresh ones of her own followed suit. She let them come. "I want you to know it's okay to hurt. To feel pain. To grieve. In this business, we'll lose more friends than we'll retire with, and there's absolutely no guarantee of tomorrow for any of us. When Vannix fell..."

She paused and brought a hand to her mouth, and closed her eyes. When she opened her eyes, all of them capable of tears cried. Quin'taa and Homer sat with their heads in their massive paws. Whirr rested one foreclaw on Harmon Gray's shoulder. Reecha wrapped both of her tiny arms around Maarg's foreleg. The words crystallized in her mind in a rapid instant, and as they came, so did more tears.

"I left everything behind to become a mercenary. By blind damned luck I found myself with good people on a good mission. I lost a bunch of them, but I gained friends I'd fight across the galaxy for on any given day. When Vannix fell, she used a word I've shied away from when I think about you all. We're taught to keep our feelings down and focus on the mission. The objective. That's all wrong, because it's the people who matter. That word was never part of the equation. But you know what? It's the only fucking word that matters right now.

"I love you. I love all of you. It doesn't matter how long you've been with Force 25. It doesn't matter your species. You've shared the battlefield with me. You've won with me. You've hurt with me. For that, I love you. There are others coming to join us, and you know what? I'll love them, too. Why? Because it's all that matters. Our tactics and our weapons don't matter. In the end, we fight for the ones at our shoulders, and I will always love you for that. Together we are Force 25, and we hold the line."

"We hold the line!"

* * * * *

Chapter Thirty-Five

Peacemaker Guild Headquarters

Location CLASSIFIED

Guild Master Rsach approved the Apex Achievement Award for Combat, with Star of Valor, posthumously for Peacemaker Vannix. The death of a Peacemaker was never easy to stomach. He settled against his multi-species desk chair and scrolled through the reports from his many-pronged efforts to determine his guild's strength and position in the Union.

With the veritable collapse of the Mercenary Guild and the infighting and distrust rampant between most of the other guilds, he had to believe the Peacemakers were in a unique and dangerous position. For him, though, information was critical, and he'd entered a period where there wasn't much to act upon.

His selector, Hak-Chet, had positioned himself at an undisclosed location in something the Humans called "deep cover." While Force 25 had secured the situation at Snowmass and had communicated accomplishment of their primary goal—the location of Snowman, he'd readied Weqq for a potential attack from the disgraced Enforcer Kr'et'Socae and sent his youngest, and undeniably most capable team of Peacemakers on a mission meant for his eyes only. Added to the mix were Captains Dreel and Kurrang as they gathered Enforcers from across the galaxy into combat-capable units. He'd undoubtedly have to use them, but when? And for what?

Preparation would be key. In his years since ascending to the guild master's position, Rsach hadn't considered the prospect of all-out war descending on the galaxy. There were too many variables to consider, and his guild, and to a certain extent his own leadership, had failed to see them before it was too late on many accounts. The Depik had almost been wiped out right under his antennae. With no greater crime than genocide to defend against, they'd collectively almost missed it. Jessica Francis and the others working with the Depik reported promising information, but Rsach couldn't help but wonder what else he'd missed, aside from the counsel of his friends. The High Council hadn't convened in months, and the rest of the council representatives clamored for a meeting soon to discuss the very things he struggled to define. If he couldn't wrap his mind around the situation, how could he unite the rest of his guild?

A buzzing noise came from his desk. The notification was similar to incoming messages or Stormwatch reports, but it was one he'd heard only once before—the day he'd become the guild master. Every outgoing guild master, if possible, conducted a familiarization for the incoming one. In Rsach's case, he'd forgotten much of the event over the course of time, but he'd never forgotten that particular sound, and the fact that no guild master in the previous two hundred years had ever had cause to hear it.

A ripple of electricity, something both excited and cautious, shot down his segmented body. He'd never expected to hear it. For the guild masters of the last two hundred years, including the dishonored Breka himself, to have never heard it made him wonder what could have cued the tone and whatever message it held. He leaned forward and touched the blinking icon with one pincer.

The screen blanked completely, and a soft monotone voice said, "Guild Master Rsach, well met."

Rsach didn't immediately respond. He tried to determine the species of the voice but was unable. Even with universal translator capabilities, there were still subtle nuances for every species in their diction and syntax. In this case, the voice was flawlessly translated into his native Jeha, but the speaker's species was still suspect. The diction was too perfect and refined. Even on his best behavior, another favorite Human idiom, Rsach never spoke with such fluency.

"Well met. To whom am I speaking, Honored One?" He added the "Honored One" as a test of the speaker's actual species. A Jeha wouldn't reciprocate the inflection or the exact wording.

"I am Counselor. No, I am not a Jeha, Guild Master Rsach. I appreciate your rudimentary effort to investigate, but I know far more than you possibly could. You are prepared to act upon my message?"

Rsach rippled several pincers across his abdomen and clutched them together. Protocol said he was to follow instructions and messages from the source immediately. "The protocols say that I should, Counselor. Though this channel has not activated for more than two hundred years, and I am wondering why I should do so."

"Because your very life depends on it, Rsach. Don't become the spoiled idiot you once were again. Faced with difficulty, the Peacemaker Guild needs exemplary leadership to take advantage of its position."

Its. So not a Peacemaker. Then who or what is this?

"You believe that I cannot lead the Guild? You threaten my very life?" Rsach bounced his antennae in agitation. "I think you underestimate my abilities."

"You have done passable work in your preparations, but there is much you have failed to do, Guild Master. Your guild is weaker for it."

Rsach rippled with furious indignation and leaned forward. "How dare you! You've insulted me and the very guild I oversee, and yet you've given me nothing to substantiate who you are and what you—"

The display flashed a singular word in his own language. The green text cut the words off in Rsach's throat instantly. The word faded from the screen, but the afterimage in his eyes took a moment longer. Rsach settled back against his chair.

Rsach replied slowly. "I meant no disrespect."

For a moment there was silence in the room. The voice returned without a sign of emotion. "I watch and remain engaged in all dealings of the guild at all times. Everything you have ever done, I have been aware of, and there are levels of information and plans I will ensure you now have. The time has come for action. The others are no match for us."

"What others?" Rsach asked.

"It matters not. You would not understand at this stage. Best hope I don't have to explain."

Rsach nodded. "Understood."

The voice continued, "You will call a meeting of the High Council at your forward location. That meeting will include mandatory attendance from representatives of Force 25, the Blue Ridge Kin, and your special operatives acting on your current initiatives. We must brief them and prepare them for war. Other guilds are mobilizing forces now, and we must be ready. The date and time of the meeting is yet to be determined, but they must be aware that when the call comes, they are to answer it."

"And Project Crusader?" Rsach asked. "You know of that initiative? Am I to include its discussion in this meeting?"

"Yes. There will be a time in the very near future when they will be needed. Until this trying time passes, Guild Master, we will converse much more frequently. The fate of the guild, and the Union, depends on it. Take your instructions and execute them. I will join you when the meeting convenes."

"What of the young ones? Their mission is riskier than anything the guild has attempted in hundreds of years. We need them to succeed to further prepare ourselves for what James Francis has found at his location."

"When they complete their mission, you will set the meeting date. By then we will know the intents of others and be prepared to stop them once and for all. Guild or not, friend or not, nothing will stand in the Peacemakers' way."

# # # # #

ABOUT THE AUTHOR

Kevin Ikenberry is a life-long space geek and retired Army officer. A former manager of the world-renowned U.S. Space Camp program and space operations officer, Kevin has a broad background in space and space science education prior to becoming an internationally bestselling author. His 2016 debut science fiction novel *Sleeper Protocol* was a Finalist for the Colorado Book Award and was heralded as "an emotionally powerful debut" by *Publisher's Weekly*. Kevin is the author of the military science fiction / thriller novels *Runs In The Family*, *Vendetta Protocol*, and *Super-Sync*. Kevin is a core author in the Four Horsemen Universe where his novels include *Peacemaker, Honor The Threat, Stand Or Fall, Deathangel*, *Redacted Affairs* (with Kevin Steverson), and *Enforcer* (with Quincy J. Allen). He is an Active Member of SFWA, and a member of International Thriller Writers as well as a member of the SIGMA, the science fiction think-tank. He lives in Colorado with his family—his home is seldom a boring place.

*****

The following is an

Excerpt from Super-Sync:

Super-Sync

Kevin Ikenberry

Available Now from Theogony Books

eBook and Paperback

Excerpt from "Super-Sync:"

The subspace radio chimed an hour later, just as Lew put aside the holonovel with dissatisfaction. There was no such thing as "happily ever after," no matter how many books she read. No one was going to carry her off into the sunset. Lew reached for the radio controls and felt the thuds of Tyler's boots on the deck in the passageway below. He burst onto the bridge and vaulted into his chair.

He looked at Lew. "Identify the transmission."

Lew fingered the controls and read off the diagnostic information, "Standard Ku band transmission from Earth. Origin point known through Houston nexus. Encryption is solid Johnson Analytics with the proper keys."

Tyler grinned. "Boss."

Lew nodded and smiled as well. "Appears so."

Their mysterious benefactor hadn't called them in more than six months, but every time he'd employed them, the take had been impressive. How he was able to garner the contracts he had bordered on magic. Lew thought the man sounded like some kind of Texas oil baron. Despite the technology, his calls were always voice-only, and there was never any interaction between them and whoever he represented.

Whatever he contracted them to acquire was delivered to a private, automated hangar on Luna. The robotic ground crew would unload *Remnant* and send them on their way again. Anonymous cash transfers always appeared in their accounts by the time *Remnant* returned to lunar orbit. The first mission had earned Tyler's company over a million Euros. The following missions were even more lucrative.

Their benefactor went by a call sign, and they talked in codes meant only for their own ears. It should have been a red flag, but the money was too damned good to pass up. A call from him could *not* go unanswered.

Tyler punched a few buttons on his console, and a drawling voice boomed through the speakers, "*Remnant*, this is Boss. Are you receiving?" The transmission ended with a chiming tone that dated back to the early days of spaceflight. The clear delineation of conversation allowed Tyler to answer.

"Boss, this is *Remnant.* Nice to hear from you. How can we be of service?"

A few seconds passed. "Tyler, it's good to hear your voice. I understand you're on a contract flight from our friend in India."

"That's affirm, Boss."

"Roger, you've got a shadow. Are you aware of that?"

Tyler's face darkened. "Roger, Boss. We're aware of the bogey."

By definition, a bogey was an unknown contact with unknown intentions. Should the situation turn bad, the radar blip would become a bandit. Lew checked the telemetry from the unknown ship. There was no change in direction or speed. It was still gaining on them.

"*Remnant*, the trailing vehicle is not your concern. I have a change in mission for you."

Tyler shook his head. "Negative, Boss. I have a contract."

"*Remnant*, I bought out that contract. The shadow on your tail is the *Rio Bravo*, under contract by me to get Telstar Six Twelve. You're going high super-sync."

*****

*****

The following is an

Excerpt from Book One of the Earth Song Cycle:

Overture

Mark Wandrey

Excerpt from "Overture:"

Dawn was still an hour away as Mindy Channely opened the roof access and stared in surprise at the crowd already assembled there. "Authorized Personnel Only" was printed in bold red letters on the door through which she and her husband, Jake, slipped onto the wide roof.

A few people standing nearby took notice of their arrival. Most had no reaction, a few nodded, and a couple waved tentatively. Mindy looked over the skyline of Portland and instinctively oriented herself before glancing to the east. The sky had an unnatural glow that had been growing steadily for hours, and as they watched, scintillating streamers of blue, white, and green radiated over the mountains like a strange, concentrated aurora borealis.

"You almost missed it," one man said. She let the door close, but saw someone had left a brick to keep it from closing completely. Mindy turned and saw the man who had spoken wore a security guard uniform. The easy access to the building made more sense.

"Ain't no one missin' this!" a drunk man slurred.

"We figured most people fled to the hills over the past week," Jake replied.

"I guess we were wrong," Mindy said.

"Might as well enjoy the show," the guard said and offered them a huge, hand-rolled cigarette that didn't smell like tobacco. She waved it off, and the two men shrugged before taking a puff.

"Here it comes!" someone yelled. Mindy looked to the east. There was a bright light coming over the Cascade Mountains, so intense it was like looking at a welder's torch. Asteroid LM-245 hit the atmosphere at over 300 miles per second. It seemed to move faster and faster, from east to west, and the people lifted their hands to shield their eyes from the blinding light. It looked like a blazing comet or a science fiction laser blast.

"Maybe it will just pass over," someone said in a voice full of hope.

Mindy shook her head. She'd studied the asteroid's track many times.

In a matter of a few seconds, it shot by and fell toward the western horizon, disappearing below the mountains between Portland and the ocean. Out of view of the city, it slammed into the ocean.

The impact was unimaginable. The air around the hypersonic projectile turned to superheated plasma, creating a shockwave that generated 10 times the energy of the largest nuclear weapon ever detonated as it hit the ocean's surface.

The kinetic energy was more than 1,000 megatons; however, the object didn't slow as it flashed through a half mile of ocean and into the sea bed, then into the mantel, and beyond.

On the surface, the blast effect appeared as a thermal flash brighter than the sun. Everyone on the rooftop watched with wide-eyed terror as the Tualatin Mountains between Portland and the Pacific Ocean were outlined in blinding light. As the light began to dissipate, the outline of the mountains blurred as a dense bank of smoke climbed from the western range.

The flash had incinerated everything on the other side.

The physical blast, travelling much faster than any normal atmospheric shockwave, hit the mountains and tore them from the bedrock, adding them to the rolling wave of destruction traveling east at several thousand miles per hour. The people on the rooftops of Portland only had two seconds before the entire city was wiped away.

Ten seconds later, the asteroid reached the core of the planet, and another dozen seconds after that, the Earth's fate was sealed.

*****

Get "Overture" now at:
https://www.amazon.com/dp/B077YMLRHM/

Find out more about Mark Wandrey and the Earth Song Cycle at:
https://chriskennedypublishing.com/

*****

The following is an

Excerpt from Book One of The Progenitors' War:

A Gulf in Time

Chris Kennedy

Available from Theogony Books

eBook, Paperback, and (Soon) Audio

Excerpt from "A Gulf in Time:"

"Thank you for calling us," the figure on the front view screen said, his pupil-less eyes glowing bright yellow beneath his eight-inch horns. Generally humanoid, the creature was blood red and had a mouthful of pointed teeth that were visible when he smiled. Giant bat wings alternately spread and folded behind him; his pointed tail could be seen flicking back and forth when the wings were folded. "We accept your offer to be our slaves for now and all eternity."

"Get us out of here, helm!" Captain Sheppard ordered. "Flank speed to the stargate!"

"Sorry, sir, my console is dead," the helmsman replied.

"Can you jump us to the Jinn Universe?"

"No, sir, that's dead too."

"Engineer, do we have our shields?"

"No, sir, they're down, and my console's dead, too."

"OSO? DSO? Status?"

"My console's dead," the Offensive Systems Officer replied.

"Mine, too," the Defensive Systems Officer noted.

The figure on the view screen laughed. "I do *so* love the way new minions scamper about, trying to avoid the unavoidable."

"There's been a mistake," Captain Sheppard said. "We didn't intend to call you or become your minions."

"It does not matter whether you *intended* to or not," the creature said. "You passed the test and are obviously strong enough to function as our messengers."

"What do you mean, 'to function as your messengers?'"

"It is past time for this galaxy's harvest. You will go to all the civilizations and prepare them for the cull."

"I'm not sure I like the sound of that. What is this 'cull?'"

"We require your life force in order to survive. Each civilization will be required to provide 98.2% of its life force. The remaining 1.8% will be used to reseed their planets."

"And you expect us to take this message to all the civilized planets in this galaxy?"

"That is correct. Why else would we have left the stargates for you to use to travel between the stars?"

"What if a civilization doesn't want to participate in this cull?"

"Then they will be obliterated. Most will choose to save 1.8% of their population, rather than none, especially once you make an example or two of the civilizations who refuse."

"And if *we* refuse?"

"Then your society will be the first example."

"I can't make this kind of decision," Captain Sheppard said, stalling. "I'll have to discuss it with my superiors."

"Unacceptable. You must give me an answer now. Kneel before us or perish; those are your choices."

"I can't," Captain Sheppard said, his voice full of anguish.

"Who called us by completing the quest?" the creature asked. "That person must decide."

"I pushed the button," Lieutenant Commander Hobbs replied, "but I can't commit my race to this any more than Captain Sheppard can."

"That is all right," the creature said. "Sometimes it is best to have an example from the start." He looked off screen. "Destroy them."

"Captain Sheppard, there are energy weapons warming up on the other ship," Steropes said.

"DSO, now would be a good time for those shields..." Captain Sheppard said.

"I'm sorry, sir; my console is still dead."

"They're firing!" Steropes called.

The enemy ship fired, but the *Vella Gulf's* shields snapped on, absorbing the volley.

"Nice job, DSO!" Captain Sheppard exclaimed.

"I didn't do it, sir!" the DSO cried. "They just came on."

"Well, if you didn't do it, who did?" Captain Sheppard asked.

"I don't know!" the DSO exclaimed. "All I know is we can't take another volley like that, sir; the first round completely maxed out our shields. One more, and they're going to fail!"

"I...activated...the shields," Solomon, the ship's artificial intelligence, said. The voice of the AI sounded strained. "Am fighting...intruder..." the AI's voice fluctuated between male and female. "Losing...system...integrity...krelbet gelched."

"Krelbet gelched?" the DSO asked.

"It means 'systems failing' in the language of the Eldive," Steropes said.

"The enemy is firing again," the DSO said. "We're hit! Shields are down."

"I've got hits down the length of the ship," the duty engineer said. "We're open to space in several places. We can't take another round like that!"

"That was just the little that came through after the shields fell," the DSO said. "We're doomed if—*missiles inbound!* I've got over 100 missiles inbound, and I can't do anything to stop them!" He switched to the public address system. "*Numerous missiles inbound! All hands brace for shock!* Five seconds! Three...two...one..."

* * * * *

Get "A Gulf in Time" now at:
https://www.amazon.com/dp/B0829FLV92

Find out more about Chris Kennedy and "A Gulf in Time" at:
https://chriskennedypublishing.com/imprints-authors/chris-kennedy/

*****